Masquerade in London

Emily L. Finch

This is a work of fiction. However, in order to set it in the mid-Victorian period, efforts were made to include historical figures, events and places where possible. As such, the characters Inspector Whicher, Sir Richard Mayne, and Mr. Poole, though their roles within the story, including any dialog, are entirely fictional, are based on their real life counterparts. All other names and characters are products of the author's imagination. Any resemblance to actual persons, living or dead, is purely coincidental.

First paperback edition March 2022

Book cover design by Bespoke Book Covers

ISBN: 978-1-7377372-0-9

www.emilylfinch.com

ONE

London. June, 1861

The early morning sun shone bright against the immaculate white stone houses that stood in neat rows on either side of Argyll Road. Half-concealed behind a decorative shrub, Samantha Kingston and her maid, Alice, squinted against the glare as they trained their eyes on house number forty-five.

"It might not come today," Alice murmured. "We should go back before we're missed."

Samantha scanned the empty street, craning her neck to see behind her. "Just…one more minute." Seeing the strain in Alice's eyes, she added, "I promise. One minute and we'll return."

A breeze rustled the leaves above them. A bird sang out as it flew past. Then she heard footsteps. A small, wiry boy emerged from behind the long row of houses. He moved at a half-run down the street. When he came to number forty-five, he skipped up the steps and stopped in front of the door. Reaching into the pocket of his faded grey trousers, he drew out a white envelope and dropped it in the mail slot.

As he turned back to the street, Samantha left her hiding place and sprinted towards him. His eyes widened in surprise and he began to run, but she'd had too much of a head start. She caught up to him at the end of the street, grabbed his arm and held fast.

"Lemme go!" the boy shouted, twisting in her grasp.

"Not until you've told me who you are," she said. "And who sent you."

He scooped up a handful of dirt and flung it in her direction. She coughed and spluttered, blinking the dust from her eyes. He tried to kick her, but she held him away from her body and his foot met nothing but air. Alice arrived just then and caught hold of the boy's other arm.

"Listen," Samantha said to the wriggling boy. "We're not going to hurt you. We just want to know who sent you."

"Yeah?" The boy stopped struggling and his mouth twisted into what he likely intended to be a sneer but which, on his pre-pubescent face, looked more like a pout. "Why's that?"

It was a simple question, but the answer was more complicated than Samantha was prepared to give to this small boy. He looked at her expectantly.

"Because he's threatening my uncle," she said simply.

"Threatening?" The boy sounded wary. She wished she knew what he was thinking. Was he surprised to learn what was in the letters he delivered, or was he part of the scheme?

"Threatening," she repeated. Then she bluffed, "and if you don't want to be drawn into a criminal prosecution, you will tell me his name."

"I don't know his name." He looked up at her with eyes that pleaded sincerity. "He's never told me and I ain't never asked. He finds me near Piccadilly some days and says he'll pay me thruppence to deliver a letter if I can get it in just after the postman."

Samantha released his arm and crouched down in front of him so that they were at eye level. "What does he look like?"

"Like a toff." He shrugged. "Nice clothes, tall hat, pocket watch."

"What color is his hair?" Samantha asked, trying to keep the frustration from her tone. "Is he clean shaven? Does he have a beard?"

The boy shrugged again.

"Is there anything else you can tell me?" she asked.

"He did say this was to be the last one," the boy said.

Samantha and Alice exchanged glances. "What does that mean?"

"I don't know," the boy answered her. "Can I go now?"

"Yes," she sighed. "Go on."

Alice released him, and he took off down the street. Samantha stood and watched until he was out of sight.

"Do you think he was telling the truth?" Alice asked.

"I think so," Samantha said, turning and starting back the way they had come. Whoever had sent the boy was blackmailing her uncle, or trying to. So far, Sir Arthur had refused to reply to any of the letters—there had been three in just under a fortnight—and dismissed the entire affair as an irritating nuisance. Samantha was less sanguine. Her uncle's monstrous sense of self-importance may have led him to believe he was untouchable, but she was not so blind. She worried that his insistence on ignoring the blackmail would lead to problems, not just for him, but for her and her aunt.

"It sounds as though the blackmailer is a gentleman," she continued. "Though, I could have guessed as much. His manner of writing in that first letter was that of a gentleman. It makes sense that he would hire someone to deliver the letters for him, not wanting to be seen and, naturally, he wouldn't tell him his name." She sighed. "I had hoped for a better description of the gentleman, though, or something to help us identify him."

If Sir Arthur refused to take action, even after such evidence, she had planned to take the information to the police herself. She refused to become a victim of her uncle's selfish pride.

Sir Arthur had read the first letter aloud to her and Aunt Victoria at the breakfast table. Samantha assumed his sense of outrage at the audacity of the writer had propelled him to be more open with his affairs than was his wont. He certainly hadn't shared the next two letters with them. She'd had to sneak them from his desk while he was at his club.

In that first letter, the writer had claimed to know some secrets of her uncle's and wanted the princely sum of a thousand pounds in exchange for his silence. Samantha had wondered if it was some sort of joke sent by a person unfamiliar with her uncle's utter lack of a sense of humor. In the second and third letters, however, the blackmailer had added threats of violence if her uncle failed to comply.

Samantha turned to Alice. "He can't expect my uncle will respond to this latest letter when he hasn't to any of the other three. So why would he tell the boy it's the last one?"

"Perhaps he's giving up," Alice suggested. "Maybe this is his last try, and if Sir Arthur doesn't give him what he wants, he'll threaten someone else."

Samantha shook her head. "I don't think so. If he knows something damaging about my uncle, as he claims, why would he abandon the possibility of reward?"

Samantha and Alice returned to number forty-five and entered through the front door. The elegant hall was empty. Silently, they removed their dusty shoes. Alice took both pairs and crept down the hall towards the back stairs while Samantha took the front stairs to her room.

Sir Arthur was Samantha's uncle by marriage. Her mother's

sister, Aunt Victoria, was his second wife. When Samantha was fourteen, her parents had sent her to stay with them at their country estate in Kent to learn decorum and ladylike graces from her proper aunt in preparation for her eventual entrance into Society. She had resented this greatly as it meant leaving the home of her beloved paternal grandfather with whom she had lived most of her life while her parents dedicated themselves to their own amusements.

Then, tragedy had struck. Cholera swept across London, taking with it both of her parents and ensuring that what ought to have been a relatively short visit became a permanent one when it was revealed that Sir Arthur and Aunt Victoria were her legal guardians. Though it was clear that Sir Arthur was no happier to have her under his roof than she was to be there, he had accepted it as his duty and, over the next six years, had dedicated himself to stamping out the spirit her grandfather had once adored.

Alice worked as quickly as she could helping Samantha to dress and re-plait her hair, but it was still twenty minutes past nine, the usual hour for breakfast, when she finally joined Sir Arthur and her aunt in the dining room. Sir Arthur sat at one end of the table, the newspaper spread out beside him. In his late fifties, he was older than Samantha's aunt by almost two decades but, despite the grey in his bushy side whiskers, he didn't look it. He was tall and powerfully built, still very much in his prime.

He looked up when Samantha entered. "You're late."

"Forgive me," she said demurely, then walked to her chair and sat. The plate in front of her was already filled. She picked up a fork and began to eat. The eggs were cold, and she fought back a grimace, aware of his gaze on her.

After a moment, he returned his attention to his newspaper. Samantha stole a glance at her aunt. Aunt Victoria, impeccably turned out in a blue rose morning dress, looking like a china doll with not a hair out of place, sat at the other end of the table, her attention on her food, eating in silence as usual.

Breakfast progressed in the same way it did every morning, with Sir Arthur lingering over the paper before moving on to the post. It seemed to Samantha, as she waited anxiously for him to open the white envelope on the top of the pile, that it took longer than usual. She had finished her eggs and potatoes and was nearly done with her mutton cutlets—always a difficult task with Mrs. Penworth's tendency to overcook them—when he finally closed his paper. She watched him lift the envelope from the tray. He inserted his letter knife under the flap and drew it across, extracting the letter. A frown creased his brow as he read the contents and then, with a grunt of annoyance, he crumpled the letter up and tossed it aside.

Unable to contain herself, Samantha spoke up. "Was it another one, Sir Arthur?"

He reached for the next envelope. "Another what?"

She glanced at her aunt, who frowned at her. She shook her head almost imperceptibly and returned her gaze to her plate.

Samantha hesitated, but only briefly. "Another blackmail letter."

Sir Arthur's eyes snapped up. "It is not *blackmail*," he said, pronouncing the word with distaste. "Blackmail would imply that the writer had some hold over me—some secret I was afraid of being made public. This letter writer—this time-waster—is nothing more than a beggar who thinks vague, unsubstantiated statements will earn him an easy reward."

"Perhaps," Samantha said hesitantly, "if you were to answer him—"

"If I require your opinion," Sir Arthur interrupted, his tone sharp, "I will ask for it. Until that unlikely eventuality, you will keep your tiresome thoughts to yourself."

Samantha closed her mouth and sat back. She was not hurt by

his comments. She had been the subject of too many of his diatribes over the years to feel anything from them anymore. But she had learned in that time that arguing with him did more harm than good. Silence fell again as Sir Arthur perused the rest of the morning post. He seemed to have forgotten the blackmail letter, which lay crumpled on a platter beside him, soaking up bacon grease. Samantha's eyes flicked to it as she ate her orange slowly and deliberately, one wedge at a time.

When Sir Arthur had finished his breakfast, he rose and announced his intention of taking a short walk through Kensington Gardens, followed by a visit to his club, where he would stay through lunch. The speech was unnecessary, as this was what he did every morning, but the announcement was as much a part of his routine as the action.

Aunt Victoria got quickly to her feet. As she and Samantha knew well, when Sir Arthur was finished eating, he expected everyone else to be too.

"I'm not quite finished," Samantha said in response to her uncle's raised eyebrow, gesturing to her half-eaten orange. "I just need a few minutes more."

She knew she was risking his wrath, but the chance to read the letter was worth it. She just hoped her recent pattern of obedience would weigh in her favor. A vein in Sir Arthur's temple twitched as she watched, but Aunt Victoria lay a placating hand across his arm and he grunted, turning back to the door and leading his wife out.

Left to herself but knowing she had only moments before the footmen arrived to begin clearing away the breakfast things, Samantha leapt to her feet. Bracing herself with one hand pressed against the fine muslin tablecloth, she leaned forward and stretched her arm as far as it would go, wishing, not for the first time, that she were not quite so short. When her fingers pinched the edge of the crumpled letter, she yanked her arm back and sat down.

Smoothing the letter out against her plate to avoid getting

grease on the tablecloth, Samantha leaned close to read the slightly smeared words.

Dear Sir,

I have been as polite as I know how, but your continued silence has brought me to a place of desperation and will, unfortunately, force me to prove my sincerity. If my request is not met by the end of the day today, you may expect a message from my associates soon. This is not an outcome either of us would desire, so I suggest you comply speedily. Do not underestimate the danger of the position in which you are placing yourself, your wife and your pretty young ward.

A noise in the hall made Samantha crumple the note back up and toss it to her uncle's plate where it lay, if not exactly where it had been, close enough. A footman entered and walked directly to the sideboard, where he began loading his arms with serving ware. Samantha pushed back her chair and stood, exiting quickly through the door he had entered.

As she hurried to her room, phrases from the note replayed in her mind. *A place of desperation…if my request is not met…a message from my associates…danger.* She grimaced as she recalled the last line. The fact that the writer had chosen to describe her as Sir Arthur's "pretty young ward" while Aunt Victoria was merely "your wife" felt sinister. She had been singled out and she didn't like to think why.

Despite an eventful, if disappointing, morning, the rest of the day proceeded at a snail's pace. They had been invited to a ball at the home of Samantha's cousin, Cyril, and Aunt Victoria, who was still recovering from a bad cold, decided to remain at home all day, saving her strength for the evening.

Unable to go out without her aunt, who was also her chaperone, Samantha tried to occupy herself, but she could not escape the thoughts that plagued her. They followed her, like a black cloud threatening rain, as she tended the garden—her only chance to be outside—and as she attempted to distract herself by refreshing her Latin, finishing her needlework and practicing the pianoforte. She could not keep herself from imagining what danger the blackmailer might have in mind and she could not conceive how to avoid it, powerless as she was. Her attempt to thwart him had failed. All her hopes now lay in one direction—her search for Charles. If she could find him, he would be able to help.

Charles was her uncle's son by his first marriage. Her friendship with him had been the one bright spot in her otherwise miserable existence with her aunt and uncle. He was the only real friend she'd ever had, apart from her grandfather. He had fallen out with his father several years ago, and she hadn't seen him since. She had, however, begun to seek him out even before the blackmail letters arrived, and she hoped, now that the situation was all the more desperate, to find him soon.

"Have you heard from your cousin yet?" she asked Alice that evening as she sat at her vanity while Alice arranged her hair for the ball. Alice's cousin worked for a family in Bath, one of the places Samantha considered likely for Charles to be living.

Alice caught her eye in the mirror and shook her head, her mouth full of pins.

Samantha sighed. "I know it's too early to expect a response, but I had hoped…It's been months, Alice. I'm beginning to worry we won't find him in time."

She had always known she would have to marry to be free of

her uncle—she didn't have the money for independence nor any desire for a life of servitude as a poor companion. Yet she had always imagined she would be able to choose her husband. Samantha's first Season had been a disappointment. As the granddaughter of an earl, she had the pedigree, if not the fortune, to make a tolerable match, yet the only offers she received were from friends of her uncle. It wasn't until the beginning of this Season, when she had chanced to overhear his conversation with one of her recent dance partners, that she realized Sir Arthur was actively working against her, discouraging any suitors he did not approve of.

Equally incensed and worried, Samantha had made the decision to appeal to the one man she knew would help her. Charles had protected her from his father when he lived at home; he would do so again, if only she could let him know she needed him. They could marry in Scotland without Sir Arthur's approval and then she would be free. Marriage to Charles would be better than to a stranger and she wondered that she hadn't considered the idea before. He was kind, funny, handsome, and she had been infatuated with him as a girl.

Locating him had been a challenge, even more so than she had anticipated. He had no contact with his father nor with any of their mutual acquaintances and, from what she had gathered, spent as much time away from London as in it.

"Have you considered," Alice began, her voice hesitant, "that if—when—we find him, he may be unable or unwilling to help you?"

"He'll help me," Samantha said confidently. It may have been years, but she and Charles had formed a strong bond. He had also made her a promise, one she was sure he would hold to.

"And if he is unable to help?"

Samantha considered the question as she watched Alice pin up several stray hairs, smoothing them as best she could with copious amounts of pomade. There were always stray hairs. Samantha's long, dark tresses were thick and curly, far from ideal when constructing the sleek, manufactured curls that were so popular. Despite nearly two Seasons of practice, Alice often spent over an hour working the curling tongs through Samantha's hair.

"If he were dead," Samantha said finally, "we would know. Estrangement or no, word would have reached Sir Arthur. The same if he were married. If he is short on funds, my dowry, though not large, will suffice to keep us independent of my uncle."

"Well, then," Alice said, straightening up and placing the remaining pins back in their little box. "What will you do if we do not find him before Sir Arthur insists you marry someone else?"

Samantha stood, moving to the center of the room as Alice retrieved the wide whalebone crinoline cage that helped to create the fashionable silhouette of her gown. She stepped into it and Alice lifted it to her hips, tying it around her waist.

"It may not matter," Samantha said. "If the blackmailer follows through on his threats..." She left the sentence unfinished because, really, she had no idea what to expect. What was true, however, was that the threat of imminent physical danger was more pressing than whatever her uncle had in store for her.

She considered telling Alice about the pointed threat to her as her uncle's "pretty young ward" but decided against it. Alice would only worry and, as they had just discussed, there was little they could do about it. So, she remained silent as Alice layered two more petticoats over the first, then the skirt of Samantha's champagne silk evening gown, kneeling on the floor to ensure the embroidered rose border was straight while Samantha turned slowly. As she went to the bed to retrieve the bodice, Alice spoke over her shoulder.

"Do you think the blackmailer will be at the ball tonight? If he is a gentleman, that is."

"Now there's a disturbing thought," Samantha said, her eyes

wide. "I suppose he might be. I shall have to be extra attentive to my partners."

Cyril had been generous with his invitations. The ballroom was nearly full when she and her aunt and uncle arrived. Gentlemen in black suits with stark white shirt fronts stood peppered throughout a sea of ladies in colorful dresses. At one end of the high-ceilinged room, musicians shifted in their seats, rustling through sheaves of sheet music and tuning their instruments in preparation for the first waltz. She could hear the gentle hum of a bow on a violin and the quick trill of a flute through the contented babble of voices and occasional laughter.

Near the door stood Cyril and his wife. Though only twenty-four, he looked much older. He'd inherited the earldom of Etwall from their grandfather at a young age and the weight of responsibility had aged him prematurely. He was his late father's only son, and with her own father also dead with no sons, the pressure for him to produce an heir had been immense. He'd succeeded—or perhaps it was more accurate to say that his wife had succeeded—within a year of their marriage, but it was clear to Samantha that Cyril resented the loss of his bachelor years.

"Sir Arthur," Cyril said, greeting her uncle with polite civility and turning to her aunt. "Lady Prescott."

His wife echoed him, bestowing a warm smile on each of them in turn.

"Thank you for your kind invitation, Lady Etwall," Samantha's aunt said.

Cyril's wife dipped her head in acknowledgement.

"Cousin Samantha," Cyril said, clasping her hand in his own clammy ones. "I'm so pleased you could be here tonight."

He smiled thinly, and Samantha responded in kind. She and Cyril had never been the best of friends, but they had gotten along well enough in childhood. Then, Grandfather had passed, Cyril had become the earl, and his manner towards her had changed. He became so chilly so immediately in their interactions that she began to wonder if he was only ever kind to her because Grandfather insisted upon it.

"Everything looks lovely," Samantha said. It was all she could think to say, but it was true. Cyril's taste was exquisite, if expensive. The amount he must have spent on candles alone that evening was unfathomable.

Cyril nodded woodenly before turning to greet the next guests. Samantha curtsied to Lady Etwall and followed her aunt and uncle into the room. Sir Arthur excused himself, promising to return for a perfunctory dance with his wife. "Perfunctory" was not the word he used, but it was clear to both Samantha and, she assumed, to her aunt, that it was the word he meant. Aunt Victoria pointedly did not meet Samantha's gaze as her husband went to join a group of gentlemen on the far side of the room. Samantha had often wished that her aunt would confide in her—that they could be a support to each other in their mistreatment by Sir Arthur—but Aunt Victoria refused to acknowledge any such mistreatment existed and the wall between them seemed impenetrable.

Within minutes, Samantha's hand was requested by an amiable young man she had danced with on a handful of other occasions but whose name she had forgotten. She had heard it briefly when they were introduced, but not since, and she had now been acquainted with him too long to ask for it again in all politeness.

Bowing to Aunt Victoria, he led Samantha to the dance floor and they took their places among the other dancers. She found herself eyeing those around her with suspicion, wondering if she was looking at the blackmailer. Was it he who smiled at her so pleasantly? Or might it be that man bowing to his partner? The music began and she made an effort to lose herself in the pleasure of the dance, ignoring the anxious thoughts that swirled through her head.

"Good heavens. How could Lord Etwall have invited him?"

Samantha followed her partner's gaze to the entrance of the ballroom. She had to twist her neck around as they spun away, but she caught a glimpse of the man he was so shocked to see. It was the notorious Mr. Archibald Kennedy, and the woman on his arm, a pretty blonde with wide dark eyes, was a young widow whose lavender dress proclaimed that she was still in light mourning.

"I doubt he did invite him," Samantha said. "My cousin is not a friend of his, as far as I know, but that won't have mattered to Mr. Kennedy. I suppose the lady received the invitation and brought him along. Cyril won't be able to turn him away now."

"That man's presence is an insult to all the ladies here."

Samantha almost laughed, but she did not want to offend her partner. From what she could tell, most of what was known about Mr. Kennedy was hearsay, and some of it downright impossible. After all, he couldn't have been born to a nabob in India and also spent his earliest years on the edge of the Sahara with his pet lion. It was true that he counted many of the sons of the nobility amongst his friends and had escorted several beautiful widows over the course of his few years in London, but, as far as she was aware, he had never trifled with any young debutantes.

"They may not stay long," Samantha said.

Samantha's partner grunted and returned his attention to the waltz. They continued in silence for the rest of the dance. When it finished, he led her to the edge of the dance floor and went to procure her a beverage.

Aunt Victoria was at her side in an instant.

"He seems attentive of late," she said, watching the young man's retreating back. "Do you know aught of his family? His connections?"

"I have no notion," Samantha said blandly. "But it's of no consequence. It is clear enough that Sir Arthur does not like him."

Aunt Victoria followed Samantha's gaze to where Sir Arthur stood in conference with another man, his brows lowered in displeasure as he watched Samantha's partner approach the door to the refreshment room.

"In that case," Aunt Victoria said hastily. "It would be best if you were to discourage him from asking you to dance again. Your time would be better spent making yourself available to a more advantageous prospect."

"No doubt," Samantha said dryly.

When her partner returned, she accepted the glass of lemonade he handed her with a polite smile and they made small talk for the prescribed amount of time before he left her, perfectly cheerfully, to ask another woman to dance. He was soon replaced by a Mr. Clairmont, a gentleman to whom her uncle had introduced her near the beginning of the Season and of whose society she was already tired.

"Good evening, sir," Samantha said in response to his greeting. "I hope you are well."

"Tolerably, Miss Kingston, tolerably," Mr. Clairmont replied with a condescending nod. "And yourself?"

Samantha replied that she was also well, though inwardly she felt ready to die of boredom. She forced herself to pay attention to her partner, however, if only to determine the likelihood of his being the blackmailer.

"The weather has been quite warm of late," Mr. Clairmont continued. "I must say, I am surprised, for I was certain we had at least another fortnight before the heat began to rise to summer."

Samantha made a noise of polite interest and mentally erased Mr. Clairmont from her list of suspects. He lacked the imagination. Not to mention that he was well-connected, both politically and socially, being the younger son of a baron.

"Would you care to dance?"

Samantha glanced at Sir Arthur, who was watching her closely. As much as she wanted to refuse, she could not upset her uncle while she was still waiting to hear from Charles. So, pasting a smile on her face, she accepted Mr. Clairmont's hand and followed him to the dance floor.

Two hours later, Samantha was tired—tired of pretending interest in partners who ranged from dull to uncomfortably solicitous, tired of smiling, and even, much as she generally enjoyed it, tired of dancing. When she saw Sir Arthur leave the ballroom, she took her chance. Claiming a headache, she excused herself from her aunt's presence, ostensibly to take a few moments rest in the ladies' retiring room. She smiled at anyone who looked her way and left the ballroom as quickly as she could. In the hall, she looked both ways and, seeing no one, slipped out the front door.

It was warm, as Mr. Clairmont had stated, for which Samantha was glad. In her haste to leave, she had not thought to get her wrap. She stood at the top of the steps, breathing deeply, happy to be away from the stuffiness and scent of perspiration that pervaded the ballroom. Horse manure was the prevailing odor outside, but she did not mind. It reminded her of the stables on her grandfather's Derbyshire estate, the only place she had ever been truly happy.

Cyril's grand townhome stood across the road from Kensington Gardens. Figuring she had at least ten minutes before her aunt would come in search of her, Samantha decided to indulge in a brief walk. She waited for a carriage to pass and hurried across the street.

Flowers of every description bordered the meandering lantern-lit paths of Kensington Gardens. As she passed between lines of flowering shrubs, Samantha inhaled their fragrance and smiled. For just these few minutes, she decided, she would indulge herself in forgetting about the letters and Sir Arthur and Charles and just be.

An odd noise, like the cracking of a twig, made her pause. A feeling of unease intruded on her bliss as she remembered that, the impropriety of walking alone aside, she was potentially in real danger from the mysterious blackmailer. She had assumed, as so many of Cyril's guests were wont to sneak out to the gardens for stolen moments together, that she could consider them almost as part of his property, but, of course, they weren't. Anyone could be lying in wait for an unsuspecting passerby.

Samantha turned on her heel, ready to return to the ball, however insufferable it had become. Suddenly, she was seized from behind and pulled into the shadow of a nearby bush. She let out a shriek of surprise and fear, but before she could draw breath to call for help, the hands at her waist spun her around and the stranger's mouth found hers.

For a moment, she didn't move—she couldn't move. Her mind and body were frozen in shock. Then everything seemed to speed up and she placed her hands on the stranger's chest and shoved as hard as she could. Caught off guard, he stumbled back.

"What the—" he began indignantly. Then he caught sight of her face and his mouth formed an almost comical *O* of surprise. He ran his fingers through his hair. "You're not Lady Clarke."

"No, I'm not." She had intended to run, but his shock at seeing her seemed genuine and she reasoned that assaulting her had not been his intention. Besides which, even in the dim light, she recognized Mr. Kennedy. His sleek dark hair and neatly trimmed mustache and beard were distinctive, but even more than his physical appearance, there was the way he carried himself—a sort of casual confidence that bordered on arrogance.

"I thought you were Lady Clarke," he said dumbly, the confident air slightly deflated.

"So I gathered." She spoke in icy tones, but she struggled to suppress a laugh at his look of dismay. She felt unbalanced by the spectrum of emotions she had just experienced—the fear, the shock, the outrage—and it was good to see him equally at sea.

"We were playing a sort of game, you see," he continued. "And when I saw you, well…It was dark and you were alone, so I just assumed…Pray, forgive me."

"I see," Samantha said. "Well, let us hope you have learned your lesson about making assumptions. If I happen upon Lady Clarke, I will be sure to point her in the right direction."

"Wait," he called out as she turned to leave. "We haven't been introduced."

"No, we haven't. Though I would be interested to hear what explanation you would give our hosts as to why you wished to be introduced to me."

"Does a man need a reason to be introduced to a beautiful lady?"

Samantha sighed. "Please, Mr. Kennedy, do not ruin your reputation as an eloquent Lothario with such trite compliments."

He uttered a surprised laugh. "It seems you do not need to be introduced to me. I am flattered to find that my reputation precedes me."

"Is 'flattered' the right word in this situation?" she asked, raising an eyebrow.

"Perhaps not," he admitted. "But I hardly think the proper rules of introductions apply here. After all, you already know me."

"I believe such etiquette was created precisely for situations such as these—to avoid unwanted acquaintances. Good evening."

She turned and began walking back to the house. He caught up to her, his long legs easily overcoming her short strides.

"At least allow me to atone for my inexcusable actions by accompanying you back to the ball. A young lady such as yourself should not be walking alone."

"And would my reputation be any less damaged if I were seen walking with you?" she asked, turning a wry smile on him.

He grinned. "You're right, of course. I suppose I have rather precluded myself from acts of chivalry."

"I cannot imagine you regret that. You have all the perks of being a gentleman without the pitfalls of propriety."

"I regret it now."

Samantha stopped and turned to him, the cool evening breeze playing with one of her stray curls as she looked up into his face. His was watching her, smiling in a roguish way—a look she was certain he had given many women who dreamed of a more exciting future than the one they faced.

"Why?" she asked, tilting her head. "Because you miss a few more minutes in my company? No, I don't think so. You have a freedom most people envy. Who would give that up? I wouldn't."

He eyed her seriously now.

"So, again, I bid you good evening, sir. As I said, I will send Lady Clarke your way if I happen upon her."

She left him there, standing beside the path, and hurried back to the house.

The front hall was still empty when she entered, and Samantha was able to slip back into the ballroom and rejoin her aunt without drawing too much attention. Aunt Victoria was engaged in conversation with another lady, so she merely nodded to Samantha before returning her attention to her companion.

Samantha took the opportunity to scan the room for Sir Arthur. She spotted him by one of the large, floor-to-ceiling windows that faced the back garden. He was speaking to a man she was fairly certain was Lord S…something, a baron. She had danced with him earlier in the evening. He had been one of her overly solicitous partners and made her quite uncomfortable. Even from a distance, she could see they were arguing. Sir Arthur's color was heightened and the baron was jabbing his finger in the air emphatically. After a moment, the latter turned and strode away, shaking his head. He approached another party, but before he joined them, his gaze swept the room and when his eyes met Samantha's, they narrowed with displeasure.

Taken aback, Samantha watched as he turned his back to her. Her eyes flicked to Sir Arthur, who was also watching the baron. His expression, easily recognizable for how often she had seen it, was one of disdain. She wondered what they had argued about. The baron's scowl, directed so particularly at her, made her think she might have been involved, though she couldn't imagine why. What with the baron and the blackmailer and even, to a lesser extent, Archibald Kennedy, she was finding herself the subject of a lot of unwanted interest and it worried her.

TWO

The morning after a ball had its own rhythm. Sir Arthur relaxed his strict schedule and took breakfast in his room, which gave Samantha and her aunt the freedom to do the same. As they had not returned home until 3 a.m., this was a welcomed luxury.

Samantha was seated at her dressing table, absentmindedly chewing a slice of toast while she read the previous day's paper, which Alice had managed to salvage from the bin, when the door opened. Her heart shot to her throat before she saw that it was only Alice.

"Who did you think it would be?" Alice asked, amused, as she shut the door behind her.

Samantha smoothed the paper where her hands had reflexively crumpled it and took a calming breath.

"I know it's silly," she said. "After all, he's never actually said I couldn't read it after he throws it out, but I just worry about someone seeing and reporting it to him. Grandfather always said it was important to stay abreast of current events. I just feel that if he takes this away too, I'll have almost nothing left of him. Not that it should matter, after what he did, but it does, somehow."

She grimaced, realizing how incomprehensible her speech had

been, but Alice gave her a sympathetic smile. Alice had been with her since she lived with Grandfather, first as a housemaid before she was elevated to Samantha's lady's maid. She had come with Samantha when she was sent to stay with her aunt and uncle, had been there when Samantha learned they were her legal guardians, had watched her write letter after letter to her grandfather asking him to help free her from her uncle, had waited with her in vain for his responses. She understood Samantha's conflicted feelings—her love for the grandfather she had known and her anger, frustration and sadness at his abandonment.

"Sir Arthur wants to see you in his study," Alice said, breaking Samantha from her reverie.

"Now?" Samantha caught her own look of alarm in her reflection in the dressing-table mirror. Sir Arthur never requested her presence unless it was to deliver a lecture or a punishment. "In my dressing gown?"

Alice nodded. With some trepidation, Samantha set down her toast and stood, brushing crumbs from her lap.

"Will you take my breakfast tray back to the kitchen while I'm gone?" she asked Alice. "And bring up a fresh cup of tea?"

Alice nodded again.

When Samantha reached the door of her uncle's study moments later, she paused to slow her breathing—it wouldn't do to arrive out of breath—and knocked.

"Enter!"

Sir Arthur's study was a reflection of his person—meticulously clean, neatly ordered, with dark shelves and a large, imposing desk that dominated the room. When Samantha entered, he was seated at the desk, scratching away at a ledger.

"Shut the door," he said without looking up.

Samantha turned and closed the heavy wooden door. When

she turned back to the desk, Sir Arthur was setting down his pen. He looked up at her and she saw resolution in his gaze. She felt her sense of unease deepen. Instinctively, she clasped her hands together in front of her and squeezed them hard to keep herself from visibly reacting to whatever came next.

"I have found you a husband," he said, with all the banality of someone commenting on the weather.

Samantha's stomach dropped, but she kept the dismay from her face.

"Have you?" she asked, replicating his placid tone with only a slight tremor.

"He is the Viscount Lord Tyrrell. A good match. Better than you have hoped for, I dare say."

Samantha had known this day would come. She was surprised her uncle had waited so long to reveal his plans for her, but she wished he could have waited just a little longer. Or that she had thought to search for Charles sooner. Steeling herself, she decided to pretend ignorance.

"I thank you for your efforts on my behalf, Sir Arthur," she said evenly, "but I believe I can find my own husband."

"Your fruitless first Season proves otherwise."

She bristled at this. As though it hadn't been through his doing that she had been unable to find a suitable match. Her fingernails dug into the flesh of her palm as she struggled to keep her composure.

"Nonetheless," she said. "I know my own mind. I can make my own decision."

Sir Arthur's brows lowered and his frown deepened.

"Your indecision has cost me a great deal of money already. Your second Season is halfway gone with nothing to show for it. You should be thanking me. I am acting in your best interests. Lord Tyrrell is a viscount. You will be titled."

Samantha's fingernails drew blood. She could see it oozing out of tiny little cuts on her palm. She ought to have turned around and left right then. It was clear that her self-control was cracking. But this was too important. If she could not find Charles in time, she couldn't let her uncle ruin her whole life.

"I won't," she said in a half-whisper.

She looked up to see her uncle staring at her.

"I won't," she repeated, her voice a little stronger. "I won't thank you. You aren't acting in my best interests. You've never cared what my interests are. You are serving yourself, building your connections through me. I know what you've done. I know you have sent away my suitors. And if you think that I would accept a man you found suitable, you are very much mistaken."

As she spoke, Sir Arthur rose from his chair and walked around the desk. His face had gone white.

"You live in my house," he said, reaching out and grabbing her by the shoulders. "You eat my food and wear clothes purchased with my money." His fingers tightened and she tensed. "Every breath you take is because of my generosity. I took you in. I take care of you."

She tried to pull away, but he held fast.

"So, when I say that I am acting in your best interests, believe that I am. Do you understand?"

She pressed her lips together against the impulse to say yes, just to appease him.

"I am the master of this house. I thought I had taught you that years ago, but it seems you need a reminder."

He raised a hand and Samantha flinched, but before he could strike her, the door that led into the study from the parlor opened and the downstairs maid peered in. Seeing that the room was occupied, she ducked back out and closed the door. The interruption seemed to check Sir Arthur's temper, though, because he lowered his hand and released Samantha.

"Lord Tyrrell will be a guest at the Hyde-Claires' dinner party tonight," he said, returning to his desk as though nothing had happened. "I suggest you pay him every attention. Do I make myself clear?"

Samantha nodded stiffly. Her whole body felt tense, as though she were bracing herself against the weight of his will on her. He waved a hand towards the door, dismissing her, and returned to his ledger. She fled.

Back in her room with the door firmly shut, Samantha collapsed onto her bed. She grabbed a pillow and held it to her mouth to muffle her sobs. She cried as she hadn't cried in years. When she had emptied herself of tears, she sat up. There was a telling wet stain on the pillow. She flipped it over to hide it and placed it back at the head of the bed.

The crying hadn't changed anything, but she did feel a little better. Brushing back the hair that had come loose from her chignon, she wiped her face with the back of her sleeve.

It had been years since her uncle had been that angry with her. She had gotten good at avoiding his triggers, at keeping her opinions to herself, at hiding behind a mask of servility and obedience. She'd had to, with Charles gone. Before Charles left, he had taken the brunt of Sir Arthur's displeasure, protecting her. If not for him, she could not have survived those first few years living with Sir Arthur. When Charles left, it had been hard not to take it as a personal betrayal. After all, he well knew what he was abandoning her to. But she knew he would have come back if he could have. His anger at his father would have blown over. Sir Arthur's would last a lifetime.

When Alice entered, her eyes flicked from Samantha's face and tousled hair to the rumpled bedcovers. Her expression turned sympathetic, but she said nothing. After all, what was there to say? She changed Samantha into a green plaid dress and brushed out her hair before twisting it into a simple bun at the nape of her neck. Then, with deft fingers, she cleaned the cuts on Samantha's palm and wrapped them in a bandage. As she worked, she hummed softly and Samantha closed her eyes, focusing on the sounds.

There were several calls to pay that day. Due to Aunt Victoria's sickness, a small pile of calling cards had collected in the silver bowl in the hall. Not all of them had to be returned with visits—for a few, Aunt Victoria simply sent her own card over—but there were enough to keep the two of them occupied for several hours. To the few solicitous inquiries made by her aunt's friends, Samantha explained away her bandaged hand, with practiced ease, as the result of an accident with embroidery scissors. She received clucks of sympathy, and conversation was soon diverted to more neutral topics by her aunt.

When they finally returned home, Aunt Victoria was frantic that there would not be enough time to properly prepare for that night's supper.

"And I must ask Mrs. Allen to remind Simmons and Oswick to return on time," she said, concluding a list of to-dos that had taken the entire ride home to recite. She held out a hand as Thomas, the footman, reached in to help her descend from the carriage. "Last time, we nearly had to prepare ourselves for bed, and Sir Arthur was not pleased. It took all my persuasion to prevent him from dismissing them both. One would have thought even a servant could understand how to honor a privilege. We don't have to give them these evenings off, after all."

Samantha grimaced at Thomas, who gave her a half smile and a nearly imperceptible shrug as he helped her down. Aunt Victoria insisted that the mark of a good servant was to be unnoticed, which was all well and good, in Samantha's opinion, but to treat them as though they were both deaf and dumb was not only inhumane, it was foolish. It was no wonder that servants always knew more than anyone the secrets of a household.

"Make haste!" Aunt Victoria called over her shoulder as she hurried up the front path.

Thomas went to help John, the coachman, with the horses. Samantha was about to follow her aunt when there was a shout, the sound of running footsteps, and she turned to see a shabbily dressed man barreling towards her. She tried to step out of his way, but he grabbed her wrist in one large hand, yanked her reticule from her and shoved her to the ground.

She could hear Thomas shouting after the man and some commotion near the door of the house, but the pain in her shin where it had made contact with the corner of the step made her unable to focus on anything else. She gasped, and tears sprang to her eyes as she squeezed them shut.

She felt a hand on her shoulder and opened her eyes to see John, blurry through the tears, leaning over her.

"Are you alright, Miss?" he asked. "Are you hurt badly? I'm awfully sorry you was attacked. 'E came outta nowhere, 'e did. But don't you worry, Thomas'll get 'im. And e'll get your bag back."

"It's alright, John," Samantha said, her head clearer as the initial pain faded. "Just help me into the house."

With John's help, Samantha was able to stand, though she found she could not put weight on her left leg without pain shooting through it. She was forced to lean heavily against the coachman as she made her way inside.

"Where is my aunt?" Samantha asked Mrs. Allen, the housekeeper, who had come hurrying towards them when they entered the front door. "And Mr. Andrews?"

"Her ladyship had a fright," Mrs. Allen said. "Mr. Andrews has taken her to the morning room to recover."

"Had a fright" was one of the polite euphemisms members of the staff used to refer to Aunt Victoria's frequent, usually contrived, fainting spells. Samantha tried not to begrudge her the indulgence. It was one of Aunt Victoria's few pleasures in life to be doted on after a faint. She did think, however, that in this instance, her aunt might have waited until Samantha was tended to.

John assisted Samantha to a couch and she sank into the cushions with a groan. Mrs. Allen shooed him away and knelt beside Samantha.

"Nothing broken," she said, speaking over Samantha's gasp of pain as she pressed her fingers along the injury.

As Mrs. Allen arranged the cushions to support her leg, Samantha was able to consider the implications of the assault. She had never been robbed before and, though it was of course possible that such an occurrence so soon after the receipt of the threatening letter could be coincidence, it was so improbable as to be unlikely. She had been on a residential street, after all, not a public thoroughfare. A quiet street, too, where a would-be robber lying in wait would find few targets, unless he was waiting for a specific one.

If the attack was deliberate, however, Samantha was at a loss to understand its purpose. She had been frightened, but only briefly. Her injury was slight and easily healed. Nothing of great value had been stolen. If this was the blackmailer's attempt at following through on his vague but ominous threats, it was a poor one.

Thomas returned at the same time as the maid Mrs. Allen had sent for tea and a cold compress.

"'E got away, Miss," he said, addressing Samantha. His skin glistened with sweat and his eyes were wide with excitement. "Do you want me to fetch a constable?"

"What? No, no, don't do that."

It was unsettling to be addressed as though she were in charge. With her uncle away at his club and her aunt indisposed, she supposed the run of the house did fall to her, but it was not a position she was accustomed to.

"When Sir Arthur comes home, I am sure he will tell us what he wants done. I don't suppose the thief dropped my reticule as he ran?"

Thomas shook his head.

"Then I will need to make a note of what was in it, in case my uncle wishes to report the theft."

"Mary, set the tea things down there," Mrs. Allen said, addressing the maid, "and get Miss Kingston a pen and paper."

"Thank you for trying to help, Thomas," Samantha said. "I'm sure Sir Arthur will wish to thank you personally when he returns."

She was not at all sure of that and no doubt Thomas knew, but he bowed and left to return to his regular duties. Samantha took the pen and paper Mary handed her and, using the end table as a writing surface, listed the few contents of her reticule that might be of value to a thief: an elegant fan, a few coins she kept to buy flowers in the street, a silver comb. Personally, she didn't care to have any of it returned, but she knew Sir Arthur would be angry if she did not make a record. They were, as he so often reminded her, purchased with his money and were more his possessions than hers.

Sir Arthur arrived home half an hour later. His reaction upon hearing the story relayed by Andrews could be easily heard throughout the house. After his tirade about miscreants and ruffians and the incompetence of the London police force, he went to check on his wife before coming to see Samantha in her room.

"It seems you won't be going to the Hyde-Claires' this evening after all," were the first words he uttered, casting a contemptuous glance at the blanket that modestly covered her propped-up leg.

Samantha wanted to respond sarcastically that, yes, he had seen through her clever plan to injure herself to avoid one interaction with Lord Tyrrell, but she held her tongue.

"Andrews said you made a list of what was stolen."

"Yes. Mrs. Allen put it on your desk."

"I will make your excuses to the Hyde-Claires. And to Lord Tyrrell. Andrews has agreed to stay behind with you while we are all out."

"There's no need—" Samantha started to say, but he ignored her, leaving as abruptly as he had arrived.

"I can stay as well," Alice offered, closing the door behind him.

"No, no, please don't," Samantha insisted. "I want you to enjoy yourself. It's so rare that you get an evening off. I will be alright with my book." She picked up the worn copy of *Oliver Twist* from her bedside table and flipped it open. "Oliver has just met the Artful Dodger, so I will have plenty of adventure to occupy myself."

Alice smiled ruefully and shook her head. "If you're certain—"

"I am."

"Well then, I'll help you dress for bed before I leave. Is there anything else you need?"

"No, nothing. I'll be just fine."

With most of its occupants away, the house was eerily quiet that evening. Samantha ate through the plate of cold sandwiches Andrews had brought her, then set it aside and returned to her reading, but the disconcerting lack of sound made it difficult to concentrate. She hadn't realized how used she was to hearing the quiet steps of the maids climbing the stairs or the distant clank of pots in the kitchen. She and her aunt and uncle were always away when the servants had the evening off, so she had never encountered the strange sensation of being so alone before. *Oliver*

Twist was not helping. She had started to imagine Bill Sykes slowly climbing the stairs and her gaze kept flicking to the closed door, certain it would open at any moment to reveal his leering face.

A crash downstairs sent her bolt upright, her heart racing. *Don't be absurd*, she thought. *Andrews is still here. He probably dropped something.* She couldn't quite believe it, though. Andrews was nothing if not careful.

Moving gingerly, afraid to jostle her injured leg, Samantha slid to the edge of the bed and threw off the covers. She grabbed the bed post for support and hobbled to the door, turning the knob and opening it enough to stick her head into the hallway beyond. From down below came the sound of voices. They were deep and their tones rose and fell in agitation. The footmen would not have returned so early. There was only one possibility she could imagine.

Burglars!

As she stood, straining to hear what they were saying, the voices became clearer and louder and she realized they were approaching the stairs. With a sharp gasp, she pulled her head back in and closed the door, turning the lock. She stood for a moment, unsure what to do. Then, she hobbled across the room to the window and lifted the sash. It was too high for her to jump. There was a ledge, but she doubted she could reach it, especially with her injured leg. Turning back to the room, she snatched the fireplace poker and held it in front of herself, acutely aware of how useless it would be if the burglars carried pistols.

Her eyes fell on the linen cupboard. It was built into the wall to the left of the door and designed to blend in with the wood paneling. The effect was so seamless, it was nearly impossible to see if one did not know it was there and even harder in the dim light of the dying fire in the grate. Trailing a hand down the wall, her fingers found the edge and she popped it open. Moving swiftly and silently, she set the poker down and gathered up the quilts from the widest shelf and tossed them onto the bed. She could hear heavy bootfalls on the stairs. Her heart beat faster. She ducked her head into the space she had created and, with a strength born of necessity, pulled herself inside.

She fit, but only just. Her back was against the wall, her knees touched her chin and her neck was at an odd angle. She reached out with her left arm—the right was pinned beneath her—and pulled the cupboard door shut. As her eyes adjusted to the sudden darkness, she heard the jiggle of a doorknob. Her heart stopped. The jiggling was followed by a series of soft clicks and scrapes of metal on metal and then the door burst open. Heavy footsteps pounded into the room.

"What the…Where is she?" came a man's voice, hoarse and deep, with the rough accents of the lower classes.

The footsteps passed Samantha's hiding place. She squeezed her eyes shut and held her breath, trying to listen through the pounding of blood in her ears.

"You sure the door was locked?" asked the other man. His voice was higher, but somehow just as menacing.

"'Course I'm sure. She's gotta be here somewhere."

Booted footsteps pounded across the room. Samantha heard the wardrobe doors open and the creak of the bed being shifted aside.

"She ain't here," the higher-voiced man said. "She's got away somehow."

"Whaddya mean, she got away?" The deep-voiced man sounded incredulous. "What, you think she popped out the window?"

"Musta done."

There was a creaking sound that Samantha thought must be the window being pushed open further.

"And how'd she get down?" the deep-voiced man asked

pointedly.

"That ledge—"

"Not a chance. Not with her leg hurt and all. No way could she reach that."

"Maybe you didn't push her as hard as you thought."

Samantha's eyes flew open in shock and she sucked in a breath. From the direction of the window, she heard a thud and a crash.

"That hard enough for you? That's how hard I done it."

"You—"

But the higher-voiced man didn't finish his sentence. Instead, Samantha heard more thumping and grunting. Another crash was followed by a volley of curses, some of which she knew but most of which she had never heard before.

"Enough!" It was the higher-voiced man who shouted. "We ain't got much time. Let's check the rest of the house. If she ain't here, we can't be blamed."

"He won't be happy."

"Yeah, well, he can't be mad at us. It's that toff what's to blame and it's the toff what'll pay for it."

The footsteps passed in front of Samantha again and she squeezed her eyes shut, holding her breath. Then, they paused.

"How much do you think we could get for that?" asked the deep-voiced man.

"For what? Oh. Er…" The higher-voiced man sounded hesitant.

"Or that?" his companion continued eagerly. "There's lots of little trinkets here what would fetch a good price with the right fence."

"We do the job we was asked to do," the higher-voiced man said, but he didn't sound convinced. "He might not be happy with us—"

"It's only a few things," the deep-voiced man interrupted.

"We'll wait a bit 'fore we sell 'em so's they can't be traced to this job. We've never had an easier time getting in an 'ouse. Seems we should get sommat for it."

"Alright…"

The word was drawn out, as though the higher-voiced man was using the time it took him to agree to finish making up his mind to do so.

"Here, give me a hand with this. We can tie it up and use it for a sack."

There was a lot of shuffling and a confusion of noise. Samantha thought she heard the soft brush of fabric against fabric, metallic clinks and wooden thuds. The heavy boots moved back and forth across the floor and then, finally, mercifully, out the door and down the hall. She heard doors opening and shutting, more clinks and clangs, and the heavy footsteps descended the stairs.

Letting out a long breath, Samantha felt some of the tension leave her arms and legs. At least one mystery was solved, she thought ruefully. The attack that afternoon *had* been planned. She had been deliberately knocked to the ground so that she would be sure to be home that evening when the men came to abduct her. Or kill her. She wasn't sure what their plan had been, only that she had foiled it. She shuddered to think how differently the evening might have ended if she had already been asleep when they arrived.

The men had mentioned a toff, which was just how the boy who delivered the blackmail letter had referred to the man who gave it to him. But from what these men had said, the toff was not ultimately in charge. There appeared to be another man, the "he" the men referred to who wouldn't be happy with the outcome of the evening. They seemed to regard him with a mixture of fear and awe, and a man who could inspire such feelings in a pair of burglars brazen enough to enter a house in Kensington scared her much more than a toff blackmailer.

Several minutes passed with no further noises from below. Silently, Samantha pushed open the cupboard door. Extending her legs, she twisted her body around and lowered herself to the floor. She was stiff and her leg throbbed worse than before, but she was alive.

As her eyes adjusted to the dim light from the fire and the candle by her bed, she saw that her room was in shambles. The bed covers had been yanked off the bed and lay in a heap on the floor beside the quilts from the linen cupboard. The doors of the wardrobe were flung open and several gowns had fallen to the floor. Her vanity had been emptied—the silk hairnet, several porcelain jars and the silver hairpin box were all missing and what was left lay strewn about. *Oliver Twist* had fallen to the floor with the bedclothes and lay open with a dirty boot print across its worn pages.

Stepping over the mess and wincing as pain shot up her leg, Samantha made for the door, picking up the poker as she went. She lifted the candlestick from her bedside and held it in front of her as she peered down the hall. Seeing nothing, she tiptoed forward. As she neared the top of the stairs, she thought she saw movement to her right and nearly jumped out of her skin before she realized it was her own reflection in the mirror above the hall table. She looked a frightful mess. Her hair had pulled free of its braid and hung in tangles, and her face was pale and drawn. The shadows cast by the flickering light of the small candle gave her a ghostly appearance and she turned away before her imagination could turn an already terrifying night into something worse.

She found the butler's pantry without too much difficulty—it was not far from the kitchen. Confident now that the burglars had absconded with their ill-gotten gain, she called out to Andrews as she approached the open door. There was no response. She was not surprised—surely, he would have come to find her if he were alright—but the silence made her pulse quicken.

She saw him as soon as she entered the room. He lay sprawled out on the floor. A dark, red liquid stained the flagstones at his feet and Samantha gasped, dropping to her knees. The poker fell to the ground with a clatter, and she put a hand over her mouth, afraid she might be sick. Then she noticed the shards of glass sprinkled about, including the large one with part of a label still attached and she took a steadying breath. Sir Arthur would not be happy to have lost a bottle of his favorite port, but at least his butler wasn't bleeding out.

Samantha stood, bracing herself against the wall for support, and stepped carefully over the glass to reach Andrews' head. There was a large knot near his temple, but she could see the rise and fall of his chest.

"Andrews," she whispered, taking hold of his shoulder and shaking him. "Andrews?"

He didn't respond, and she found herself wishing she had her vinaigrette. Smelling salts would have been the simplest way to revive him.

"Andrews!" She shook him harder. He did not stir. With deft hands she loosened his collar and cuffs. She stood, with difficulty, and hopped one-legged to the other side of the room. She emptied a small crate of the bottles it contained, setting them on the wooden counter, and flipped it upside down. Careful to avoid the pool of port, she set the crate beside Andrews' feet and lifted his legs onto it. His legs were much heavier than her aunt's, who she was used to reviving in such a way, but she managed it. She returned to his head and waited, straining her eyes and ears for signs of continued breathing.

Finally, Andrews' eyes opened. He blinked several times and then, seeing her no-doubt anxious face hovering above his, he made a move to sit up.

"No, no, no," Samantha said hastily. "Stay still. You took a nasty blow to the head."

"Head?" He looked confused, then alarmed. "Miss Kingston! There are burglars in the house!"

"Not anymore," she assured him. "They left. You've been unconscious for quite a while."

"They left? But…are you hurt? Did they take anything?"

"They took some things. I haven't had the opportunity to ascertain what all they took, but they didn't harm me. They didn't even know I was here."

Relief and concern warred across Andrews' countenance, but in the end his usual inscrutable look won out.

"I'll send for a doctor," Samantha said, getting to her feet. "And a constable."

Before Andrews could object, Samantha hurried out of the room. She went first to her own room to grab her dressing gown, throwing it over her nightgown. Then, she went outside via the servants' entrance. She climbed the first few steps of the short flight of stairs that led to the ground level until she could see out through the gate to the street. Then she pursed her lips together and whistled.

To her immense relief, considering the lateness of the hour, one of the odd-job boys who patrolled the neighborhood looking for work was nearby. He looked surprised to see her standing in the well of the servants' entrance in her dressing gown, but he took the coin she offered him eagerly and ran off to fetch the help she had requested.

Unfortunately for all concerned, Sir Arthur's carriage pulled up to the house in time to see the constable being shown in through the servants' entrance. The doctor had arrived only a few minutes before. Leaving the coachman to help his wife down, Sir Arthur leapt from the carriage and hurried down the steps after the constable.

"What's this about?" he demanded on entering the butler's

pantry.

Doctor North knelt beside a pale Andrews, who had graduated to a sitting position. Samantha stood beside the constable, who had not yet had the opportunity to introduce himself.

"You must be Sir Arthur," the constable said, inclining his head.

"Of course I'm ruddy Sir Arthur," Samantha's uncle shouted, apoplectic with indignation. "Who the blazes are you? And what are you doing in my house?"

"My name is Constable Dobbs, sir," the constable said, "and this young lady was just about to tell me what I'm doing here."

Samantha's uncle rounded on her, and she could see a vein pulsing in his temple.

"We were robbed, Sir Arthur," she said, cutting him off before he could speak. "Two men broke into the house. They hit Andrews over the head and stole—"

"Robbed? What do you mean, robbed?"

"I—"

"Andrews, what happened?"

Samantha let out a huff of frustration which no one, except perhaps the constable, heard.

"As Miss Kingston said," Andrews explained. "Two men broke in. I was counting the inventory and they surprised me. I—"

"Tell me, have any of the servants returned?" Sir Arthur interrupted.

"Not yet, sir."

"Samantha," he snapped. "Your aunt is waiting outside. Go let her in the house."

"But surely—"

"Now."

Samantha closed her mouth and turned on her heel. There was

no use arguing and the quicker she performed her task, the quicker she could return.

She led her aunt into the living room and onto a settee before telling her briefly what had happened. Aunt Victoria promptly fainted, as Samantha had known she would. Laying her back against the cushions, she reached into her aunt's reticule and extracted the vinaigrette. She removed the lid and held the smelling salts under her nose. With a gasp, Aunt Victoria came to.

"The doctor is here already," Samantha assured her. "Why don't I go get him for you?"

"There's no need to make a fuss," her aunt said unconvincingly.

"I'll send him right up."

Doctor North was packing up his bag when she returned, but he stopped when he saw her.

"There's no need to explain," he said before she could open her mouth. "I will look in on Her Ladyship before I leave. Is she in the drawing room?"

Samantha nodded.

"Very well. If you will excuse me, Miss Kingston, Sir Arthur, Constable."

Nodding to each, he left the room.

"I will be returning with the constable to Scotland Yard," Sir Arthur said, replacing his hat, which he had removed on entering the house. "Be sure to tell Lady Prescott. I do not know when I will return."

Constable Dobbs closed his notebook and pocketed it. With a short bow to Samantha and a brief but polite farewell, he put on his helmet and went out.

"Sir Arthur," she said before her uncle could follow. "What about me?"

"What about you?"

"Shouldn't I speak with the constable about what happened?"

He looked annoyed.

"Why?"

"To tell him what I saw, of course," she said, her brow knitted in confusion.

"You saw the burglars?"

"Well, no, but—"

"Then I fail to see what useful information you could have for the constable."

"But, Sir Arthur, I think the blackmailer sent them."

That made him pause.

"Why do you say that?"

"I overheard them talking. They…that is, it seems they came to abduct me. On another man's orders."

He frowned.

"Perhaps the constable should hear what I overheard."

"There's no need. I will tell him."

"But—"

"Good evening."

He swept from the room.

"Do not worry, Miss Kingston. Sir Arthur has the situation well in hand."

Samantha jumped. She had forgotten Andrews was still in the room. She thought she heard him chuckle, but when she turned to look, his face was its usual mask of polite indifference. He placed a hand on the counter and began to lift himself unsteadily to his feet.

"I am feeling much better," he assured her, seeing her about to object. "I will just go to the kitchen and rest for a while until Thomas or one of the other young men returns and can help me up the stairs. You should be in bed, if I may say. It's quite late."

Samantha thought she would have trouble getting to sleep with all that had happened. Her leg still throbbed and she had developed a dull headache behind her temples. Yet, within a few minutes of lying down, with her leg once again supported by pillows, she found herself drifting off, though not before wondering what her uncle was doing in Scotland Yard.

THREE

Evening had fallen and the gas lamps were lit by the time the hackney carriage rolled up to a modest house on Bedford Row in Holborn. Sir Arthur opened the door and stepped out, holding out a hand for his wife. Aunt Victoria remained frozen to her seat, staring out at the wrought-iron gate that opened to a short front stoop.

"Come along, my darling," Sir Arthur said impatiently, beckoning her forward.

"I don't understand," she said, her voice strained. "What are we doing here? I thought we would be staying with friends. Surely you don't know anyone in Holborn?"

Samantha was as surprised as her aunt, though she didn't voice her opinion aloud. Sir Arthur was quite snobbish despite, or perhaps because of, the fact that he himself was only one generation removed from trade. He cultivated friendships primarily with the nobility and a few influential gentlemen. If he knew anyone who couldn't afford to live in Mayfair or Kensington, he certainly didn't advertise it.

When Sir Arthur had ordered them to pack and sent the servants, including Alice, on to the house in Kent, she assumed they would be following shortly. But then he had sent the carriage on its way and led her and her aunt to the mews, at the back of the house, where a hired carriage awaited them. They had traveled across the city, jostled until their teeth rattled, in the poorly hung chassis of the hired coach and, rather than heading south across the river, they had come to Holborn. Samantha was utterly at a loss.

"Of course I don't know anyone in Holborn," Sir Arthur scoffed in answer to his wife's question. "This is our house. For a few days."

"Our house?" Aunt Victoria repeated in a strained voice. Beside her, Samantha struggled to keep her face the bland mask she tried to maintain around Sir Arthur.

"Yes. Now get out of the carriage before this man charges us extra."

Aunt Victoria continued to stare at her husband, so Samantha reached over and lay a hand on her knee.

"I think we had better move," she said softly. "You don't want to upset Sir Arthur."

Galvanized, her aunt gathered her reticule and got up, ducking her head as she exited the carriage. Samantha followed and they stood beside the gate while her uncle spoke with the driver. Aunt Victoria's eyes swept up and down the street, confusion mixed with disdain as she took in the soot-stained grey brick houses with their flat exteriors, no doubt comparing them unfavorably with the stately white mansions of Argyll Road.

Sir Arthur joined them and added his own frown to the atmosphere of disapproval.

"Where are they? I was assured they would be ready for us."

No sooner had he finished speaking than the front door opened and a woman appeared, followed by a boy. The woman was thin and greying, with rounded shoulders that gave her a hunched appearance even when standing tall. She ordered the boy, a small, wiry child of around twelve or thirteen, to help the coachman unload the bags and strode forward.

"Good evening," she said, dipping her head to Sir Arthur and Aunt Victoria and bending her knees slightly. It looked as though she had been unable to decide whether to curtsey or not and had given up halfway through the effort. "I am Mrs. Dunbar, the housekeeper. We keep a skeleton staff here while the family are away and, with the cook absent at the moment, Davy, the footboy, and I are the only members of staff currently in residence. But we'll do our best to make you comfortable."

The coachman and Davy made short work of unloading the baggage and soon the hired coach was rumbling away down the road. Samantha watched it go, a feeling of nervous anticipation twisting her stomach as she wondered what was to come.

"If you will follow me, Mr. Avery," Mrs. Dunbar said, lifting her skirts as she mounted the steps, "I will show you to your rooms."

Samantha did a double take at the false name. Out of the corner of her eye, she saw Aunt Victoria's mouth gape open in a most un-ladylike fashion. Sir Arthur gave them both a quelling look and followed Mrs. Dunbar.

Inside, moonlight filtering through the windows cast eerie shadows over the furniture. Samantha's imagination filled the darkest parts of the room with sinister figures and she squeezed her eyes shut, hoping to speed their adjustment to the gloom. When she opened them, Mrs. Dunbar was picking up a candle from the hall table. By its flickering light, she led the way up the narrow stairs. Sir Arthur followed, then Aunt Victoria, leaving Samantha to scramble up after them in near darkness.

When they reached the landing, Mrs. Dunbar showed Sir Arthur to his room first, then Aunt Victoria. Samantha's room was across the hall from her aunt's. She entered it with some trepidation, but was pleased to find a lit candle in the sconce beside the bed. She lifted the candle from its holder and carried it with her as she explored the corners of the room.

It was smaller than what she was used to, as was to be expected, but not unpleasant. The windows, which were open to let in the warm night air, faced the back garden. There was a bed, a chair, a wardrobe, and a washstand. She was just bending to sniff the sheets for freshness when Davy the footboy entered with her bags.

"Thank you," Samantha said as he set them down in front of the wardrobe.

He looked surprised at being addressed and, after a hesitant nod, he seemed to doubt himself and sank into a deep bow. Samantha put a hand over her mouth to stop herself from laughing. When he straightened, she smiled, and he hastened out.

Left alone, Samantha eyed her bags with trepidation. She had never unpacked for herself and, without Alice or someone else to assist her, she wouldn't be able to change out of her traveling garments, anyway. With a sigh, she went to the washstand and splashed her face with the tepid water in the ewer, then went back downstairs.

Sir Arthur and Aunt Victoria were already in the lounge. The curtains had been drawn shut and a fire lit in the grate. Several braces of candles sat on surfaces throughout the room, dispelling the gloom and making it possible to see that the lounge was a comfortably appointed, if over-stuffed, room. Sir Arthur sat in a high-backed armchair, angled to the fire. Aunt Victoria was nearby, poised on the edge of an embroidered couch, the cup of tea beside her untouched.

"Have you settled in?" Sir Arthur asked.

"Yes, thank you," Samantha said, sitting beside her aunt on the couch. "Is there a reason all the servants have gone on to Kent without us?"

It wasn't quite sarcasm, but it was as near to it as she ever dared come with her uncle. However, he seemed not to notice, still too pleased with whatever secret he had kept from them.

"We'll be joining them shortly," he said. "Just as soon as we've caught the fellow."

"Caught the fellow?" Aunt Victoria echoed. "What fellow?"

"The one with the almighty gall to try to blackmail me," he replied. Then, he lowered his voice conspiratorially. "We've laid a trap for him."

"A trap?" Aunt Victoria repeated at the same time that Samantha said, "We?"

"Yes, a trap. We've sent the servants on to Kent so he'll think we've gone there, too, but we'll be safely hidden away in London."

"But, why Holborn?" Aunt Victoria asked. "Why not stay with someone we know?"

Sir Arthur chuckled and shook his head.

"My dear Victoria, the fellow clearly knows us. He knew where we lived and the perfect time to break into our house when the servants were away and Samantha was alone. He could be any one of our friends."

Now his wife laughed, but the quaver in her voice showed she was more nervous than amused.

"That's ridiculous," she said. "No one we know would need to blackmail anyone for money."

"Excuse, me, Sir Arthur," Samantha tried again. "When you say 'we'—"

"But who could it have been?" Aunt Victoria interrupted, sounding almost hysterical. "The Pollards? They have taken some financial losses lately and Mrs. Pollard has always been jealous of my gowns. But, no, I couldn't see them associating with criminals. The Pritchards, then? Or the Carltons?"

Sir Arthur stood and walked over to the window. He clasped

his hands behind his back and turned to face them.

"There's no use speculating," he said. "Though, for my part, I could see any of them being responsible."

Aunt Victoria paled. "Then we are to remain here until the culprit is caught. How long will that take?"

Sir Arthur smiled. "With luck, only a day or two."

But they had no luck, and as the days stretched to a week, the atmosphere in the house became strained. Sir Arthur went out most days, though, where he went, he refused to say. He wore a false beard that Samantha thought looked like a small, furry animal clinging to his face. Each day, he returned more irritable than the last, so that Samantha and her aunt took to retreating to their rooms as soon as they saw him coming up the path. Aunt Victoria was also irritable, though her frustrations revealed themselves in different ways. She would sit in the front parlor, staring out the window for hours on end. Every so often, she would sigh and turn to Samantha with tears glistening in her eyes.

"What can your uncle have been thinking?" she would moan. "This Season is so crucial for you. We have spent so much already on gowns. If we have to come back next year, you will require a whole new wardrobe. Oh, how can he think to keep me—you—locked away like this?"

Sometimes her complaints were trivial—her fears of missing out on the latest gossip or being upstaged by her rivals—and sometimes they were more serious.

"What will everyone think? What will people say? No one leaves in the middle of the Season when they're in the market. People will think there is a reason we had to leave."

Samantha had been so caught up in the mystery of the blackmailer and her near-abduction that she had not thought about her Season since the argument with her uncle. Now the implications of her aunt's comments hit her. It was true. People were always ready to believe the worst. If they did not return to Society soon, people would think she had been taken away because she had gotten herself with child. With her meager fortune, she would never recover.

On a practical level, the family's forced seclusion had been a lesson in adapting, particularly for Aunt Victoria, who had never been without her lady's maid. Sir Arthur's apathetic suggestion that she use Mrs. Dunbar had been met with objections on both sides. So, Samantha and her aunt wore their hair simply and helped each other with their corsets. Samantha found that, much as she missed Alice, she enjoyed being without a maid. It wouldn't have been possible to go without under normal circumstances, but in that tiny house in Holborn, with Sir Arthur insisting they turn down every neighborly invitation and with no one to impress but one another, she was able to manage on her own and was happy to discover that she could.

There was another benefit to dressing herself, which Samantha discovered two days after they moved to Holborn. Desperate to understand what her uncle was doing and tired of being rebuffed, she slipped out the back after he left and followed him. Unfortunately, after walking to the end of the street, he hailed a cab and drove off, foiling her intentions. Rather than return to the house, though, she continued down the street. She walked for several blocks, but she received curious looks from so many people—a young woman of her status walking unaccompanied was a rare sight—that she entered the first secondhand shop she saw and bought a dress. It was several years out of fashion and simple in design—perfect for a servant on her day off.

The next day, after Sir Arthur went out and Aunt Victoria was settled on the settee in the parlor, Samantha left by the back door and went for a walk. She wore her new dress. No one called out to her or stared or seemed in the least interested in her at all. It was the freest she had felt since entering her uncle's household.

She repeated the breakout every day thereafter and grew bolder each time, walking farther and taking in more of the city. If the servants marked her absence, they said nothing. Aunt Victoria was too wrapped in her own misery to notice Samantha's afternoon jaunts and Sir Arthur was rarely home before supper.

Nine days into their stay in Holborn, Samantha was awakened by a crash. She sat up with a start and the book that lay across her chest slid to the floor. She had fallen asleep in her chair again, waiting for her aunt to retire so they could help each other out of their corsets. The room was dark, but by the candle she had left burning, she could make out its sparse furnishings. Everything was where she had left it, even the dress she had thrown across the bed after removing it; nothing had fallen over. She was just wondering if she had dreamed the sound, in some nightmarish re-creation of the night of the attempted abduction, when she heard more noises. They were muffled and sounded like furniture shifting and men's voices. Her heartbeat quickened.

The doorknob turned. Fear paralyzed her and she could only watch as the door slid open silently. Then Aunt Victoria appeared, carrying a candlestick. Samantha let out a breath as her aunt slipped in and shut the door behind her. But when she turned, her eyes were wide and, even in the candlelight, Samantha could see that she was white as a sheet.

"They found us," she said in a panicked whisper.

"Are you certain?"

Aunt Victoria nodded.

"I had fallen asleep waiting for you to help prepare me for bed," her aunt explained. Samantha repressed her irritation at the implied criticism. "When I woke, I came to find you and I heard voices from downstairs. Angry voices. Your uncle was speaking, but there were other men too. They were arguing. Something about money. Then there was a crash."

As she spoke, another crash came from below.

"You have to hide!" Aunt Victoria said with a gasp, grabbing Samantha's arm and pulling her from the chair.

"What? Why?"

"They'll take you if you don't. Hurry!"

Samantha tried to protest that, if persuading Sir Arthur to pay was their aim, they had no need to abduct her while they were currently arguing with him downstairs, but Aunt Victoria wouldn't listen. Her hand gripped so tightly on Samantha's upper arm that she was cutting off the circulation, she pushed her towards the wardrobe.

"Get inside," she said, throwing open the doors. "I'll tell you when it's safe."

Then, releasing Samantha, she hurried back to the hall, her skirts swishing behind her.

"Where are you going?" Samantha hissed, as loudly as she dared.

"To help Sir Arthur," Aunt Victoria replied, pausing in the doorway and looking back. "They will hardly dare attack a lady. Perhaps I can calm them down."

It was such a brave and foolish thing to do that Samantha was momentarily stunned. She watched her aunt disappear through the door and then shook herself. She was still in her chemise and corset, so she grabbed the secondhand dress from the wardrobe—it was the easiest to put on without assistance—and threw it on, determined to follow her aunt.

She was doing up the buttons, fumbling a little in her haste, her breath coming in hard, when the muffled voices from below rose to shouts and a sharp crack resounded through the house. Samantha froze, her heart pounding in her ears. Then there was a shrill, terrified scream and another gunshot. The screaming stopped.

Samantha's frozen limbs seemed to melt and she sank to the floor, breathing shakily. Below, she could hear male voices raised in argument. They grew louder and she realized, in some distant, logical part of her mind, that they must be coming into the hall. A third gunshot resounded so loudly it left her ears ringing.

Her body moved before her mind had caught up and she rose to her feet, heading for the window. She could hear the men arguing again. The only thought in her mind was that she had to get out before they found her too. She threw up the sash and stuck her head out the window. A breeze caught the hair that had come loose from its pins and blew it across her face as she turned to clamber out. She shook her head to clear it away and grabbed the windowsill, placing her toes securely on the trellis below.

She was halfway down the trellis, splinters of wood biting into her bare feet, when the back door burst open and a man came running out. Samantha couldn't hold back her gasp of surprise. He came to a sudden halt, halfway between her and the back gate, and turned.

For several heartbeats, they stared at each other. His face was half hidden behind a thick growth of facial hair and a long brown coat covered most of his body, blending in with the darkness, but she could see his eyes. They were bright blue and seemed to pierce right through hers. He lifted his right arm and she saw the glint of metal in the moonlight as he pointed his gun at her. Her fingers tightened reflexively on the trellis and she squeezed her eyes shut.

The unmistakable clack of a police rattle sounded nearby. Samantha, expecting a gunshot, started violently and her foot slipped on the trellis. As her eyes snapped open, she saw the retreating form of the blue-eyed man as he sped out of the garden.

Weak with relief, Samantha half climbed, half-slid down the rest of the trellis, landing with a thump. The ground beneath her feet was cold and rough. She crouched behind a potted plant, expecting to see the second man follow the first. Seconds ticked by and no one came out. She wondered if he was still looking for her in the house and decided she would feel safer waiting out front for the police, where the neighbors could see her. She stood and hurried across the small back garden to the gate, feeling tiny pebbles and sharp-edged rocks cutting into her feet with every step.

The police rattles grew louder as Samantha came out onto the street. There were shouts too. Doors were opening as neighbors stuck their heads out, trying to see what was going on.

"Were those gunshots?"

"Did you hear gunshots?"

"Has someone been shot?"

Samantha couldn't see the blue-eyed man anywhere, but as she stood, unsure, on the edge of the street, she heard footsteps running up behind her. Turning sharply, she saw the gangly form of Davy. His eyes widened as they met hers and he came to a stop, bent over and panting.

"They're dead!" he gasped. "They're all dead!"

"Dead?" Samantha echoed dumbly. "Sir—Mr. and Mrs. Avery? Are you sure? They're not just…"

Davy shook his head.

"Blood everywhere. Not moving. Not breathing. And Mrs. Dunbar."

"Mrs. Dunbar? Mrs. Dunbar too?"

Davy nodded. "Those men killed them all and now they've scarpered. We've gotta get outta here!"

"Wait!" Samantha grabbed his sleeve before he could run off. "We need to wait for the police. We have to tell them what happened."

"You can if you want, but I ain't waiting for them to pin this on me."

"They won't pin anything on you," Samantha said with exasperation as he pulled against her. "They don't pin things on people."

Davy gave her an incredulous look. Then he wrested himself from her grasp and took off up the street. As he crossed in front of the house, Samantha saw the front door was ajar. Had the other man gone out the front, then? A faint, flickering light from within drew her attention and she began to walk towards it. She could hear the neighbors shouting after Davy, heard more running feet, but she found herself transfixed by the doorway and what she knew, and feared, lay beyond it. She was at the threshold before she fully realized what she was doing and then, a moment later, she was inside.

The first thing she noticed was the smell. Gunpowder mixed with the heavy, metallic scent of blood. She put a hand over her nose and mouth, breathing shallowly. The fireplace in Sir Arthur's study was still lit and its flickering light shone through the door into the hall, casting deep shadows throughout. On the floor by the door, a large shape was outlined by the firelight. She stepped towards it, moving as if in a dream, the soft whisper of her bare feet against the wood floor the only sound apart from the crackling of the fire.

It was Mrs. Dunbar. She lay on her side with her head tilted up. The hair near her temple was matted with blood. A red stain spread across her chest, a pool of liquid beneath it. Her eyes were open, blank and staring. Samantha felt her stomach twist and she clamped her hand more tightly over her mouth as bile rose in her throat. She swallowed convulsively and felt her throat burn.

Samantha turned from the grisly sight and her feet, almost, it seemed, of their own accord, carried her into the next room. As she stepped inside, she felt a sharp pain in her foot and looked down to see the shattered remains of a glass vase. Flowers lay scattered across the floor and there was a dark stain on the rug where the water had soaked it.

Her gaze trailed across the flowers towards the bookshelf. The heel of a man's black shoe peeked out from behind the desk. With mounting trepidation, she stepped carefully around the shattered vase, bringing the rest of the body into view.

Sir Arthur sat propped against the bookshelf, his head at an odd angle and his eyes staring, unfocused at a point near her feet. Blood soaked his white shirt and trickled from the corner of his slack mouth. Beside him lay Aunt Victoria, her pallid face turned towards Samantha, a pool of blood beneath her. Samantha let out a strangled scream that was muffled by the hand she still held to her mouth and took an involuntary step backward

How long she stood there, transfixed, she did not know. Eventually, propelled by a sense of propriety drilled into her by the woman who lay motionless before her, Samantha crouched down and closed her aunt's eyes.

"Don't move."

The words, spoken in sharp, harsh tones, broke Samantha from the daze that had fallen on her from the moment she had entered the house. She startled, unbalancing herself, and threw out a hand to stop her fall. Her hand landed in the blood beside her aunt and she gasped, jerking it back and falling on her backside.

"I said, don't move!" the harsh voice shouted. "Stay where you are, and show me your hands."

Fear coursed through Samantha as she lifted her hands, the right one sticky with blood, above her head. Heavy footsteps sounded behind her and she heard a crunch as one of the booted feet ground the remains of the vase further into the rug.

"Check her for weapons," the speaker said as he came into view. He moved cautiously, his truncheon held out in front of him defensively. Samantha was relieved to see the blue coat, almost black in the darkness, and the glazed hat that shimmered in the firelight. He was a constable. Of course he was. She had known they were coming. She felt foolish to have imagined, even for a moment, that one of the killers had returned to finish what he had started.

"Stand up," said a voice behind her. "But keep your hands up."

Samantha got awkwardly to her feet. Her arms were beginning to ache, but she kept them raised. A second constable stepped around her. His eyes scanned the ground on either side of her, then he scrutinized her person, ducking his head to look under her arms, but he did not touch her.

"None," he grunted finally, stepping back.

"Where is the gun?" the first constable asked.

"I don't know," Samantha said, her fear rising again at the look of accusation in the constable's eye. "That is, I didn't shoot them. But the man who did, I think he took it with him. I saw it."

"You think he took it? Or you saw it?"

"I saw it," Samantha amended. "He pointed it at me, but then he heard the police rattles and he ran."

"Who are you?" the constable asked.

"I'm…" she began, but she hesitated. They had been living under the name of Avery. Should she give that name? It was what the neighbors knew them by and what they would corroborate. Then she remembered that she had never met any of the neighbors. Mrs. Dunbar had been instructed to turn them all away. Did any of them know there was a young lady living with the mysterious Mr. and Mrs. Avery?

The constable's eyes bored into hers and she knew her delay was only making things worse.

"I'm their niece," she said finally, gesturing to Sir Arthur and Aunt Victoria.

The constable looked her up and down and she knew he was

taking in her simple dress, ripped in several places where she had caught it on the trellis, her bare feet, and the hair that was falling down around her face. No doubt she looked more like a street waif than the niece of someone as clearly genteel as Sir Arthur, though she thought her polished accent must give the constable pause.

"Did you know the boy?" the constable asked. "The one who ran?"

"Yes, that's…" She stopped short of giving Davy's name, remembering his fear of having the murder "pinned" on him. She didn't want to send the police in the wrong direction when she knew who the murderers were.

"How about we start with your name?" There was an edge of impatience, underlaid with suspicion in the constable's tone.

She was spared the agony of deciding how to answer when a third constable entered. He took in the room at a glance, looking very pale, and addressed the first constable.

"There's no one else here," he said. "But the back door's standing open."

"That's how he left," Samantha said, and both men turned to look at her. "The man I saw. He went out by the back door."

"This man you saw," the first constable said, and she could not fail to note the skepticism in his tone. "Are you telling us that he shot…?" He gestured to Sir Arthur and Aunt Victoria, glancing at them and then looking quickly away.

"He or his companion. There were two of them."

"You saw them?"

"No," she admitted, and she saw the constables exchange glances. "Not this time. I only saw one of them this time, but I could hear them and there were two of them before."

She knew she was doing a terrible job explaining, but she was finding it difficult to arrange her thoughts. The bodies of her aunt and uncle drew her eyes and it was taking most of her willpower to keep from looking at them. She was also avoiding looking at her hand, though she could feel the warm, sticky blood easily enough. Her stomach churned at the thought of what and whose it was and she longed to scrub it off.

"Before?" the constable asked, dragging Samantha's attention back to him. "What do you mean before?"

Samantha drew a breath, clamped her mouth shut against the foul taste of the air, swallowed and spoke, trying to be as clear as she could. "Two men broke into our house a fortnight ago. They attempted to abduct me, but they failed. We came here to hide from them, but they found us and they killed my aunt and uncle. And the housekeeper."

All three of the constables stared at her. The first was disbelieving, the second skeptical, the third merely looked confused.

"It's the truth," Samantha said, a little desperately. "I know it sounds strange, but it's true. You can ask…" She stopped as she considered who could corroborate her story. None of the neighbors. No one nearby. If she could contact them, there were any number of acquaintances who could identify her and her aunt and uncle with their real names, but they didn't know about the blackmail. Except the blackmailer himself, of course.

A sense of panic began to blossom in Samantha's chest. She had never felt so alone, so isolated. Her guardians were dead, Alice was miles away and Charles was nowhere to be found. There was no one else who cared about her, certainly not the three men who now watched her with a mixture of suspicion and revulsion.

"You need to come with us," the first constable said, and he took hold of her upper arm.

"What?" Samantha gasped. "Where? Why?"

"Scotland Yard. You can explain yourself to the detectives

there."

"But I didn't do anything," she protested.

"What's this?" The constable grabbed her wrist and lifted her hand, the one covered in blood.

"I fell when you came in. You saw me."

"What I saw was a house with three dead bodies and a young woman kneeling over one of them. That's highly suspicious, if you ask me, and that's without your convoluted stories."

Samantha's heart was racing. Her eyes darted from one man to the next, searching for pity, for understanding or a willingness to listen. What she saw did not give her hope. She did not know what would happen if she went with them, if she would be given the opportunity to bring in witnesses to her identity, if she would be sent to prison first. All she knew was that she did not want to find out.

When the constable was distracted, giving instructions to his colleagues about the bodies, Samantha saw her chance. Grabbing his shoulder for leverage, she kneed him as hard as she could in the place she knew would hurt most. It was a move Charles had taught her and one she had never needed to use before, but it worked as promised. The constable doubled over in pain, releasing her arm, and she ran.

She ran past the body of Mrs. Dunbar and out the door to the street. A small crowd of neighbors had gathered around the front of the house. She slipped through them easily, but she heard the questions they threw at the constables who followed her, and their angry replies as they pushed their way through the crowd. By the time she reached the end of the street and had turned down the next, she could hear the sound of boots pounding across the ground. She ran faster, propelled by a mixture of adrenaline and desperation. She ran so fast she hardly felt the stones cutting her feet.

Eventually, the sound of pursuit faded, but Samantha continued to run, turning up one street and down another, hardly aware of where she was going.

In the dark, with only the streetlamps to guide her, London was a different city altogether from the one she had been used to strolling through. As she ran through residential areas into commercial ones, the streets grew more populated and she was forced to slow down to navigate the crowds. But the people of Nighttime London were a different sort from those who inhabited it during the day. To Samantha's frightened gaze, they seemed more sinister and vicious. Their voices were harsh, their faces leering.

A man lunged at her as she passed under the swinging sign of the Bear and Badger. She scampered out of the way, and the woman he was with grabbed him by the coat and yanked him back to her.

"Wotcher, dearie!" she said with a cackle of laughter. The man laughed, too, and pulled his companion deeper into the alley.

Samantha hurried down street after street until she found herself in front of a Gothic building with a tall steeple—a church. The doors were closed, but she scrambled over the fence and tried them, anyway. They were locked. Turning, she leaned back against the door and slid to the ground, wrapping her arms around her knees.

She expected to cry. She thought that, after all the running and looking over her shoulder, she would break down. Or even just think over all that had happened. But she didn't. She felt numb. A hazy buzzing filled her mind and she stared straight ahead, listening to the sounds of the city around her, blank.

FOUR

She was standing on a rope ladder, swaying five feet above the ground and laughing. Above her, a young man with blond hair stuck his head through the trapdoor of the treehouse and pretended to hack at the rope with an imaginary sword.

"No sabotage!" she said, swiping his arm away and setting the ladder swaying even more. "I got out first, Charles. You have to wait."

"I don't think so."

Samantha's shriek of surprise dissolved into laughter as Charles grabbed the side of the ladder and leapt down, swinging away from her and dropping to the ground. He straightened and winked.

"No fair!" she called to him. "Your legs are longer!"

She descended the ladder, skipping the last two rungs, and took off after him. They were halfway to the house when he suddenly stopped and turned to face her.

"What?" Samantha asked, nearly running into him. "What is it?"

"It's the gorgon."

Samantha followed his gaze and saw Miss Caxton, the

governess her uncle had hired for her, hurrying down the garden path towards them.

"Oh, what now?" Samantha said petulantly. "I've finished all my lessons. She can't keep me inside all day. Can't you hide me, Charles?"

"It's too late," he replied, leaning back against the tree beside them. "She's spotted us. But cheer up. I'm sure I can think of something to get you out of whatever horrors she has in store for you."

But as Miss Caxton drew nearer, it became apparent that, whatever her errand, it was not one she relished. Gone was her habitual expression of haughty disapproval and in its place was something Samantha had never seen there before: pity.

"What is it?"

In her anxiety, Samantha spoke sharply, but Miss Caxton did not reprimand her.

"There's been a telegram," she said, looking from Samantha to Charles and back. "From London."

Samantha felt her breath catch. Her parents were in London—had been for four months. In all that time, she'd only received two letters from them. For them to write to her out of nowhere and via telegram, it could only be bad news.

"What happened?" she asked.

Miss Caxton cleared her throat. "Perhaps you had better sit down," she suggested.

"Tell me!" Samantha snapped. Beside her, Charles moved closer and took her hand.

"They're dead," Miss Caxton said simply.

Samantha slid to the ground, hardly noticing the way the bark of the tree scraped against her as she did.

"How?"

It was Charles who asked. She could barely breathe, much less speak.

"Cholera. There was another outbreak. It was swift, it seems, which is why they were unable to write in time."

Miss Caxton continued speaking, but Samantha wasn't listening. She turned to Charles, her eyes wide.

"What's going to happen to me?" she asked, feeling more like a child than the young woman she was supposed to be becoming.

"Don't worry," he said, brushing her hair from her eyes. "I'll take care of you. I promise."

She smiled at him and turned to look at Miss Caxton. Only, Miss Caxton was gone. In her place was a man in a long brown coat with piercing blue eyes and a thick beard. He leered at her and reached out a hand. She screamed.

Suddenly awake, she didn't move for several moments. She wondered if she were still dreaming and that the shooting and the running were all part of an extended nightmare she was still in the middle of. Then someone kicked her and the sharp pain in her shin brought her to reality.

Uncurling stiffly, she sat up. The stone steps beneath her shone pale yellow in the early light of dawn. She couldn't have slept more than a few hours. There was a crick in her neck and an ache in her lower back. She stretched and looked to her right to see who had kicked her. A young man with shaggy brown hair and an even longer beard was sitting up and stretching. He was so dirty and blended so well with the brown stone around him that she thought he might have been there when she sat down and she had simply not noticed.

"Sorry about that," he said, grinning and displaying a mouth with several missing teeth. "It's me leg. Can't always control what it does."

He reached down and patted a leg that was considerably

shorter than the other.

"It's not a problem," Samantha said, trying not to stare.

He paused in the middle of lacing a pair of boots that were more patch than shoe and regarded her.

"Where you from?" he asked.

She hesitated, unsure if his question was prompted by mere curiosity or if he had picked up on her upper-class accent. If the police were still searching for her, she didn't want to stand out in anyone's memory.

"Buxton," she said, naming a village near her grandfather's estate in Derbyshire.

"Where's that?"

"The midlands." She spoke in an imitation of Alice's native accent. It was easy enough, as she heard it so often, and she considered that it would be better to try something she was familiar with than to attempt a London accent with a native.

"Huh. Never been out of London meself. Bit hard to travel with this." He patted his leg, then returned to lacing his boots. "You best get moving. We're lucky the peelers ain't got here yet."

He stood, using a rail for support, then grabbed a gnarled crutch and stuck it under his arm. He gave a mock salute and hobbled off down the stairs. Samantha got to her feet and watched as he joined bustle of activity in the street below. She could see costermongers setting up their wares, shopkeepers cleaning their windows and countless other people hurrying up and down the street.

She felt strangely detached from what she was seeing, as though she were watching a play or a pantomime. It seemed so odd that life could be continuing when it felt to her as though it had come to a crashing halt.

Sir Arthur was dead. Aunt Victoria was dead. And a woman she had barely known was dead as well. Images of what she had seen in the house kept flashing through Samantha's mind and she squeezed her eyes shut as though by doing so she could keep them at bay.

A feeling of despair swept over her—a feeling so powerful that she sank back to the ground, pressing her forehead into the iron bars of the stair rail. What was she to do? What *could* she do? She knew she had only strengthened the suspicion against her when she ran. The police would be looking for her. For her and for Davy. While the real killers walked free, she was a wanted woman.

Samantha's stomach growled, reminding her of her most pressing needs. She would have to eat soon. She had no food nor any money to buy food. The house in Kensington was shut up and returning to Holborn wasn't an option. She needed help.

As she mentally reviewed a list of her acquaintances, Samantha dismissed one after another. Even without the spectre of the unknown blackmailer, there was no one she could trust in her current state. She regarded her right hand, still stained with blood and decided, loath as she was to turn to him, that her cousin Cyril was the only person she could go to. He would not be happy to see her, but he would help her, if only to protect the family name.

Relieved to have settled upon a course of action, Samantha rose to her feet and walked through the gate onto the street. She turned back for a last look at the church and realized, in the light of day, that she recognized it from her daily walks. For all her running the night before, she had ended up only a few streets from where she started. Though disconcerted, she was relieved not to be lost. She knew how to get to High Holborn from here and High Holborn became Oxford Street, which she could take most of the way to Cyril's.

She had gone only a block, though, when she had to stop. In her panicked state the night before, with adrenaline coursing through her, she had hardly noticed the pain in her feet. Now, however, it was excruciating. Lowering herself to the ground with her back against the soot-stained brick of a shop front, she turned her feet to inspect the soles.

They were scored with cuts and gashes. Dried blood mixed with dirt had stained them brown. A couple of the cuts still oozed fresh blood. A pebble was caught under the flesh of her left foot, but her attempts to remove it left her gasping in pain.

When she got to Cyril's house, she would have her feet properly cleaned and bandaged. For now, though, it was clear she could not keep walking without doing something. Angling her body to screen herself from view, she lifted her skirt, exposing the edge of her petticoat. She tugged at the hem of the fabric. It did not tear easily. She found a sharp rock nearby and used it to start the tear. After she had removed a long strip, she dropped her skirt and brushed the loose dirt from her feet. Then, she split the strip of fabric into two and wrapped her feet.

It wasn't very neat, but at least her cuts were all covered. She rose gingerly to her feet and, after a few tentative steps, continued on. But only a few blocks later, she stopped again. This time, it wasn't her feet. On the street corner, a boy was selling newspapers and calling out the morning's headlines:

"Murder in Holborn! Three dead! Suspects on the run! Read all about it in the London Tattler! Penny a paper!"

Samantha felt the blood drain from her face. She closed her right hand into a fist over the incriminating stain and sped up her pace. A few blocks later, she heard another boy shouting headlines.

"Holborn Horror!" he cried. "Gentleman and his wife shot dead in their home! Servant girl seen running away just after! Girl outruns police! Did she do it? Is anyone safe in their home? Find out in The London Inquirer!"

Samantha wondered what information the papers had. Was there a description of her? She decided she had to find out. She watched a gentleman buy a paper from the boy. He tucked it under his arm and continued on his way. Samantha hurried after him, following as he turned onto a busy street. Then, when the crowd began to jostle them both, she reached out and snatched the paper, ducking behind another passerby as she hurried to the side of the road.

There was no shout of surprise or anger. He seemed not to have noticed the theft. Samantha breathed a sigh of relief. She headed for Lincoln's Inn Fields and sat down on the edge of the lawn to read.

The article, written by a reporter called George Canard, was thin on information but full of speculation. The London Inquirer was not a paper her uncle regularly took, so she had never read it before, but she could see that it was not a paper that bogged itself down with facts. Mr. Canard had, to her surprise, given how little time he'd had to gather information, learned the false names her aunt and uncle had been living under. He also described the crime scene with such detail she realized he must have been there.

Samantha's attention sharpened as she reached a description of her own role in the tragedy.

> *Police refuse to name any suspects at this time, but neighbors saw a boy of around twelve running away moments after the shots were fired. Even more intriguing, a constable who arrived early to the scene and who asked to remain anonymous, revealed that a young woman was found standing over the bodies of two of the victims, blood dripping from her hand. When confronted, the woman refused to answer questions put to her and, when she was restrained, broke free and fled with nigh-inhuman speed into the night. Who was this mysterious woman? Were the killings part of some satanic ritual? Will the killer strike again, or has her bloodlust been satisfied? This reporter will stop at nothing to find answers.*

If the matter had not been of such serious concern to her, Samantha might have laughed at the absurdity of Mr. Canard's prose. "Nigh-inhuman speed"? Was he suggesting she was a witch or a vampire? She did note that he gave no physical description of her. Presumably, he would have included one if his constable informant had given it to him. That was a comfort, at least.

The walk to Cyril's house took much longer than she had anticipated. The pain in her feet kept her from moving quickly and, once she reached the more prosperous commercial part of Oxford Street, she had to keep ducking into side streets to avoid patrolling police officers.

By the time she reached the white pillared entrance to Cyril's London townhome, Samantha was exhausted and her feet had bled through their makeshift bandages. She nearly had to drag herself up the steps. When she had knocked, she leaned against one of the pillars, panting.

Gregson, Cyril's pompous butler, opened the door. He scowled. "The tradesman's entrance," he said imperiously, pointing to the servants' staircase below.

"I'm here to see Cyril," she said, standing straight. "I know I look a frightful mess, but—"

"The tradesman's entrance," Gregson repeated. He stepped back and made to shut the door.

"Wait!" Samantha cried out. "It's me, Gregson. Miss Kingston."

The butler's hand dropped from the door and he stepped forward, narrowing his eyes as he surveyed her.

"I must speak with my cousin," she said. "It's urgent."

It occurred to Samantha then that she had only met Gregson on a handful of occasions, what with the infrequency of her interactions with her cousin. Each time, she had been in evening dress with her hair done up and Sir Arthur and her aunt by her side. It was highly unlikely he would recognize her in her current state.

"If this is some bizarre scheme for getting money from his lordship, it won't work," Gregson said, stepping back behind the door. "And in any case, the family are not at home. They left for the seaside not an hour ago."

He shut the door in her face. Samantha was stunned. Cyril was gone? She had been dreading meeting with him, dreading asking him for help, but it had never occurred to her that he might not even be available to ask. She sank onto the steps and buried her face in her hands. She could not think what to do next. She had already thought through her options, and speaking to Cyril had been the only reasonable one. If she knew to which seaside resort he had gone, perhaps she could follow him, but she had no way of knowing. Nor, she realized, did she have the money for transportation if she did.

Samantha felt suddenly overwhelmingly tired. Her whole body was heavy with exhaustion and a headache was forming behind her eyes. All she wanted was a place to sleep. She wished Alice were there to re-dress her feet and help her into bed. If only Sir Arthur hadn't sent all the servants to Kent, she might have been. If Andrews and Mrs. Allen and John and all the others had been at the house in Holborn, things might have turned out differently.

As it was, they were miles away, completely unaware that their employer had been murdered. And they weren't the only ones who deserved to know what had happened to Sir Arthur. Charles needed to be told too. Despite all the bad blood between them, Sir Arthur was his father.

Samantha sat up straighter as a plan began to form in her mind. While Sir Arthur was alive, she had been too afraid to ask Andrews how to contact Charles, but she felt sure he would know. He would have kept Charles' addresses in case Sir Arthur ever changed his mind and wanted to reach out, however unlikely the possibility. If she could get Andrews' help finding Charles, Charles could vouch for her, and his word as a gentleman would carry far more weight than hers.

Pushing her tiredness to the back of her mind, Samantha descended the steps to the street. She didn't know how much a train ticket to Kent cost, but as her assets were currently nonexistent, it didn't really matter. She would have to beg.

She could not beg near Hyde Park. There were too many police officers. Also, she might be recognized. With some trepidation, Samantha began the long trek back across Oxford Street, through Mayfair and into Soho. Someone was sure to have enough to spare for a ticket, especially once she had explained her circumstances—or some of them, anyway.

When Oxford Street became High Holborn, Samantha stopped. She stood at the edge of the street for several minutes, searching for a friendly face. Most people hurried by, staring determinedly ahead, too preoccupied with their own interests to notice their surroundings. Samantha's stomach twisted. Whether it was from hunger or anxiety she was not certain, but she thought it likely to be some combination of both. She didn't want to beg. Just the idea of it made her feel vulnerable and predatory at the same time. She knew the pity and revulsion she felt when she was approached by beggars in the street. She was not a beggar, though. She was a young woman whom circumstance had brought to a place of temporary need. She was certain she could find someone to help her.

A man in a silk hat with curly side whiskers walked past her. He tipped his hat in greeting as he went. It was the first acknowledgment of her presence and she felt she must take advantage of it. She hurried after him. He looked taken aback, then wary, but before he could move away, she spoke.

"Please, sir," she began, then, realizing she sounded like a beggar, she amended. "If you would, sir. I need to get to Kent as soon as possible…"

He was already backing away and shaking his head.

"You don't understand," she said hastily. "It's imperative. I will repay you if you give me your address."

He was gone. Cheeks red with embarrassment and frustration, she walked back to her post on the side of the road and watched the crowd again. Twice more she was rebuffed. She spotted a plump middle-aged woman with a round face and a cheerful expression and tried again.

"Good morning, ma'am," Samantha said hopefully as the woman and her companion neared her. "I don't wish to bother you. I hoped you might—"

"Away with ye, ye grubby wench!" the woman cried, shooing Samantha. "I won't be accosted like this."

Stumbling back to avoid the woman's swinging arms, Samantha tripped and fell on her backside. The woman turned back to her companion as though nothing had happened. Samantha lifted her stinging hands from the ground and examined them. They were covered in mud and horse dung, as was her dress, she did not doubt. Tears of frustration sprang to her eyes.

"Pitiful."

Looking up, she saw a thin girl with dirty blonde hair that hung in tangles to her elbows. Samantha guessed her to be fourteen or fifteen, though it was difficult to tell. The hem of her dress was several inches too short and, beneath it, a wooden peg leg was easily visible. Samantha swallowed the angry response she had planned to give in the face of such pitiable circumstances.

"See," the girl said, her face twisting into a crooked smile. "You gotta have an angle."

Samantha frowned in confusion. The girl leaned down and offered a hand. She took it and stood, brushing as much dung as she could from her clothes.

"No one gives any notice to a beggar," the girl continued. "Especially one what looks like they've eaten a few times."

She winked at Samantha, picked up a cane that had been lying on the ground and hurried across the street. Samantha was just thinking that if she wasn't careful, she was going to get knocked to the ground, when she was. A well-dressed gentleman stepped out of a carriage and turned without looking, running right into her. He looked annoyed, then, seeing the peg leg, embarrassed. He helped the girl stand. When he tried to leave, she clung to him. He stepped back, trying to extricate himself, but she held fast, saying something Samantha could not hear. His eyes flicked desperately from one passerby to another, as though one of them might rescue him. Finally, he pulled some coins from his pocket and handed them to her. She released him and he hurried away.

The girl returned to Samantha with a grin, showing her the shiny coins before pocketing them.

"You gotta make 'em feel guilty," she said. "And you gotta keep hold of 'em. Make 'em wanna do anything for you to go away so's they can feel good about themselves again. It don't always work. Usually don't, actually, but when it do, you can make a tidy sum."

Samantha stared at her. She wasn't sure what to say. The girl laughed. Then something seemed to catch her eye and she hurried off. She returned a few moments later.

"Like I said, it don't always work." She displayed empty hands.

"Can you help me?" Samantha asked tentatively.

"Thought I just did."

"I know. I mean…" she trailed off, not sure what she meant. She had perhaps been thinking she could ask the girl to share some of her coins, but that was incredibly selfish.

The girl gave her a look of understanding.

"You knapped?"

"I beg your pardon?"

"Are you in the family way? Got a little one coming?"

Samantha's eyes widened as she understood what the girl was saying.

"No! Absolutely not!"

The girl frowned.

"Then what's a toff like you doing on the streets looking like that?"

Samantha teetered on the brink of telling the girl, who certainly wouldn't run to the police, but she was too afraid, so she told a partial truth.

"I'm hiding from a man," she said, thinking of the man who had come running from the house. "And I don't want to go to the police because, if I do, he might learn where I am and come after me."

It was only as she said it that she realized there was a real possibility that if she went to the police, the killer might come after her to prevent her from identifying him, if by some miracle she was not charged herself.

The girl's face softened and she held out a dirt-stained hand. "I'm Annie."

"Sa-Sarah," Samantha said, extending her own mud-covered hand and shaking Annie's. "I need to get to Kent to see my… friends, so I need a train ticket, but I don't have any money."

"Well, I can't get you a ticket," Annie said, "but if you can earn your place, you can come stay with me for a bit. Then at least you won't be sleeping on the street."

"That would be wonderful," Samantha said.

"You might want to work on that," Annie said, gesturing to Samantha's mouth. "Unless you want him to find you right quick. Nobody here sounds like that."

"I know."

"That I probably could help you with. We'll see."

"Thank you," Samantha said.

"It's not charity I'm doing. You'll have to earn it, as I said."

"I know. I'm still thankful. You're the first person who's been kind to me since…in a while."

Annie laughed. "Don't think I've ever been called kind. Can't afford to be kind. But, if I can train you up proper, we could do well together, you and I."

FIVE

Five Weeks Later. August 1861

In the library of the United University Club on Pall Mall, a young man sat beside a table littered with papers and the remains of his half-eaten breakfast. He was reading a newspaper and biting on the end of a pencil, his brow furrowed. His name, scrawled on a note that was making its way towards him, was V.T. Wyatt, the Honourable—when he chose to be—and he was late for lunch.

An elderly man in a crisp suit handed him the note on a silver tray and stepped back.

"Thank you, Alfred," Wyatt, as he preferred to be called, said, taking the note and flipping it open. He scanned its contents, his eyebrows rising as he reached the end.

"He is waiting at the entrance, if you wish to meet with him, sir."

"Regrettably, I must." Wyatt stood and buttoned his coat. "As he reminds me, I did offer him lunch today." He ran a hand through his tousled dark hair and looked down at the papers he had left on the table. "I don't suppose you could gather these up for me and have them waiting at the front desk when I return? I'm sorry to leave you with such a mess."

"Not to worry, sir. Enjoy your afternoon."

Waiting for Wyatt just inside the front door of the club was a man not much older than himself. His rumpled coat and limp tie earned him suspicious looks from a few of the members as they passed by, but he seemed not to notice. As Wyatt approached, the man pulled a pocket watch from his vest and flipped it open.

"Ah." He shook his head and snapped the watch shut. "Half an hour late, Wyatt. Tsk, tsk. I've been getting the evil eye from your doorman."

"Since I just received your note, I assume you've only just arrived yourself, George. Don't try to trick me into an apology."

George laughed as Wyatt accepted his hat and cane from an attendant.

"I will admit to nothing," he said, following Wyatt down the steps and out into the street, "though I don't understand why we can't eat at your club."

"I want to stretch my legs a bit."

"In a cab?" George asked sardonically as a large black hansom drew up and they got in.

Wyatt grinned. "I want a change of scene?"

"I think you're just cheap," George said with a snort. "Or you're ashamed to be seen with me."

"Well, that's definitely true," Wyatt said. He gave the driver an address and the cab lurched forward. "In all seriousness, though, I wanted to talk where we mightn't be overheard."

George raised an eyebrow. "I'm intrigued. What about?"

Wyatt leaned back and drummed his fingers on his cane. "Do you have any more information about the Holborn murders?"

George sighed dramatically. "Sadly, no, I don't. I'm doing my best to keep them in the public eye, though."

"Do you mean with all the lies you've been printing?"

"Not lies," George said, as though explaining a simple concept to a stupid child. "Possibilities, I think you mean. They aren't lies unless they are proven false. I'm the one who found out about that girl sneaking out every day, remember? Then it was a simple matter to consider why she did it and link it to the murder. Sneaking out to meet a lover, of course. Mother and Father don't approve. There's a row, she grabs Father's gun and shoots them both in a fit of passion."

Wyatt laughed. "I thought you said she was a witch. Or was she a servant girl?"

"No," George said with deliberation. "She only dressed as a servant girl to help her sneak out. And she may well be a witch too. How should I know?" He gave a little shrug, but his grin undermined the innocence of the action.

"How, indeed. But do you dare continue to write about her? She may be angry at how you are portraying her and choose you as her next victim."

George rolled his eyes. "I know you're just trying to get a rise," he said, "but if it weren't for me and my efforts—"

"And those of the fifty other papers…"

"Which are all spurring one another on," George said with a bite of annoyance, "and keeping the public's interest. If it weren't for us, the police wouldn't be so motivated to solve the murder. I'm doing the city a service."

"How very public-spirited of you."

"That can't be what you really wanted to talk about," George said shrewdly. "You know if I knew more, I'd've written about it. So, what do you want?"

"Whatever you have on the latest housebreaking. Anything and everything, not just what you put in the paper."

"Is that all? Here." He tossed Wyatt a notebook. "It's all in there. You can copy it down while we eat."

The cab slowed to a stop outside a pub on Drury Lane. The atmosphere was a world away from the Pall Mall with its stately gentlemen's clubs and wide thoroughfare. Drury Lane lay in the heart of bohemian London, the home of the literary set, streets away from the newspapers and publishing offices. It was noisy, crowded and dirty.

George opened the door and jumped down.

"Have you graduated then?" he asked when Wyatt joined him after paying the driver. "From missing brooches to housebreaking? That's quite a step."

Wyatt didn't answer. He just pushed past his friend into the pub. Inside, they were greeted by the smells of simmering meat and strong ale. The place was nearly full, but after they ordered, they found a table near the back and sat down.

"I've figured it out," George said, taking a swig of beer and setting his tankard down. "You've joined the peelers. You didn't want to tell me, because you're embarrassed to finally be making an honest living, but, as I've outed you, I'll let you know, I'm proud."

"Of course I haven't joined the ruddy police," Wyatt said. "I was asked to look into it by one of the homeowners. She didn't think the police were doing enough and thought I might be able to help. That's all."

"She?"

Wyatt raised an eyebrow at George's lopsided grin. "'He fashioned hell for the inquisitive'," he quipped.

"'Curiosity is, in great and generous minds, the first passion and the last'," George countered.

"Yes, well, you need a great and generous mind for that one to apply."

"Fine, I won't ask about this 'she'—just promise me you'll let me know if you turn up anything about these robberies. They aren't nearly as interesting as a triple murder, but whatever keeps me employed is of interest to me."

Wyatt spent the rest of the meal scribbling down George's notes while George devoured a cottage pie and another pint of beer. When they had both finished, George left for Fleet Street and Wyatt decided to walk back to the club. Although the smells were often overwhelming, he found the sights and sounds of the city invigorating.

The fastest way to get back to the Pall Mall would have been to cut through Covent Garden, but Wyatt decided he really did want to stretch his legs. He went back out to Drury Lane and took it to the Strand. He was almost to the crossing when someone knocked into him. A girl hurried past. Instinctively, Wyatt reached for his pocketbook. It was gone.

"Stop!" he yelled.

The girl picked up speed, and Wyatt chased after her. She was fast—turning onto the Strand and cutting back north through a small, unfamiliar street. Wyatt matched her pace, gaining on her. As he drew near, he grabbed her arm and yanked her back.

"I'll have that," he said, plucking the pocketbook from her hand and sliding it back into his coat.

The girl twisted and pulled, trying to escape his grasp. When that failed, she balled her other hand into a fist and swung at him.

Wyatt caught her hand midair. "Nice try. Next time, don't pull your arm so far back, and you might actually catch someone by surprise."

"Let go of me!" she yelled, struggling even harder.

He had assumed she was a child—one of the myriad of unfortunate waifs who worked the streets either for themselves or to supplement their family's income. He could now see that she was a young woman, though with her long, dark hair pulling free of a messy plait and half-concealing her dirty face, it was hard to tell. Something about her eyes, though, as she shook her hair back and glared at him, seemed familiar. He couldn't quite think why.

His momentary distraction proved detrimental. With a swift, unsportsmanlike kick, she brought him gasping to his knees. He released her and she snatched the pocketbook back out of his coat and fled.

*****

Samantha ran for several blocks and then, sure she had not been followed, slowed to a walk. Her hands holding the stolen pocketbook shook and she felt ready to vomit from the combination of fear, adrenaline and self-loathing. Was this what she had become—a common street thief?

Ducking into an alley, she sank to her knees beside an empty crate. It was hard to believe that, less than two months ago, she had been dancing in some of the finest houses in London, eating her fill of cakes and tarts. Her stomach grumbled at the thought of cake, and she groaned. She had lost so much weight in her month on the streets that her dress, once a bit tight, hung loose on her thin frame.

"Sarah?"

From the entrance to the alley, a voice called out uncertainly. Samantha raised her head above the crate. When she recognized Annie, she sank back down.

"In here," she said despondently

Annie shuffled in. Her false peg leg was gone and, in its place, she had opted to wrap her left foot in bandages and drag it behind her. Her dirty blonde hair was tied back in a clean kerchief, and she had washed her face. When she came around the crate and saw Samantha, she set down the basket of flowers she had been carrying and knelt in front of her.

"You alright?" she asked with concern. "I seen you running by and I thought you might've popped in here to hide. Didn't see nobody following you, though."

Samantha tossed the pocketbook onto the ground between them.

Annie frowned. "Not again. I've told you before, it's too risky, and you ain't no good at it, neither."

Samantha laughed, then groaned. "I need more money."

"Who don't?" Annie said, accompanying her words with a shrug.

"I'll pay it back."

"Right," Annie said, drawing out the vowel. "With all that money your friend in Kent's got. Look, it don't matter to me what you do, so long's you pay your part of the rent. All I'm saying is, if you wanna stay outta stir, pinchin' ain't gonna help. Stick to legitimate enterprises like mine."

She gestured to the basket.

"Didn't you pinch those flowers?" Samantha asked.

"From dead people," Annie said. "Off their graves. I don't think they're too bothered. In fact, they might be glad to help a poor girl like me. It might even count as good deeds for 'em."

Samantha shook her head.

"It's only…whatever I make goes to rent and then food if there's enough. I haven't been able to put any aside for my ticket."

"I don't know how things work in Buxton," Annie said, "but that's pretty much how it goes here in London." She stood up. "Try not to get yourself nicked, alright? I'd hate for you to miss your rent. And, much as I hate to admit it, I'd miss you."

She picked up her basket again and left, whistling as she went.

Samantha sighed and reached for the pocketbook. Annie was right. Not only was stealing wrong, but she was not particularly good at it. This was her fifth attempt and she'd been very nearly caught every time.

She flipped it open and reached inside. Her fingers found several coins and she gasped as she pulled out a crown and three pennies. She held the crown up, turning it over and marveling at its realness. It wasn't enough for a ticket, but it was almost enough, and the *almost* was worth celebrating.

Samantha stuffed all but a penny back into the pocketbook. Then, checking that no one was coming, she pulled her dress up over her right thigh. A strip of her petticoat, the remains of which had been sold to the rag-and-bone man the week before, was tied around it like a bandage, creating a hidden pocket. She slid the pocketbook into it and dropped her skirt. Then she stood and ran to get the first bite of food she'd had since the previous morning.

The rest of the day was less productive. She joined the mudlarkers searching the banks of the Thames for anything that could be sold, but she came up empty-handed. However, as she returned to her lodging house that evening, she held onto the sense of optimism the coins had given her.

The faded sign hanging above the weather-beaten door read Lampton Manor. Annie had assured her it was one of the nicer of the low-end lodging houses in the city. There were separate rooms for men and women, the stray cats ate most of the mice, and the furniture had been purchased from a junkyard, rather than the vacated homes of smallpox victims, as was distressingly common.

None of these assurances had prepared Samantha for the shock when she first arrived at her new home. The room she occupied with Annie and four other girls was half the size of her bedroom in Kensington. There was only one narrow bed, which three of the girls shared. Samantha, Annie, and the fourth girl slept on mats on the floor. Even in this, they were lucky. On the ground floor, there was a room whose furniture consisted of two long benches and a rope strung in front of each. Those who could not afford a room could pay to sleep on the bench, leaning across the rope to keep from falling while they slept. If they could sleep.

Samantha entered the front hall and ascended the stairs. She barely noticed the smells anymore. The whole city reeked, and the mixed aromas of hundreds of lodgers crammed into a space designed for half as many did not alter it overmuch. Besides which, she was sure her own unique scent was pungent enough to inure her to any others.

As she moved down the narrow third-floor hallway, she tried to block out the voices of the occupants of the other rooms. The sounds were harder to get used to than the smells. Babies cried at all hours of the day and night. Heavy feet clomped across rickety floors. Doors slammed. People argued and fought. Tired as she was after long days spent trying to earn what she needed, Samantha hadn't had a full night's sleep in weeks.

The room was empty when she entered. The other girls would filter in over the next hour or so. Sitting on her mat with her knees against her chest, Samantha pulled out the pocketbook she had taken earlier that day. It was good quality—a fine leather—but it was old, well-creased and tarnished with age. She thought of the man she had taken it from. He was young, unlikely to be the original owner of so old an object. Too, though his dark, curly hair had been somewhat unkempt, everything else, from his perfectly tailored suit to his polished black shoes, showed him to be a man of means. No doubt, he could afford to replace the pocketbook, which likely meant it held sentimental value.

Samantha flipped it open and searched the side opposite the one with the coins. Her fingers found a thin metal case and a piece of paper. The paper was a photograph of a pretty girl no older than twelve or thirteen. On the back was the name Helena and a date, 1852. An old photograph in an old wallet. Samantha opened the case and found a small stack of calling cards with the name V.T. Wyatt printed on them in bold letters. Beneath the name was an address in Knightsbridge.

The name Wyatt was familiar, but she could not place it. She shut the card case and slid it back in the pocketbook. Helena looked accusingly up at her from the photograph. Samantha grimaced and flipped the photograph over before putting it back with the card case. Her conscience had been plaguing her for weeks as desperation had reduced her to thievery. But this Mr. Wyatt would surely not miss one crown. He might miss his photograph, though, and his wallet.

Helena must be his sister, she had decided, for what man keeps a photograph of his sweetheart from when she was a child? It seemed apparent, also, that this sister must now be deceased, for, if she were alive, she would be close to Samantha's own age and would certainly have sat for a formal portrait when she came of age. Samantha had no siblings, apart from those who lay buried beside her old home, never having lived more than a few months beyond the womb. She could well imagine that, had she been granted the privilege of twelve whole years with them, she would never want to lose their likenesses. She would have to return the pocketbook to Mr. Wyatt tomorrow. The money she could mail to him once she was safely back in Kent.

SIX

When Wyatt came down for breakfast, there was a beggar girl across the street. He could see her through the window of the dining room, walking away, then returning, and glancing frequently at the door. As he poured himself a cup of tea and shifted through the collection of newspapers that had been delivered that morning, Wyatt wondered why she did not knock, but he was distracted by the entrance of his housekeeper.

"Any interesting news today, Mrs. H?" he asked as she set a plate of eggs and toast in front of his chair.

Mrs. Hexam was a short, plump woman in her early fifties who had been with the family since his elder brother, Thomas, was born. Perhaps it had been unwise to employ a former nanny as a housekeeper, but Tom was not going to have children any time soon and Wyatt hadn't had the heart to send her away.

"You know I never read the papers, Mr. Wyatt," Mrs. Hexam said with a sniff. "I'm far too busy for that, but I *can* tell you that the front parlor will have its annual deep clean this morning, if you find that interesting."

"Oh, I do. Absolutely. I cannot imagine how it can have slipped my mind. Tell me, is there a particular form of dress for a parlor cleaning or will my frock coat do?"

"There is a form of dress, Mr. Wyatt. It is an apron, and if you wish me to iron one out for you, I should be more than happy to. Otherwise, I suggest you and your smart comments keep to your study this morning if you know what's good for you."

Wyatt laughed and sat down, spreading *The Times* before him and picking up his fork.

"That girl has been out there since I set the table, sir," Mrs. Hexam said, walking to the window and pulling back the curtain. "Would you like me to send Jenny to clear her off?"

Wyatt looked up. The beggar girl was still there, wavering on some point of decision.

"No," he said, as an idea entered his mind. "Invite her in for a bite. Take her into the kitchen."

Mrs. Hexam frowned at him.

"You don't want to go starting a thing like that, Mr. Wyatt. Once you invite one in, they all come running."

"Don't worry, Mrs. H. Just do as I say."

He could hear the housekeeper's brisk tones as he walked down the stairs to the kitchen, minutes later. They were followed by the low responses of the girl. She sounded nervous, worried. Had she been sent by someone? Did she bring a message?

"Ah, Mrs. Hexam," Wyatt said, stepping into the room. "There you are. I was wondering if I might bother you for a…"

He stopped as the girl, seeing him, gasped and turned to run.

"The door, Mrs. Hexam," he commanded.

She never argued with him when he used that tone. She cut in front of the girl and locked the door to the outside. The girl stopped and turned, clearly terrified.

"I'm not going to hurt you," Wyatt said, stepping forward.

She threw something at him, and he caught it. It was his

pocketbook.

"I brought it back, sir," she said, a quaver in her voice. Then, more firmly, "You can have no reason to keep me here."

It was the thief from the day before. She had re-plaited her hair so that it no longer concealed her face, but she wore the same filthy dress.

Wyatt looked down at the pocketbook in his hand. He had been upset to lose it. It had been his father's and it contained one of his only photographs of Helena. He flipped it open and found the picture in its usual place. He didn't remember exactly how much money had been inside, but there was none left.

"No reason?" he asked, raising his eyebrow at the thief. She looked down, and he could have sworn he saw her blush.

"Why did you return it?" he asked. The wallet was in poor condition—she wouldn't have been able to get much for it, but she could have earned a few pennies at least with the right buyer.

"I thought…" she began hesitantly. "I thought you would want your photograph back. She was your sister, wasn't she? You must have loved her very much to carry it around. I'm not a thief. At least, not really."

He watched her twisting the folds of her skirt in her hand and felt an overwhelming sense of curiosity. Who was this woman? She'd fought him off to take his pocketbook in the first place, then brought it back, albeit with money missing. The trip to his house from the part of the city in which he'd encountered her would have taken an inordinate amount of time on foot. It was a lot of effort to make to return a beat-up old wallet. And she knew the photograph was of his sister. How?

"Mrs. Hexam, would you move the breakfast things to my study? And Mrs. Plummet," he said, turning to the cook, who had been pretending to clean counters while watching the proceedings. "Prepare another pot of tea and some extra scones to send up."

His housekeeper gave him a stern look that plainly displayed her disapproval, before ascending the stairs. Mrs. Plummet, who was much more in awe of him, merely nodded and complied with his wishes.

"You must be hungry," he said, turning back to the young woman. "Would you like some tea?"

"In your study?" she asked warily.

"The chairs are much more comfortable there," he said. "I'd prefer not to sit on these hard, wooden stools while we talk."

"Talk?" Her suspicious frown deepened.

"Yes," he said. "I have some questions for you, and I think we might help each other."

"How?"

"We can discuss it in my study," he said, gesturing impatiently to the stairs. "But, whatever you decide, you needn't worry that I'm going to have you arrested. I'm not."

She seemed to deliberate for a moment before nodding.

"Thank you," he said, and he led her upstairs.

Wyatt's study was a mess. Stacks of paper were piled on his desk and the floor surrounding it, while books lay strewn across every available surface, some open with purpose, others having reached that state by negligence. The wall behind the desk was mostly taken up by a blackboard on which hastily scribbled words were connected by wriggling lines of chalk, or set apart and surrounded by question marks. Across from the desk was a large map of the city in which little pins tied with ribbon were stuck like tiny flags.

Wyatt walked around the desk and tossed the newspaper he'd been holding on top of the pile. He looked up to see the young woman examining his map with interest.

"Don't touch that," he said.

She withdrew the hand that had been reaching for one of the

pins.

"What is it?" she asked, turning to him.

"A map of London."

"I can see that," she said. "I meant, what are the pins for?"

He didn't answer her immediately. Now that they were speaking more calmly, he noticed something odd about her speech. Her vowels weren't consistent. They fluctuated between sharp and soft in a way that wasn't natural.

"They indicate the locations of the robberies I'm investigating," he said slowly.

"Investigating?" she said in surprise. "What do you mean? You can't be a police officer. You're a gentleman."

"True," he said, amused by her assessment. "I'm just helping a friend."

"By investigating," she said, a question in her tone.

Wyatt moved to one of the armchairs by the fire and gestured for her to do the same. She sat stiffly on the edge of her seat, and he settled into the chair across from her. Leaning back, he studied her with unabashed curiosity. She was uncomfortable to be sitting with him, but it wasn't the discomfort he'd seen in Finn, the errand boy he hired from time to time. It wasn't the fanciness of the room, such as it was, that bothered her. In fact, she had barely given it notice, apart from the map. No, it was his presence that bothered her.

The door opened and Jenny, the housemaid, entered with a tea tray. She shifted a few books around so that she could set it down on the desk while she poured. She carried two cups over and handed one to Wyatt and one to the young woman. The woman looked up at Jenny and over at Wyatt, and her cheeks reddened.

Was she blushing? Was it some sense of propriety that made her uncomfortable? That would explain her bizarre accent. If she didn't grow up on the streets, her voice would be the biggest giveaway.

"I've just realized I don't know your name," Wyatt said. "I am Mr. Wyatt, though I assume you learned as much from my card when you found my address."

"Sarah," the young woman said, looking down at her cup. "My name is…Sarah."

Jenny left, and they sipped their tea in silence for several minutes. Wyatt took note of how daintily Sarah—he doubted that was her real name—drank and how straight her posture was. She was definitely of the gentry. Upper middle class, at least. What had happened to cause her to fall so far? Pregnant by the chauffer? An illicit affair? She must have been involved in some scandal for her family to cut her off and leave her to starve in the streets.

"Is there something on my nose?"

"What?"

"You're staring at me. What fascinates you?"

She spoke with a frosty hauteur that further cemented Wyatt's suppositions, but her words reminded him of his manners.

"I beg your pardon," he said smoothly. "I was lost in thought. Would you like a scone?"

Jenny had left the plate of scones on the table beside him. He gestured to it and "Sarah" took one almost before the words had left his mouth. She ate it with much less poise than she had drunk the tea and was soon done. He smiled as he handed her the plate, and she took two more, abandoning manners altogether as she gobbled them down.

When she had eaten her fourth, some sense of shame seemed to settle upon her, and she flushed and looked down at her crumb-covered lap. The flush brought a becoming color to her cheeks and he reflected that, with her wavy black hair and high cheekbones, she was quite pretty, if unfashionably thin.

"You said we could help each other?" she said, looking up.

There was a defiant blaze in her eyes that he liked, as though daring him to mention the crumbs.

"I did." He took a sip of tea in order to collect his thoughts. "I told you I'm not a police officer, but I…like puzzles. I'm quite good at them. And sometimes I apply my talents to real-world problems. I've helped several friends over the past couple of years to conceal or uncover secrets, find lost items, et cetera."

She was watching him closely, but he couldn't read her expression.

"I've found it helps," he continued, "to connect myself with people who can obtain information difficult for someone in my position. People who can go places I can't and speak to people who wouldn't talk to me."

"Places you can't go?" she echoed, her brow furrowed.

"Places where a gentleman wouldn't be welcomed. Where I would be an unwanted outsider. Servants' halls. Certain parts of the city."

"Why are you telling me this?"

"I'd like to hire you to be one of those informants."

She uttered a surprised laugh. "What?"

"The more people I work with," Wyatt explained patiently, "the faster I can obtain information. As for my specific choice, you've proven yourself to be fairly clever, and, I would hazard a guess that you are resourceful as well. I think you could be a valuable asset."

After her initial outburst, she had schooled her features into an inscrutable mask. He could not tell what she thought of his proposal as she considered him over the rim of her teacup while she took another sip.

"Are you looking for any particular information right now?" she asked finally.

"Have you heard about the housebreaking spree?"

She looked startled, but shook her head. "Housebreaking… spree?"

"There have been a number of houses robbed over the past several weeks. All of the robberies happened while the homeowners were away and there either weren't many servants to begin with or a number of them were not at home."

She raised her eyebrows. He had surprised her again.

"I am trying," he went on, continuing to watch her reactions, "to find a connection between the victims, but so far, there have been few. What I'd like you to do, is to find out what you can about the thieves. They must be selling their stolen goods somewhere or bragging to someone about what they've done."

She closed her mouth and took a sip of tea before replying. "How much?"

"I beg your pardon?"

"How much will you pay me for information?"

"It depends on how useful it is."

"I need two shillings and sixpence."

He was taken aback by her forthright specificity.

"Why?" he asked, though he knew it was none of his business.

She sipped her tea again and did not reply.

"Very well," he said. "If what you bring me is useful, I'll give you two and six."

She held out a hand, and he fought back a laugh as he realized she meant to shake on it.

"Gentlemen's agreement, is it?" he asked as he took her small hand in his. His grin faded as he felt callouses, a reminder of the difference in their situations.

"Thank you for the tea and scones," she said. "I will return as soon as I can."

"Not here," he said hastily. "I'm usually at my club during the day or out somewhere. You would be more likely to find me on the Pall Mall."

She nodded and stood. He rose as well and led her out the door. When they reached the hall, Mrs. Hexam appeared and escorted Sarah down the back stairs and out through the kitchen.

Wyatt locked himself in his study for the rest of the day, unwilling to face Mrs. Hexam. She did not approve of his recent choices, and seeing "Sarah" would have reinforced her greatest fears as to the classes of people he was consorting with in the course of his work. He wasn't ready for her lecture, especially because he didn't feel right about the situation himself.

If he had met Sarah before her fall from grace, their interactions would have been markedly different. She would have been Miss Surname; she would never have had tea with him alone at his home and he would have felt honor-bound to help her if he had discovered that she was in trouble. Why was it so different now? Why had he not simply given her the money she so clearly needed? It wasn't as though she would plague him forever with begging. She had a specific need and he had ignored it. He resolved that, when next he saw her, no matter how useless the information she brought him, he would give her what she wanted.

Guilt assuaged, Wyatt turned his mind to other matters, re-reading his notes on the previous four robberies and comparing them with the most recent, but his mind kept returning to Sarah. How she had deduced that the photograph was of his sister and that she had passed away, he did not know, but it demonstrated a cleverness that intrigued him. She had also managed to survive on the streets after falling from her former life, and that took bravery, as well as intelligence. Who was she? What had happened to her? And why was there such a nagging sense of familiarity when he looked at her?

*****

Knightsbridge was little more than a half hour's walk from

Samantha's lodgings in Westminster, but she had so much to think about that the journey home seemed to take no time at all.

Mr. Wyatt was not what she had been expecting. She had been wavering between ringing the bell so she could be sure someone got the pocketbook and leaving it on the stoop to an uncertain fate when she was invited in by his housekeeper. Wary, but unable to resist the promise of food, she had entered the house. When he came down to meet her, she was sure no good could come of it, but he'd surprised her by treating her well.

He was somewhat ordinary in appearance—handsome enough, but with no standout features—so she was not surprised that she did not remember ever meeting him. She had placed the name, though. He was the younger brother of Thomas Wyatt, Viscount of Boxley. Viscount Boxley she remembered as pompous, meticulously attired, and deeply boring. Mr. Wyatt, on the other hand, was unaffected, with an office as disorderly as his hair and a face that hid more than it showed. She could hardly believe they were related.

Thoughts of Mr. Wyatt and his mysterious investigative work were set aside as Samantha reflected on the information he had relayed to her. There had been several houses robbed in much the same way as her uncle's. Were the same men involved? Was it the same blackmailer? Was he blackmailing all of those people?

Then a horrible thought struck her. If more people were being robbed and possibly blackmailed, then the men who had killed her uncle were not concerned only with him. They might kill again, and the police had not made any progress because they were chasing after a servant girl who had nothing to do with the murders.

A weight seemed to settle over Samantha and she felt, more than ever, the urgency of her need to get to Kent and find Charles. She would complete her task for Mr. Wyatt, get the money owed her, and continue with her plan. Once she found Charles, they could identify Sir Arthur and Aunt Victoria and point the police in the right direction.

Annie was there when Samantha got back, changing into the relatively clean and mended dress she wore for selling flowers.

"If I were interested in finding someone who breaks into houses," Samantha asked when they had greeted each other, "where would I go?"

Annie paused with her arms and head partway through the dress and gave her a searching look. "And why would you be looking for an houseman?"

"I was only curious," Samantha said, busying herself with brushing off her bed mat. "I've met lots of pickpockets and cut-purses and the like, but no housemen."

Annie wiggled into her dress and shook out the skirt.

"That's because this house is full of *independent* workers what avoid any run-ins with Skinny Jim. And, far as I know, there ain't many independent housemen."

"I've heard the name, but who is Skinny Jim?"

"Someone you'll steer clear of, if you know what's best for you," Annie said, rearranging the flowers in her basket so that the best blooms lay on top. "He's got his claws in most everything, but they can't never prove nothing, so he's never been arrested, though all the peelers knows he's crooked. He's paid some of them off, too, I'm sure. Knows a lot of powerful people, he does, and don't nobody never cross him."

Noting Samantha's interest, she warmed to her theme.

"He works out of a pub by the river in Blackfriars, and anyone wants a job done but don't know how to do it can come to him. He's got all kinds as works for him, and he can put together a job quick as you like, depending how much you pay him."

"So, all the housemen work for him?"

"Most do, far's I know. For him or with him, though it's

almost the same thing. It's hard not to work for him. He's got a lotta snakesmen with him as well." Seeing Samantha's confusion, she clarified. "Snakesmen's little kids what fit in small places. Makes it easier to break in."

Samantha considered Annie's words. She could go back to Mr. Wyatt with this information, but she doubted he would pay her much for it. He would probably ask why she hadn't gone to the pub to learn more. With Annie's warnings about Skinny Jim, visiting the pub was the last thing she wanted to do, but she couldn't see any way around it. Getting paid by Mr. Wyatt was the surest way to get what she needed, and it was legal.

When Annie had left with her flower basket, Samantha went to the crate that held her friend's meager belongings. She shifted aside the dress Annie had just changed out of and found the third and final outfit her friend owned—a shirt and trousers. Annie had told her that, when she was younger, she'd tried to be a chimney sweep, dressed in her brother's clothes, but she hadn't lasted long. She kept the trousers, though, in case she found a new use for them or needed to sell them down the line.

Samantha stepped into the trousers. They were a little too long, but they fit at the waist. She rolled the cuffs up until she could see her feet. Then, she removed her dress. She had long since gotten used to the awkward acrobatics that were required for her to tie and untie her own corset and she removed it easily. The skirt of her chemise had been mostly sacrificed to bandages, reducing the garment to little more than an undershirt. She took some of her remaining bandages and wound them over the chemise and around her chest, binding it. Then she slipped on the shirt. Her hair she twisted and knotted under the cap she found at the bottom of the chest.

With no looking glass, it was hard to know how effective her disguise was, but she felt different. The trousers gave her an odd sensation when she walked and she wasn't sure that she liked feeling the fabric against her legs with every step. She was also uncomfortably aware of how exposed they were, each leg distinct in its own half of the trousers. The act of walking itself was different, as well, and she realized, as she stepped with her legs farther apart than usual, trying to keep the trousers from brushing each other, that she might need to observe how men walked before she continued.

Outside the lodging house, Samantha leaned against the wall in what she hoped was a casual manner and watched people go past. Then, as unobtrusively as she could, she mimicked the gaits she had seen. She knew she must look ridiculous, but she also knew how important moving like a boy would be when she did not look exactly like one.

Traveling at a slower pace than usual as she implemented her new walk, it took an hour for Samantha to reach Blackfriars and another quarter of an hour to find someone to direct her to the correct pub.

The Lion and Eagle was situated almost at water's edge. It was a Tudor-era building with a single large window at the front and no exterior decoration apart from the sign. Inside, dark wood paneling lined the walls. There was a long bar and an assortment of tables, most of them empty. It was clean and well-kept and carried an air of respectability that Samantha found surprising in a place she had been building up in her mind as a den of depravity.

She scanned the room, looking for a place to sit where she might overhear as much as possible. There were five patrons: two men at a table near the front, two at a table near the back and a fifth man, also at the back.

Her eyes were drawn immediately to the fifth man. It was impossible not to notice him. Apart from the fact that he was the largest man she had seen in her life, taking up an entire side of the table at which he sat, alone, he had a magnetism about him and an undefinable energy that made it immediately apparent he was the most important person in the room. Whether he had once been thin or he found a perverse amusement in throwing people off their guards, it was clear that Skinny Jim did not match his name.

He watched her navigate the tables to a chair near the back, but before she could sit, he caught her eye and crooked a finger, indicating for her to join him. Samantha's heart beat faster, but she had little choice but to obey. He watched her appraisingly as she approached.

"You must be a snakesman," he said. His voice was deep with a raspy edge. "You've got the build for it. What brings you here?"

Samantha stared at him. The words she had prepared on the way over seemed to have gotten lost on the way to her mouth. She had expected to find a busy pub, had imagined watching for a while, looking for an opportunity to approach him. She hadn't expected to be called to him or for him to be so direct.

Skinny Jim's eyebrows lowered in displeasure. "I'm a busy man. I haven't got all day. You looking for a job?"

"I'm…looking for an houseman," she said finally, her voice hoarse as she attempted to disguise it.

He scoffed and shook his head. "That's not how it works. I organize the jobs. I put together the teams. I sort out the pay. You want a job, you go through me."

Samantha started to shake her head, to explain that she only wanted to talk to the housemen, but Skinny Jim quelled her with a look that sent a ripple of unease down her spine.

"I've got a job tonight," he said, taking a swig from the mug in front of him. "Should be easy. You'll do it for free. If you can prove yourself, I'll consider taking you on."

Samantha hadn't even started to object when he called over the barman, a burly black man with tattoos on his muscled arms.

"I've got some help for you, Daniel. This here's…"

He looked expectantly at Samantha.

“Sam,” she managed to squeak out.

“Sam,” he echoed. “Sam’s gonna do a job tonight, and I don’t wanna have to hunt him down, so he’s gonna help out at the bar ’til then.”

He put a strange emphasis on the words “him” and “he” as he spoke them, and the accompanying sinister grin made Samantha realize that he must have seen through her disguise. He did not, however, seem inclined to do anything about it or to feel anything but amusement. He just gestured to the barman and said, “Go with Daniel, Sam. He’ll show you what needs doing.”

Numbly, Samantha followed the barman as he took her to the back room, handed her a broom and cleaning cloth and told her to start behind the bar. As she wiped the counter, her hand moving in repeating circles, she marveled at how rapidly everything seemed to have spun out of her control.

SEVEN

At a quarter to seven that evening, after a day wrestling with several puzzles he could not solve, Wyatt bade a hasty goodbye to Mrs. Hexam, informing her of his intention to dine at the club. He hailed a cab and headed to Boodle's, eager for the company after a long day of solitude.

He had just handed over his hat and coat when he was hailed from across the room.

"Val!"

He turned as his old school friend came hurrying towards him. Francis "Bingo" Beaumont, Lord Aston, was the only person who still called him by that ridiculous nickname.

"Bingo! I didn't realize you were in town."

"Only just arrived, old sot," Bingo said, embracing him and clapping him on the back. "It was a bit of a last-minute decision. My mother's idea, or rather, because of her idea. How are you?"

"Better for seeing you."

"Let's catch up. Have you eaten yet? No? Henry, a private table for Mr. Wyatt and me, there's a good chap. You really must tell me all you've been up to, Val. It seems an age since we last spoke."

They were escorted to a table in the corner of the room and ordered their meals.

"What brings you to the city, Bingo?" Wyatt asked. "Shouldn't you be making the rounds at the shooting parties?"

"I was," Bingo replied. "I'd done a week at our grouse moor in Scotland and a weekend with Lord Marlborough when I decided to come home for a stretch. I invited some friends back with me and we had several spirited nights of cards when I hit a bit of a bad streak."

Wyatt shook his head and grinned. "What did you lose this time?"

"Just the East Wing," Bingo said breezily. "I knew I'd win it back in the next hand. The trouble is, my mother happened to have popped in for a moment right when I lost it and then she rather lost her temper. She banned cards from the house and made everyone return whatever they had won to the original owners. Caused quite a bit of embarrassment for me, as you can imagine, but the worst of it was when she decided to cure me of my 'gambling problem,' as she calls it, by marrying me off."

Wyatt laughed. "Hasn't she already tried that? Weren't you engaged to some girl last year? When I saw you at Christmas, she was with you."

"Engaged?" He looked confused for a moment, then brightened. "Oh yes, Mabel. I'd nearly forgotten about her. My mother rather fancied her political connections, and her father liked our money, I believe, but in the end, she ran off with an American, and that was the last anyone saw of her."

"I'm sorry."

"Don't be. Can you imagine me, married? At my age? Mother may be upset now, but that will pass, which is why I'm here. The way I see it, I have at least five more years of eligible bachelorhood before she becomes entirely desperate. Why should

I marry before then? It would be a waste of opportunities. And with my money and title, I'll still be quite the catch for the young society debutantes. I'll have my pick of the crop."

"So, you've come to the city to escape your mother?"

"Yes, she made wild threats about a series of house parties or balls or some similar horrors, and I legged it. Caught the first train here. My man should be following tomorrow with the bags. Mother will expect me to visit friends in the country somewhere. London is the last place she would look for me outside of the Season. I'll stay at the club for a few weeks. By the time she discovers my whereabouts, I expect the whole thing will have blown over."

A waiter arrived with their food and conversation stalled for the next few minutes as they ate.

"How's the detecting going?" Bingo asked, swallowing a mouthful of beef and reaching for his glass of Bordeaux.

"Tolerably well."

"I confess, I am surprised you've stuck at it this long. I thought you were just doing it to spite Tom, yet here we are."

Wyatt cut into his steak with such force that the knife hit the plate with a loud clang. "I didn't do it to spite Tom," he said, setting the knife down. "I did it for myself. I enjoy it. I enjoy the challenge and the opportunity to exercise my brain."

"I haven't done that since Cambridge," Bingo said with a dismissive wave of his hand.

"You didn't do it in Cambridge," Wyatt pointed out, and Bingo laughed.

"Fair," he said. "And look how happy I am. Embrace the mediocrity of our existence. Everyone else does."

"Not everyone has your *joie de vivre*, my friend. Most of us get bored; we're just trained not to show it. I hate being bored."

"Yes, but you already have a solution to that. A much more

entertaining solution and one I whole-heartedly support."

Wyatt gave him a quelling look, but Bingo merely laughed.

"And I appreciate your support," Wyatt said. "I couldn't do it without you. But *that* is not intellectually challenging."

"What a burden a brain is," Bingo said with an exaggerated yawn. "Are you going to eat that?"

He reached across to Wyatt's plate and stabbed a potato with his fork.

"I was, actually, but go ahead. By rights, it's yours, anyway."

"What do you—ah. I see. Planning to stick me with the bill, are you?"

"I told Henry to put it on your tab before we even started."

"Touché, my friend. Touché. This round to you."

They ate their way through two more courses, after which Wyatt announced that he was ready to go home.

"Surely not," Bingo protested. "The night is young, and I only just got here. You can't want to retreat to the fires of hearth and home at this hour."

"I can and I do. I've had rather a long day, and tomorrow promises to be another."

Bingo sighed. "I suppose I am tired after my escape. Call for your carriage, and I'll walk out with you."

"I don't keep a carriage anymore, but you're welcome to come watch me hail a cab."

"You don't keep a carriage?" Bingo looked shocked. "Not even a gig?"

"It seemed superfluous. I generally walk most places, and cabs are abundant. It was a wasted expense."

"How long have you been without a carriage?" Bingo asked, standing up and following Wyatt out of the dining room.

"Six months now."

"Does Tom know?"

"Not yet." Wyatt stopped and spun around to face Bingo. "And neither does my mother, and I'll thank you not to tell either of them. I think my mother would die of shame, or at least come as near to it as she could manage without giving us too much hope."

"You do still keep a valet, though?"

"Naturally, though he is away visiting family at the moment."

Bingo visibly relaxed at this evidence of Wyatt's escape from utter depravity. Wyatt did not think it needed to be mentioned that Summers was visiting family only because Wyatt had compelled him to in an effort to get rid of him while he found a replacement. Summers had become too familiar in the past year, feeling it not only acceptable to comment on the master's choices in everything from clothing to female companionship but to attempt to direct them as well.

"I say, old thing," Bingo said with a yawn, "do you mind if I don't follow you out? The journey is starting to catch up and I'm feeling a bit used up."

Wyatt nodded and they parted, Bingo to his room and Wyatt to the street to hail a cab.

*****

Samantha spent most of the day working as a lackey for the barman. She served drinks, cleaned up spills, and was generally grateful for her foresight to dress as a boy as the number of rowdy, drunken men grew. None of them seemed to see through her disguise as Skinny Jim had, or if they did, they said nothing. She considered trying to escape but decided, ultimately, that it made more sense to stay. Skinny Jim hadn't hurt her, and she might still learn something useful.

She had already learned a lot about the business at The Lion and Eagle. Some people—men mostly, though there were a few women—came in for a few drinks, spoke with Skinny Jim, and left. But there were many more customers who sat down at a table, paid more than the listed price for their drinks, and were joined by someone they appeared to be meeting for the first time.

Skinny Jim kept busy. There was almost always at least one person at the table with him. Samantha never saw money change hands, but she overheard parts of several negotiations. Skinny Jim never wrote anything down but seemed to remember exactly what was owed and who was working with whom.

As night fell, the clientele of the pub changed. The customers were paying the regular price for drinks and some were even getting their drinks free of charge. They were rougher-looking and, for the first time since she spoke with Skinny Jim, Samantha was afraid.

She was soon called to the big table. A man with thick arms, thick brows and an anchor tattoo on his right bicep sat with Skinny Jim.

"He's new," Skinny Jim was saying as she joined them. "So, I'll give you a discount. I want to know how he does, so let me know when you get back. And Kieran—" The man paused in the act of standing. "No damage to this one, you hear? Or I'm adding you to the list."

The man nodded. Samantha struggled to mask her reaction to Skinny Jim's last words. *This one?* How many others had Kieran "damaged"?

"Go with Kieran, Sam," Skinny Jim said. "He'll let you know what needs doing. When you're done, he'll bring you back, and we'll see if you're worth keeping on."

Samantha nodded and followed Kieran out of the pub.

"Where are we going?" she asked as she caught up to him.

"You'll see when we get there. Until then, keep your mouth shut, stick to the shadows and follow me."

Samantha did as she was told, half-running to keep up with the man's long strides. He led her up one street and down another, out of the docks and into areas she was unfamiliar with. The dense, putrid London fog did not discriminate between the rich and the poor, and it followed them wherever they went. It felt as though they had been dodging in and out of alleyways and avoiding streetlamps for hours when they finally stopped in front of a row of houses with whitewashed front steps and wrought-iron fences.

"Go around back," the man said in a low voice, handing her a metal bar that curved at one end. "There's a small window. Use the rook. Get inside, go to the back door, and unlock it for me, then come back here and wait."

"Which house?" Samantha asked, trying to keep the tremor from her voice.

He pointed to the one on the end, and she nodded. She stole across the street and crept behind the house. There was a small rectangular window at ground level. Examining the bar Kieran had called a rook, she saw that it tapered at each end. She felt along the window and slid the long end under it. Using all her strength, she pushed down on the curved side of the bar. It popped up, losing purchase on the window and nearly hitting her. She let out a squeak of surprise. Dropping to the ground, she scooted to the side of the window, making herself as small as possible as she listened hard. Nothing, apart from her own labored breathing and the wild beating of her heart. She remained undiscovered.

Turning the bar around so the curved end went into the window, Samantha tried again, more carefully this time. She was relieved when the window made only the tiniest of creaks as it lifted open. Lying flat on the ground, she stuck her head inside. The kitchen was empty but for a few pots and pans left out on the table. She pulled her head back out and turned, sliding her feet through first, then inching slowly down. It was a tight squeeze and one she could not have managed a month ago. Once she was inside, hanging from the windowsill by her fingertips, she dropped down softly, her calloused feet hitting cold stone much sooner than she had expected.

She waited, listening for sounds within the house, holding her breath. All was still. Tiptoeing to the kitchen door, she opened it just wide enough, slipped through and hurried upstairs.

The back door was easy enough to find, but as she stood with her hand on the lock, she paused. What was she doing? She had been following Kieran blindly, caught up in the role she was playing, but this was no longer a role. She was a houseman…a snakesman. She wasn't just pretending to be one to get information for Mr. Wyatt. She was actually breaking into a house. What she was about to do was not only immoral, but illegal.

Kieran couldn't get in the house without her. Maybe she should wait him out, stay here until morning and…and what? She could hardly expect the family to understand what a filthy boy was doing in their front room. They would call the police. Theft was no longer a capital crime, but it would mean prison. If she ran away, Kieran would catch her or would at least tell Skinny Jim, who would probably hunt her down and make an example of her. And where would she run? Would Mr. Wyatt help her? Perhaps, but she could not be sure.

She had to go forward, even though every decision she made seemed destined to carry her further and further from her former life, even as the chances of ever returning to it grew smaller.

Resignedly, Samantha turned the lock and opened the door. She stepped aside as Kieran entered the house, and made her way to the pre-arranged meeting spot to wait. It couldn't have been more than five minutes later when a large, shadowy figure crossed the street and joined her. The pockets of his long coat bulged.

They went back as they had come, running through the fog and shadows until they reached one of the poorer parts of town, at which point they slowed to a walk.

"I'll be back," he said. "Wait here."

He held out a hand to hold her back. Samantha tried to protest, reminding him that he had promised to bring her back to Skinny Jim soon, but he ignored her, ducking into a rundown pub and leaving her alone on the street.

No sooner had he closed the door than it burst open again, banging against the wall. Three boys, none of whom could have been older than fifteen, came stumbling out. They were laughing and walked with their arms around each other. One of them tripped over the step and all three went sprawling onto the street. Samantha watched as they righted themselves, with difficulty. She heard footsteps behind her and turned to see a girl in a green dress running towards the boys. When she reached them, she jabbed her finger in the chest of the middle boy and shouted something Samantha didn't catch, gesticulating wildly behind her. The boy laughed and tried to brush her off, but when she continued to argue, he grabbed her by the arm and threw her to the ground.

Samantha gasped. Without stopping to think, she ran over and reached down to help the girl.

"What're you playing at?" the boy said. "Leave off!"

"Yeah, go saw your timber, ratbag," said one of the boy's friends.

"I'm not gonna let you hurt her," Samantha said, straightening up and facing them.

The boy stepped towards her, puffing out his chest. "If I wanna batty-fang my wife for disrespecting me, it ain't none of yours."

"Your...wife?"

The girl looked to be about fourteen, the same as the boys.

"Yeah," the boy breathed, his alcohol-soaked breath making Samantha wrinkle her nose in disgust. "Though I am starting to regret it."

"You can't treat your wife like that," Samantha said angrily.

"I reckon I can," he said. "Anyway, it's what they expect, ain't it? The girls'd probably be confused if we was to treat 'em any other way."

The other boys laughed. Samantha looked down at the girl. She was wiping blood from her lip and frowning at Samantha. She didn't appear happy to be rescued at all. Quite the contrary. Samantha was confused. She stepped back and turned to leave.

"That's what I thought," the boy said with a laugh. "Now, get up, you scummy wagtail, 'fore I lose me temper."

She heard his shoe skid on the ground and a groan from the girl, and Samantha knew he'd kicked her. She balled up her fist, spun, and punched the boy as hard as she could.

It was not a great punch—she'd never punched anyone before—and it didn't draw any blood, but it did cause the inebriated boy to topple to the ground. He landed hard. Samantha gasped as pain shot through her fist. She cradled it with her other hand, looking down at it in surprise. In her distraction, she missed the boy's friend's sudden movement and, seconds later, she was staggering back, pain exploding through her head, radiating from a point beneath her right eye.

Almost immediately, her eye began to swell. She threw up an arm to protect herself from another attack and saw Kieran exiting the pub. He came running over. In one swift movement, he knocked her attacker to the ground. Then he grabbed her roughly by the arm and dragged her away.

"You're gonna explain this to him," he said, yanking her forward. "I am not going on the list for your idiocy."

He stopped abruptly and whirled around. Grabbing her face in his rough hands, he turned it one way, then the other, examining her eye.

"You've copped a mouse," he said, shoving her away.

He paced back and forth a few times before turning to her and pointing a stubby forefinger at her chest.

"You're going to bring it up," he said, "before he even asks. Tell him you picked a fight and I had nothing to do with it. Swear it!"

Samantha nodded emphatically. "I will," she said. "I'll swear it wasn't you."

It was well into the early hours of the morning when Samantha returned to the lodging house. She had not relished telling Skinny Jim the black eye was her own fault, but it was the truth and he seemed to believe it. He told her he didn't care what she did on her own time, as long as she didn't injure herself to the point of being unable to work. Then he sent her away, telling her to return for another job the next day.

She stumbled up the three flights of stairs to her room, the darkness hampering her already impaired vision. When she finally reached it, she collapsed onto her mat and was asleep within seconds.

When she woke, she experienced a brief panic when her eye would not open. Then the events of the night before became clearer in her mind, and she groaned. How long had she slept? Judging by the light coming in through the hole in the roof, not very long at all.

"What happened to you?" Annie asked with a laugh.

She was always the first one awake, and it was her shuffling footsteps that had awoken Samantha.

"Some cockeyed boy got me when I wasn't looking," Samantha said.

She winced, partly from the pain and partly from the shame of hearing how easily coarse language now flowed from her mouth.

Annie laughed again and was rewarded with a loud shushing from one of the other girls—Mary, or Edith, possibly. One of the girls in the bed, anyway. She rolled her eyes heavenward and mimed hitting the shusher with her basket.

"Where were you yesterday?" she asked, her voice lowered to a whisper. "I was planning to ask you to join me in a new grift I've thought up."

"I…er…went to see Skinny Jim," Samantha whispered back, rubbing a hand over her uninjured eye to avoid seeing Annie's reaction to her news.

"You did what?" Annie's voice rose in pitch and she struggled to keep it quiet. "You went to see Skinny Jim after what I told you?"

"I told *you* I needed to learn about housemen," Samantha said. "I went in disguise; don't worry."

"I can see that." Annie looked her up and down. "You're still wearing it. Are those mine?"

Samantha grimaced and looked down. "I was going to return them. And I would have done last night, only I was so tired."

She expected Annie to chastise her or yell at her, but she didn't. Instead, she threw back her head and laughed. Mary sat up in the bed and glared at her, but Annie kept laughing.

"What's so funny?" Samantha asked warily.

"It's just…" Annie wiped a tear from her eye. "You've turned out even better than I thought. When I brought you home that day, I figured you'd last a week at most. But now, you're stealing my clothes and walking into Skinny Jim's place bold as brass."

The laughter subsided but a huge grin remained on her dirt-stained face. Samantha did not return it. She didn't know what to think of what she had become. Part of her was appalled at the depths to which she had sunk, but another part felt proud to hear Annie's assessment of her—to see herself as not only a survivor, but an adapter. She'd always had a strong inner drive and a practical mind, but even she was surprised by how well it had served her in this alien environment.

After Annie left, Samantha lay back down, but she could not go back to sleep. Her body ached all over. She felt muscles she had never known she had protesting the rigors to which she had subjected them. It wasn't just the running, but the lifting and the scrubbing and the kneeling. Her eye continued to throb and felt puffy to the touch.

And what had she gained for all her efforts besides this pain? Nothing. She knew what Annie had told her—that most housemen worked for Skinny Jim and therefore, in all likelihood, the men who were currently ravaging London did—but she had learned nothing else. Should she give up, return to Mr. Wyatt and tell him she had tried to learn more but been unable to? He would surely be sympathetic when he saw her eye.

Even as she considered the idea, she rejected it. That might be the most sensible course of action and the one she would have taken had she been in the same position a month ago, but Annie was right. She was different now and, illegal activities aside, she liked it. Why should she hurry home to find Charles when she could be much more useful here in London? She would first help Mr. Wyatt find the housemen and set him on the right path. Then, when she did find Charles, they could approach Mr. Wyatt together, explain her circumstances and connect the housemen to the murders of her aunt and uncle. Solving the murders would go a long way to helping her fix the mess she was in.

That evening, Samantha returned to The Lion and Eagle with renewed determination. Her eye was still swollen, but she had come to consider it a blessing in disguise as it detracted all the more from her femininity. She had managed a few hours of sleep after her fellow tenants left for the day and she felt rested, if not sated. Her stomach rumbled at the sight of a meat pie being delivered to a patron, but she had become accustomed to ignoring its complaints.

The pub was full of activity and Samantha took a moment to observe the customers before heading to the back. A dark man with a thick beard and piercings covering the whole curve of his right ear drew her eye, and she wondered how much the piercings had hurt and whether he had done them all at once or spread them out over a period. A burly sailor with a cap pulled low over his brow was telling his table a joke that would have made her face burn with embarrassment a month ago but now only made her shake her head in amusement. The amusement was not at the joke, which she still considered vulgar and obscene, but at his overeager method of delivery that caused him to botch the punchline.

A man entered. Though he was dressed like a dockworker, he didn't look like one. He was slim, with skin untouched by the sun, and the soft, unscarred hands of a gentleman. He had endeavored to disguise his features with a set of ludicrous false whiskers that did more to draw attention to him than to deflect it.

"I don't know why they bother."

Daniel, the barman stood beside her. She hadn't heard him approach. He was watching the man with wry amusement as he moved awkwardly to a table near the front and sat down.

"As if he didn't make it his business to know exactly who he's dealing with," Daniel continued. "And it ain't that hard to find out."

He chuckled to himself and continued on to the bar. She watched him pick up a glass and fill it, passing it to one of the men at the end of the bar. He caught her eye and nodded to the back of the pub. She grimaced and turned away, winding her way through the tables to the place where Skinny Jim sat. He was in a meeting, so she hung back, not wanting to interrupt. The men sitting beside him were rough-looking. One of them had his back to her, but the other was everything she pictured when she imagined a villain. His hair was long and lank, tied back from a craggy face, pockmarked and scarred. She shuddered inwardly and avoided looking at him.

Skinny Jim caught her eye and gestured her forward with an impatient wave of his hand.

"You can have Sam," he said to the men. "He's eager to prove himself, so he'll work well for you. My other lads are busy tonight."

Samantha came to stand beside Skinny Jim and froze. She could see the face of the villain's companion now. It was the face that haunted her dreams, the face of the man who had come running out of the house after the shots were fired, who had pointed his gun at her—her aunt's and uncle's killer.

"Alright," the killer said dully, glancing up at her with those piercing blue eyes and returning his gaze to Skinny Jim. "How much?"

They began to negotiate over rates. Samantha was vaguely aware of the indignity of being haggled over, but mostly she felt numb. How could this be? How could he be here?

But of course he was here. He was a houseman, besides being a murderer. This was exactly what she had come to find. And yet seeing him in the flesh was almost more than she could bear. Did he recognize her? He didn't seem to, but then, he'd barely looked at her. Though he would be looking again soon if she didn't pull herself together and stop staring.

Mentally shaking herself, Samantha felt the shock melting, to be replaced by a torrent of emotions. She was scared, of course, but even more so, she was angry. What was he doing sitting in a pub, haggling over wages and planning a robbery when he had murdered three people in cold blood? How could he sit there with that bored look on his face when he was responsible for her misery?

Years of practice with her uncle meant that none of these emotions showed on her face, but she dug her nails into her palm with the effort to remain neutral. To her relief, the negotiations didn't take long and soon the men were standing and pushing back their chairs. When she made to follow them, Skinny Jim held her back.

"Do well tonight," he said in a low voice, "and you may be set here. Slater and Palmer are some of the best. If they like you, it'll go a long way in my book."

Samantha nodded and followed the robbers out of the pub.

Except for turning back once as they started off to make sure she was following them, both men ignored her as she trailed behind them. They didn't skulk in the darkness, as Kieran had, but walked nonchalantly along as though they didn't have a particular destination in mind. Samantha followed several paces behind them and tried to appear as casual as they were, but it was difficult. She felt as though her heart were in her throat. She couldn't believe she had found them and that they had no idea who she was.

When they reached Doughty Street in Camden, the men stopped. The scarred man—Palmer, his partner had called him—turned and motioned for her to join them.

"That one," he said, his deep voice pitched low. He pointed to the house third from the right. "We'll get in through the garden. There's a window in the back you'll fit through. Let us in and go back to wait."

They entered at the end of the row and had to climb several fences to get to the correct garden. Samantha was even gladder that she had chosen to wear trousers as she swung her legs over the last fence and dropped into the garden of the third house. Behind her, she heard the two heavy thumps of the robbers hitting the ground as she approached the house.

The window they had referenced was below ground level. She lowered herself into the narrow alcove that had been dug to accommodate it and knelt down. After some jiggling, it opened easily enough, but it stopped after she had raised it about a foot. There was a bar in the upper part of the window that prevented it going any further. Keeping it open with one hand, she sat down and slid through the narrow opening, feet first. When her feet touched ground, she twisted around and pulled herself the rest of the way through.

The house was silent. Letting out a shaky breath, Samantha reached up and lifted out the bar that prevented the window opening further. Palmer jumped down into the alcove and she opened the window for him. He entered with practiced ease and dusted himself off as his partner, Slater, followed.

"Wait for us outside," Slater said.

Samantha crawled back out the window, sliding it shut behind her, and hauled herself out of the alcove. Then, she waited. She was just wondering how long the robbery would take when she heard the booming barks of a large dog coming from inside the house. Seconds later, the back door burst open and first Slater, then Palmer, came charging out. Close on their heels was a huge black dog.

"Go!" they shouted, running past her to the fence. They vaulted over it in one movement. Samantha scrambled up after them. The dog snapped at her heels, tearing off the cuff of one of her trouser legs. She pulled herself over the top and landed with a thump on the other side, then ran to the opposite fence. She could hear the robbers sprinting across the next garden, but by the time she had jumped down into it, they were gone.

Panting for breath, Samantha scrambled up the last fence. She caught her sleeve on a nail and yanked. The fabric tore, and she fell over the top, landing hard on the other side. The wind was knocked out of her, and she lay stunned for several seconds before her panic returned and she rolled over and pushed herself up. She ran out to the street.

It was a quiet residential street, so there were few people around. She didn't see Slater or Palmer anywhere. She started running again, wanting to distance herself from the robbery when it was discovered, but she had to stop after only a few blocks to catch her breath.

There was no point in going back to Skinny Jim. She had what she needed now. She could tell Mr. Wyatt she knew who the housemen were. She could give him a description of both of them. And their names. She could get the money she needed and be back in Kent tomorrow evening.

With a laugh of relief, Samantha limped back to Westminster for her final night of sleeping in the slums.

EIGHT

Wednesday morning, Wyatt joined Bingo as he went to Saville Row to visit his tailor. It had been two days since he had asked Sarah for her help, and he'd heard nothing from her. He wavered between concern that something had happened to her and annoyance that she had not been more useful. The thieves might strike again any day, and he was no closer to stopping them than he had been a week ago.

"I have to say," Bingo said as they set off in his carriage. "I'm starting to regret, ever so slightly, my rash decision to come to London in August. I don't remember it smelling quite this foul during the Season."

"Weren't you here a few years ago when it was especially bad?" Wyatt asked, leaning back in his seat. "They called it 'the Great Stink.'"

"No, thank heavens. I was back in the country in early June that year. I could already tell it was going to be hotter than blazes that summer."

"The smell does worsen in the heat," Wyatt conceded. "But I'd still rather be here than at Boxley Abbey with Tom and my mother."

"You could have come with me," Bingo said. "I'd have put you up."

"And if I had, I'd be right back here now," Wyatt pointed out with a laugh. "As it happens, I'm glad I stayed. I wouldn't have known about the robberies otherwise."

Bingo quirked an eyebrow at him. "If you'd come with me, you would have had days full of amusements, good food and good friends. But, robberies, yes—quite the trade off."

"The shooting would have been nice," Wyatt admitted. "But you know I don't play cards."

"I know. It's been my theory that you don't play merely so you can look down on us lowly mortals from your high horse of moral superiority."

"Don't be ridiculous. I don't play because it's dull."

"It's only dull to you because you don't risk enough."

Wyatt laughed.

"Ah. I see. So, if I were to lose my house on a hand, I would really enjoy myself."

"That is just what I mean," Bingo said. "Moral superiority. And, as I said, it was only a wing of the house, and I was about to win it back."

The carriage stopped in front of number 15, and the two men climbed out. Bingo instructed the driver to wait.

"This shouldn't take too long," he said to Wyatt. "Let's lunch at the club afterward."

Wyatt was about to follow his friend through the door of Henry Poole & Co when he noticed a young boy begging in front of one of the nearby shops. He must have just arrived for the shop owner not to have chased him off yet.

"You go in," he said to Bingo, backing down the steps. "I'll be right there."

He walked down to the shop the beggar boy had positioned

himself in front of, nodding to a few acquaintances as he passed them. When he reached the boy, he pulled out a sixpence and dropped it in the tin cup he held in his grimy hand.

"T'were an awfully long way to travel for sixpence, sir," the boy said, grinning slyly up at him.

"You can have more if your information is worth it," Wyatt sighed. Of all of his informants, Jamie was the cleverest and most difficult to handle.

"I was hanging around Camden when I heard some talk about a robbery last night."

"Where?"

"Number 59 Doughty Street. There was this toff kicking up a fuss about how his wife's favorite earrings had been taken, and some of her best jewels, and the peelers wasn't doing nothing to help."

"Did you hear anything else?" Wyatt asked.

"Maybe I did, and maybe I didn't, but you ain't gonna know without a bit more tin in my tin."

Wyatt complied, something he regretted an instant later when Jamie said that he hadn't heard anything else and legged it.

As he walked back to the tailor's, Wyatt contemplated what Jamie had told him. If this robbery had been committed by the same people, it was a shame, but he would at least have more information to work with. If he could get there before the end of the day, he might be able to speak with the homeowners directly and ask them some questions while the event was still fresh in their minds.

Bingo was in front of the mirrors when Wyatt entered the shop, being fitted for a shooting jacket by the proprietor himself. Mr. Poole, dressed with the exquisite taste one would expect of a tailor on Saville Row, moved with speedy precision, re-positioning the fabric and making tiny chalk markings on the sleeves.

"Ah, Mr. Wyatt," Mr. Poole said solicitously. "Are you here to get something for the hunting season too?"

"Sadly, no," Wyatt said with a shake of his head. "I'm only here to keep his lordship entertained."

"What do you think?" Bingo asked, holding out his arms.

"It looks good," Wyatt said. "Though I'm not sure I understand why you need another one. Didn't you get a new jacket last year?"

"Yes, but if you'll remember, I accidentally set fire to it on Christmas Eve. Too much port."

Wyatt grinned.

"Of course. How could I forget? I'm suddenly less surprised that Mabel left you for that American."

Bingo laughed.

"That was a happy consequence."

"Bingo, would you mind if we postponed lunch? Something's come up, and I'm going to be rather busier today than I thought."

"Busy?" Bingo said skeptically. "With what?"

"If you'll just step down, sir," Mr. Poole interrupted. "I'll take the garment, and you and Mr. Wyatt can be on your way."

Bingo allowed the tailor to help him out of the jacket and received his own coat back from an assistant.

"Thank you, Poole," he said, shrugging it on. "Have it sent to the United when it's ready."

"Of course, your lordship. Have a good afternoon. And you, Mr. Wyatt."

"Now, what's this about being busy?" Bingo asked as they left the shop and climbed into the carriage.

"Nothing you'd find interesting," Wyatt said wryly.

"Ah, so it's related to your investigation of the robberies."

"Yes."

"Some news, then? A new break-in?"

"I don't want to bore you."

Bingo laughed.

"Oh, you know how changeable I am. At any rate, I am suffering from a lack of amusements until the evening, so go ahead."

Wyatt sighed loudly, but then he smiled. It might be fun to have his friend tag along.

"There was another break-in," he said.

"Aha!" Bingo said triumphantly. "You see, I can be clever too."

"Yes, you're brilliant," Wyatt said. "Good guess. This one was in Camden on Doughty Street. I was planning to go there and see what I could learn."

"Now, that does sound interesting," Bingo said.

"I know."

"Let's go, then."

Bingo leaned out the window and gave the address to his driver. Less than thirty minutes later, they pulled up in front of number 59 Doughty Street. Wyatt followed Bingo out of the carriage and they went to the door. Wyatt knocked and waited. He knocked again. Finally, the door opened.

The woman who answered looked flustered. Her cheeks were flushed, and she panted slightly as she greeted them.

"I apologize for my late response to your knock," she said. "Unfortunately, the cook is visiting family and my maid is laid up in bed. I'm not used to answering the door. And I wasn't expecting visitors."

She looked at them expectantly.

"I understand completely," Wyatt said, slipping into character. "And I apologize that we were unable to send advance notice of our visit. My name is Artemis Signet and this is my friend and colleague…"

"Lord Aston," Bingo said with a short bow. "I realize this is a difficult day for you, but I hoped we might have a few moments of your time to talk with you about the robbery."

"The robbery," the lady repeated. Her eyebrows rose almost to her hairline. "How do you know we were robbed? And why would you want to talk to me about it?"

Before Wyatt could answer, Bingo spoke again.

"My father is a friend of the commissioner," he said. "They were at Cambridge together. From time to time, Sir Robert asks me to check in on investigations to make sure his officers are treating respectable citizens with decency."

Wyatt sighed and closed his eyes, sure they were about to be turned away after such a ridiculous lie.

"Indeed?" the woman said, and Wyatt's eyes snapped open at the eagerness in her tone. "It's about time someone in government took their responsibilities to heart. As a matter of fact, I have a few complaints to make. Do come in."

She stepped back and gestured for them to enter.

"I thought we agreed to use false names," Wyatt hissed to Bingo as they followed her down the hall and into the parlor.

"And I thought we agreed that my status was our most important asset," Bingo whispered back. Then he slipped into the room before Wyatt had the chance to argue back.

"I would offer you tea," the woman said, gesturing for them to sit, "but with my maid unavailable…"

"We understand, Mrs. James," Wyatt assured her, hoping he was correct in his assumption that the "Mr. and Mrs. James" needlepoint in the hall was hers. "You've had a distressing few days."

"True," she said, finally sitting down so that Wyatt and Bingo could follow. "Mr. James and I returned home from a party and there was Eliza with a lump on her head and all of my jewelry gone!"

Bingo let out a gasp of horror and Wyatt shot him a repressive frown. Bingo waited until Mrs. James wasn't looking and grinned back.

"Did the police arrive in a timely manner?" Wyatt asked, pulling out his notebook.

"More or less," Mrs. James said, furrowing her brow as she thought. "There were two of them. I can't recall their names, but no doubt there is a record somewhere. They were quite rude. They nearly overwhelmed us with questions from the moment they walked in the door."

"What sorts of questions?" Wyatt asked.

"Mostly what you would expect," Mrs. James said, sitting straighter in her chair. "They asked us to describe the house as we discovered it and I told them that the front door was locked, though the back door was wide open. I suppose that must be how they got in, though I was sure it should have been locked after we left. Eliza is so particular about such things. She is quite afraid of being alone in the house, and now I fear she will be even more so. Oh, dear. I hope she does not give notice."

"Is she badly hurt?" Wyatt asked.

"She received a hit to the back of the head, poor dear, but the doctor says she will recover so long as she rests for a few days. That is another inconvenience this robbery has caused me. As though having the safety of my home threatened and my family jewels stolen weren't enough, I must be without a maid for several days."

"When does your cook return?"

"She should be back sometime this afternoon. She was only gone for a few days to visit her mother. I would like it recorded," she said, looking pointedly at Wyatt's notebook, "that the constables last night became quite rude. They asked my husband where we had been. We were at a dinner party, you see, which is why we were not here when it happened. They asked who had hosted the dinner, and when my husband said he didn't see how that was relevant, they become positively insistent and said they would need to verify our statement. As though we had been suspected of the crime ourselves!"

"I will be sure to tell Sir Richard," Bingo said as Wyatt pretended to write. "Shocking. Most shocking, indeed."

There was more than a hint of laughter in his voice, and Wyatt sought to move the interview along before his friend lost what was left of his composure.

"Mrs. James," he said. "Might you show us the back garden? Where the thieves escaped?"

"Of course," she said, standing. "Though, I should warn you, we have a rather large dog out there."

"A dog?"

"Yes. It belongs to a friend of my husband's. He asked us to watch it for a few days. He was called away unexpectedly and did not want to bring the dog. Really, we have the dog to thank that the thieves did not make away with more."

"What do you mean?" Wyatt asked.

"Well, we kept it in the house while we were gone because Eliza was concerned it might be too cold outside. Apparently, it started barking when it met with the robbers and chased them out of the house. The neighbors made certain to complain to us about the noise until we told them we had been robbed." She looked smug. "Then, they were tying themselves in knots apologizing for not sending for the police."

Bingo laughed and Mrs. James' smile broadened. She led them down the hall and out the back door to the garden. A large black dog was playing in the rose bushes. When it saw them, it came bounding over.

"Down, Champion!" Mrs. James said in a scandalized voice as the dog leapt on Bingo, its front paws landing on his chest.

"I don't mind," Bingo assured her, rubbing the dog's head. "I love dogs."

Wyatt walked past them to the right side of the garden. "If they came and went through the back they most likely went this way. It's the shortest distance from the street."

"Yes," Mrs. James agreed. "That's what the constables thought. My roses have been crushed."

Wyatt noted the broken stalks. He knelt beside them to look more closely. "I'd say they almost definitely left this way." He reached out and picked up a torn piece of fabric lying beneath one of the bushes. It was almost the same color as the dirt, so he didn't wonder that the constables hadn't noticed it.

"What's that?" Mrs. James asked. Bingo was too busy playing with the dog to notice.

"It looks like it was torn from their clothes," Wyatt said. "Probably by the dog as they were climbing back over the fence." He rocked back on his heels and stood up. "You said you thought the door was locked?"

She nodded.

Wyatt walked back to the house and peered down at the window below ground level. He jumped down into the alcove and attempted to lift it. It opened. Mrs. James gasped.

"That shouldn't be able to open," she said.

"Does it have a lock?"

"No, but there's a bar that prevents it opening."

Wyatt knelt down. "Do you mind?" he asked, gesturing into the house.

She shook her head, so he climbed in through the window and landed in the kitchen. A quick glance around was all it took to find the bar she spoke of on the floor near the fireplace. He closed the window, then picked up the bar and put it in place and tried to raise the window again.

"It's tight," he said as he clambered back out of the alcove moments later, "but a child, possibly even a small adult, could fit through that gap. I'm guessing the thieves sent a snakesman in first. You should get a bigger bar for that window."

"Thank you!" Mrs. James exclaimed. "I will tell Mr. James to get it replaced this afternoon."

"Thank you for your time, Mrs. James."

"Yes, thank you," Bingo echoed. "Is there anything else you would like us to know?"

"I don't suppose so," she said. "The constables examined my window, but they didn't let me know what they found and they certainly didn't tell me how to make it more secure. It would have been nice if they had."

"Duly noted," Bingo said.

They took their leave and returned to Bingo's carriage.

"So that's what investigating looks like?" Bingo asked as the carriage lurched forward. "It wasn't nearly as entertaining as I hoped. I felt like I was accompanying my mother on one of her visits to the poor, only without the hamper of food weighing me down."

"Please, don't hold back in your criticism," Wyatt said sarcastically.

"The dog was nice," Bingo said with a grin. "I wish I'd thought to bring one of mine to London."

The carriage hit a bump in the road, and they braced themselves against the sudden jostling.

"Did you hear what she said about the dog?" Wyatt asked.

"That it chased the robbers away? Another reason I should have brought mine."

"No, that she was watching it for someone else. It wasn't their dog."

"What of it?"

"I think whoever tipped the thieves off about the Jameses' being out that night and the cook being away didn't know about the dog. The thieves weren't expecting it."

Bingo flashed him an amused smile. "You say that with an air of significance, but I'm afraid you've lost me. Ought I to infer something from what you say?"

Wyatt sighed and leaned his head back against the upholstery. "I don't know exactly. But it's the first mistake they've made, and that has to be significant."

*****

The Pall Mall was a beautiful street, with its wide thoroughfare and elegant buildings. The large windows, columned porches and gold adornments had put Samantha in awe when she first came to London. Now, she was thoroughly sick of the sight of them.

The day had started well. Knowing that she would be heading home to Kent that night, she had risked spending a penny on a hot potato for breakfast and she felt pleasantly full. She had gathered up her belongings—just the rest of her bandages and the small handful of coins—and bid farewell to the girls she had not said goodbye to yet. She and Annie had spoken the night before, and she was still annoyed at the girl's reaction to the news that she would be leaving.

"No fear," Annie had said with a laugh. "I'll keep your mat waiting for you when you return."

The clothes Samantha had borrowed from Annie were once more in the trunk, and Samantha again wore the secondhand dress that had been her only garment, day and night, for weeks. If it weren't that the city itself smelled so bad, she might have worried that her smell would offend those around her.

She had hurried to the Pall Mall, not sure when Mr. Wyatt would be arriving at his club. It was only after she had begun walking down the street, being alternately ignored or watched with suspicion by the wealthy passersby, that she realized he had not told her which was his club. She cast her mind back to their conversation. He had said he was most likely to be at his club during the day and that the best place to find him was the Pall Mall.

Inwardly berating herself for not demanding more specifics, she decided there was nothing for it but to walk the length of the street until she met with Mr. Wyatt. This she did and for so long that she was certain she might have walked to the far side of Regent's Park and back by the time she finally caught sight of him.

It was early afternoon and she was leaning against a building, resting her feet, which were in considerable pain from all the walking, when she saw him exiting the United University Club. To be leaving, he must have entered, and she cursed the ill fortune that had caused her to be away when he did.

He stood for a moment under the columned entryway, adjusting his hat and cane, and began to walk towards St. James' Street. Samantha hurried across to him, dodging out of the way of a carriage and a hansom cab.

"Sarah!" He looked surprised to see her, and possibly a little relieved.

"How long have you been in there?" she asked, pointing to the club entrance. It was not a polite greeting, but she was annoyed to have wasted so much time walking while he was tucked away in the smoking room or playing billiards.

"I don't know," he said. "A couple of hours at most. Why? Have you been waiting for me?"

"Since early this morning," she said, not trying to conceal the anger in her voice. "Why did you not tell me which club was yours?"

"Did I not? I'm sorry."

She had been holding up a hand to shield her eyes from the glare of the sun. He shifted his position, allowing her to drop her hand.

"Blo—" Mr. Wyatt started to say, but he coughed and cleared his throat. "Forgive me, but, what happened?"

He was staring at her black eye.

"It's not important," she said. "I came to tell you—"

"Not important?" He cut her off. "You look awful."

"Thank you," Samantha said mildly.

"I didn't mean to be rude. It's just that—it's hard to miss."

"I could certainly wish it had been easier."

He stared at her, then a smile turned the corner of his mouth. "It's not something to joke about," he protested.

"If I don't mind, why should you? But I am endeavoring to tell you that I have information for you about the housemen—the thieves."

"You do?" he said, sobering. "Then by all means, tell me. Only, not among all this traffic. Why don't we step over to the square?"

He led the way to St. James' Square, where there were fewer people and they could hear themselves speak without raising their voices.

"They work for a man called Skinny Jim," Samantha said, as they began to walk around the perimeter.

"Skinny Jim?"

"Yes. Have you heard of him?"

"I have," he said gravely. "I know he's a dangerous man who's avoided arrest by a combination of cleverness, bribery, and violent threats. How do you know they work for him?"

"I met them at his pub in Blackfriars."

"You met them?" He gaped at her.

"This would be much easier, Mr. Wyatt, sir, that is, if you would not interrupt," Samantha said. "There is much to tell."

"Of course. Forgive me."

She went on to explain how she had come to learn of Skinny Jim and how he had mistaken her intentions and allowed her to stay in his pub.

"Wait," Mr. Wyatt said, stopping and turning to her. "I know I said I would not interrupt, but are you telling me that you spent a whole day serving drinks in a pub run by a criminal?"

"I should have explained. I was disguised as a boy."

"Disguised as a—how?"

He looked at her in disbelief, and Samantha felt her cheeks redden.

"I borrowed some clothes," she said. "And my hair was in a cap. Without going into detail that would embarrass us both, I will ask that you assume I had some modicum of sense and intelligence to have done the thing properly." He still looked skeptical, so she added, "It was not well-lit and when we went out, it was nighttime."

"When who went out where?"

Samantha decided against telling him of her first venture into housebreaking. No need to reveal her lawbreaking when it was not relevant.

"I accompanied the housemen—their names are Slater and Palmer—on a robbery," she said.

She had been unable to decide whether to look ashamedly at the ground or defiantly into his eyes as she said this and so ended up rather stupidly staring at his waistcoat. As a result, she was unable to see his immediate reaction to her words. When several seconds passed in silence, she gathered the courage to tear her eyes from his watch chain and look into his face. He was staring at her, but she could not read his expression.

"They weren't boasting about the robberies, as you had hoped," she said, "but Skinny Jim told me they were two of the best, so it seemed likely that they were the ones you were looking for."

She couldn't tell him that her main reason for suspecting them was that she had recognized one of them from her uncle's house —not yet, anyway.

"By following them, I was able to see into which house they went, so I can tell you, that you may confirm your suspicions. And I can describe them both."

"Did you follow them, or accompany them?" Mr. Wyatt asked.

"Why do you ask?"

"Following implies observation. Accompanying implies participation."

"Is that relevant?"

"I suppose not," he said, but his tone implied otherwise.

"The house was on Doughty Street," she said.

"Fifty-nine Doughty Street?" he asked.

"I don't know the number," she admitted. "It was the third house from the right after the crossing with James Street."

"That's fantastic," he said, smiling broadly.

"Is it worth the payment you promised?"

His smile vanished. "Yes, yes, of course." He looked away and cleared his throat. "Absolutely. Only…" He pulled out his pocketbook and opened it. "I don't have any coin with me."

"Can you not ask to borrow from a friend?" Samantha asked anxiously. "Surely someone at your club…"

"Yes, of course. Wait here. I'll be right back."

He set off across the square and Samantha found a bench to sit and wait.

*****

It took Wyatt longer than he would have liked to find the coin he needed. Many of his friends did not travel with cash on hand and those who did carried mostly paper money. At last, by promising him a game of whist, Wyatt was able to persuade Percy Bainbridge to lend him a few shillings. Pocketing the coins, he hurried down the grand stairs, determined to give the whole sum to Sarah.

"Mr. Wyatt."

Wyatt stopped halfway to the door and turned to see a man detach himself from the wall he had been leaning against and come to join him. He was shorter than Wyatt and stout, with a face scarred by smallpox. He wore a bland expression, but Wyatt wasn't fooled.

"Inspector Whicher," Wyatt said. "To what do I owe the pleasure?"

"There is a matter of some delicacy which I must speak to you about," the inspector said. "Is there somewhere we can talk?"

"I'm rather busy at the moment, actually," Wyatt said. "Another time, perhaps."

Inspector Whicher fingered the brim of his hat, which he still held in his hands, but made no move to leave.

"It won't take long," he said calmly. "And I thought you might rather speak here than in my office."

Wyatt's eyes flicked to the door as he thought of Sarah, waiting for him. She must be wondering where he was.

He sighed. "It can't wait?" he asked, making no effort to hide his irritation.

"I would prefer if it didn't."

"Very well, but it had better be quick."

He led the way to a salon. Large windows faced the street. Wyatt chose a spot near one of the windows so he would be sure to see Sarah if she came looking for him. He dropped into a chair and eyed Inspector Whicher expectantly, drumming his fingers on the red leather armrest.

Whicher sat more slowly. He seemed to be formulating his words as he watched Wyatt. "I have just been to Camden," he began. "I was following up on a robbery investigation on Doughty Street."

Wyatt stopped drumming. "Oh?"

"Yes," Whicher said. "The owner of the house told me how pleased she was with the visit of some friends of the commissioner who came to see how she had been treated by my constables."

He paused and looked at Wyatt, as though expecting him to say something.

"I see," Wyatt said. "And the reason you are telling me this is…?"

"Lord Aston is a friend of yours, is he not?"

"Yes, he is," Wyatt said, inwardly cursing Bingo for using his real name. "Was I not clear enough earlier? I am in a hurry. Please say what you came to say."

"Lord Aston and his friend, a Mr. Artemis Signet"—Inspector Whicher's tone bordered on sardonic as he spoke the second name and he raised an eyebrow at Wyatt—"used Commissioner Mayne's name to gain entry to a private residence. They did not do any damage, as far as I could tell, and I am inclined not to take the matter further, if they can assure me they will not do so in future."

"Are you saying you think they did not go on the commissioner's authority?" Wyatt asked, keeping his voice light and even.

"I know they did not."

"I thought you came here directly after leaving Doughty Street. How did you have time to check?"

"The commissioner does not send members of the aristocracy

to evaluate the personable qualities of his officers."

"He might," Wyatt said. "After all, public opinion of the detective branch, at least, is rather low after the Kent case."

He had hoped to throw the inspector off by mentioning the notorious murder investigation that had so damaged his reputation, but Inspector Whicher merely shook his head and continued to watch him with that disconcerting gaze of his.

"Are you certain the man was Lord Aston?" Wyatt asked nonchalantly. "If the men lied about their purpose, they may have lied about their names as well."

"Mrs. James' description of the man matches that of Lord Aston."

"A general description of Bingo would match half the gentlemen in London."

Inspector Whicher sat forward. "Mr. Wyatt, you may continue to play your game, but I will speak plainly. The reputation of the police force in London is tenuous at best, but its work is important, and that work cannot be done without public confidence. I take seriously any threat to that confidence. What you and your friend did may have been harmless, but had anything gone amiss while you were sailing, as it were, under false colors, it would have been my men hurt by it, and by extension, the people of this city they protect.

"Now, you are your own man, a free citizen, and if you choose to masquerade as Artemis Signet or Joe the fisherman for your own purposes, that's of no mind to me, but don't you involve the reputation of this police force."

Wyatt did not respond immediately, matching the inspector's stare as he collected his thoughts. "I can assure you," he said deliberately, "that no slight on the reputation of the police force will be of my doing."

"That is not quite what I asked of you."

"But it's what I'm willing to give."

Silence stretched between them. Wyatt was determined not to be the first to look away.

"Mr. Wyatt," Inspector Whicher said finally. "I know that we have had our differences in the past. I admit that I disapprove of your hobby, but I must ask you, in the interest of the justice we both profess to promote, what you were doing in the James house. Or, if you prefer, what do you think Artemis Signet might've been doing there?"

Wyatt considered. He believed Whicher when he said that he would not pursue the matter of his, or rather, Bingo's, ill-conceived lie to gain entry to the James house, but admitting to his part in it would be to prove Whicher right. Though they both knew it to be true, he wasn't sure his pride would allow him to admit it. After all, it had been laughably easy for Whicher to make the connection between Artemis and himself, and it rankled him.

"Not knowing the gentleman," he said at last, "I'm sure I couldn't say."

Inspector Whicher sighed. "Very well, Mr. Wyatt. I am sorry to have held you up."

"Out of curiosity," Wyatt said, as they stood, "how are things progressing with the Holborn murders?"

"Why? Do you have new information?"

"I was merely curious."

Inspector Whicher eyed him shrewdly, then shook his head. "The investigation is ongoing. There's nothing more I can tell you."

His mouth drew into a tight line and he looked so harassed that Wyatt did not press him. They walked in silence to the door and bade each other farewell once they had stepped onto the street. Inspector Whicher hailed a cab, and Wyatt walked back to St. James' Square. Sarah was not where he had left her and, after some searching, he was forced to realize that she was gone.

NINE

She had thought better of him. In all her dealings with him, Samantha had come to regard Mr. Wyatt as an earnest, honest man, but after waiting for such a long time for him to return with her money, she was forced to conclude that he had abandoned her.

She ought to have demanded the money first before giving him the information he had asked for. There was no doubt that she had earned it ten times over. She was furious, and her anger only grew on her long walk to his home in Knightsbridge. She planned to camp outside his door until he returned and demand her payment.

Mr. Wyatt's house faced a square, and she took up her post on a bench in the square. She was soon shooed from it by a passing constable and spent the rest of the day on the lookout for the constable, hiding whenever he came by and sitting beside a tree the rest of the time.

As evening fell, elegant barouches with liveried footmen began to crowd the square. It appeared one of Mr. Wyatt's neighbors was hosting a dinner party. Ladies and gentlemen in evening finery descended and hailed one another in cheery voices, laughing and discussing the fine weather. They seemed unreal to Samantha, like spirits of long past. Then one of the ladies turned back to unsnag her gown from a bush and, for a brief moment, their eyes met. In that moment, Samantha saw herself through the lady's eyes. She saw a thin, dirty girl in a fraying dress sitting alone and friendless and she felt pity, but no empathy. For how could she understand someone whose life was so far removed from her own? And what was it to her? A voice called from within the house and she turned back, the moment forgotten.

Samantha had fallen asleep and woken several times when Mr. Wyatt finally arrived. She was relieved to see him, for she had been afraid she had missed his coming altogether while her eyes were closed. She hauled herself to her feet, brushing dirt from her skirt, and hurried across the square.

Her feet made little sound as she padded across the grass and onto the street. Mr. Wyatt stood in front of the steps to his house, looking down at something in his hand. As she reached him, he whipped around and she found herself with a knife at her throat.

"Sarah!" he gasped, letting the hand holding the knife fall to his side. "What were you thinking sneaking up on me like that? I might have hurt you."

Samantha stepped back, rubbing her throat. "Sneaking? I wasn't sneaking."

"What else do you call coming up behind a person in the dark without announcing yourself?"

It was a fair point, but Samantha was too angry to care. "It wouldn't have been dark if you had been here earlier. It's been hours."

"What happened?" he asked with concern. "Why didn't you wait for me?"

"Wait for you?" She stared at him in disbelief. "All I've done all day is wait for you. I waited on the Pall Mall and I waited at St.

James' Square and I've been waiting here ever since."

"Yes, but you left St. James' before I returned."

"You were gone for ages," Samantha retorted. "I assumed you were not planning to return. So, I came here to catch you out."

Mr. Wyatt opened his mouth to say something, then closed it and shook his head. "I'm sorry I took so long. I was forcibly delayed."

"Oh." Samantha hadn't expected him to apologize. Her anger deflated, and she suddenly felt tired. "Well, I'm sorry I thought the worst of you."

"It was understandable," he conceded. "I assume you're here for your money?"

She nodded.

"Won't you come in and have a bite to eat first? I feel I ought to recompense you for all your time. I doubt you had opportunity to eat, running after me all day."

He smiled at her and reached up to knock on the door. He had knocked only once when it opened.

"There you are." The woman who answered the door sounded exasperated. She stepped back to let Mr. Wyatt in and continued, "I saw you walking up and I could not conceive what took you so long to knock but…oh."

She stopped speaking as Samantha entered. Samantha recognized her as the housekeeper who had welcomed her in the first time. She was short, close to Samantha's own height, and stout, with a round face. Her thick, grey brows were drawn together in a slight frown as she watched Samantha.

"Is Mrs. Plummet still awake?" Mr. Wyatt asked as he placed his hat and cane on the stand.

"She is, sir," the housekeeper said, her eyes still on Samantha.

"Would you ask her to put together some light repast? And

have Jenny bring it to us in my study. No need to set the table."

The housekeeper gave Samantha a final, suspicious look, then nodded to Mr. Wyatt and bustled away down the hall.

"If you will." Mr. Wyatt gestured for Samantha to precede him into his study.

It was as messy as it had been the last time she had entered it, possibly more so. Books were still piled haphazardly on every available surface. Papers covered the desk. A dark green coat had been thrown over a marble bust of Aristotle, covering one eye and giving the old philosopher an oddly rakish look.

Wyatt led her to the chairs by the fire in which they had sat on her previous visit. The fabric was faded and worn. When they were seated, she found some of her discomfort returning. Apart from Charles, who was, after all, practically family, she had never been alone with a man not related to her. If Aunt Victoria could have seen her, she would have been horrified. But then, if Aunt Victoria were alive, Samantha wouldn't be there.

"A penny for your thoughts?"

Samantha started and looked up to see Mr. Wyatt watching her. "I can't imagine my thoughts are worth even that."

"They seemed to be troubling you," Mr. Wyatt pressed. He was frowning at her with every appearance of genuine concern, but she didn't have the luxury of sharing.

"You said you have my payment?" she asked instead.

"Yes, of course." He reached into his pocket, looking flustered, and handed her several coins. "I'm sorry that it took so long to get it to you."

Samantha counted them. "This is more than I asked for." She tried to hand the extra back to him, but he shook his head.

"It's no more than you deserve."

"Thank you."

She couldn't modestly access the hidden pocket of her skirt

where the rest of her savings was hidden, so she rolled back her left sleeve a few times and slid the coins into the folds of the fabric, rolling it over one more time.

"Why did you need that specific sum?" Mr. Wyatt asked.

"I'm not sure how that's your business," she said. "Begging your pardon, sir."

He sighed and passed a hand over his brow. Then he leaned forward and fixed her with a determined stare.

"I've been wrestling with my conscience for some time," he said. "And I've decided that I cannot be party to allowing a lady to live on the streets without trying to help her in some way."

"Lady?" Samantha repeated, and she was unable to hide the tremor in her voice. What did he know?

He huffed impatiently. "Please, Sarah, or whatever your name is, allow me some amount of intelligence. You are too well-spoken to have been long on the streets. You carry yourself like a lady. There are myriad ways in which you reveal yourself. I cannot be the first to have noticed."

Samantha's breathing eased. He didn't know anything after all. "I need the money to get home. It's the cost of a train ticket."

"But will they take you back?" he asked earnestly.

"Take me back?" She blinked. "What do you mean, take me back?"

"Presumably the home you are speaking of is the one you were cast out of. Was it a tryst? Were you with child?"

"I… What…" Samantha spluttered, flabbergasted. "Cast out? What are you talking about?"

Now Mr. Wyatt looked confused. "I assumed that was why you were left to fend for yourself. Why no one has helped you."

"Absolutely not!" she insisted. "I was never cast out. They would help me if they knew where I was."

"Then why do you not write to them?"

She gestured to her sleeve with its hidden collection of coin. "Money," she said with annoyance. "It costs money to buy paper and ink and to send letters. And even then, it's something that's best explained in person, where there is no chance of the message being misinterpreted or intercepted."

"If you weren't cast out," Mr. Wyatt said, "how did you end up in the slums of London with no money and no friends?"

Samantha bristled at his assessment of her current position. She had not been sleeping on the street, after all. She had taken care of herself and worked to pay for her lodgings.

"I got lost," she said, which was true enough.

Mr. Wyatt laughed. Then, he became serious. "I cannot help you if you don't tell me what's wrong."

"I don't need your help." When he started to object, she pressed on. "I have gotten along perfectly fine without your help and I don't need it now. I have a plan."

Mr. Wyatt stood up and began pacing. "You call this perfectly fine?" he asked, gesturing to her rags.

"I'm alive, aren't I?" she said, standing as well, her voice rising. "Do you know how long I've been on my own? Five weeks. Five weeks caring for myself. I've fought and I've begged and I've worked myself to the point of exhaustion and nobody gave me anything. But I survived. On my own. So, I don't need your pity and I don't need your sense of obligation to me because you have suddenly recognized me as a lady. Why should my situation of birth earn your assistance when my circumstances did not?"

All of the bitterness that had built up inside her was pouring forth. It felt good to let it out and to rail against the man who had raised her hopes and quashed them over and over again that day. But as she wound down, it occurred to her that he wasn't listening. He had stopped pacing and was staring, unfocused, at a spot behind her head. His lips were moving silently and he seemed to be thinking. Suddenly, he smiled.

"I could be wrong," he said, looking back at her, "but I don't think I am. You're the missing witness from the Holborn murders, aren't you? And not a witch or a servant, therefore… Miss Avery, I presume?"

Samantha felt the blood drain from her face as she stared at him, open-mouthed. She knew there was no point in protesting as his expression turned triumphant.

"How could you possibly know that?" she asked in a half whisper.

He shrugged. "It just fits. The timing, your class, your current circumstances, everything I know about the murders."

"Are you going to turn me in?" she asked.

"Did you kill them?"

"Of course not!"

"Then why have you been hiding?"

Samantha hesitated. "It's complicated."

"But surely, if you had explained what happened to the police…"

"No," she said. Then, more firmly, "No. I tried that. They wouldn't listen. They thought I was making things up, that the footboy and I had killed them together. And I had no one to vouch for my identity or my character. That is why I need to go home and return later. There are some…complications that must be dealt with."

At that moment, the maid entered. She was carrying a tray laden with an assortment of hand pies, cakes, and fruit. She set it down on the desk.

"Would you like anything else, sir?" she asked Mr. Wyatt.

"No, thank you, Jenny," he said absently, looking down at the floor with his hands in his pockets. Jenny curtsied and left.

When the door closed with a click, Mr. Wyatt looked up. "I

want to help you," he said. "And before you object, hear me out. If you want to go home and gather a few friends or family members to return with you to speak to the police, that's your decision. However, as I'm sure you have considered, the matter will not then be settled. The murder will still be unsolved. There will be questions, and not only about your involvement. People will want to know where you have been all this time. I don't know what circles the Averys moved in, but I imagine the people in them are much the same as those in higher society. You will find it hard to ride out the scandal."

Samantha suddenly felt very weary. She returned to the chair and sank into it. Mr. Wyatt picked up a couple of hand pies from the tray and handed one to her, sitting down opposite her once again.

"I have some skill as an investigator," he continued. "I won't pretend I've ever inquired into a murder before, but I think I could do it. If you can tell me everything that happened that night, I could begin to investigate. And with the information you give, we might be able to find the killer and bring that part of your difficulties to an end."

"And the scandal?" Samantha asked, looking down at the pie, but unable to summon the energy to bite it. "How will you fix that?"

"I have a cousin, a lady of respectability. If I write for her help, she will come here and act as chaperone for you. We will both swear that you came to me directly after the murders and she stayed with you here. It won't quell all the gossips, but it should go a long way to keeping your reputation intact."

Samantha considered. Her conscience rebelled at the idea of lying so blatantly. Thus far, the only real lie she'd told was her name. She may have hidden things, but she'd kept to the truth as much as she could. What Mr. Wyatt was suggesting was significant. It wasn't one lie, but several, and ones she would have to tell over and over.

He was right about the scandal, though. If people knew the truth—that she'd lived in the slums of London on her own for over a month—her life would be over. Her loss of virtue would be assumed. No gentleman would marry her and no respectable woman would agree to hire her as a companion. No parents would see her as a fit governess for their children. She may as well return to live in the lodging house with Annie, scouring the Thames for salcable trash and fending off drunk men's advances until she died of starvation.

It was a harsh truth, and one she had been avoiding as she focused on her plan to find Charles. Yet, however much of a comfort it would be to have Charles by her side, he wouldn't be able to safeguard her reputation. He didn't have any respectable female relatives who would stoop to subterfuge. The fact that Mr. Wyatt did was odd, but if true, could be the difference between respectability and ruin for her. Yet, she could not help but be suspicious of his motives.

"And why would you do this for me?" she asked.

He took a bite of his pie and chewed thoughtfully for a moment before replying. "I would love to give you a noble reason, Miss Avery," he said, and Samantha felt a jolt of surprise at his use of her false name—a reminder that she was still pretending. "But the truth is that I find your story intriguing, and I'm curious. It's a puzzle."

Samantha took a bite of her own pie, catching the crumbs with her other hand as she considered. His solution seemed her best option. However, it would require that she tell him who she really was. Not Miss Avery, but Miss Kingston. She didn't trust him enough yet to do that. But perhaps, in time, if he showed himself to be capable of helping her and finding her aunt and uncle's killer, she would.

"Very well," she said. "I accept your help."

When Samantha awoke the next morning, she thought for a moment that she was back in her uncle's house on Kensington Square. Instead of the thinly padded hard wood she had become used to, she felt the softness of a mattress beneath her. Her head lay in a cloud of pillows and she was warm underneath a layer of blankets.

The door to the room opened, startling Samantha from her state of half-wakefulness. A maid entered, Jenny, followed by the housekeeper, Mrs. Hexam, and memories of the night before rushed to mind.

"Good morning, miss," the maid said. She curtseyed and walked across the room to open the windows.

"What time is it?" Samantha asked, blinking as sunlight streamed in.

"It's half past nine, miss."

"Half past nine?" She had never slept so late before. She sat up and the sheets that had covered her slid down, exposing her old, dirty dress.

"You'll be having a bath this morning," Mrs. Hexam said. "I would have insisted last night, only you were so tired, I didn't like to. There's a tub in the corner there behind the screen and Jenny's already brought up two bucketsful of nice, hot water while you were sleeping. Just give your clothes to me. I'll be giving them to the rag-and-bone man."

"What am I to wear?" Samantha asked as she went behind the screen to undress.

"I brought down a few dresses from the attic," Mrs. Hexam said. "They were Mr. Wyatt's sister's. With a few alterations, they should fit you. Until then, there is a dressing gown by your bed you can put on when you get out."

Samantha lay her old dress over the screen and watched it

disappear as Mrs. Hexam pulled it from the other side. She felt an odd sentimentality over the garment—the first she had bought herself as well as almost her only possession for all this time.

"Your breakfast will be on the bed when you get out," Mrs. Hexam said. "I will return later to get your measurements. Jenny will help you with your bath if you need it."

"Oh, no thank you," Samantha called back. "I shall manage on my own."

She listened to their footsteps recede and the door close. Then, she was alone. Samantha dipped an experimental toe into the water. It was still warm. She stepped in and lowered herself into the tub. It was the most wonderful feeling in the world. The warm water enveloped her like a cocoon. A sigh escaped her lips and she leaned back against the edge of the tub and closed her eyes. A bath must truly be the most luxurious experience in the world. She hoped she would never again take it for granted.

*****

Wyatt strolled through Hyde Park that morning with so many thoughts parading through his mind that he hardly noticed where he went. He had dispatched a telegram to his cousin, Madge, that morning, explaining obliquely that he needed her help with a problem and hoped she might come stay with him a few weeks. She would be at her country estate, but he felt certain that she would oblige him and he could expect her shortly.

With the problem of Miss Avery's reputation well in hand, he turned his mind to the matter of the murders of Mr. and Mrs. Avery. He would need to find out what the professional investigators knew already, which would mean trying to get information either from George or Inspector Whicher, preferably both.

"Wyatt!"

Wyatt looked up sharply to see Bingo walking beside him. It was he who had shouted.

"What was that for?" he asked, pointedly rubbing his ear. "You nearly deafened me."

"I called you several times," Bingo said.

"Sorry. I was lost in thought."

"So, I see. Anything in particular on your mind?"

"Yes, but nothing I feel at liberty to share."

Bingo put up his hands in mock defense. "As you wish," he said. "I only came to ask if you might pass on an invitation to Archie for me." He grinned.

"What invitation?" Wyatt asked.

"There's a ball tomorrow night," Bingo said, nodding to an acquaintance they passed. "It's the last one before the few stragglers still here head off to the country."

"I heard about that. Are you planning to go?"

"Only if Archie does. I don't think I could stand it otherwise."

"I'll let him know you feel that way. I'm sure he'll be touched that you so enjoy his company."

"I don't want it to go to his head. I do have other friends, you know. None of them quite so interesting, of course."

"Of course."

They walked in silence for a few minutes, then Wyatt asked, "Would it lessen your enjoyment if Archie were to bring a guest?"

"Guest? What sort of guest?" Bingo asked. His eyes narrowed. "Not Mrs. Lanham again, I hope."

"I'm only asking, in case he wishes to bring someone, if you would rather he didn't."

Bingo sighed. "I don't suppose I mind, so long as he does not spend too much time with her."

"Good."

"Is she handsome?" Bingo asked. "This mysterious guest, I

mean."

Wyatt laughed. "I don't know," he said, throwing up his hands. "She's young."

"But not handsome? And likely naive, a combination I rather enjoy. I believe I shall have her head turned from you to me before the night is over. Shall we make a wager?"

"Her head is not turned in any particular direction, nor shall it be. That is not why I am bringing her, if I do."

"Why are you bringing her?"

"I don't want her wandering off while I am away. Also, I think her presence will add to Archie's colorful persona."

"Is she likely to wander off? What a sad reflection on you, my good friend."

Wyatt punched Bingo lightly on the arm. "That's enough from you," he said. "Perhaps I won't pass on this invitation after all."

"Whatever you say." Bingo hefted his cane and adjusted his coat. "I must be off. I'll see you tomorrow night."

When Wyatt returned home, in considerably better spirits than when he had left, there was a telegram from Madge saying that she would be at his address in two days.

"Mrs. Hexam," he said, hanging up his hat and cane. "I will be attending a masked ball tomorrow night."

"Very good, sir," Mrs. Hexam said.

"I would like Miss Avery to accompany me. Would it be possible to find her something to wear?"

Her eyebrows raised, but she refrained from voicing her thoughts. Instead, she said, "Well, sir, as your sister never came out, she has no ballgowns for me to alter. But there is a charity shop on Green Street that takes ladies' cast-offs and deconstructs them to sell the fabric. I could see if they have anything they haven't picked apart yet."

"Thank you, Mrs. Hexam," Wyatt said, smiling at her. "And before you go, would you send Miss Avery to see me?"

"Yes, sir." She curtseyed and left, and Wyatt went to his study, whistling.

Sometime later, the sound of someone entering the room caused him to look up. For one heart-stopping moment, he thought he was seeing a ghost. Helena was walking towards him, a smile on her face. Then he blinked, and the vision was gone. It was Sarah—Miss Avery—who stood before him in Helena's old dress, looking nothing like his sister.

She didn't look like herself either, or, at least, the version of her he had come to know. Her face was clean; the bruise around her eye had faded. Her hair was brushed and styled in a simple knot at the nape of her neck and there was a serenity in her countenance he had not seen yet. Somehow, a bath and a change of clothes had transformed this wild young woman into a lady.

The nagging sense of familiarity that had pulled at him when he'd first seen her had grown so strong that he felt it must be just behind a door in his brain, and if he could only open the right one, he would finally realize where he had seen her before. It was possible that Helena's dress was affecting him, though. He had been happy for Mrs. Hexam to use his sister's old clothes when she suggested it, but now, seeing them worn for the first time in years, he wished he hadn't given his consent.

"You asked to see me?" Miss Avery prompted, and Wyatt realized that he had not yet spoken.

"Yes, yes, I did," he said hastily. "Won't you sit down?" He came around the desk and pulled out a chair for her. She thanked him and sat.

"I assume you would like me to tell you about the murder now," she said as he returned to his seat.

"Well, yes," Wyatt said. "Though I was planning to ask how

you slept first. And whether you were comfortable, enjoyed your breakfast, et cetera. All the pleasantries, you know."

She laughed. "I'm sorry. My mind has been so focused lately. I find it difficult to think about anything else."

"Completely understandable," he said. "How *did* you sleep?"

"Very well, thank you. I..." She stopped and frowned to herself.

"What is it?"

"I must confess," she said. "I thought I would have difficulty readjusting to a mattress and pillows. And baths. To all of it, really. And yet, I've found it the most natural thing to have someone help me dress and bring me a hot meal."

"And that disappoints you?" Wyatt asked.

"A little, yes."

She stared, unfocused, at a corner of his desk and Wyatt waited for her to elaborate.

"Why does it disappoint you?" he prompted, when she continued in silence.

"I don't think you would understand."

"Try me."

She sighed. "It's different for men," she said. "Men grow up. They go away to school and then they join the world. Women, we're never allowed to leave childhood. We're told what to do by our fathers, then our husbands, and then our sons, and what we're told to do is sit quietly and don't bother the men while they handle the important matters. We're dressed, fed, put to bed by our servants.

"When I was out there, I was starving and tired and scared, but my life was my own. No one told me what to do. Then, one night in a nice house, and I've melted back into the same person I was before."

She had been animated as she spoke, gesturing with her hands, but as she uttered the last few words, she fell back into the chair and was silent. Wyatt did not know quite how to respond. Part of him wanted to dispute her characterization of women. After all, his mother had never once listened to him. But he knew her to be right, in a general way. It wasn't something he had spent much time thinking about, but of course he was aware that men and women lived very different lives.

"I suppose that's true," he conceded. "But men and women are different. Men are more suited to governing and to handling weighty manners. Women are better at other things."

She frowned at him. "Other things, like what?"

"Matters of the home," he said vaguely.

She leaned forward and rested her elbows on his desk, clasping her hands together in front of her.

"Matters like raising children?" she asked. "Nursemaids raise the children. Running the household? It's hardly difficult if one has good servants. Anything women of our class might be allowed to do is taken away, and we are left with nothing but to attend social functions and be dressed like dolls multiple times a day."

"There are plenty of men whose lives are exactly that," Wyatt countered. "Those who don't have estates to run or seats in parliament to fill. Why do you think I do what I do? I can't abide idleness."

"Yes, yes. Idleness is a curse of the upper classes, irrespective of gender, but it is forced upon women in a way that it is not on men. And what do you mean men are more suited to weighty matters?"

Wyatt reeled from the speed at which she changed the subject. "I…they just are," he said lamely. Rallying, he added, "Men have a greater capacity to understand mathematics and the sciences. It allows them to—"

"My grandfather taught me to manage his books," she

interrupted. "He said I had a head for numbers that even my father did not."

"I'm not saying that no woman could learn—"

"What *are* you saying?"

He frowned at her. "I don't know how you expect to know that when you keep interrupting me," he said testily. "I'm only saying that men, generally, have a greater capacity for certain things than women, generally."

"What are you basing that assumption on?" she asked.

"Science."

"And by science, you are referring to that field of study dominated by men."

"How did we get onto this subject?" he asked, annoyed by the self-satisfied smile that played across her lips. "I thought we were going to discuss the murder of your family."

That wiped the smile from her face.

"I'm sorry," he apologized. "That was indelicate. I know it must be a painful subject for you."

"Not as much as it should be," she said enigmatically. "Do you wish to ask questions? Or shall I just start talking?"

"Go ahead." He shifted books aside, searching for his notebook. "I'll ask questions when I need clarification."

The notebook was under a pile of letters. He flipped it open and grabbed a pen. When she saw that he was ready, she began.

"I'd fallen asleep in a chair getting ready for bed. It was a crash from below that woke me. Then, my aunt came. She—"

"Your aunt?" Wyatt interrupted. "I thought they were your parents."

Samantha gave him a half smile. "You didn't figure everything out. No, my parents have been dead these six years. It was my aunt and uncle who were…who died."

"I see," he said. Then, feeling he ought to say something else, he added, "I'm sorry about your parents."

She pursed her lips and glanced away. "Thank you. As I was saying, my aunt entered my room. She had heard men downstairs —"

"Men?" Wyatt interrupted again. "How many?"

"Two. At least..." She faltered. "I do not recall her saying specifically, but I believe there were two. They were speaking with my uncle and they sounded angry. Aunt Victoria was worried. She told me to hide. Then she went to help my uncle. I planned to follow her, but I wasn't...I had to finish getting dressed. Before I could join her, I heard the shots."

"How many?"

Miss Avery had gone pale, and he was sorry to press her on what must be painful memories, however necessary it was.

"Three," she said in a small voice. "The first one was followed by a...a scream. There was another shot, and the screaming stopped."

She sat back and covered her face with her hand, her elbow resting on the arm of the chair. For a moment, he thought she might be crying. Then she lifted her head.

"You can relax," she said with a laugh. "I'm not falling apart. There's no need to look so petrified."

"I wasn't petrified," he said indignantly.

"If you say so."

"You said there were three shots?"

"Yes. The third wasn't until after they came into the hall. That will have been Mrs. Dunbar. I can only assume she was unconscious before they shot her and that was why she made no noise. There was a wound on her head when I saw her later."

"You saw the bodies?" he asked, surprised. "Do you mean you went downstairs? After the shots?"

"Not right away, no." She shook her head. "I was afraid they were coming for me next. I went out the window. I was halfway down the trellis when one of the men came running out. He saw me and pointed his gun at me. I thought I was going to die." She was silent for a moment, staring down at her hands.

When she spoke again, it was at a much brisker pace, as though she were in a rush to finish her story. "He ran at the sound of the police approaching. I waited for a moment, lest I meet his partner, then I went out front. The footboy joined me and told me they were all dead before running himself. I went in through the front door—it was open—and that's when I saw them."

"Had the police arrived yet?" Wyatt asked, his hand cramping from the speed of his note-taking.

"I suppose they must have at least reached the street," she said, "because they asked me about Da—about the footboy. They saw him running."

"Is there a reason you aren't telling me the footboy's name?" Wyatt asked, looking up.

She grimaced. "I don't suppose it matters, especially as I only know his Christian name. It's only that he was so afraid of having the murder 'pinned' on him, and I know he wasn't involved."

"Do you? How can you be sure?"

She looked down at her hands again. "It was two men," she said firmly. "Not a man and a boy."

"But you didn't see two men, did you?" he asked, checking his notes. "You only saw the one and you said your aunt didn't say how many—"

"I *heard* two men," she said heatedly. "There were two men arguing after the second shot."

"Still," Wyatt pressed. "It could have been two men and a boy. You can't dismiss him entirely."

"Yes, I can." Color rose in her pale cheeks and she glared at him. "He'd been with us less than a fortnight. What reason could he have had for killing my aunt and uncle?"

"What reason could the other men have?" Wyatt asked, diverting her attention, having established that she had no valid reason not to suspect the footboy.

Miss Avery looked unaccountably flustered by the question. "I…No doubt it was a question of money. A robbery."

"In the middle of the night, when the owners of the house were still awake?"

"I…how should I know why they came?" she said. The defensiveness of her tone belied her words, and he was almost certain she was concealing something from him. Before he could press her, she continued, "Discovering that is your task, is it not? Speaking of which, I hope you will allow me to continue with my narrative now. Without interruptions, it shouldn't take much longer."

He fought to conceal a smile as she frowned at him pointedly. He gestured for her to continue.

"My aunt and uncle were in my uncle's office," she said. "I was closing my aunt's eyes when the constables entered. They startled me, and I fell. My hand landed in…There was a puddle…of blood. My aunt's. They questioned me, and I suppose I did look suspicious with blood on my hand, but they were rather closed-minded. And stupid. After all, I didn't even have a gun. They were going to take me to Scotland Yard, and perhaps I ought to have gone and explained myself, but they hadn't exactly filled me with confidence as to the sort of reception I would have there, so I ran."

Wyatt twirled the pen between his fingers. There was more to what she was saying. He was sure of it. He almost pressed her, but he caught her eye and could see from her expression that she was determined not to speak further. He would have to bide his time.

"Would you like me to describe the man I saw leaving the

house?" she asked. "I'm not much of an artist, but a verbal description ought to help."

"Did you get a good enough look at him? It was dark, and you don't seem to have seen much of him."

She gave him a self-satisfied smile. "I saw enough of him that night to recognize him when I saw him again. And we spent quite a bit of time together on the second meeting."

"What?"

"He was one of the men who robbed that house on Doughty Street. One of the housemen you are chasing. Slater is his name."

Wyatt was stunned. He had not been expecting that. And she had been sitting on the revelatory information the whole time without betraying the slightest hint. He had to admire her audacity, even as he wanted to throttle her for it.

"You couldn't have told me that earlier?" he asked.

"There would have been no point before I told you how I recognized him," she said, a spark of humor in her eye. "And we both agreed last night that we were too tired to get into that discussion then."

"Still…" He ran his hands through his hair.

"Would you like my description?"

"Yes, I would."

She was able to give him more detail than he could have hoped, down to the tattoos on the man's arm. He wasn't yet sure what he would do with the information, but it was exhilarating to have made such a step in the investigation.

*****

Samantha watched Mr. Wyatt scribble away with evident excitement, but she could not share it. She had begun to wonder just what they would be able to do with what they knew. Did Mr. Wyatt plan to track down Slater and force a confession out of him? That seemed unlikely. Besides, Slater worked for Skinny Jim. He had powerful allies.

"These robberies," she said, on sudden inspiration. "Did they start before or after the murder?"

"After," he said. "Why?"

"It strikes me as odd," she said, "that they would kill the first time and wait until the houses were empty all the other times."

He furrowed his brow. "The Holborn murders were high-profile news. They may have felt they had drawn too much attention to themselves. It has worked out well for them. With so much focus devoted to the mystery of the murders, these robberies have passed by almost unnoticed. Maybe," he said, sitting up straighter, "they did that on purpose. They created a distraction that drew focus from their true intentions."

"That's a risky distraction," Samantha said. "I hope you are wrong, for I would hate to think my aunt and uncle had died for so trivial a reason."

He looked chagrined and seemed to be searching for a suitable reply, but Samantha's mind had already raced off in another direction. They were speaking as though the murders had been a botched robbery attempt, but she knew that was not the case. Those men had followed her family across town. They had targeted them. And before that, her uncle had been blackmailed, which must be connected. *But why kill someone you are blackmailing?*

"Miss Avery?"

Samantha started and looked up to see Mr. Wyatt watching her with amusement.

"I beg your pardon," she said. "I was thinking."

"So I gathered," he said. "I was attempting to tell you that there is a ball tomorrow night, and I thought you might like to accompany me."

She stared at him. "Are you mad?"

He put up his hands in a defensive posture. “I thought you might enjoy some entertainment after your ordeal. It’s not as though anyone would recognize you.”

He was thinking of her as Miss Avery of Holborn, who would have only dreamed of traveling in such exalted circles as he did. But Samantha Kingston would most certainly be recognized. How would she explain her presence when everyone thought she had returned to the country with her uncle?

“ shouldn’t be overcrowded,” Mr. Wyatt was saying, “as so many people have left for the season. It’s a sort of last hurrah for those of us who are still here. Mrs. Hexam thinks she can find you a dress, and the mask should hide whatever you can’t cover with powder.”

He was looking at her eye. The swelling had gone down completely and what was left was a much smaller bruise than it had first threatened to be.

“Did you say mask?” Samantha asked, belatedly processing his words. “The ball is a masque?”

“Yes,” he said. “I wish it weren’t. Masks are so uncomfortable in the heat of a ballroom. Though I suppose I might get away with not wearing one…”

He trailed off, apparently lost in thought. Samantha mulled over what he had said about the ball—that it would be a “last hurrah” for those still in town. That should mean that anyone still in London would be going. She had not given up her plan to find Charles and let him know about his father. In agreeing to stay with Mr. Wyatt and help him find Slater and Palmer, she had merely postponed it. If Charles was in London—and he was just as likely to be in Bath or even York—he would probably be at this ball. He would have heard that Sir Arthur had returned to Kent and know that he was free to attend without fear of running into his father.

“If your housekeeper is going to the trouble of procuring me a gown,” Samantha said finally. “I suppose it would be rude to refuse. Thank you for the invitation."

The rest of that day and most of the next, Samantha found herself reluctantly in the position of dressmaker's dummy as Mrs. Hexam and Jenny pinned and tucked and added fabric to two dresses and a ballgown. The day dresses were so far out of fashion that the skirts did not fit over the crinoline the housekeeper had found for her and some creativity was needed to enlarge them. The burgundy silk ballgown, however, was only a few years old and the addition of fresh ribbon and lace improved it.

Jenny had little experience in dressing a lady's hair, so Samantha did most of the work herself. She pulled part of her hair forward and braided it, then wrapped the braid around the simple knot she had twisted up in the back. Jenny added fresh flowers, which softened the look. Alice would have done some intricate work with curls, but Samantha was pleased with her efforts.

Powder applied near her eye helped to make the bruise almost invisible and she pinched her cheeks to add some color to her face. Then, when she was ready, she stepped into the crinoline and Jenny tied it on.

"I am sorry to put you to all this effort, Jenny," Samantha said as the maid lifted the first petticoat over her head. "I know these are not your usual duties."

"I don't mind, miss," Jenny said. "I like the experience. I might like to be a lady's maid one day."

"I'm sure you will be very good at it," Samantha said. "Perhaps when Mr. Wyatt is married, if his wife does not already have a maid or cannot bring her, you might take that position. Then you wouldn't have to look elsewhere."

Jenny laughed. "I don't think I'd want to wait that long, miss. I don't think it would suit him to have a lady about the place. Like as not, she'd make him hire more servants and keep the rooms tidier, and he wouldn't like that."

"I can imagine," Samantha said with a smile. "Well, then, when I have returned home, I might recommend you to a friend."

"Would you?" Jenny asked, her eyes wide. "I would be so grateful if you did, miss. Not that I don't like to work for Mr. Wyatt, you understand."

"I understand."

Jenny handed her a pair of white gloves, and she slid her hands into them. Then Jenny picked up the button hook from the dressing table and fastened the row of tiny buttons at the wrist. When she had finished, Samantha collected her fan and mask and went down to meet Mr. Wyatt.

As she descended the stairs, Samantha felt ill at ease. She ought to have been focusing on her goal of searching for Charles at the ball and on what she would say if she did, finally, find him. Instead, she could not stop thinking about how strange it was to be attending a ball on the arm of a single gentleman. Even though no one would know who she really was and no aspersions would be cast against her own character, she felt tainted at the thought. And what did it say about Mr. Wyatt, that he would arrive at a ball with a woman who was not his wife?

Mr. Wyatt himself stepped into the entry hall at that moment and she felt the air go from her lungs as all thoughts of propriety vanished from her mind. Because, though she knew he must be Mr. Wyatt, the person she saw before her was Archibald Kennedy.

TEN

Wyatt heard Miss Avery descending the stairs and tore himself away from the newspaper article he'd been reading. It was from the *Times* the day after the murder, and he was scouring it for anything he might have missed. He felt a twinge of annoyance at being forced to abandon it but reminded himself that attending the soiree had been his idea.

When he stepped into the hall and saw Miss Avery, he was momentarily speechless. It was the transformation, more than anything, that had stunned him. He knew she was pretty. He had noticed that before. But in the ballgown with flowers in her hair, she was…elegant. Poised. Sophisticated. No trace of the ragamuffin he had brought into his house was visible.

She, too, seemed at a loss for words, and he realized that he had forgotten to tell her he would be going to the ball as someone else. No doubt she was confused by the sudden growth of facial hair that partially obscured his face. He'd never been a fan of side whiskers himself, but they did a lot to aid in his disguise. He had learned, over the years, that expectation played the biggest part in deception—people saw what they expected to see—but a raspier voice, shoes that added height, hair lightened with pomade and clothes tailored and padded to suggest a different build, all helped.

"Mr. Kennedy?" she said incredulously.

He blinked. He had not expected she would know him. Archie Kennedy was generally fairly discerning in his choice of entertainment. He ought not to have been familiar to a tradesman's niece.

"At your service." He gave a mock bow. "I trust you will keep my secret as I keep yours."

He walked forward and held out a hand to escort her to the door. She continued to gape at him, and he noticed that her eyes were a beautiful shade of hazel. Perhaps bringing her along wasn't such a good idea after all. He had thought she would blend in.

"How?" she asked. Then, answering her own question, she gestured to his false whiskers. "Well I see how, but why?"

He hesitated. The real answer was complicated. He and Bingo had invented Archie in their school days as a convenient scapegoat for some of their more ill-advised pranks. When it became necessary for him to make an appearance, they took it in turns to dress as him until Wyatt was discovered to be the superior actor and Bingo the better impresario. When Wyatt moved to London, they thought it would be amusing to resurrect him. But, if Wyatt were being honest, Archie's continued existence was almost entirely due to himself. He had become addicted to the freedom of being someone else and being able to do things that V.T. Wyatt, younger brother of the Viscount Boxley, couldn't do without consequences.

Archie had become useful, however, when Wyatt was handling delicate problems for his friends. And, as that was a more agreeable reason, that was what he told Miss Avery.

"And how does escorting widows to balls and chasing ladies through gardens help with that?" she asked, her eyebrows raised.

"Chasing ladies through gardens?"

"Yes," she said, adding hastily, "one of many stories circulating about you."

It was as though a door in his mind had finally opened.

"We've met before, haven't we?" he said, his eyes raking over her features as he finally realized why she had seemed so familiar. "At Lord Etwall's ball back in June. You were there when I was looking for Lady Clarke."

"Lord Etwall?" she said, looking unnerved. "I don't think—"

"I know it was you, Miss Avery. I've been trying to place you in my memory since we met."

To his confusion, her face lightened at his words.

"Oh," she said with a nervous laugh. "Well, I might dispute the word 'met.' We weren't properly introduced, after all. I'm surprised you would acknowledge the incident. It doesn't reflect particularly well on you."

He cringed. That was true. He'd regretted his stupidity that night for some time afterward and had been thankful that the woman he had accidentally accosted was so understanding. He didn't know what he would have done otherwise.

"I must beg your forgiveness again," he said. "I truly did think you were Lady Clarke. I don't make a habit of kissing women without their permission."

"I am relieved to hear it," she said, and there was a smile playing around her lips, as there had been the night when she'd given him that setdown. He found himself wondering what it would be like to kiss those lips—to really kiss them—and to feel her respond.

At that moment, Mrs. Hexam entered to announce the arrival of the carriage. Wyatt shook himself mentally and took Miss Avery's arm, escorting her outside. He handed her up and climbed in after her.

"Am I to be the latest conquest of Mr. Kennedy?" she asked, raising an eyebrow at him as the carriage lurched forward.

"Perhaps Mr. Kennedy is your conquest," he said. "After all, nothing is known about…Mrs. Hartley is the name we chose, is it not?"

She laughed.

"Archie's reputation is more embellishment than substance, you know," he said seriously.

"So I've always assumed," she said with a wry smile. "But why are you telling me that?"

"I wanted to reassure you, now that you know I'm Archie and you're a guest in my house. I'm not sure which rumors you've heard, but—"

"I do hope you're not about to tell me you don't actually have a pet lion cub," she interrupted him. "Because I was quite looking forward to meeting it."

There was a hint of humor in her expression and a knowing smile that said she understood him. He smiled back.

"Unfortunately, I do have to disappoint you. I sold the lion two years ago."

She gave a surprised laugh, and they settled into a comfortable ride. Wyatt reflected that a tension seemed to have broken between them. Their relationship was no longer wealthy employer to urchin employee, but it had hung in an odd limbo since she had entered his house. He wasn't sure what precisely had pushed past that divide—whether the realization they had met before, their shared secrets or something else entirely—but something had changed, and he found he did not regret it.

*****

When they arrived at the house where the ball was being held, Samantha put on her mask—a large beaded one that hid half her face.

"Is it on right?" she asked Mr. Wyatt, adjusting it so that she could see better.

"It's perfect," he said. He leaned forward to open the door.

"Where's your mask?"

He gave her a wry smile. "I thought you knew Archie. You must know he hates to play by the rules."

He hopped down, turned, and held out a hand. She lay her gloved fingers in his and stepped down. The hackney moved off behind them and was replaced by the next in a long line of carriages waiting to discharge their passengers. On the pavement in front of the house, about a dozen people mingled, meandering towards the door, where they were ushered in a few at a time.

"Doesn't Mr. Kennedy generally arrive late?" Samantha asked, touching her mask to make certain it was in place as the woman in front of her turned to look back at them.

"Yes," he said. "I thought you would prefer to be on time, though, so as not to miss anything."

They were soon inside. Mr. Wyatt handed over his hat and cane and they greeted their hosts. Samantha was not concerned about being recognized by them—she knew them only in passing—but as soon as she and Mr. Wyatt moved forward into the ballroom, she saw just how many people were still in town.

"Oh, dear," she breathed.

Samantha felt her breath catch as nearly every eye in the ballroom turned their way. She tightened her grip on Mr. Wyatt's arm, afraid her legs might buckle. She had never enjoyed the attention of strangers, and having so much directed at her at once was suffocating.

Slowly, the eyes turned away and dozens of lips moved as conversation resumed. That was all she could see with the masks. Eyes and lips. An occasional nose, but mostly just eyes and lips. And the eyes continued to flick towards her in a way that made her want to sink into the floor.

A man approached them. He was tall—taller than Mr. Wyatt —and she almost had to crane her neck to look up at him. She recognized him even with the mask, though they had never been properly introduced. It was Lord Aston. He was heir to a marquessate, outrageously wealthy and handsome. He was the elusive white hart that every scheming mama and debutante had hunted for years. How he had managed to avoid being trapped into marriage so long was a testament to his elegant diplomacy and cleverness.

"Archie!" he said, clapping Mr. Wyatt on the back. "I'm so glad you could make it. And who is this angel? I insist on an introduction."

She had forgotten Mr. Kennedy and Lord Aston were friends. Their friendship only enhanced Lord Aston's appeal in the eyes of the young ladies who vied for his hand, and his social standing was too high for him to be brought down by the association even in the eyes of the most conservative mama.

"Mrs. Hartley, may I present my friend Lord Aston," Mr. Wyatt said. "Aston, this is Mrs. Hartley."

"A pleasure." Lord Aston bowed and kissed her hand. "Mr. Hartley is a fortunate man."

There was a question in the statement and a twinkle in his eye that indicated he already knew the answer, but Samantha supplied it anyway.

"My husband," she said, the word sounding foreign on her tongue, no matter how many times she'd practiced it earlier that day, "was not so fortunate as you might think. He passed on to his reward two years ago."

Lord Aston's smile belied his words as he said, "Such a pity. How sad to be widowed so young."

"Yes, I'm afraid I look rather ill in black."

He laughed at her irreverent comment. "I hope you won't

think me presumptuous, Mrs. Hartley, if I ask for the pleasure of a dance?"

Mr. Wyatt made a sound of surprise or possibly annoyance beside her, but Lord Aston ignored him, so Samantha did as well.

"It would be an honor, my lord," she said with a brief curtsey.

The first waltz was just beginning, so Lord Aston held out an arm and escorted her onto the dance floor. She laid a hand on his shoulder, he took her waist, and the music started. At first, they glided along in silence, spinning and floating across the floor. Samantha loved to waltz. It was a pleasure she had missed very much.

"How long have you known Archie?" Lord Aston asked, effectively destroying her ease just as she had begun to enjoy herself.

"Mr. Kennedy?" she said, attempting to sound nonchalant. "Not long."

"So, you wouldn't say you had a particular attachment to him?" he asked.

"No…" She drew out the word, looking at him questioningly.

He grinned. "Only curious. I know it is indelicate to mention his previous…acquaintances, but with a few exceptions, he doesn't generally arrive accompanied."

She blushed.

"There is something different about you, though," he continued. "I don't know what it is, but there's something he isn't telling me."

"I don't know what you mean, my lord," she said. "I can't imagine why he wouldn't want you to know all the details of his private life."

She kept her face neutral when she said it, hoping both to put him off questioning her and to appear innocent in case he took offense at her sarcasm. He gave her a searching look, and his smile broadened.

"I like you, Mrs. Hartley," he said, "even if that isn't your name. I don't know what you are to do with my friend, but I like you."

"I hope you won't be offended, my lord," Samantha said, "if I tell you I prefer to reserve my judgment for now."

He laughed again. "Not at all, not at all. Although, I should warn you: I am very likeable. Indeed, it is one of my few redeeming qualities. Archie will tell you. You won't be able to reserve judgment for long."

When the dance had finished, he escorted her to the edge of the floor and brought her a drink. She was then approached by another man and Lord Aston excused himself. Samantha danced several more times with a succession of strangers. She thought she recognized a few of them by their voices, but she could not be sure. None of them were Charles. They tried clumsily to discover her identity, but she evaded most of the questions. They were not put off. After all, the guessing game was half the fun of a masquerade. Pretending to be someone other than you were was the rest.

Samantha grew more relaxed as the evening wore on. No doubt the sips of champagne between dances contributed to the feeling, but it was more that she had become comfortable in the role she had created for herself. Mrs. Hartley didn't have to worry that a murderer knew she had seen his face or that the police regarded her as a suspect in a notorious triple homicide. Nobody was going to shun Mrs. Hartley for having to survive on the streets. In fact, most of the guests didn't even know her as Mrs. Hartley. She was just another mysterious, mask-wearing lady enjoying herself at the last dance of the season.

Occasionally, Samantha caught a glimpse of Mr. Wyatt. Sometimes he was dancing, sometimes he was talking with friends. He was so different from the enigmatic man she had come to know that she could hardly believe that he and this easy, jocular gallant were the same person.

After supper, Mr. Wyatt sought her out. She was talking with the gentleman who had just danced with her.

Mr. Wyatt walked right up to them and took her elbow. "So sorry to cut this short," he said to the gentleman, "but I must dance with this lady before the night is over or she will be quite out of sorts with me."

Samantha allowed herself to be led away. "That was rude," she said when they were out of the gentleman's earshot.

"Was it?" he said disinterestedly. "Well, it hardly matters now. I promised you a dance, Mrs. Hartley, and a dance you shall have."

"I'm not sure I want a dance, Mr. Kennedy. Not after the way you have behaved. Escorting me here, then abandoning me for other partners."

He raised his eyebrows and she smiled ever so slightly, letting him know she was playing her part and was not in earnest.

"I believe it was the other way 'round," he said, a half-smile undermining his haughty tone. "You left me for Aston almost as soon as we had stepped inside."

"It would have been rude to refuse him. And you have had ample opportunity since then to dance with me. You need not have waited until after supper to do so."

"You can hardly expect me to tie myself down at such an event, my dear," he said as he led her onto the dance floor. "You knew that when you met me."

Mr. Wyatt took her hand in his and placed his arm around her waist. She lifted her other hand to his shoulder and they waited for the music to start.

"How many partners have you had this evening, Mr. Kennedy?"

"Four."

"Ha! I have had seven."

"Lord Tennant may be as large as two men, but that does not allow him to count for two."

"So, you were watching me."

"Hardly. I happened to notice."

"I counted Lord Tennant only once. There were still seven."

"I see I have work to do if I am to best you."

Samantha smiled. "Shall we make a wager?"

"I cannot take your money."

"No money. The loser will have to walk home."

"I cannot allow a lady to walk home alone at night."

"I won't have to."

"Very well," he agreed with a grin. "I accept. I'll send a footman with you."

When they had finished their dance, Mr. Wyatt was called away by Lord Aston and Samantha welcomed the chance to rest her feet for a moment. She watched the people around her with interest. Some of them had removed their masks, despite the fact that the official unmasking was still a few hours away. She recognized several of them, making her all the gladder for her anonymity.

In one corner of the room, she saw two men in heated discussion. One of them was facing away from her, but the other, she recognized. It was the baron she had seen arguing with Sir Arthur at Cyril's ball back in June—the one who had scowled at her when she caught his eye. She had wondered at the time if she had been the subject of their disagreement, though she was barely acquainted with the baron. Was it all related to the blackmail, somehow? Was that why she had been singled out in the threats?

Samantha rose to her feet and made her way along the edge of the ballroom towards the baron with the vague idea that she might eavesdrop on his argument in order, if nothing else, to at least catch his name. However, before she had gone ten feet, she froze. It had only been a fleeting glimpse, seen through the crowd leaving the dance floor before someone moved to block her vision, but she could have sworn she saw Charles. Abandoning her path to the baron, Samantha pushed forward into the crowd, hardly noticing as she bumped into several people in her haste.

It was him, without a doubt. His sleek, blond hair glinted in the candlelight and his mask-less face was turned to the lady beside him, returning her smile with one of his own. Though it had been several years since Samantha had last seen him, she would recognize that smile anywhere.

Samantha stood less than ten paces from the object of her months-long search, watching him chat happily with his partner, unsure how to approach him. He must have sensed her stare, because he suddenly looked up. Their eyes met and she smiled. She couldn't help it. His eyes were the same blue she remembered and, looking into them, she felt transported back in time.

Charles smiled in response, and she felt emboldened.

"I am sorry to interrupt," she said. Turning to Charles' partner, whom she had recognized as a debutante known to have a formidable chaperone, she added, "It's Miss Somerson, isn't it? Mrs. Ellis is looking for you."

"Oh, really!" Miss Somerson huffed. "Pray excuse me, Mr. Prescott. I will only be a moment."

She hurried off, seething with indignation, and Samantha turned to Charles.

"Was that true?" he asked, grinning at her. Oh, how she'd missed that grin.

"Probably," she said, and he laughed. "I must confess that I was hoping for the opportunity to speak with you privately."

His eyebrows rose, and she flashed him a smile, trying not to cringe. It felt wrong to flirt with him while he thought she was someone else. She did not know how else to get him alone, though, without revealing herself to the room at large.

"Have you been to the gardens?" Charles asked. "I hear they're lovely. I've been meaning to see for myself. Will you join me?"

She nodded, and he held out an arm and escorted her outside. They took a path that led away from the house. She listened with half an ear as he commented on the large number in attendance and the quality of the food. When they were no longer in view of other couples, Samantha stopped and turned to him, feeling her anxiety mounting Would he even recognize her after all this time?

Charles had stopped talking and was watching her with bemusement while she reached up and untied her mask with unsteady fingers. As she lowered it, she watched his face. There was a moment when he merely looked at her, a smile at the corner of his mouth, and then his eyes widened and his lips parted in surprise.

"Samantha?" He stared at her as though unable to believe what he was seeing, and she struggled to read anything but shock in his expression. Then he caught her up in an embrace.

She hadn't realized how much she had missed him until that moment—how much she had missed that close human connection. In her life, only Charles and her grandfather had ever held her like that—with warmth and affection, with a promise of love and protection. She found herself melting into his embrace, a feeling of relief overwhelming her. She was not alone.

She wasn't aware she had begun to cry until Charles pulled back and looked at her with concern.

"What's wrong?" he asked. "Here, sit down."

He led her to a bench and handed her his handkerchief. She took it and dabbed under her eyes.

"I'm sorry," she said thickly. "I just can't believe it's you."

"Nor I you," he said. "I heard my father had taken you all back to Kent. In fact, I was assured of it. I wouldn't have come if

I thought he'd be here. Where is he?"

He looked around in alarm. Samantha shook her head.

"He's not here. He's…He's dead, Charles."

"Dead?" Charles blinked at her, looking nonplussed. "That's not possible. I'd have heard. Someone would have told me."

Samantha took a shuddering breath. "He was murdered. He and Aunt Victoria. No one told you because no one else knows. You see, he didn't die under his own name. I know it sounds strange and unbelievable, but…the Holborn murders? That was Sir Arthur and Aunt Victoria."

He stared at her. In the dim light of the decorative candelabras placed throughout the garden, it was difficult for her to make out his features, but she could imagine what he was thinking.

"I'm so sorry I didn't contact you immediately, but I…didn't know where you lived." She decided this simple explanation would do for now. There would be time later to explain more fully.

"No, no." His voice was rough and low. He took her hand. "Don't apologize for anything. You're not to blame. What you must have been through…I'm sorry I wasn't there to help." He released her hand, his brow furrowed.

"But what are you doing here? The Holborn murders—they killed a housekeeper, too, didn't they? How did you escape? And what was my father doing living under another name?"

"It's a long story." She sighed and leaned back against the bench. He put an arm around her, and she relaxed into him, relishing the sense of familiarity that came so easily, despite their long time apart. "It started with the blackmail."

"Blackmail? Someone was blackmailing my father?" He laughed darkly. "Well, that was a stupid thing to do. He would never give in."

"He didn't," she agreed. "Some men broke into the house and

tried to abduct me. For ransom, I assume." Charles stiffened. "They didn't succeed, but that was what made Sir Arthur decide to go into hiding. He had an elaborate plan, which he did not share, for tracking down the culprit." She sighed. "Obviously, we were discovered. Aunt Victoria went to reason with them, and I was about to join her when I heard the shots. I was afraid they would come for me next, so I escaped out the window."

"Where did you go?"

"Back to the house, initially."

"Why?" he asked incredulously.

She lifted her shoulders in a tired shrug. "I was fairly certain the men had escaped. One of them went out the back and I presume the other went through the front door. I don't know why I went inside, precisely. I may have been thinking I could help. I don't know that I was thinking much at all. I just…went."

Charles squeezed her shoulder. "I'm sorry you saw what you did. But, does that mean you were the woman mentioned in the newspapers? The one the police spoke with who disappeared?"

She nodded. "I tried to tell them what happened, but they wouldn't listen. They were going to arrest me." She turned to face him, determined to make him understand what she knew must seem insensible. "I had to run, Charles. They thought I did it. I ran and I hid. And I've been hiding ever since."

"Hiding?" Charles repeated. "Hiding where?"

"She's been staying with a friend of mine."

Samantha gasped, and Charles jumped up. From the shadow of a nearby hedge, Mr. Wyatt stepped forward.

She put a hand to her heart, her breathing coming in fast. "Mr. Kennedy!" she said reproachfully.

"My apologies." He gave her a mock bow.

"Were you spying on us?" Charles asked as he helped her to her feet.

"I've been looking for you," Mr. Wyatt said, addressing Samantha and ignoring Charles. "The ball is winding down. There's no one of interest left. I'm ready to take you home."

Charles turned to Samantha. "How do you know this man?"

Her eyes flicked from him to Mr. Wyatt and back. She hadn't intended for them to meet like this, not before she'd had the chance to explain each to the other.

"As he said," she began slowly. "I've been staying with a friend of his since…since the murders. With a chaperone, of course. He's been helping me."

"I can't believe any friend of his is someone you ought to know," Charles said, glaring at Mr. Wyatt. "But now that I'm here, you can stay with me."

He took her hand and seemed ready to drag her with him.

"Don't be ridiculous," Mr. Wyatt snapped. "She's not going with you."

"I beg your pardon," Samantha said haughtily. "*She* can speak for herself, thank you." She turned to Charles. "You know I can't go with you. I can't stay with you unchaperoned. How would that look?"

"Who cares what it looks like?" he said hotly. "It would be better than you staying with some low—"

"He's respectable, Charles, I swear it," Samantha said, pulling her hand from his. "It's only temporary until we sort things out. Come by tomorrow. I'll explain it all then."

She gave him the address and then, ignoring Mr. Wyatt, embraced him one last time.

"Until tomorrow," Charles said. He squeezed her hand, glared at Mr. Wyatt, and departed.

*****

Wyatt escorted Miss Avery, hidden once more behind her

mask, back through the ballroom to the carriage, outwardly charming to everyone they passed, but inwardly seething. He had been watching her all night, keeping track of her partners and ready to step in if needed. He wasn't needed, though. She was as good an actor as he was, it seemed, effortlessly embodying the role they had created for her. It made sense, he supposed, considering that she had been pretending to be someone she was not for several weeks.

Confident that she was enjoying herself, he had stepped out to talk to Bingo, and when he returned, she was nowhere in sight. For an irrational moment, he had feared that she was in danger. Perhaps some drunken lord had forgotten himself enough to presume to accost her, or her past had somehow caught up with her. The likelihood of the second event was scant, however, and he considered that she may have simply stepped into the garden, so he'd gone out to look for her.

At first, he thought he'd stumbled across a pair of lovers, so close were they sitting, and he had begun to back away and search elsewhere when he heard her voice. "It started with the blackmail," she had said.

Apparently, she was an even better actress than he gave her credit for.

Wyatt handed in Miss Avery, or whatever her name really was, and climbed in after her. The anger he felt was reflected in her face as she sat across from him and yanked off her mask, though he couldn't imagine what cause she had to be angry except that he had cut short her secret rendezvous.

"When were you going to tell me?" he snapped.

"Tell you what?"

"Don't play coy with me now. You were willing to spill all your secrets to a stranger a moment ago."

She glared at him. "Charles is not a stranger. He's family."

"Family," Wyatt scoffed. "If he's family, what was he doing while you were on the streets?"

"He didn't know that I was, and I didn't know where he was. We haven't seen each other in years."

"You seemed awfully close for not seeing each other in years."

She rolled her eyes in a most unladylike fashion. "That's because we *were* close. My uncle is the reason we haven't seen each other in all this time."

"Right. Your uncle, who was his father. So, I'm guessing Avery is not your surname?"

She shifted in her seat and looked down. "No, it's not."

"And your uncle?"

"Sir Arthur Prescott. Charles is his son by his first marriage. My aunt was his second wife."

Wyatt nodded, his mouth in a tight line. "And you didn't think that was important for me to know? After I agreed to risk my reputation for you?"

"I didn't ask you to do that!" she burst out. "All I asked was that you give me the money you owed me so I could go back home and sort this out!"

"Because you've done such a good job of that so far."

She looked stung, and he immediately regretted snapping at her. After all, he did think she had done remarkably well, considering her resources.

"Stop the carriage," she said icily.

"Don't be ridiculous. You can't walk home from here."

"I don't intend to walk to your house. I'm going back to find Charles. I ought to have gone with him in the first place." She put a gloved hand on the door handle.

He covered it with his own. "Wait, Miss—er," he said conciliatorily. "I apologize for my harshness just then. It was unwarranted. Please, let us talk about this."

She looked up at him, and he could see a slight softening in her expression. He sat back, and she leaned back in her seat with an impatient huff.

"What do you want to talk about?" she asked, looking out the window rather than at him.

"Why don't we start with your name? Is it Sarah, at least?"

"It's Samantha," she said. "Samantha Kingston."

He extended a hand. "How do you do, Miss Kingston?"

She frowned, but he saw the ghost of a smile as she shook his hand.

"So, Miss Kingston, how did you and your aunt and uncle end up in Holborn?"

"It's a long story."

He nodded in understanding. "Perhaps we should wait until we're a bit more comfortable."

It wasn't long before they were back at Wyatt's house. As he helped Miss Kingston down from the carriage, she avoided eye contact with him. They went inside, and Wyatt asked Mrs. Hexam to brew a strong pot of tea and bring it to his study.

"Do you want to change into something more comfortable?" he asked Miss Kingston.

"I don't have anything more comfortable," she said. "Everything requires these ridiculous crinolines."

"So you think they're ridiculous?" he asked, happy to discuss neutral topics. "I thought all ladies loved fashion."

"I don't know any woman who *loves* walking around in a cage," she said pointedly.

"I will never understand women," he said. "Why be the perpetuators of your own torture?"

"I'm too tired to discuss the nuances of women's fashion with you," she sighed, "and who really drives it, but I must agree with your assessment that you will never understand women, especially when you gather and dismiss the entire sex in one patronizing comment."

He was taken aback by her quick wit, especially considering that she did look very tired. She brushed past him into his study and he followed her in, wanting to be annoyed at how possessively she had taken to his personal space, but not feeling up to the battle.

*****

"Are you going to take those farcical whiskers off?" Samantha asked as they sat in their usual chairs by the fire.

"I can't." He pulled at the end of the mustache to demonstrate. "It's attached quite firmly. I have to rub a special mixture in to peel it off."

She sighed and leaned her head back. She felt more than tired. A weariness had descended upon her. It had all happened so quickly: seeing Charles for the first time in years, discovering that Mr. Wyatt had overheard at least part of what she'd told him, and now having to tell him the whole story much earlier than she had planned.

Looking up, she saw Mr. Wyatt watching her with an unreadable expression, and she realized he must be waiting for her to speak. So, she did. Beginning with the blackmail notes, she told him everything that had happened to her. At some point, Mrs. Hexam arrived with the tea, but Samantha was too absorbed in her story to pay much attention. Mr. Wyatt listened well, his eyes on her the whole time in a manner she found as disconcerting as it was reassuring. She sensed that he was watching her expressions for evidence that she was telling the truth, but she saw no point in hiding anything.

When she finished, he was silent, seeming to consider what to say.

"Miss Kingston—" he began finally, but she interrupted him.

"Samantha."

"I'm sorry?"

"It does seem a bit absurd, don't you think?" she said. "You continuing to address me so formally when we are sitting here in your study late at night discussing murder and scandal? It's hardly conventional."

"True." The corner of his mouth quirked in the hint of a smile. "Is this it, though? The final name I am to call you? After all, first you were Sarah, then Miss Avery, then Miss Kingston. Is Samantha official? You don't have another name I might be asked to use in future?"

"I do have a second name," she said, "but I've never liked it, so, yes, Samantha it is."

"Very well, Samantha. And you may call me Wyatt, if you wish."

"You don't have another name?" she asked, half in jest.

"Not that I care anyone to know, much less use," he said. Then, abruptly changing the subject he added, "I think there is still much we need to discuss, but it doesn't need to happen tonight. We're both tired. Let's leave it for the morning."

They stood and she followed him to the door. He opened it and stepped back to let her precede him.

"Just one thing," he said before she could go. "How did you get the black eye? You never told me."

"It really was nothing important," she said. "Just a boy. A very intoxicated boy. I punched his friend, and he was upset about it."

He let out a surprised laugh.

"You *punched* someone?" he asked incredulously. "*You* punched someone?"

"It wasn't very impressive," she admitted. "He wouldn't have fallen to the ground if he hadn't been so deep in his cups, but I expect it looked serious to his friend."

He continued to stare at her. She gave him a small smile and walked past him. When she reached the hall, she turned back.

"Thank you for the tea."

ELEVEN

The next morning, when Wyatt came down for breakfast, Miss Avery—Samantha, as she now was—was already there, reading the newspaper. It gave him an odd feeling to see her. He was so used to living alone that, to see anyone at his breakfast table, much less a woman, was unusual and yet, he was glad she was there.

"Good morning," he said.

"Good morning."

Her smile was tight, restrained. She was uncomfortable. As was he. There was no established propriety for the circumstances in which they found themselves, and he realized, much as he usually deplored it, how useful propriety could be.

"My cousin should be arriving today," he said, sitting down and reaching for the plate of sausages. "I think you'll like her. She's nothing like me, if it helps."

She took a sip of tea and leaned towards him.

"Do you mind if I speak plainly, Mister....erm...Wyatt?"

"By all means."

"Our situation is unusual, and I think I would feel better if we simply acknowledged it as such. I just spent more than a month on the streets, hiding from the police as a murder suspect and you are now harboring me in your house in a way that has every appearance of scandal. Your cousin, whom I've never met, is coming today to add a veneer of respectability to our situation, and we can only hope she does not arrive at the same time as my friend Charles."

Wyatt smiled at her curt assessment. "Duly acknowledged." He added a generous amount of butter to his toast. "Now, if you don't mind, I would like to return to the subjects we were discussing last night."

"Of course."

"You said that your uncle was being blackmailed, and you think it was the blackmailers who attempted to abduct you?"

"Not precisely," she said. "I think they were sent by the blackmailer. Or, at least, by associates of his. His last note implied that he had unsavory connections, and he said he would regret their involvement as much as we would. I believe abducting me was meant to be a way of carrying out his threat as much as it was of securing the money he wanted."

"But to track you all the way to Holborn?" Wyatt said. "That takes dedication. Quite a lot of effort for an uncertain reward."

"Unless he already knew where we were."

Wyatt looked at her sharply. "What do you mean?"

"My uncle told us he had a plan," Samantha explained. "Well, what he actually said was 'we' had a plan. He wouldn't say who the 'we' was, but he did say they had decided to lay a trap for the blackmailer by making it seem as though he and my aunt and I had returned to Kent. Clearly, the trap failed, and it makes me wonder if he put his trust in the wrong person."

"You think he accidently confided in the blackmailer?"

She nodded.

"If that were so," Wyatt said slowly, thinking it through, "why wait so long to act? He could have sent his enforcers right away, as soon as you were all settled in that house. As you came to learn, relative anonymity is as dangerous as it is protective. If he was desperate for money, as his actions imply, why wait nearly a fortnight for his reward?"

She frowned and scooped up a forkful of eggs, looking thoughtful as she chewed.

"Something else to consider," Wyatt added. "If the men who killed your aunt and uncle—those men who are now robbing houses all over town—were there at the behest of the blackmailer, why would they kill? Dead men cannot pay their blackmailers."

"It may have been an accident," Samantha suggested.

Wyatt made a disbelieving grimace.

"I think it's worth considering," she said, frowning at him. "If they came for the sole purpose of murder, they would have shot him the minute they entered the house, but they didn't. They spoke to him long enough for my aunt to come to me and then to join them."

It was, after all, a valid point, but Wyatt was saved from replying by a knock at the door. They looked at each other in surprise. It was far too early for any social calls.

"Your cousin?" Samantha asked him.

"Or yours?" he replied, arching an eyebrow.

They heard Mrs. Hexam open the door and the muted tones of the visitor drifted down the hall. Mrs. Hexam entered the room moments later with a card. Wyatt took it, glanced down and handed it back, nodding.

"Yours, it seems," he said to Samantha. Then, "Show him into the parlor, Mrs. Hexam, and get the tea ready."

"I don't consider him my cousin, you know," Samantha said, standing and pushing her chair back. "He's more of a friend."

"Let's go see your friend, then." Wyatt stood and held out an arm to escort her to the parlor. She started to take it, then paused.

"Wait," she said, her eyes wide. "How do you know Mr. Kennedy?"

"What?"

"I mean," she said, "that I forgot to ask how Mr. Wyatt and Mr. Kennedy know each other. How do I explain how I came to be here?"

"Oh, yes, of course." He glanced at the door and lowered his voice. "Archie and I know each other from Cambridge. You met him at that party at Lord Etwall's, just as you really did. He will have told you about how I—Wyatt, that is—helped him assist a friend of his to regain some incriminating correspondence from a lady's house."

"Did you really?"

She looked surprised and, he thought, disappointed, when he nodded.

"But how did I know how to find you when I needed you?" she asked sensibly.

"Archie will have told you about how much time I spend at the United University Club, and you will have waited outside 'til you saw me, I think."

She bit her lip and nodded. Then she took his arm and they proceeded to the parlor.

Mr. Prescott was standing at the fireplace when they entered, examining a small Chinese vase on the mantle. When he saw Samantha, he smiled. She detached herself from Wyatt and hurried over to greet him.

In the light of day, Mr. Prescott seemed less the sinister villain he had the night before. He was fair, with light blond hair that swept away from a face which, free of whiskers or moustaches, retained a sort of boyish charm. His thin frame contributed to that image of boyish good looks. Wyatt's own face was not, perhaps, so effortlessly handsome, but he was broader and taller than his guest, and he found himself thinking that, in a boxing match, he would come out the winner.

Immediately after the thought crossed his mind, he wondered at the childishness of it. What had possessed him to imagine something so petty about a perfect stranger?

"It's so good to see you again," Prescott said to Samantha. "You can't imagine how much I've missed you."

"And I you," she replied.

She smiled with such undiluted joy as she said it that Wyatt had to mentally shake himself to avert the jealousy he felt. What had he to be jealous of? Yes, she was pretty, and perhaps the most interesting woman he had met, but what of it? He hardly knew her. Even if he were to consider shackling himself to a wife, his family would be up in arms at his tying them permanently to such scandal as would soon surround Samantha. And there would be quite a scandal, as much as he would try to help her mitigate it.

Samantha turned to Wyatt, and he stepped forward.

"Mr. Prescott, I presume," he said. "I'm V.T. Wyatt. I welcome you to my home."

Prescott bowed. "Your servant, sir."

Wyatt acknowledged the bow with a nod and gestured for them all to sit.

"I'm glad you came," Samantha said as soon as she was seated. "We have a lot to talk about."

"Indeed, we do," Prescott agreed. "I still can't believe he's dead."

"It must be quite upsetting for you," Wyatt said.

Prescott eyed him shrewdly. "You may have heard that we didn't get along. That, in fact, I hated my father. It's no secret. He was an angry, tightfisted old man who thought he deserved the world. Just ask Samantha—Miss Kingston. News of his death is, nonetheless, upsetting to me, if only because I know the trouble it has caused her."

Prescott leaned forward and took Samantha's hand in his.

"I am sorry about your aunt," he said earnestly. "I know she wasn't the warmest, but she was your family, and it's never pleasant to lose family."

"Thank you, Charles," she said, bestowing on him a sad smile that somehow made her look even more beautiful. Wyatt looked away.

"Will you tell me now what happened?" Prescott asked. "How did you come to be here of all places?"

Samantha glanced at Wyatt, coughed, and began to explain. Wyatt watched her as she spoke, but Prescott was still holding her hand, and she kept her gaze on him.

"I came to a church," she said as she neared the end. "It was locked, and I was so tired that I fell asleep on the steps. The next morning, news of their deaths was all over the papers and I was described as wanted for questioning in their murders. I went to Cyril—you remember my cousin, Cyril—first, but he had left that morning for the seaside. Then I...remembered Mr. Kennedy telling me about his friend Mr. Wyatt, who had helped another friend with some delicate problems, so I waited outside his club until I saw him. When I had explained my situation, he brought me here for my safety with his cousin as my companion and chaperone. She's out at the moment, but we expect her back soon."

"I wish you could have come to me," Prescott said. He held up a hand to curb her protests. "I know why you could not. I only wish the circumstances had been different."

"As do I," she said. Her eyes widened and she turned to Wyatt. "Not that I don't appreciate your help," she added hastily. "It's just —"

"I understand," he said, and smiled to show he meant it,

though he was beginning to feel irritated with his role as third wheel in his own parlor. Seeking a change of subject, he directed a question to Prescott. "Do you know who may have wished to blackmail your father?"

Prescott shrugged. "It could have been anyone. I told you that he was a terrible father and guardian. He was also a scheming louse determined to forward his own ambitions in any way possible. I'm sure he had enemies, but I am equally certain he had lots of powerful friends. Any action taken against him would have to be subtle."

"Do you know what the blackmail might have been about?"

Prescott smiled wryly and shook his head. "A dalliance? A business dealing? Take your pick."

Wyatt sighed. "Can you think of anything that would be useful?"

"I'll let you know if I do."

At that moment, Mrs. Hexam entered with a tea tray. They took their tea in silence. When she had left the room, Prescott spoke.

"So, do we go to the police today or would tomorrow be better?"

Samantha choked. Wyatt's reaction was equally strong, but fortunately, he had already set down his cup.

"What do you mean?" he asked.

"We need to report my father dead," Prescott said, sitting back in his seat as Samantha regained her composure. "I understand why you didn't want to go forward before. Miss Kingston was afraid she could not prove either her identity or her innocence, and Mr. Wyatt was doing as she instructed, but now I'm here, we can clear everything up."

"But I'm still a suspect," Samantha said.

"Only because the police did not know who you were,"

Prescott said airily. "You were dressed as a maid. They won't impugn a lady."

"What about Miss Kent last year?" Samantha asked. "They arrested her. She went to jail and stood trial."

"She was hardly a lady," Prescott said. "Upper middle class. And it wasn't London."

"It was a London detective."

"And he is now in disgrace for how he handled the whole affair. They won't be likely to make such a mistake again, especially not so soon."

Samantha twisted her hands in her lap. "You weren't there, Charles. You didn't see their faces. I can understand why they were suspicious, when I look back on it. For some time, I've thought as you do—that it was simply a matter of clearing a misunderstanding—but I am less sure now. Supposing it goes to trial? Even if I am cleared of the murder charges, there are certain things…"

She trailed off, looking up at Wyatt, and he knew she was worried about the truth of her time on the streets being revealed.

"What, then?" Charles asked. "Are you going to wait forever, hiding in a stranger's house?"

"No," she said, a hint of irritation in her tone. "We are going to find out what happened, clear my name, and then I'll reappear."

"And if you don't find out what happened?"

She looked stricken, but Wyatt was certain she must have considered the possibility. They had never voiced it aloud, though. Perhaps it was hearing it said so boldly that upset her. Wyatt threw Prescott an annoyed look but Prescott, speaking to Samantha but looking at Wyatt, said, "I'm only being practical. You should have a plan in case of such an eventuality."

Samantha nodded. "No, you're right. I just keep hoping there is a way I come out of this situation without becoming the center of some hideous speculation."

"I think it's too late for that," Wyatt said. Compassionately, he hoped. "But we can try to minimize the damage. Would you consider imposing a time limit? Give me a week to see what I can do, and then we can evaluate."

Prescott looked doubtful, but Wyatt ignored him and, fortunately, so did Samantha. She nodded.

"In the meantime," Prescott said, "you look as though you could benefit from a diversion. Allow me to go see about a carriage and I will come take you for a ride. Say, in an hour?"

"That would be lovely," she said.

They all stood and Prescott, after kissing Samantha's hand and nodding to Wyatt, took his leave.

*****

Charles' visit left Samantha feeling almost cheerful. A ride would be wonderful. She would need a large bonnet to hide her face. She hoped Wyatt had one in his sister's collection of clothing. It really was inconvenient to keep borrowing clothes. She would need to be fitted for some of her own soon. Perhaps when Wyatt's cousin came, she might ask for her help.

Turning to Wyatt to ask him about the bonnet, she noticed he was looking at her, his brow furrowed.

"What is it?" she asked.

"I'm considering a possibility," he said. "What if your uncle wasn't the target?"

"I beg your pardon?"

"You said that the men who came to abduct you spoke of being sent to get you. They never mentioned Sir Arthur. We have been assuming they were taking you for ransom because of the blackmail letters. What if they came for you?"

Samantha was confused. "What possible reason could they

have to take me other than as ransom?"

"They may have intended to get money from you."

"It would have been a waste of their time if they did," she said with a dark laugh. "I haven't any."

He raised an eyebrow.

"Well, not none, of course," she amended, "but not much."

"I just thought with all the revisions you've made to your story, it was possible you forgot to tell me you had a fortune."

She rolled her eyes. He was deliberately provoking her. "I thought we had moved past this already. I didn't tell you the whole story at first, true, but I hardly know you, so I don't think you can judge me so harshly. And now that we are all working together, I would hardly keep such a secret. Of course, if I had a fortune, I would have recognized that as a possible motive. I do not, however. My grandfather—the Earl of Etwall, if you must know so that you cannot charge me with concealing details—settled a modest dowry on me, and my father left me a similarly modest sum that I will inherit when I reach my majority or marry, whichever comes first. But even if that amount were enough to tempt so bold an action as abduction, I have no access to any of the money until next month."

"Your grandfather was the Earl of Etwall?" Wyatt asked, focusing on the least important detail.

"As I said. Is that so very surprising?"

"Only in that it means the current Lord Etwall is related to you. I didn't realize that when we met at his party."

"My cousin and I have never been close. Our grandfather's death only drove us further apart."

"I'm sorry," Wyatt said sympathetically. "I don't know your cousin, but my father knew your grandfather. He always spoke highly of him. He was a good man."

She pursed her lips and made a noncommittal noise. She had

thought so, too, before he abandoned her. Now, she did not know what to think.

"I'm sorry to have resurrected painful memories," Wyatt said. "It does seem unlikely that you were the target, as you say. I just wanted to be certain to explore all possibilities."

"I understand," she said, masking her feelings with a smile. "If you'll excuse me, I need to get ready."

An hour later, Samantha sat atop a hired gig with Charles as they traveled slowly down a green path in Hyde Park. The sun was out, but the cool of morning still lingered.

"Is that really necessary?"

Samantha had to turn her head completely to see Charles because her deep slat bonnet acted like the blinders on a horse. She saw him looking askance at the top of her head and realized it was the bonnet he was referring to.

"I can't see you," he complained.

"Precisely," she said with a smile. "Supposing we were to come across someone I know?"

He gestured expressively to the almost empty path around them. Samantha sighed. Perhaps she was being overly cautious. It would be nice to feel the fresh air on her face. However, as she started to lower the bonnet, a couple came walking around the bend. She recognized them as Lord and Lady Lynstock. Hastily, she shoved the bonnet back on and tied the ribbons, keeping her face turned away. Charles tipped his hat to the couple as they passed.

When they were out of hearing distance, Samantha said, "Now you see I was right."

"Did you know them?" he asked.

"They were friends of my parents," she explained. "Funnily enough, the last time I saw them was the day I met Mr. Kennedy."

He did not respond, and she was forced to turn her head to look at him. She was surprised to see him frowning. He flicked the reins and glanced over at her. Catching her eye, he looked away again.

"I still don't see why you went to the masque with him," he said. "I understand coming to Mr. Wyatt for help, but why go to a ball with his profligate friend when you are supposed to be staying hidden?"

"It was a masque," she said. "I *was* hidden. No one recognized me. And I went hoping I might find you."

He was silent again, his frown deepening.

"What's wrong?" she asked.

"You shouldn't have had to find me," he said. "I should have been there for you."

She started to respond, but he cut her off, reining in the horse and turning to face her.

"Samantha, I am truly sorry for abandoning you to my father. I know I promised you—"

"Don't concern yourself with it," she cut in. As long as she had wanted an apology or explanation from him for his abrupt and complete departure, she suddenly found it unnecessary. After all, so much of the blame lay with Sir Arthur. "You did what you had to do."

"But I promised—"

"You told a young girl what she wanted to hear," she said with a sad smile. "You gave me hope to hold onto when times were bleak. I don't hold that promise against you any more than I hold your departure against you."

"Your kindness is making me feel worse," he said with a groan.

She laughed. "Shall I be cruel then? Will that help?"

"I doubt you could be if you tried."

"It's in the past, Charles. I survived. You survived. Now we can both move forward."

*****

Wyatt returned from sending a telegram in time to see a barouche pulling up in front of his house. A footman jumped down, and Mrs. Hexam came out to greet the visitor. His cousin Madge alighted and, on seeing him walk up, smiled. She was almost his height, with strong features, an athletic build, and unfashionably sun-bronzed skin. Her traveling dress was plain and practical, and her hair was tugging loose from its low bun.

"I'm glad to see you weren't waiting up," she said pointedly. He started to apologize, but she cut him off. "No need. I'm early. The journey wasn't nearly as bad as expected. I could use a cup of tea, though."

"Of course," Wyatt said. "Mrs. Hexam?"

The housekeeper had been directing the footman and Madge's maid, Higgins. She nodded and followed them inside. Wyatt started to lead his cousin to the parlor, but she stuck her head through his study door and entered.

"I like what you've done with the place," she said, her eyes sweeping the room.

"Well, I—" He began to defend himself, but she cut him off again.

"I like a cluttered study," she said with a satisfied nod. "It shows you've got something going on up there." She jabbed a finger in the direction of his head. "I always think a study reflects the mind, don't you?"

"So, my mind is hopelessly disorganized?" he asked ruefully.

"No, I'm sure you know where everything is."

"I thought we would…" he said helplessly, gesturing to the parlor, but she shook her head.

"I'm fine right here," she said. "We have a lot to talk about and I'm guessing this is the room where you do your best thinking."

Shrugging, he joined her.

Madge was his father's cousin. She and his mother had never gotten along, so, after the death of his father, Madge had not set foot in the Wyatt family home. He had been to stay with her a few times on holiday from school. She was an avid sportswoman with a passion for hunting that was matched only by her strong dislike of the city. Her separation from London society combined with her unconventional manners made him think she would be perfect for the proposition he had to make her. However, now that it had come to it, he felt awkward explaining everything.

"You weren't very forthcoming in your letter," Madge said, taking the lead. "Afraid someone else might read it, I suppose?"

"Just being careful," he said. "There's a lot at stake. I need your help protecting a young lady's reputation."

He explained how he had met Samantha and what had happened to her family, omitting the part where he spent most of their short acquaintance in the dark and making it seem as if he had known her full story from the moment she moved into his house. He also glossed over her time on the street, completely avoiding mention of any illegal activities or Skinny Jim. By the end, Madge was on the edge of her seat, watching him wide-eyed, the cup Mrs. Hexam had brought suspended between the saucer and her lips.

Wyatt finished by explaining the plan to see what progress he was able to make in a week and decide the way forward from there. He was interrupted by a knock at the front door.

"That must be her," Wyatt said, getting to his feet.

"Where has she been?" his cousin asked.

"Out with Mr. Prescott, her uncle's son."

"The one she discovered at the masquerade?"

"Yes."

"I should like to meet him."

She rose and, before he could stop her, had made her way out the door into the hall. Wyatt followed, arriving as Samantha and Prescott entered. Samantha looked happy. There was a color in her cheeks as she removed her hideous bonnet. Her eyes widened when she saw Madge, but she schooled her features.

"Did you enjoy your ride?" Wyatt asked.

"Very much," Samantha answered, as Prescott said, "Yes, we did."

They laughed, and Wyatt caught Prescott watching Samantha with an expression that demonstrated more than cousinly affection.

"This is Mr. Prescott, Madge," Wyatt said, laying a hand on his cousin's arm and holding the other out to indicate Prescott. He paused as realized his error. Sir Arthur had been a baronet, which meant his son would have inherited the title. "Or, rather," he resumed, with an apologetic glance at Prescott. "This is Sir Charles. Sir Charles, this is my cousin, Lady Bradwell."

"Mr. Prescott will suffice for now," Prescott said, bowing. "I'm not sure how I feel about using the title just yet. It is a pleasure to make your acquaintance, my lady."

"Likewise, I'm sure," Madge said. "I'm sorry I could not meet you earlier. Always been an early riser, me. I was out this morning."

"I understand," he said, flashing her a charming smile before taking his leave of them all.

When the door closed behind him, Wyatt turned to Samantha and officially introduced her to his cousin.

"Call me Madge," she said when Samantha addressed her as Lady Bradwell. "All my friends do, and I am sure we will become fast friends. Wyatt was telling me about your plight, and I can tell that you are just the sort of plucky girl I like."

Samantha looked taken aback, but then she smiled, and Wyatt was sure he had made the right choice in calling on his cousin.

"Now," Madge said, taking Samantha's arm in hers. "You can help me and Higgins unpack while we talk. After all, if we are to maintain this ruse that I have been here for some time already, we will need to know quite a lot about each other."

She led Samantha up the stairs, stopping only long enough to tell Wyatt he might as well disappear to his club as they wouldn't be needing him until dinner. Samantha caught his eye over her shoulder and raised an eyebrow. He smiled and shrugged.

*****

Over the next two days, Samantha found herself in two minds. She enjoyed her time with Wyatt's cousin. Madge was good company. She spoke candidly and often. Her favorite subjects were her dogs and shooting, and, while Samantha would have been happy not knowing the details of Caesar's gastrointestinal distress, she found it easy to converse on both subjects. Having Madge around put Wyatt in a better mood, too. No doubt he felt relieved to have one part of the problem solved, and it helped that Madge teased him almost constantly.

Yet, despite this domestic tranquility, Samantha was increasingly dissatisfied. Wyatt had taken full charge of investigating her aunt's and uncle's murders. He posted several letters but refused to tell her what they contained. He visited Sir Arthur's club, Boodle's, of which he was also a member, to speak with some of her uncle's friends, but did not relay what he learned. He had become very high-handed in his dealings with her, and she was tired of being ignored.

On the third morning after Madge's arrival, while Wyatt and Samantha were breakfasting and Madge was out riding in the park, Mrs. Hexam came to tell Wyatt that a boy was at the kitchen door asking to see him. Swallowing the last of his orange juice, Wyatt set down his glass and stood up.

"If you'll excuse me," he said to Samantha. "I'll just be a minute."

Samantha waited until she heard his footsteps heading down the back stairs before jumping up and hurrying after him. He had left the door open, so she stood at the top of the steps, out of sight, and listened. It sounded as though the boy was describing a robbery in another part of the city. Samantha heard the clink of coins and then Wyatt telling Mrs. Hexam that he would be going out. Samantha ran to the hat tree and grabbed her parasol, turning to face him as he came up the stairs.

"Where are you going?" he asked with a frown.

"With you," she said, flashing him a bright smile.

"No, you most certainly are not." He brushed past her and lifted his hat off the tree.

"This is about Slater and Palmer," she said.

"Possibly." He shrugged into his coat and picked up his cane. "But I don't know that for certain."

"More than possibly," Samantha insisted. "Probably. And I intend to be part of it."

"No."

She bit back an angry retort. He would only say she was being emotional and use it as an excuse to leave her behind. She switched tactics. "I'll follow you."

"On foot?" He raised a supercilious eyebrow. "Running after my carriage?"

"You really are an incredibly irritating man," she said. "Don't be ridiculous. I heard the address. I will simply make my own way there."

"And how would you pay for the carriage?"

"With this." She held up his pocketbook.

He stared at it, then patted his pocket reflexively. Finally, he gave her a grudging smile. "When did you take it?"

"You left it in your coat," she said. "I saw it when I grabbed my parasol."

"What is the world coming to when a man's money isn't safe in his own home?" He sighed. "Fine. You can come. But don't say anything. If anyone asks, you're my sister."

"I thought I wasn't to say anything," she said innocently.

He ignored her and reached for his wallet.

"Perhaps I ought to hold onto it," she said, dancing out of his reach. "You do seem to have trouble keeping it safe."

"Don't try my patience, Samantha."

She handed it over but couldn't resist one more barb as she walked past him to the door.

"Frowning is not a good look for you," she said. "Those little lines are aging you prematurely."

*****

Once they were outside, Wyatt took off down the street at a brisk pace. Behind him, he heard Samantha hurrying to catch up.

"Aren't we going to hire a carriage?" she asked, a little breathlessly.

"I thought we'd walk," he said.

"The whole way?"

"It will be invigorating, don't you think?"

He hadn't planned to walk until she'd made that jibe about his frown lines, but it seemed like a good revenge. If she wanted to tag along with him, she had to be prepared to keep up. They went for several blocks without speaking. He kept expecting to see her flag or hear her beg him to slow down, but she didn't, and eventually even he grew weary of the pace.

"Tired already?" she asked as he slowed to a stroll.

"Of course not," he said. "I thought you might be. I didn't like to be ungentlemanly."

"Didn't you?"

She was smiling at him as though she knew exactly what he had been up to. It irritated him to be so transparent, so he ignored her, certain that any response he made could only be rude.

"Who was that boy?" she asked, stepping deftly around a pile of fresh horse manure.

"Jamie."

"Is he another of your informants?"

"Yes."

"Wyatt."

Her use of his name made him pause, and he turned to look at her.

"I know you are used to working alone," she said. "But you can't keep ignoring me."

"I'm not ignoring you," he said automatically.

"Yes, you are. You won't tell me anything you've learned. When I ask questions, you refuse to give me proper answers. You seem to expect me to follow you blindly."

Wyatt raised an eyebrow. "Hello, Pot," he said, reaching over to grasp her hand and shake it. "I'm Kettle. I don't believe we've met."

"I had good reasons for not sharing what I knew," she said, batting his hand away. "I didn't know if I could trust you yet. I would like to know what reasons you have for concealing information from me that must be much more relevant to me than it is to you."

"I wasn't doing it from any malicious intent," Wyatt said.

"I never thought you were. No doubt you meant to spare me the sordid details and solve all of my problems for me."

"Would it be so terrible if I did?"

She looked up at him shrewdly. "Would you like someone to do as much to you? To handle all of your affairs while you wait at home?"

"No. But then, I am—"

"If you are going to tell me that you are a man, you may save your breath," she said.

"I would never dream of using such an argument with you," he said, the corner of his lips twitching. "I was, in point of fact, going to say that I am doubtful I know anyone who would like me well enough to take on such a task in the first place."

She grinned reluctantly. "You can see what I mean, though," she pressed. "I am sure there are people who are happy to hand over their affairs to someone else and to while away their days on amusements, but I know you are not one of them and I need you to understand I am not, either."

He looked down at her earnest face and thought how strange it was to speak so openly and plainly with another person. Most people he knew hid their intentions in a bouquet of trite compliments and false modesty. Samantha, when she was not concealing facts about herself for what he had to admit were understandable reasons, was always direct. Moreover, he could not fault her logic.

"I told Jamie to let me know if he heard about any more robberies similar to the others," he said after a moment. "It was he who told me about the one you were involved in."

She glanced up at him in surprise and smiled. "He sounds like a much more useful informant than I was," she said with a laugh.

"Well, he does have the advantage of you in almost every way when it comes to knowledge of the London underworld," Wyatt said. "But only you could have made the connection between the housemen and your aunt's and uncle's killer."

"Yes," she said, frowning. "For however much good it's

done."

"It's helped a great deal," Wyatt said, tossing a coin to a crossing sweeper as they traversed a busy street. "I've wondered how the robbers knew when the homeowners would be away. The odds of them finding loose-lipped servants willing to divulge their masters' schedules at so many houses seem slim. It would also be risky to use servants, because there's always the chance one of them might be persuaded to tell what they know and identify the robbers."

She nodded. "That makes sense."

"But knowing the robberies are connected to the killings opens up another possibility. If the housemen are involved in both, why not the gentleman?"

"Do you mean the blackmailer?" she asked doubtfully. "How?"

"A gentleman of a certain stature might reasonably have acquaintances in both the upper and middle classes. He could be giving the robbers information on people he knows."

"But why would he do that?"

"If he was blackmailing your uncle, he needed money. Perhaps, when that failed, he decided to rob people instead."

She looked thoughtful. "Why would the robbers give him anything they stole, though? Why wouldn't they just keep it for themselves?"

"They'd need him to continue supplying them with information," he said. "So, they'd give him a portion of their loot. A simple business arrangement."

"That still doesn't explain why they killed my aunt and uncle. What was the benefit there?"

He sighed. "I don't know. And now that I say it out loud, I'm not sure how much sense my business-arrangement theory makes, either."

He reached up to run his fingers through his hair but remembered his hat in time and ended up swinging his arm awkwardly. He thought he saw her smile, but when he turned to look, she was thoughtful again.

"What are you hoping to learn from this latest robbery?" she asked. "You already know who committed it."

"Anything that might help establish a pattern," he said. "Details about their home or possessions that would link them to the other robberies. If I could find support for my theory that they share a mutual acquaintance, that would be ideal, but I'm at a loss to know how to go about it. I can't exactly ask them to list every friend they have."

"No," she chuckled. "Though it would be entertaining to watch you attempt it."

*****

However, there was no opportunity for Wyatt to do so. When they arrived at the address Jamie had given, they found the family away from home and the servants unwilling to speak with strangers, no matter how polite or genteel. With understandable frustration, Wyatt and Samantha began the long walk back to Knightsbridge.

Without the distraction of conversation, Samantha paid more attention to her surroundings on the walk back. To her chagrin, she realized that, in her haste to accompany Wyatt, she had not remembered to bring the wide-brimmed bonnet she wore on her excursions with Charles, leaving her face exposed. She shifted her parasol to block as much of the street as she could and looked around her, her gaze bouncing from one well-dressed passerby to another, afraid both to recognize and to be recognized herself. A nervous energy bubbled up from within her, and it took considerable strength of will to prevent her from walking faster and drawing unwanted attention to herself.

As though he sensed her unease, Wyatt laid a hand over hers where it rested on his arm in a calming, somewhat restraining manner and leaned towards her.

"If you go on like this, you will alert our pursuer, and he'll get away before I've had the chance to question him."

She looked up at him in alarm. "Pursuer?" She would have turned to look behind them if he hadn't pulled her tighter to his side.

"Don't," he said.

"I won't look," she said, and he eased his grip. "But what pursuer?"

"I thought you had seen him too. He's been following us for the last several blocks at least."

"I didn't notice him," she was forced to admit. "If I was acting strangely, it was from fear of being recognized. Who is he?"

"I don't know. I've never seen him before, but there's no doubt it's us he's after. Every time I've stopped and pretended to look into a shop, he's stopped somewhere farther back and waited."

"What do we do?" Samantha asked.

"I have a plan," Wyatt said. "But we'll have to act quickly."

He explained his idea and, at the next intersection, they turned down a side street. Wyatt released Samantha's arm, and she picked up her skirts and half-ran to a bookseller's stand midway down the street. She glanced behind her and saw Wyatt step into the shadow of a pillar. Her hands shaking with excited energy, she dropped her skirts and smoothed them, then pretended to scan the spines on the shelf before her, ignoring the bewildered, wary stare of the bookseller.

It took all she had not to turn around to see if she had been followed. She did not want to alert their mysterious pursuer before Wyatt had the chance to set upon him. Only when she heard a shout did she allow herself to turn, along with the rest of the patrons of the bookseller, to see Wyatt running back out to Oxford Street after a man in a dark coat.

Echoing with a barely repressed smile the words of surprise and confusion around her, Samantha turned back to the bookstand and began to search in earnest for something she might like, not knowing how long it would be before Wyatt returned to fetch her.

She had just found a well-worn copy of *Oliver Twist* and was checking to see that all the pages were within when Wyatt returned, the look of vexation on his face enough to preclude any inquiries into his success.

"Let's go," he said, reaching out to take her arm.

"In a moment." She held up the book for him to see.

Wyatt pulled out his pocketbook. "How much?" he asked the bookseller.

Sizing Wyatt up in one calculating look, the bookseller named an absurd price.

"Here." Wyatt handed him the coin, took Samantha by the elbow, and steered her away.

"You know this isn't worth half that amount," Samantha said in surprise as they rejoined the traffic of Oxford Street.

"I know," he said. "I wasn't in the mood to argue."

"I find that surprising," she said.

He looked at her sharply but, seeing her determinedly mild expression, grinned.

"Touché, Miss Kingston. But I think you will find that, in general, I am a hopeless haggler. I inevitably pay more than I mean to when I buy from street vendors."

Mrs. Hexam let them in, informing Wyatt that the post had been delivered and was on his desk. He disappeared into his study, and Samantha set her new book on the hall table and went to the parlor to find Madge sitting on a sofa by the window, reading a magazine.

"*Great Expectations*," she said, holding it up for Samantha to see. "Mr. Dickens' latest. Can't say I like it as much as the last one. Quite a lot of unpleasant characters."

"I believe I've missed too many issues to catch up now," Samantha said, sitting on the other end of the sofa and propping her sore feet up on a footstool. "I'll have to wait for the book."

"Don't bother," Madge said, shaking her head. "It won't be worth it, I assure you. I'm only reading it now because my neighbor, Lady Anstruther, will want to discuss it when I return, and I need to be prepared to disagree with all of her opinions."

Samantha laughed. Then Wyatt entered, looking grave, and the smile slid from her face.

"What is it?" she asked.

"I received a reply to one of my inquiries," he said, holding up a letter.

"Oh?"

He walked over and sat opposite her, leaning forward on his elbows and watching her with a serious expression. "This letter is from your grandfather's solicitor. It seems that he left you some money in his Will."

"But he didn't," Samantha said, shaking her head. "My cousin, Lord Etwall, was his heir."

"He was," Wyatt agreed. "But he wasn't the only one. It seems your uncle attended the will reading on your behalf, as he was your legal guardian. He assured the solicitors that he would convey the information to you."

"He never said anything. But it can't have been very much money. He always complained what a drain I was on his finances and how difficult it would be to get me married well."

"I'm not sure why he told you that. It is a sizeable sum."

Samantha stilled. “Sizeable?”

He nodded, and a smile spread across his face. “If you consider one hundred thousand pounds sizeable, that is.”

TWELVE

Samantha gasped. She couldn't help it. Beside her, Madge choked and began coughing.

"One hundred thousand pounds?" Samantha asked breathlessly.

"Yes," he said, smiling at her and Madge's reactions. "The lawyers will no doubt contact you with the details, but you come into it on your twenty-first birthday or your marriage, whichever comes first."

"I turn twenty-one next month," she said, her eyes wide. "I had no idea that Grandfather…That he…"

She couldn't finish the sentence. She had spent years being angry with her grandfather for abandoning her. Had he really left her such a fortune? Why? And why could he not have talked to her about it?

"There's another letter," Wyatt said. From within the first letter, he slid out a second folded paper. "The solicitors sent it along with their response to me. It's from your grandfather."

He held it out to her. She stared at it. She could see her name on the outside, written in her grandfather's wide, even hand, but she did not reach for it. She felt an unreasonable fear of what it might contain.

"Here, dear," Madge said, taking it from Wyatt and forcing it into her hand. "Why don't you take it upstairs to read?"

"Yes, thank you," Samantha said in a hollow voice. She held the letter delicately, as though it might disintegrate in her hand, and stood. "I'll return shortly."

In her room, she sat for several minutes on the bed with the letter laid out before her, just staring at the handwriting, but not reading the words. She couldn't help thinking of the last time she had seen his writing, on the letter of condolence after the deaths of her parents. It had been a disappointing letter because it contained no plan to remove her from her uncle's house and return her to his. She had meant to speak with him about it at the funeral, but they had not had an opportunity to talk in private. That was the last time she saw him. She remembered driving away from the funeral, watching him wave to her from the front steps of the house. In her memory, at that moment, it was raining, and he stood with rain dripping down his face until she was out of sight.

With a deep, shuddering breath, Samantha steadied herself and began to read her grandfather's last words to her.

My dearest Samantha,

I have often, in these past years, had occasion to regret my accession to your parents' wishes in sending you away. I thought at the time that I was doing what was best for you. I was, after all, ill-equipped to prepare you for the life that lay before you, and your mother feared I might have already damaged your prospects by giving you as much freedom as I did. I cannot, however, regret the hours, months, and years we spent together in such harmony of mind and thought. I am an old man and I have made many mistakes, but taking you in was never one of them. Perhaps if I had been as attentive to my own children, they would not have repeated my mistakes as their own.

I understand why you have severed communication with me. I hurt you deeply. I want you to know that was never my intention, and I hope someday you may forgive me, if not for my sake, then for yours. Anger can turn so easily to bitterness, and that bitterness eats away at the soul.

I cannot turn back time, however much I may wish it, but I can try my utmost to create the best possible future for you. The estate must go to your cousin Cyril. He inherits the title and it is only fitting that he have the property to support it. There is a good deal of money not tied up in the estate, however, and that I leave to you in the hopes that you may make better use of it than he would. Think of this gift, not in financial terms, but as I truly intend it—the gift of freedom. I free you to marry whomever you choose, without that desperation that comes from a need for security. I free you to remain unmarried, if that is your preference, because I cannot imagine a man I would consider worthy of you, my dearest.

It is not far from my mind as I write this, that if you are reading it, it means not only that I am dead, but that I went to that death without ever seeing you again. A heaviness settles upon my heart at the possibility, but I cannot banish the hope that it will not come to pass and that I will have the opportunity of conveying my wishes to you in person. To see your beautiful face again and to hear that laugh that fills my dreams is the dearest wish of my heart.

My doctors tell me I am not long for this world. Every day brings more relatives, eager to reassure me of the devotion they have thus far demonstrated by their absence. I do not blame them. If they see me now as nothing more than a source of material gain, it is because I led them to that conclusion. My harshness and greed in my younger years bred the same in those I influenced. I thank God every day that, in your case, the influence ran the other way. Your light and joy filled a void in my heart. I loved you selfishly, but you made me a better man. The irony that your influence led me to the very act that tore us apart is not lost on me, but perhaps it was for the best. I took you for granted when you were with me. I hope your aunt and uncle cherish you.

How to end such a letter as this? It is, unless a miracle occurs, my final goodbye to the joy of my existence. There are no words I could pen that would convey how I feel in this moment, so I will not make the attempt. Instead, I will write these simple, inadequate words and hope that you will understand.

I love you.

Samantha could barely make out the final paragraph. Every time she wiped away the tears, her eyes filled again until she gave up and let them run down her face. A lone tear dripped onto the last page and she snatched the paper up, dabbing it dry with her pillow.

Her heart ached for her grandfather, for the sadness that filled every word and the loneliness he felt in his final days. How could he think she had not wanted to be near him? She hadn't severed communication with him; he'd done that to her. Unless… If her grandfather thought she had not wished to write to him, he couldn't have received her letters. Who else could have stopped her letters but her uncle?

Hatred roiled up in her, rapidly replacing the sadness. She pounded the mattress with her fists and screamed into her pillow. What monster would do that? He had cut her off from one of the only people who cared about her, and for what? His own sick pleasure at seeing her broken and beaten down? The surge of power he felt from completely controlling her life? For the first time, she imagined confronting the man she had seen coming out of the house, not to demand justice or for him to prove her innocence, but so that she could shake his hand.

The anger died within her, snuffed out like a candle. What was she thinking? That man had killed three people in cold blood. Her aunt, who had never harmed anyone, was dead. As was the housekeeper who had done nothing but her duty. And what was the satisfaction in knowing that Sir Arthur was dead, too? She would rather he were alive so she could confront him with what he had done, to ask him why. And then perhaps, for her own satisfaction, to punch him as she had done the mattress. But not to kill him. He had always thought too much of his own image. He should have lived to see it shattered.

Samantha drew a shaky breath and stood up. She carried the letter to the wardrobe and opened the top drawer. Folding it carefully, she slid it under her borrowed linens and closed the drawer. Then, she went to the mirror and took in her appearance. Her eyes were red-rimmed and bright with tears. She blinked and wiped them with the back of her hand. Then, she let down her frazzled hair and brushed it, braiding it quickly and twisting it into a clean bun at the nape of her neck. She pinched her pale cheeks and practiced smiling until she came up with an expression that didn't look forced.

Wyatt and his cousin were at the table when she entered the

dining room. Wyatt stood up and pulled out a chair for her.

"You're just in time," Madge said briskly. "Dinner is on its way up. We would have waited for you, but we didn't want to presume."

"I understand," Samantha said, fixing on her practiced smile. "I appreciate your consideration."

Wyatt watched her closely, but he said nothing. They had a hearty meal and Samantha was made aware, in a way she could not have appreciated before her time on the streets, how much easier it was to face problems when one's stomach was full.

Charles arrived not long after lunch to take her on a walk, as had become their daily habit, and she felt almost her old self as they stepped onto the pavement, arm in arm.

"Which way today?" Charles asked genially.

"Towards Hyde Park, I think," Samantha said. "I would like to see the flowers."

He agreed and they set off down the street. "Have you had a pleasant morning?"

Samantha considered telling him about the letter. Of all people, he would understand her anger with her uncle. But she found she was not ready to share it yet. Instead, she told him of her frustration in learning nothing useful from her visit to Mayfair.

"Wyatt let you go with him?" he asked with a frown.

"Let me go with him?" Samantha repeated. "Of course, he *let* me go with him. It's not as though we were visiting the slums of St. Giles. It was Mayfair."

"Still," he said. "I thought he was investigating for you. He should be able to do it on his own."

"Perhaps he could," she said, frowning in her turn, "but I see no reason why I could not help. Would you rather I sat twiddling my thumbs?"

"Not twiddling your thumbs." He laughed and patted her hand. "But certainly not putting yourself in danger."

"What danger?" she asked. "As I said, it was Mayfair."

"I don't know." He shrugged. "But you ought to leave looking for a killer to Mr. Wyatt and focus on…"

"On what?" She stopped walking and slid her arm from his. "What would you have me do, Charles?"

"Spend time with me," he said. "We have so much to make up for."

"And we have been, but that doesn't take up all of my day. I am anxious for this to be over."

"It will be," he assured her. "Soon. At the end of the week, we'll go to the police—"

"You mean, we'll talk about going to the police," she corrected him. "And we will determine what the best course of action is."

"Which will be going to the police," he insisted. "What other option is there?" When she started to answer, he talked over her. "What *viable* option is there?" he amended.

She sighed, but before she could reply, her attention was distracted. A large, black landau carriage with the sides enclosed drew up beside them on the curb so precipitately that it rocked. Samantha stepped back, annoyed at the carelessness of the driver. Then the door opened and two men jumped out. They ran forward, grabbed her by the arms and dragged her back with them. She shouted and pulled against them, trying to twist from their grasp, but they were too strong. She could hear Charles yelling and turned in time to see the driver jump down and knock him to the ground. He didn't move.

"Charles!" she screamed, but her voice was muffled by a piece of foul-smelling cloth pressed roughly over her mouth. Then she was hauled up into the carriage and thrown inside.

Samantha's skirt caught in the door. She heard swearing. There was a bang from above and the carriage rumbled off. She spit out the dirty cloth and looked up. From where she lay on the floor, all she could see was a mass of fabric as the skirt of her dress towered above her.

"Get that down!" one of the men roared, and she threw her arms up to protect herself, twisting away as a heavy boot descended above her. She heard a crack, but she felt no pain and, looking through her arms, she saw that he had stamped on her dress, breaking the whalebone rings of the crinoline cage. Thick, hairy arms gathered the fabric of her skirt and shoved it down, out of sight of the window.

They drove on at a rapid pace. The men above her were talking, but their voices were so low that she couldn't hear what they were saying over the rattle of the carriage wheels across the uneven pavement. Her body was jostled and bumped from side to side, but she was too afraid to move from her uncomfortable position.

Eventually, the carriage stopped. One man stepped over her and jumped down. The other grabbed her roughly and hauled her into a sitting position, bringing her face level with his. She gasped when she recognized Slater. He leered at her and for a brief, panicked moment, she thought he recognized her, whether from Skinny Jim's or the night of the murder, she didn't know, but his next words made it clear he did not.

"Miss Kingston," he said. "So glad to finally make your acquaintance. We keep missing each other."

"Is that so?" she asked faintly.

"I'm glad you ain't in an 'ysterical mood," he continued, "because I need your cooperation now. You see this?" He held up a small pistol.

She nodded as her body tensed with fear.

"I'm gonna put it in me pocket 'fore we get out," he said. "But if you make so much as a sound between the carriage and where we're headed, I'll shoot you. Understand?"

She nodded again, but she was thinking fast. The reactionary part of her was terrified, but her rational mind was doubtful. He and his partners had gone to the trouble of snatching her from the street and driving her away. If they wanted to kill her, they could have done it in the carriage and dumped her body in the river. They must have some other purpose for her, one that required her alive.

Slater jumped down from the carriage, still holding tightly to her wrist. She stepped down after and glanced around. They were in an area of town she did not recognize. The buildings were packed together, three stories high, with shops on the ground level. The shops appeared dingy and cluttered.

Slater led her down the sidewalk. She tried to catch someone's eye, but everyone she saw was either engaged in conversation, focused on their shopping, or studiously avoiding eye contact with her. Samantha began to despair.

Then a miracle happened.

Slater tripped over an uneven patch of sidewalk and in that moment, when he released her to catch himself, Samantha grabbed up her skirts and ran.

Down the street, past vendors and shoppers, she ran. Behind her, she could hear Slater in pursuit, his heavy boots hitting the pavement closer and closer to her. She turned down a side street and felt a hand close around her arm. It tightened and yanked hard, pulling her backwards so that she fell into his chest. Then, in one swift movement, he had flung her over his shoulder and was carrying her into a small alley between two shops.

Slater kicked a metal bin aside and flung her from him. She landed on her backside and crashed into a bin, the wind knocked out of her. He loomed over her, his mouth contorted into a snarl.

Then he reached into his coat pocket and pulled out the pistol, aiming it at her heart. She froze, her eyes on the barrel of the gun.

"What'd I say?" he asked. "What'd I tell you 'fore we got out that carriage?"

"Not to make a sound," she said, her voice high and thin with fear. Without thinking, she added, "And I didn't."

With a growl, he spun the pistol in his hand so that the butt was facing her, leaned over, and slammed it against her temple. Samantha collapsed to the ground. Pain shot across her head. Her vision blurred and her ears rang. In the confusion, she thought she heard someone shouting, but she couldn't be sure. Pain was her whole world. Black edged her vision and she lay down, certain she was about to faint.

Hands grappled with her shoulders, rolling her onto her back. Above her, a blurry face loomed. The mouth moved, and she could hear something, but it sounded like it was coming from a long way off. She just wanted to close her eyes and make the pain go away. The hands at her shoulders shook her. Another face appeared, and she felt something wet and cold on her temple. The faces came into focus, and she saw that a man and a woman, both middle-aged with rough, lined faces, knelt over her, wiping her face with a wet cloth.

"Where…" The words seemed to be travelling through sludge to get to her mouth. "Where'd he go?" she croaked.

"Ran off down the road," the woman said. "He'll be long gone now. Are you alright? That was quite a blow you took."

"I'm…I'll be alright," Samantha said. Her head felt like it was splitting in two, and opening her eyes more than a squint made it worse. The ringing had stopped, though, and her vision was clearing. "Could you help me to a cab? I need to get home."

"Are you sure you should be moving?" the man asked in surprise.

"No," Samantha said, wincing and groaning as she sat up. "But my friends will be worried about me."

"I think—" the man began, but his companion interrupted him.

"I'll send Meg to find a hackney," she said. "You'll be able to pay?"

Samantha started to nod, then stopped as the throbbing in her head ramped up exponentially.

"Yes," she gasped. "When I get home. They'll pay."

The woman stood up and hurried away.

"Put your arm around my shoulders," the man said, wrapping his arm around her back. "I'll help you stand."

She did as he asked and, with his help, she rose shakily to her feet. She gasped again as the pain spiked.

"What's wrong?" the woman asked, hurrying back to them.

"My head hurts," Samantha said. "But it will pass."

"You need a doctor," the man said.

"I'll get one," Samantha assured her. "When I'm home."

The woman came around to her other side and slid an arm around her back. Together, the three of them hobbled to the street. Samantha felt the broken pieces of whalebone crinoline pressing against her as her rescuers leaned in to support her. Her face still felt wet even with the rag gone and she wondered if she was bleeding.

When they reached the street, a hackney was pulling up. It must have been nearby. Half a dozen people stood around, staring as she emerged from the alley, but she was in too much pain to care. When the driver asked for an address, she gave him Wyatt's, and the man and the woman helped her into the cab.

"Thank you," Samantha breathed, as they lowered her onto the seat. She leaned her head back and closed her eyes.

"Good luck," the man said. He and his companion stepped

out and closed the door. The cab started off. The bumpy ride did not help Samantha's splitting headache, but she was at least able to close her eyes and shut out the light.

When they arrived in front of Wyatt's house, she was half-conscious, so she did not immediately realize they had stopped. When she opened her eyes, it was to see Wyatt flinging open the carriage door, worry written across his features. He made a sound somewhere between an oath and a growl and leapt inside.

"I'm fine," she said faintly as he leaned over her, taking her face in his hands and turning her head to examine her temple. "My head does hurt…rather a lot. Can you not move it like that?"

"What happened?" he asked. "Prescott said some men pulled you into a carriage and knocked him out. We were just on our way to the police to report you missing. How did you get back? What happened to your head?"

Samantha winced at the noise. Wyatt sat down heavily in the seat beside her. As he pulled his hands away, she saw that the right one was covered in blood.

"Blood," she said, staring at it.

"Yes." He whipped out a handkerchief and wiped his hands. "It's yours."

She reached up and felt her head. It was sticky. She brought her fingers down and examined them. They were reddish-brown with blood. Wyatt took his handkerchief and dabbed at her face.

"Can you stand?" he asked. "We need to get you to the house. Mrs. Hexam will clean you up."

"I might need some help," she said, wincing as she spoke.

Wyatt folded his bloody handkerchief and shoved it into his pocket. Then, he stood and helped her up. When he had stepped onto the pavement, he pulled her into his arms, carrying her into the house. Samantha was about to protest that she could walk, but the pain spiked again. She squeezed her eyes shut and turned her head into his shoulder.

"What happened?"

She could hear Charles' anxious voice as they entered the house, but she didn't look. She was afraid if she moved, her head would split wide open.

"Mrs. Hexam," Wyatt said, ignoring Charles. "Get something to clean the wound and have Mrs. Plummet prepare some peppermint tea."

"Is she going to be alright?" Charles asked.

"She'll be fine," Wyatt said. "Wait down here."

Samantha felt herself being carried upstairs and through the door to her bedroom. She could hear Jenny bustling around them, emitting little squeaks like a mouse.

"Here you are, Mr. Wyatt," Jenny said. "Lay her right here."

She felt the softness of blankets and the give of the mattress, and Wyatt's arms retreated. There were footsteps and Mrs. Hexam hurried in.

"I've brought water and rags," she said. "Out of my way. Let me see the damage."

Splashing and dripping. Then something warm and wet.

"There, that's not so bad," Mrs. Hexam said. "It was just a lot of blood. That's what happens with head wounds. They bleed something fierce, but as you can see, it's not a large cut. What was it hit her?"

"I don't know," Wyatt said. He sounded anxious.

"A pistol," Samantha murmured.

"What was that, love?" Mrs. Hexam asked.

"A pistol," Samantha repeated, a little louder. "He hit me with the handle of a pistol."

Wyatt swore. She could hear him pacing the floor. "Who?" he asked. "Who hit you?"

Samantha opened her eyes one at a time. The room was dim

enough that it wasn't as painful to look around as it had been outside. Mrs. Hexam was smiling reassuringly down at her. Wyatt had stopped pacing and was watching her too.

"Slater," Samantha said at last.

Wyatt swept a hand through his hair and turned away.

Mrs. Hexam wrung out her rag. "Jenny, get me some fresh water," she said, handing Jenny the bowl. "I'll be right back, Miss Kingston. I'm going to get you some peppermint tea. It will do wonders for that headache."

With a nod to Wyatt, she followed Jenny out of the room. Wyatt watched them leave and turned to Samantha.

"You're sure?" he asked.

"Yes," she said. "And he knew who I was. He called me Miss Kingston."

Wyatt blew out a long breath. Then, he grabbed the chair from the table by the window and carried it over to the bed. He plunked it down beside her and sat.

"Tell me what happened," he said.

She told him, speaking slowly and softly to avoid aggravating her headache.

"Why, though?" he asked when she had finished. "Does this mean you were the target all along?"

"I don't know," Samantha said, covering her eyes with her hand. "But what did they want me to do? I don't inherit the money for another month. Were they going to hold me until then?"

"Maybe they were going to threaten you," Wyatt suggested. "Or scare you, so that you would give it to them once you received it. I don't know. It doesn't make any sense. All I know is that you're in more danger now than before. I think we have to get the police involved."

"I know."

"You're not going to argue with me about it?" He sounded surprised.

"It makes sense," she said. "They can offer us some protection, and they have more resources. Perhaps this attack will convince them of my innocence." She smiled. "A silver lining."

A hand wrapped around hers and pulled it back from her face. She opened her eyes to see Wyatt watching her with concern.

"You will get through this," he said seriously. Then his lips quirked and he added, "And, if it gets as bad as it could, you can always use all that money to buy yourself a castle in the highlands."

"Don't make me laugh," she chided. "It hurts too much."

"Get some rest. Mrs. Hexam is probably standing in the hall with your tea. We'll go to the police tomorrow."

He squeezed her hand once and left the room. Moments later, Mrs. Hexam entered, bringing with her the soothing scent of peppermint.

*****

Prescott came over after breakfast the next day and the four of them, Madge included, went to Scotland Yard together. Wyatt had written to Inspector Whicher the day before to let him know they were coming, but he had not included any details, saying only that he and some friends were coming to share information related to an ongoing investigation. That Whicher would see them, he did not doubt. The man would know that only desperation would bring Wyatt to him. But he did wonder how long the detective would make them wait.

The headquarters of the Metropolitan Police Service was a former private home located at 4 Whitehall Place. However, since its purchase by the government several decades earlier, the public entrance had been from the courtyard at the rear of the building, which faced Great Scotland Yard.

Wyatt had been to the offices before, but it was the first time for the others.

"It makes one feel like a servant, entering through the back this way," Madge said with a sniff of disapproval. "Is that why they do it, do you think?"

"I think it's just convenience," Wyatt said, holding the door open for her and stepping out of the way. "They were still using the front of the house for other purposes when the offices were first opened, and it made the most sense to have people enter through the back."

"Are you certain Inspector Whicher is the one we should talk to?" Prescott said, voicing his doubts for what felt like the hundredth time. "He is a bungler, and that's a fact."

"No, it's not," Wyatt said, not bothering to keep the exasperation from his tone as he followed Prescott and Samantha inside. "And, yes, I am certain. Whicher is intelligent, he's discreet, and he knows me."

"In that case, perhaps we ought to find someone else," Samantha said with a slight smile. "If he knows you, he may not agree to speak with us at all."

He was glad to see she was in a good mood. She had been silent on the journey over, and he was worried she was having second thoughts.

The lobby was quiet. They were the only visitors. Behind the large wooden desk that faced them stood a man in the dark blue trousers and long-tailed coat of a constable. Imprinted on his stiff, buckled collar was the letter A, for the Whitehall division, and the number 43. He was polishing the brass buckle of his thick belt when they entered but set it aside as they approached.

"Good morning," he said placidly. "Do you have an appointment?"

"Yes," Wyatt said. "With Inspector Whicher. I'm V.T. Wyatt."

The constable checked the ledger open before him and ran his finger down one of the columns. When it landed on Wyatt's name, he nodded and looked up.

"He'll be waiting for you, then," he said. "Upstairs and first door on your right."

Wyatt thanked him and led the way to the stairs. When they reached the first floor, they found the correct office and Wyatt knocked.

"Come in."

Inspector Whicher's office was as plain as his person. If not for the nameplate on the desk, it might have been anyone's. There were no photographs, no children's drawings, nor trinkets collected on travels abroad. A coat hung on a stand near the door, and an open bottle of brandy sat on the desk beside a stack of papers.

When they entered, he rose to greet them.

"Mr. Wyatt," he said, coming around the desk to shake his hand. "A pleasure."

"These are the friends I wrote you about," Wyatt said. "My cousin, Lady Bradwell; Miss Kingston; and Mr. Prescott. This is Inspector Whicher."

"A pleasure to meet you all," Inspector Whicher said, bowing to the ladies and shaking Prescott's hand.

He gestured to the seats in front of his desk. There were only two, so the ladies took them, and Wyatt and Prescott stood to either side. Inspector Whicher resumed his seat and scooted his chair forward. He tented his fingers and watched them expectantly.

"We have some information about the Avery case," Wyatt said.

The inspector nodded, and Wyatt went into the speech he had rehearsed in his head on the way there. He introduced Samantha and explained who she was, then Prescott. He included everything from the blackmail to the murder, omitting nothing relevant. Then, he told the story they had concocted about how Samantha had come to him right after and how Madge had joined them. When he got to the part about why they had not come forward earlier, he had to work to keep his voice even. By pretending that Samantha had been with him since the day after the murders, he was implying that he had spent weeks attempting to solve them on his own before finally coming to the police. It galled him to do so because it made him seem both incompetent and foolish.

He finished by describing Samantha's abduction and her identification of the man who did it as her uncle's killer, prompting their visit.

The inspector reached into a drawer in his desk and drew out a notepad and pen. He scribbled in silence for a few minutes while Wyatt and the others sat awkward and still. Then he looked up.

"I hope you are feeling better after your knock on the head, Miss Kingston," he said.

"A little, thank you," Samantha said. There was a slight quaver in her voice and Wyatt knew she must be anxious to know Whicher's reaction to their revelation.

"Quite a harrowing experience overall," the inspector continued. "I am sorry that you didn't feel comfortable coming to us earlier, but I'm glad see that we have some use." He spoke so mildly, it was almost possible to miss the sarcasm. "We'll set up a watch on your house to see if we can prevent any future catastrophes."

"Thank you."

"I hope you will understand when I ask that you stay at Mr. Wyatt's residence for now."

"I do."

"I would like the opportunity to interview you there later, when I have questions. For now, I'd appreciate it if you would give a description of the men you call Slater and Palmer to my constable downstairs so that we can attempt a likeness."

"Of course."

She looked bewildered. No doubt, she had expected more questions, possibly even feared detainment. To be so soon dismissed had put her at sea. Wyatt was no less confused, but he smiled at her as she stood and left with Madge.

"Mr. Prescott," Inspector Whicher said as Wyatt and Prescott took the vacated chairs. "My condolences on your loss."

"Thank you, Inspector," Prescott said evenly, "though, as you will no doubt learn, it was not much of a loss for me."

If Whicher was at all surprised, he didn't show it. In fact, Wyatt thought he saw a slight smile flicker across his lips as he glanced down to turn a page in his notepad.

"I will need details of your whereabouts on the night of the murder and the days immediately preceding and following," he said, scratching out a few words as he spoke. "Leave them with my constable, and we'll follow up shortly."

"As you wish," Prescott said. "Though I may have to go home and check my diary about specifics."

"Just tell the constable what you remember and return later with the rest. I would like to speak with Mr. Wyatt alone before you all leave."

Prescott frowned at the abrupt dismissal, but he rose and took his leave, casting one last look over his shoulder as he shut the door behind him. When he was gone, Inspector Whicher gave Wyatt a hard, searching look.

"There are a few things I would like to make clear," he said. "Firstly, I know that Miss Kingston has not been with you since the murders. If I had to guess, I would say you have known her a week, possibly two." Wyatt started to protest, but Whicher cut him off. "I understand your reason for cultivating this lie, and I see no reason to contradict it publicly. Contrary to popular belief, I don't derive a perverse pleasure from sullying the reputations of respectable young ladies."

He reached into his desk and pulled out a file, setting it down and spinning it so that it faced Wyatt. There was a label on the front that read "Prescott/Avery." Wyatt's eyes widened and he didn't even bother to hide his shock as he looked up at Whicher.

"You knew who Avery was?" he asked.

"Of course we knew," Whicher said. "He was a friend of the commissioner. Sir Richard is the one who told him about the house for let in Holborn."

"Then why haven't you released that information?" Wyatt asked.

Whicher sighed and retrieved the file, sliding the notes he had just taken into it. He tapped it against the desk to straighten the papers and replaced it in the drawer.

"Sir Richard knew that, as soon as the murder hit the papers, it would become a sensation, especially so soon after the Kent case. We had received an unprecedented number of letters during that case with members of the public claiming to have solved the mystery or just claiming to know something we did not. It was hoped that, by keeping the true identities of the victims out of the press, it would be easier to sort the true informants from the attention seekers."

"And was that the case?"

"It has certainly added validity to the information you brought me," Inspector Whicher said placidly. "I've told you all of this to say that I would be willing, in exchange for complete honesty from you and Miss Kingston, to say that you have both been cooperating with us from the beginning. I don't need to explain to you how helpful that could be in alleviating some of the negative attention she is bound to receive when her involvement is made public."

Wyatt nodded, staring absently at a corner of the desk as he considered. It could help. It wouldn't only be him, Samantha and Madge claiming she had been living safe and protected, but the office of the commissioner of police as well.

"I must add," Inspector Whicher said, speaking carefully, "that, though I do not believe Miss Kingston shot her aunt and uncle or their housekeeper—I never did—I cannot dismiss her merely on my own assumptions. Until the killer is caught, she remains a suspect. She herself admits she was there."

"Which makes her even less likely to be the killer," Wyatt said heatedly. "If she were guilty, she would place herself as far as possible from the scene."

"She might," Whicher allowed. "And that can certainly be argued in her favor, but it will not preclude her from trial, should it come to it."

"But…"

"Mr. Wyatt, may I remind you that I agree with you. That does not allow me to circumvent the law. Until the killer is caught, Miss Kingston may not leave the city. I am making you responsible for her."

"How long do you expect it will be before he is caught?" Wyatt asked testily.

"I hope it will be soon, now that we have a description of him, but I can't make any promises that he will be convicted. Miss Kingston did not see him pull the trigger, and though his running from the house after the shots is highly suspect, it will be difficult to prove him guilty without a doubt."

Wyatt frowned. He had known that was likely to be the case, but he didn't like hearing it.

"There is something you can do to help me," Whicher said, leaning forward and clasping his hands together. "I am interested in this cousin of Miss Kingston's. The one who inherited their grandfather's title and lands. It would be easier for you to learn more about him than it would for me. People, particularly those of the peerage, tend to be reticent when talking to police officers."

Wyatt laughed. "A very political way of putting it. I have already made some inquiries into Lord Etwall, but I will make more and share my findings with you."

"Thank you," Whicher said. He sat back and began shuffling the papers on his desk. "That is all, Mr. Wyatt. Thank you for coming in today. I will see you soon, I am sure."

Wyatt left the room, his mind whirling.

*****

It was with a sense of dejection that Samantha left the police station and walked to the hackney carriage. The inspector was quieter than she had expected. He had listened to Wyatt's abridged version of events without interruption and, though his eyes had flicked to her several times, he hadn't asked her to clarify anything. They had agreed to let Wyatt do the initial talking for the sake of simplicity and clarity, but she had expected to be interrogated afterward. She felt that, somehow, she had missed an opportunity to defend herself and her actions.

What were the police planning to do with the information she had supplied? Did they have a way of finding Slater and Palmer? Would they let her know when they had? She ought to be allowed to know the plan. It was her future that was affected, after all.

"You're awfully quiet," Charles said, drawing her mind back to the present. He had just sat down opposite her in the carriage.

"I have a lot to think about."

"I would have thought you'd be relieved," he said. "The police have taken charge now. They'll be watching the house. You're safe, and it will all be over soon."

Samantha found his optimistic confidence irritating. She had good reason to be still concerned. And, as he well knew, once the killer was caught, she would only trade one set of troubles for another.

Feeling another pair of eyes on her, she chanced a glance at Wyatt. He met her gaze and gave her a half smile and slight shrug. At least he understood her frustration. She returned the smile and angled her body to the window, hoping to discourage further discourse.

When they got home, Charles showed signs of wanting to stay, but Samantha pretended to misunderstand all his subtle hints and he was forced to bid them farewell. She felt a little bad, but not enough to change her mind. Years ago, she would have given anything to have him look at her the way he did now, with fascination and admiration. She had dreamt of the day when he would whisk her away with him on his white horse. But she was older now, and wise enough to know that her infatuation with Charles had been as much about her desire to escape her uncle as it had been about any childish notions of romance. They were different people now, and though she loved him dearly as a true friend, when she considered that she no longer needed to marry him to escape her uncle, she felt relief.

Madge went up to change. She planned to take Samantha to a dressmaker to have a few gowns made up for her return to Society. Samantha was about to follow when Wyatt pulled her aside.

"I thought you would want to know," he said, lowering his voice as Jenny hurried past them, dust rag in hand. "It seems that Sir Richard Mayne, the commissioner of police, helped your uncle get that house in Holborn."

"What?" she gasped. "Are you sure?"

"They were friends, apparently. Or friendly enough that your uncle approached him for help and Sir Richard told him about the house."

"Then the police have known all along?"

"I believe it was only Sir Richard and, later, Inspector Whicher who knew. They've kept the information from the public while they try to find the killers."

"Still," Samantha said, her mind reeling. "If I had gone with the constables to Scotland Yard that night…"

"You had no way of knowing it was Sir Richard your uncle approached."

"I knew he'd gone to the police the night of the break-in," she insisted, determined to fully examine her own foolishness. "I ought to have guessed the 'we' Sir Arthur spoke of in his plan was the police."

"Stop," Wyatt said sternly. "First, we don't know that the person he made his plan with was Sir Richard. It probably was, but it may be that he got the house from Sir Richard and made his plan with a completely different person. Second, whether he made the plan with Sir Richard or not, the fact remains that Sir Richard, the commissioner of police, knew where you were hiding and Sir Arthur still died. I have little confidence in his ability to protect you, had you surrendered to the police. I'm glad you didn't know."

Samantha was silent, unsure what to think. She had been prepared to dismiss Wyatt's attempts to make her feel better over her inability to connect the dots, but he made a fair point.

"There's something else," Wyatt said, and Samantha's eyes flew to his, afraid of what he might say next. "Inspector Whicher guessed that you haven't been with me the whole time."

"He guessed?" she asked, panic rising in her chest.

"He knew a lot more about the case than we thought he did," Wyatt reminded her, "and he's very quick-witted. Besides which, he has more information than the public ever will, even once the general facts become known."

Samantha sighed and massaged her temples, trying to calm her anxiety.

"He assured me," Wyatt continued, "that, if we cooperate with him, he'll support our claims about where you've been."

"Why would he do that?"

Wyatt shrugged. "For all I know, it may be out of charity, but I would guess it's also a bit mercenary. He told me he will say you stayed under my protection at the recommendation of the police, which implies that the police have been much more aware and in control of the investigation than they have been. It will look good for them."

"I see," Samantha said hollowly.

They stood in silence for a moment.

"Do you want to play cards?" Wyatt asked.

Her eyes flicked up to meet his. "What?"

"I know I've been busy lately," he said. "And I'm sorry it's taken me away so much. I could stay home this evening, and we could play piquet or something."

Samantha smiled at his somewhat clumsy attempt to ease her worries. "There's no need. I don't require entertainment. Even if I did, Madge and I can play."

"No, you can't," Wyatt said. "Madge hates piquet."

She laughed. "I'll read then. I haven't had the opportunity to do more than glance through the book you were so kind as to purchase for me."

"I'm sure you've read it a hundred times before," he said. "Is there a reason you are trying to avoid playing with me? Are you terrible at cards, perhaps?"

"Quite the opposite. But, knowing how loath you are to lose at anything, I wanted to spare you pain."

"Piquet it is," he said with a laugh.

Wyatt went out just before Samantha and Madge left for the dressmaker's and was not back until just before supper. They ate together, and Samantha enjoyed the novel experience of participating in an interesting dinner table conversation in which her opinion was valued. The topic of discussion was the recent defeat of the American army by the Southern Confederacy at the battle at Bull Run. There was a consensus that the rebellion, which many had hoped would be quickly quashed, was now on track to become a long and costly war. Concerns were rising in Britain about the impact it would have on the cotton mill industry and the economy in general.

Samantha found Wyatt a skilled opponent in piquet. He was also just as competitive as she, and they played for more than two hours because neither wanted to stop while the other was ahead in points. Finally, Madge declared that she was going to bed, and they were forced to abandon the game mid-hand.

Samantha went to bed in expectation of a long, restful sleep after the drama of the past day and a half. However, when she woke, it was still dark outside, and she was confused to see Mrs. Hexam leaning over her, one hand on her shoulder. By the flickering light of the candle placed on the table beside her bed, Samantha could see that she was worried. She sat up abruptly, causing the housekeeper to jump back in surprise.

"What is it?" Samantha asked in a hoarse whisper. Her heart felt as though it were in her throat. "Are they here?"

"Who?" Mrs. Hexam asked.

Samantha gripped the edges of her blanket and tried to will herself into a state of calm. Her pulse beat rapidly and the muscles in her arms and legs were taut, as though she were preparing to spring from her bed. She caught Mrs. Hexam's expression of alarm and forced a smile.

"No one," she said. "It was only a dream."

Mrs. Hexam's face relaxed, though she retained a hint of

suspicion in her eyes. "It's Inspector Whicher," she explained. "He's downstairs with Mr. Wyatt. He says a body's been found. He needs you to come identify it."

THIRTEEN

It only took a moment for Samantha to grasp the situation. The abruptness of her return to wakefulness and the panic that had coursed through her had served to energize her mind. There were just two people she knew only she could identify: Slater and Palmer.

Mrs. Hexam offered to help her dress, but Samantha declined. She brushed her hair into a loose chignon, pulled off her nightgown, and slipped on a chemise and drawers. She had gotten used to tying her own simple corset, and her fingers moved deftly in the dark. A crinoline cage would only get in the way, so she threw on one of Wyatt's sister's dresses and a pair of boots and hurried down the stairs, stepping lightly so as not to wake Madge.

Wyatt was waiting for her. He had clearly dressed in a hurry—the buttons on his coat were off, and his hair stood on end. Inspector Whicher was beside him, hat in hand, looking tired but alert.

"Ah, Miss Kingston," Inspector Whicher said when she joined them. "I'm sorry to rouse you at such an hour, but I think we have found the man you described as Slater. I thought it best you identify him as soon as possible and without the added hassle of having to explain this trip to your neighbors."

She caught his meaning. If they went out during the day, accompanied by a police inspector, they might excite interest they did not want.

"Of course," Samantha said. "Any way I may be of help."

The inspector opened the door and led the way down the steps to the waiting carriage. He and Wyatt sat down opposite Samantha, and he tapped the roof. The driver set off.

"What happened?" she asked, feeling jittery with anticipation.

"A body was pulled out of the river this evening," the inspector said. "A man. He does not appear to have been dead long."

"Do you know how he died?"

Inspector Whicher and Wyatt exchanged a look.

"He was shot," the inspector said. "My guess is that he was thrown in the river after death, though when I left, the inspection of the body was not yet complete. There may be more to learn."

"And if it is Slater?"

The question hung in the air for several moments. Wrapped up in it was all the dread that Samantha had felt since she realized who the body must be. If it was him, how would they ever solve her aunt's and uncle's murders?

"We will have to follow other lines of inquiry," Inspector Whicher said finally.

"Such as?"

"I'll send constables to your neighbors in Holborn. Now that we know what he looked like, we can learn if anyone saw him that night. We'll start searching for Palmer, as well. There are several paths we can take."

Samantha might have taken his words at face value, if she had not seen Wyatt glance at him and look away. There was something they weren't telling her. Likely, it was related to whatever they had discussed after she had been dismissed from the inspector's office. She turned her face to the window, careful to betray none of her frustration, and resolved to speak with Wyatt as soon as she could to find out what he was up to.

They rode in silence the rest of the way. Inspector Whicher appeared to be at his ease with the lack of conversation. Wyatt glanced at her frequently but seemed unwilling to say anything to her with Whicher there.

The cab stopped a few blocks from the morgue when the streets became too narrow for it to continue. They went the rest of the way on foot, through the sludge and muck of the slums. As they walked, bodies that lay curled up against buildings for warmth reached out hands towards them, begging for money. In the dim light cast by Inspector Whicher's lantern, the pale hands appeared to float, bodiless, out of the dark. Samantha felt a mixture of fear and empathy at the sight. Wyatt put an arm around her, urging her forward.

The morgue was a small cinderblock building near the water's edge. From her position on the south side of the Thames as she stood beside it, she could see the outlines of the buildings across the river and the sprinkling of mystical dots of lamplight. Samantha paused to look and Wyatt stopped beside her.

"Hurry along," Inspector Whicher said, beckoning them forward.

They followed him inside. It was a dismal place—sparsely lit, stark, and cold. The inspector led them to a room at the back where a body was laid out on a stone table. Samantha froze in the doorway.

"You'll have to get a lot closer than that," the mortician said, laughter in his voice. He was young, perhaps eighteen or nineteen. He wore a large brown apron over his clothes, and his long black hair was tied back.

"I was starting to worry you weren't coming back," he said,

addressing Inspector Whicher. "Shift change is soon, and I need to process the body before then."

"Thank you for waiting," the inspector said with a nod.

He turned to Samantha and motioned for her to join him at the table. She walked forward cautiously, Wyatt beside her.

Samantha swept her gaze over the body, postponing the moment she would have to look at the face. The clothes were sodden and bedraggled, ripped in several places. The skin under the rips was free of blood, though it was badly scratched. Near the middle of the chest, the fabric had been pulled back to reveal a small hole—the entry point of the bullet.

Steeling herself, Samantha tore her eyes from the sight and looked at the face. Drained of all color, it was empty and emotionless, except for the eyes. The eyes, the same bright blue she remembered, were open and staring. From where she stood, they seemed to be staring right at her.

She backed away quickly. Looking up, she saw Inspector Whicher and Wyatt watching her. She gave a brief nod and hurried out of the building. She had hoped that fresh air would calm her writhing stomach, but there was no fresh air in London, and the smell near the river was worse than anywhere. Her stomach heaved, and she hurried around the side of the building to the relative privacy of the tiny alley.

As she stood up, wiping her mouth with the edge of her sleeve, Samantha fought back the images that assaulted her mind. Mrs. Dunbar, lying in a pool of her own blood, Aunt Victoria, crumpled on the floor, and Sir Arthur, his head at an odd angle, his eyes looking past her. Now, added to them was Slater, staring up at her, pale and bloodless.

When she returned to the front, Wyatt and the inspector were waiting for her. Wyatt was paler than usual and there was a grim set to his mouth. He held out his arm and she took it, leaning on him for the walk back to the carriage. Being ill had left her a little shaky. When they reached the cab, she let him hand her up and she leaned against the cool leather seat back with a groan.

"I'm sorry you had to see that," Wyatt said as he joined her and shut the door.

"I'm not." She rubbed a hand over her eyes. "I don't know that I would have believed him really dead if I had not seen it for myself." She glanced around as the carriage started to move. "Where is Inspector Whicher?"

"He had to go back to Scotland Yard. He said he'd find himself another cab."

Samantha nodded and covered her mouth to stifle a yawn. "Who do you think shot him?"

"I don't know," Wyatt sighed. "It could have been the man who hired him. He could have seen the pictures around town, known the police were looking and wanted to shut him up before he could reveal anything to us. Or it might have been Skinny Jim, ensuring that he couldn't be connected to the crime. Or it could be completely unrelated. He was a criminal. No doubt he had a lot of enemies."

"That would be quite a coincidence."

"I agree. It probably was one of the first two options. Either way, we've lost a valuable witness."

"Palmer is still out there," Samantha said. "Maybe finding him will prove useful."

"It will be harder, though. The police will have to change their methods or risk another body turning up in the river."

Samantha groaned and put her head in her hands.

"Samantha."

She felt a hand on her shoulder and looked up to see Wyatt's face inches from hers. She could see tiny flecks of gold in his deep brown eyes.

"We're going to figure this out," he said, and his voice carried an authority that made her believe him in spite of her doubts. "This is a setback, I won't disagree, but you aren't going to be waiting forever. Whatever his flaws, Inspector Whicher is a brilliant detective. With him on our side, it won't be long before the mystery is solved."

Samantha smiled. Even more than his assurances about Inspector Whicher, she found comfort in his use of "our" and "we."

Madge was up when they returned, and so was the sun, though just barely. Wyatt's cousin was in the parlor, torturing herself with *Great Expectations* and seemed glad for the excuse to set it aside.

"What does this mean for Samantha?" she asked when Wyatt told her where they had been. "What are you going to do?"

"Inspector Whicher has some ideas," Samantha said before Wyatt could answer. "But there's something he asked Wyatt to do when we went to Scotland Yard that I assume is still relevant."

"Oh?" Madge asked, looking at Wyatt curiously.

Wyatt gave Samantha a shrewd look, then sighed. "I didn't tell you because I didn't want to upset you if it turned out to be nothing. Inspector Whicher asked me to learn all I could about your cousin, Lord Etwall. If you were the target, after all, he has a strong motive. No doubt he feels cheated out of the money your grandfather left you."

"It might explain his coldness towards me since Grandfather's death," Samantha said. "I always assumed he was simply showing his true feelings without Grandfather to force politeness from him."

"He certainly knew about the inheritance right away, even if you didn't," Wyatt said.

"What could he have gained in kidnapping me, though? I don't have the money yet."

"It might have been meant to scare you," he suggested. "Like we talked about earlier. To show you that he can get to you wherever you are so that when the time comes, you'll sign the money over to him."

"It doesn't explain the murders of my aunt and uncle. What did that accomplish? I can understand trying to scare me, but murdering three people even by proxy is a big risk, especially for someone in Cyril's position. He has a legacy to protect. A wife and child. He would never be so foolish."

"With your guardians dead, would your cousin not be the most likely person to take their place?"

She nodded.

"If he could prove you were unfit to manage your own affairs, as your guardian, he would have control over your money."

"How would he prove me unfit? No one would believe that."

Wyatt shrugged. "I don't think it would be hard to find a few doctors short on funds and with few enough scruples to sign the papers to have you sent to an institution."

Samantha's eyes widened. Mental institutions had a terrifying reputation. And for good reason.

"I can't think him capable of that," she said. "That would be monstrous. Even Sir Arthur didn't do that."

"A hundred thousand pounds is a strong motivator." Madge gave her a sympathetic smile. "Men have done worse to each other for much less."

"As I said," Wyatt continued. "It may turn out to be nothing."

"Do you think he did it?" Samantha asked, searching his face for a reaction. He eyed her seriously, then looked away.

"I don't know," he said. "It makes logical sense, but I've yet to find a connection between him and either Slater or Palmer."

Samantha nodded, feeling a lead weight settle in the pit of her stomach. When she thought a friend of her uncle's was the villain, she had been worried, but mostly intrigued. The idea that her own cousin might have been responsible for all that had befallen her was devastating.

*****

After breakfast, Wyatt locked himself in his study to think of a plan for seeking out Lord Etwall, but after half an hour of distracted unproductive waste, he gave up and allowed himself a few hours of sleep. Refreshed, he went to Boodle's, thinking he might engage a few of the young earl's friends in a game of cards.

Just outside the entrance to the club, Wyatt was met by George. The reporter was leaning against one of the columns, ignoring the glares of the doorman. He stood straight when he saw Wyatt and hailed him.

"I need to speak with you," he said, giving Wyatt a rare serious look. "Take a walk with me, will you?"

He strode off down the street. After a moment's hesitation, Wyatt followed.

"I've heard rumors that that Inspector Whicher has a lead in my case," he said when Wyatt had caught up to him.

"Your case?"

"The Avery murders, of course."

"In what way is that your case?" Wyatt asked.

"I'm the one who's been keeping it alive," George said defensively. "If not for me, people might've forgotten all about it. What kind of justice is that?"

Wyatt laughed. "This isn't about justice for you."

"Maybe not," George admitted, "but if anyone deserves to know when there's about to be news, it's me."

"Why are you telling me this?" Wyatt asked.

"I've been keeping an eye on Whicher. He's been to your club, and you visited him at Scotland Yard a few days ago."

"And?" Wyatt asked with an air of unconcern.

"I also have it on good authority," George said slyly, "that you've been walking about town with a young lady. Mayfair, to be precise."

"Are you having me followed?" Wyatt asked indignantly. "Was that your man I chased down the other day?"

"Then you don't deny it?"

"That I took a stroll with a lady? Why should I?"

"The thing is," George said, "I can't seem to find out who she is."

"She is none of your concern."

George shrugged. "I'm not normally one to care about your private life, but I'm sure my friend in the society column would be most interested to hear about the woman who lives with the Viscount Boxley's younger brother."

Wyatt grabbed George's arm and swung him around. "If you dare slander a lady's name…" he threatened through clenched teeth.

"If it's printed, it's technically libel, not slander," the reporter said, grinning wickedly, "and libel laws are notoriously complicated." He shrugged out of Wyatt's grip and brushed imaginary dust from his sleeves. "But there's no need for any of it to reach the paper. I just want to know what you know about the Avery murders. And there's no use denying it. I know Whicher's break is connected to you."

Wyatt continued to glare.

George's expression softened. "Listen. I like you, and I'm not interested in ruining you or your brother. You know this is all going to come out sooner or later. If you tell me now, I will be in your debt. We both benefit tremendously."

Wyatt scrutinized the reporter's narrow face as he considered his options. Would George follow through on his threat? He was passionate about his work and fiercely ambitious. If it came down to a choice between preserving a friendship and furthering his own career, he might well choose the latter. However, it needn't come to that. George was right. They could both benefit from working together. An ally in the papers could be a great help to Samantha.

"You're right," he said finally. "I do know something about the Avery murders."

George grinned.

"It is sensitive, though, and I'm not ready to reveal it yet. However," he said before George could protest. "I can promise you that, when the time comes, I will give you an exclusive, as long as you say nothing until then."

"I won't wait forever," George warned.

"I wouldn't expect you to."

They shook hands and Wyatt watched George saunter away, his thoughts in turmoil. Then he turned and entered the club.

In the smoking room, he was surprised to find Bingo lounging in a chair by the fire.

"Val!" Bingo said with delight, bouncing up and clapping Wyatt on the back. "Where have you been? It's been an age."

"Less than a week, actually," Wyatt said mildly, taking the seat Bingo offered him.

"Yes, well, even one day feels like an age now. I've never been in London outside the Season before. Is it always this miserable? There's no one here, and everyone who is here is dry as toast. Take that man." He pointed to a white-haired gentleman sitting not far from them who was reading a paper. "No, don't worry about him overhearing. He's been asleep for two hours."

"He isn't now," Wyatt said, lowering his voice. "His eyes are open."

"That's where you make your error," Bingo said. "His eyes

were open when I got here, and I thought he must be awake, too, but that paper hasn't moved an inch, and if you listen carefully, you can hear him snore."

Wyatt laughed. The old man didn't move.

"I'm surprised to see you here," Wyatt said. "I thought you preferred White's."

"Yes, well, it's even deader than this place, if you can imagine. And I can't go back to the United for a while because I took the blame for letting those pigs loose in the dining room."

"I wondered if that was you." Wyatt shook his head and grinned.

"*I've* been wondering," Bingo said, narrowing his eyes, "if your absence is related to that lady you brought to the masque."

"Why would a lady prevent me from seeing you?" Wyatt asked, hoping to deflect.

"Why, indeed?" Bingo said, arching an eyebrow. "I've been pondering that very question, and I've come to the conclusion that you are hiding something. Though why you would be keeping secrets from your oldest and dearest friend whose history of secret-keeping is as long as his friendship with you, I cannot fathom."

Wyatt smiled ruefully. "I know you can keep secrets—"

"Absolute vault."

"—but it wasn't mine to share. How about this? Come to dinner tomorrow. If she says no, I'll send you a note. Otherwise, be there at seven."

Bingo grinned. "I'll be there."

There were only a handful of other club members there that day, and though Wyatt endured several hours of whist, he learned very little about Lord Etwall. The earl was twenty-four, married with an infant son, had good land for shooting, and bred race-winning horses. He never backed down from a bet, but no one liked to play cards with him because he was a poor loser. He had a new filly and *wasn't she just the prettiest you'd ever seen but she couldn't run worth anything and, no, you're thinking of Lord Sayers' mare, oh wait, maybe you're right. Lord Etwall's newest stallion, though…*

When Wyatt got home, Prescott's gig was turning the corner at the end of the street, driving away. Tossing his hat on the rack, he went to find Samantha in the parlor, but was informed by Madge that she had gone to her room.

"I'll be in my study if you need me," he told Madge, who nodded and returned to her magazine, the crease between her brows deepening as she did.

It had been a difficult transition, but Wyatt had gotten used to having ladies in his house. He had even begun to like it. Madge was always good fun, and Samantha challenged him at every turn. The house felt lighter, and even the food was better. He'd never paid much attention to the menu before, but Samantha and his cousin had insisted on some alterations that he was quite pleased with.

What he could not abide were the constant visits from Prescott. It felt to Wyatt as though he could not step out of his study without tripping over the man. He knew how important he was to Samantha, so he wasn't about to turn him away or banish him from the house, but he had begun to wish he could. It wasn't that Prescott was unpleasant. In fact, he was absurdly polite to Wyatt. It was the proprietary way that he treated Samantha. He had assumed he had the right to visit whenever he wished and spoke often of places he would take her once she had been released from the prison of Wyatt's home.

If Wyatt had been her legal guardian instead of just her physical one, he would have insisted that Prescott either show he could support her and propose or back off. He sometimes wondered if Samantha wouldn't have appreciated some such action on his part, but he couldn't be sure. She guarded her emotions with an expertise that could only stem from years of practice, but sometimes he saw a glimmer of irritation or frustration when Prescott arrived unannounced.

*****

The next evening, Samantha prepared for dinner with Wyatt's friend, Lord Aston. She had consented readily when Wyatt proposed the idea. It would be good, she thought, like a testing of the waters before she rejoined Society at large. Lord Aston had been charming and amusing at the masque, and she looked forward to spending time in his company.

She hadn't told Charles about the dinner. She could hardly, as a guest, have invited him, and it would have been rude to discuss it with him when he was not invited. That was what she told herself, anyway, but she knew it was not the only reason. Wyatt would have permitted her to invite Charles if she had wanted to.

No, the real reason was that she was irritated with him. He was always around and always talking. After their visit to Scotland Yard, he seemed to take it for granted that the police would soon solve the murders and everything would return to normal. He could not understand her continued worry or her desire to discuss who might be behind his father's and her aunt's deaths. There was no need, he insisted, and no use in her troubling herself about it. Yet, she was troubled, and his failure to understand that troubled her all the more.

Samantha's dress for that evening was one she had ordered with Madge. It was black satin, with full, bell-like sleeves that ended in a wide ruffle. The flounces of the skirt were similarly ruffled. At the modiste's suggestion, and to her relief, considering the ill-effect of black against her skin tone, the upper part of the bodice, though bordered by a black ruffled V that began at her shoulders and ended just below her bust, was white. It had the effect of softening the garment's stark color, and she was pleased with the ensemble. Her hair had been drawn into a loosely braided bun by Madge's maid, Higgins, and when she looked in the mirror, Samantha thought she might be able to endure the constrictions of mourning, after all.

When she came downstairs, the door to Wyatt's study was closed, so she wandered into the empty parlor and sat down on a seat near the window. It was a cozy parlor, though the furniture was outdated, and the wallpaper was not to her liking. She considered how she would decorate it differently if it were her home and was struck by the realization that she would soon have the opportunity to decorate her own house, if she so chose. Until that moment, she had not regarded her imminent inheritance as anything more than a possible motive for her abduction, but the reality of being an heiress was suddenly before her. As long as she did not get killed or arrested before her birthday, she would very soon have complete control over her own life.

Madge entered, interrupting Samantha's thoughts. She rose and greeted her.

"I like this," Madge said, stepping back and looking Samantha up and down with approval. "I think we made the right choice in not going all black. Your hair is too dark for that. And the ruffles are just enough without being overly decorative. Yes, it was a good choice."

"I'm glad you approve," Samantha said, half in jest. "Do you know where Wyatt is?"

"He and Lord Aston are having a tête-à-tête before supper," Madge said. "No doubt Wyatt is catching him up on our activities."

Samantha frowned. She ought to have been included in the conversation.

At that moment, the door to the study opened, and voices from the hall spilled in. Wyatt entered the parlor, speaking over his shoulder to his friend, who followed behind. Seeing the two of them together, with Lord Aston's face free of the mask he had worn at the ball, Samantha was struck by the contrast between them. It wasn't only the physical difference, though that was evident enough. Lord Aston was taller, with curly auburn hair, where Wyatt's was dark. He had a neatly trimmed beard and mustache, while Wyatt was clean-shaven.

The main difference between the two men, however, came from something less tangible. Where Wyatt was controlled, restrained, even, showing only glimpses of his true emotions, Lord Aston exuded an energy that was infectious, making his presence felt the moment he entered the room.

"Miss Kingston," he said, hurrying over and taking her hand in his. "Such a pleasure to see you again." He bent to kiss her hand, then straightened up. "And, if I may say, you look even lovelier without the mask."

"Thank you." She smiled back at him.

"And Lady Bradwell, I am always happy to see you."

Madge let him kiss her hand as well, then tapped him on the arm with her fan. "When are you going to come see my new pointer?" she asked in a playfully accusatory tone. "You told me you were interested, and I've put several buyers off."

"A thousand apologies, my lady. I had planned to come after the grousing, but circumstances precipitated my immediate removal to London. Perhaps in October I might come for a visit?"

"Let me know when, and I'll kill the fatted calf."

Samantha glanced at Wyatt where he still stood near the door and found he was watching her. He caught her eye and looked away.

"I believe this is the smallest dinner party I have ever attended," Lord Aston said, looking around him, as though expecting to see more people.

"We may have set a record," Wyatt agreed, walking forward.

"I like it," Madge declared. "No standing on ceremony. No tiptoeing around controversial topics. No guests invited only out of politeness. Shall we go in?" She took Wyatt's arm and steered him back out the door, leaving Lord Aston to offer his arm to Samantha. She took it, and he lay his free hand on hers, leaning over to whisper.

"I hope Wyatt has been good company. He's wound a bit tight, my friend," he said conspiratorially. "You wouldn't think it to look at him, but once he's loosened up, he actually possesses a sense of humor."

Samantha laughed. Wyatt cast them a quizzical look, but Madge pulled him along impatiently.

Wyatt's cook had spared no effort with the food, and the place settings were more elegant than any Samantha had yet seen at her host's house. It seemed almost ridiculous to have put so much effort into a meal that included only one extra person, but the pomp and circumstance did serve to remind her of what she would be returning to.

"I must tell you, Miss Kingston," Lord Aston said, addressing her, but not bothering to lower his voice, so that Wyatt and Madge broke off their conversation to listen, "how much I admire your bravery."

"My bravery?" She shot Wyatt a frown across the table. What *had* he told his friend?

"Yes, bravery. Fortitude, too. Not many people—certainly not any women I know—could stand to spend as much time as you have with my friend and yet here you are, smiling and none the worse for wear."

Wyatt threw a dinner roll at him. Lord Aston ducked and it bounced off his shoulder. Madge laughed.

"You overestimate your friend's adherence to his duties as a host, I think," Samantha said wryly. "It has not been such a feat as you think to endure the little of him I've seen."

Lord Aston gasped in mock horror. "Well," he said, turning to Wyatt. "What have you to say to that?"

"Only that Miss Kingston well knows the reasons for my absence, but had I known she felt it so keenly, I would have made every effort to be at her side."

He bowed his head to her and, when he lifted it, there was a challenge in his eyes.

"I was not thinking merely of myself," Samantha said, raising a supercilious eyebrow, "but of your poor cousin who came all this way to be met only by your negligence."

"I do think you might've made a bit more effort on my account," Madge agreed, taking a sip of Madeira. "When I think of the joy I felt on receiving an invitation from my favorite cousin, and all the evenings I imagined we would enjoy together, listening to that monotone reading voice of yours reciting Shakespeare's sonnets, I am saddened."

"May I remind you all that this is my home," Wyatt said, trying and failing to conceal a smile. "It doesn't do to mock one's host, you know. I could send you all out."

"Into the perils of a late summer evening?" Lord Aston asked. "Oh, the horror!"

"Without the rest of this delicious meal, yes," Wyatt said.

Lord Aston held up his hands in surrender. "There is no need to threaten such drastic measures, Val. You win."

"Why do you call him Val?" Samantha asked.

"Because he thinks he's being funny," Wyatt answered as Lord Aston laughed.

"I don't understand."

"It's short for Valentino," Lord Aston explained.

"Is that what the V stands for?" Samantha asked in surprise.

"No," Wyatt said emphatically.

"I've known Val since we were boys at Eton together," Lord Aston continued, "probably longer than anyone else, apart from his family, and even I don't know what the V stands for."

"Truly?" Samantha asked, her eyebrows raised.

"Truly. Wyatt's name is one of his best-kept secrets. I have tried to get it out of him for years with no success. So, halfway through our time at Eton, I started making up names to call him, all starting with V, of course. I believe I hit upon Valentino after a particularly embarrassing incident involving him and a young lady."

"Valentino for Saint Valentine?" Samantha guessed.

"Yes. It caught on with the other lads and stuck."

"Your name must be quite dreadful for you to prefer Valentino to it," Samantha said to Wyatt.

"That is something neither you nor Bingo will ever be able to discover for yourselves," he said.

"Do not underestimate my determination," Lord Aston said, then laughed. "Or overestimate my interest."

"Surely you know," Samantha said, addressing Madge, who had been eating her soup with a half-smile throughout the exchange.

"Oh, I know," Madge said. "And there's no need to look so panicked, Wyatt, my boy. I won't betray you. I wouldn't give your mother the satisfaction." She turned confidingly to Samantha. "She's the one who named him, you see. Wyatt's father never could stand up to her. It was one of her whims, and I daresay she regretted it later, but she could never admit that, of course."

Wyatt's expression was stormy and he attacked his soup with vigor. Madge lay a calming hand on his and continued.

"I've told him he ought to be glad that his surname at least is palatable. Imagine if he'd been a Wigmore or a Carburton or something similarly bizarre ."

"Like Pumblechook," Samantha suggested.

"Or Sowerberry," Lord Aston added helpfully.

"Or Squeers."

"Gradgrind."

Samantha giggled. "Quilp."

"Fezziwig," Lord Aston said. "Definitely Fezziwig."

He and Samantha laughed heartily and Madge chuckled along.

"Yes, you're all very amusing," Wyatt said. "And you all have perfectly ordinary names, so you've no business commenting on mine."

"Francis is hardly ordinary," Lord Aston said. "A bit too French for my liking."

"Yes, but nobody calls you that," Wyatt said. "They call you Aston."

"For now. Once my father dies—and long may he live—I'll be Rotherham, which, besides being a mouthful, is all too easily turned to Rottenham or Rotten 'un as the locals are fond of calling him."

"I would also like to object," Samantha said. "I am the only Samantha of my acquaintance. I don't call that ordinary."

Wyatt gave a growl of frustration and Madge patted him on the back.

"You'll never win," she said soothingly. "Not when you stack the odds against yourself like this. Too many clever opponents."

Samantha smiled.

"I can't say I've ever been accused of cleverness before," Lord Aston said. "I am even sorrier now that I was forced to delay the pleasure of your hospitality, Lady Bradwell. If these are the sorts of compliments I am to receive on my visit, I may never leave."

Madge laughed and drained her glass. "Where is that next course? I am ready to be impressed."

When the meal had ended, Madge caught Samantha's eye, and they rose to take their leave.

"You gentlemen had better not be too long at your port," she said, following Samantha out of the room. "It would be decidedly rude to keep us waiting when there are so few of our party to begin with."

In the parlor, Samantha lowered herself into the leather armchair by the fire that had become her favorite, reflecting on how comfortable she had become in Wyatt's house and how unsure she was of her future. Where would she live? Would she find a chair she liked as much?

"Quite an enjoyable dinner party," Madge said, settling into the settee with a sigh. "I do think I will host a few of these small affairs myself."

"Small affairs may be all I'm able to host," Samantha said dourly, "once Society has learned my secrets."

"Oh, no, my dear," Madge said with a chuckle. "I think you will be surprised by how popular you become. There will be some who shun you initially, but they will soon forget why. You are too sensational to be brushed aside, and I imagine you'll be inundated with invitations. Everyone will want you at their events because everyone will want to come wherever you are to see the spectacle."

"I don't want to be a spectacle," Samantha said with revulsion. "I want to be left alone."

"That will not be possible, much as you may wish it. However, you will have the money to set your own fashion, as you like."

"I don't want to set my own fashion. I don't even know what my own fashion would be." Samantha blew out a breath, and several loose curls bounced. "Until this year, my only goal was to marry away from my uncle and run my own household."

"Well, then," Madge said seriously, "before all this comes down around your ears, it might be time to think about what you want. Money, for all people with it like to disparage it, is quite freeing. Think about it. What is something you always dreamed of but never imagined you could do?"

"Returning to Derbyshire," Samantha said without hesitation.

"A country girl at heart," Madge said with a smile. "I knew there was a reason we got on so well. So, do it! Perhaps not right away, as there will be a lot to sort out, but I am certain there will be plenty of friends eager to have you for a guest. Count me among them. In fact, I hope you will visit as soon as you might."

"And see your dogs?" Samantha asked.

Madge's smile widened. "Clearly, we were destined to meet."

The men entered shortly after, and they all passed such a pleasant evening that Samantha gave no more thought to what was to come.

FOURTEEN

Dawn was breaking when Wyatt was awoken by Mrs. Hexam shaking him. He rubbed sleep from his eyes and rolled onto his side with a yawn.

"It's that inspector again," she said in a harsh whisper. "He says it's urgent."

Still half-asleep, Wyatt nodded and sat up, swinging his legs over the side of the bed and stepping onto the woven mat that protected his feet from the cold floor. He stretched and stopped midway, surprised to see his housekeeper still standing there, frowning at him.

"Mrs. H," he sputtered, snatching his dressing gown from the hook. "I thought you left. I'm not…dressed."

"I changed your nappies for years," she said waspishly. "Nothing I haven't seen before. I wanted to say that I hope this isn't going to become a pattern, being woken by police inspectors at unholy hours."

"I have no control over what another man chooses to do with his time," he said, walking over to the ewer and pouring water into the bowl to wash his face. "I don't know what you expect me to do about it."

She grumbled and stalked out of the room, leaving him to wonder again about the wisdom of employing his former nanny.

Inspector Whicher was pacing the floor of the parlor when Wyatt joined him a few minutes later. He stopped abruptly and gave Wyatt such a grim look that he was immediately filled with dread.

"What's happened?" he asked, his voice cracking with early morning disuse.

"I wanted to tell you before you read the morning papers," Whicher said. "Lord Etwall is dead."

"What?" Wyatt was stunned. "What happened?"

Inspector Whicher sighed and rubbed his eyes with a calloused hand. "It appears he killed himself. A housemaid discovered him yesterday evening, hanging from the ceiling of his private study. Scotland Yard got a telegram from the Brighton police almost as soon as they learned of it, and I've been up all night handling it."

"Why would he kill himself?" Wyatt asked, still reeling.

"He left a note. It's still being examined, but I have a copy and I fear the newspapers will too."

He handed Wyatt a folded piece of paper. Wyatt shook it open, skimming the important facts first, then reading through it again more slowly.

I, Cyril Everard Kingston, fifth Earl of Etwall, am no longer able to live with the guilt of my sins. I leave this note to be found beside my body and ask that it be distributed to police and newspapers alike that it may help to right the wrongs I have done. To my cousin, Miss Samantha Kingston, I can only say how very sorry I am to have caused you such pain.

Upon the death of my grandfather, the fourth Earl, it

was expected that I would inherit his title and lands, as I did. The bulk of his fortune, however, was not settled on myself, but on my cousin, Miss Kingston. This will come as a shock to many who assumed, as I had, that the estate would pass undivided. I have lived beyond my means for years in an effort to keep up appearances, hoping all along to find a way to contest the will and grant me my rightful dues.

No way was found, however, and I despaired until I devised a plan, which I now recognize as desperate and ill-conceived, to have my cousin abducted and to force her to sign over her inheritance before the truth could be discovered. I hired men to do the deed, but they failed, alerting my cousin's guardians, Sir and Lady Arthur Prescott. Out of fear, the Prescotts hid themselves and my cousin under a different name, that of Avery.

Indeed, it was that Avery family about whose brutal murder you read this summer. I found where they had hidden and sent the same men again to force my cousin's hand. There was a struggle, and in the confusion, Sir Arthur and his lady, along with their housekeeper, were shot and killed. I have lived with the guilt of their deaths for months now. I did not pull the trigger, but if not for me, they would be alive.

As for my poor cousin, though she escaped, she has doubtless lived in fear all this time, not knowing what to do or whom to turn to. It is my hope that, with these admissions, she may at last return home in peace.

This is my last confession. May God have mercy on my soul.

Wyatt looked up to find the Inspector watching him intently. "It seems Miss Kingston is exonerated."

"It does," Inspector Whicher agreed, his face an inscrutable mask.

Wyatt glanced back at the letter. Although he had theorized just such a motive for her cousin, it seemed almost too convenient how neatly the matter had come to a conclusion.

"What about the blackmail letters?" he asked.

"I don't have all the facts yet," Whicher said, holding out a hand to take the letter. "I have a lot of work to do. I have, however, confirmed that the note is in his own hand. Not only does it match other examples we found, but there were ink stains on his fingers."

"It's awfully theatrical," Wyatt said doubtfully, handing over the paper.

"What aspect of this case has not been? It carries all the absurdities of an amateur village farce." Inspector Whicher stuffed the note into his pocket and jammed his hat on his head. Then he rubbed his face with both hands and sighed. "My apologies, Mr. Wyatt. It's been a long night."

"I understand. I don't wish to detain you any longer."

"I'll keep you informed."

With a stiff bow, Inspector Whicher departed and Wyatt sank into a chair, putting his head in his hands. It wasn't long before he heard shuffling footsteps, then a cough.

"Yes," he said without looking up.

"Should I wake Miss Kingston?" Mrs. Hexam asked.

Wyatt groaned and sat up.

"So, you heard?"

"The door wasn't closed," his housekeeper said unabashedly. "Do you want me to get Miss Kingston?"

"No." He stood and walked past Mrs. Hexam. "Let her sleep. There will be time enough to deal with all this when she wakes. Send some breakfast up to my study. And the papers, when they arrive."

An hour later, there was a loud knocking at the door. Wyatt heard Mrs. Hexam answer it and the angry tones of the visitor as they carried through the closed door of his study.

"Do not be alarmed, Mrs. Hexam," Wyatt said, entering the hall. "He's only a writer."

Mrs. Hexam stepped aside as George Canard pushed past her and marched up to Wyatt, breathing heavily and waving a folded newspaper at him.

"You hypocritical prig!" he shouted, shoving Wyatt back with his free hand. "I agree to wait for you to send something my way, and then this?"

"How is it my fault?" Wyatt asked, knocking George's hand off his shoulder. "I didn't know he was going to kill himself."

"You promised me a story. You said you knew something. This was my story, and now it's all over the whole blasted city!"

"Keep your voice down. We can talk about this in my study."

"Keep my voice down?" George laughed incredulously. "Who am I gonna wake? The girl I agreed to cover up for you? I held up my end of the bargain, Wyatt. What did I get for it? Well, I can tell you now, the next scandal to break will be yours!"

Wyatt tried to usher George into his study, but it was too late. Samantha appeared at the top of the stairs, Madge behind her. She seemed to have been interrupted in the middle of getting ready, for, while she was dressed in one of his sister's simple day dresses, her hair was still in the long braid she had no doubt slept in. It draped over one shoulder and the tendrils that escaped from it framed her face.

"What's wrong?" Samantha asked as she descended the steps,

looking between Wyatt and George with concern. "We heard shouting."

To his credit, George had the sense to look abashed. He removed his hat and bowed as the ladies came to stand before them.

"I gather this is the newspaperman friend you spoke of," she continued, nodding to George.

"Yes. Samantha, George Canard. George, this is Miss Kingston."

She looked at him sharply and he realized he had forgotten to give her false name. In his agitation over the events of the morning, it had completely escaped his mind. He swallowed back the list of apologies, excuses and qualifications that leapt to his tongue at the look on George's face. There was no going back now. Perhaps it was best. After all, the public would expect Samantha to reappear after the note her cousin left.

With a sigh, he addressed Samantha, ignoring the agitated movements from George. "I'm afraid I have some bad news. Your cousin, Lord Etwall, is dead."

Samantha gasped. Madge put an arm around her. "How? When?"

"He hanged himself. Yesterday. It's all over the papers."

"Hanged himself?" Samantha regarded the newspaper George still gripped tightly in one hand. "May I?" she asked, holding out a hand.

He shuffled his feet and coughed. "I'm not sure a lady should…" he started to say, but Samantha scoffed and rolled her eyes heavenward.

"Am I a lady now?" she asked in a voice dripping with sarcasm. "I thought I was a girl you agreed to cover up, though it seems you were about to go back on your word."

Wyatt caught Madge's eye and looked away before the

impulse to laugh overtook him.

"I…" George began, uncharacteristically at a loss for words, before muttering, "He'd gone back on his."

"And, naturally, the sins of others always excuse our own," Samantha said, her eyebrow raised in such perfect disdain that Wyatt wondered if she'd practiced it in front of a mirror.

George, never one to be down for long, grinned and handed over the newspaper.

"Thank you," she said. "I'll return it as soon as I'm finished."

She swept off to the parlor, with Madge following behind.

"That's…" George said, watching Samantha leave.

"Yes, she is," said Wyatt.

"She's been…"

"Yes, she has."

"I need a drink."

Wyatt steered George into his study and sat down at his desk. He didn't bother to shut the door. George went to the wall cabinet and poured himself a shot of whiskey.

"I can't believe you didn't tell me," he said, tossing back the shot and setting the glass down.

"I can't believe you didn't figure it out for yourself," Wyatt said. "Maybe if you spent less time making things up and more time investigating the truth…"

"How long has she been here?" George asked, pacing restlessly.

"She came the day after the murders," Wyatt lied. "We had a mutual friend. She thought I could help her."

"So, all the time we've been talking about this, you had the main witness hidden away in your house?"

Wyatt nodded, keeping his face placid.

"I must have looked like such an idiot to you, with my theories and suppositions. How did you keep a straight face? I thought I knew all your tells."

"Practice," Wyatt said simply. "Now, do you want to go on wallowing, or do you want to learn how I live up to my end of the bargain?"

George stopped pacing and turned to him. "And how is that?"

"By giving you an exclusive interview with the infamous Miss Kingston."

George's eyebrows rose. "Exclusive? No other paper gets her?"

"Exclusive."

"What aren't you telling me?"

"We get to read it before you publish, and Miss Kingston has the right to remove anything she doesn't like."

George gave a thoughtful hum and crossed his arms over his chest, leaning against the wall.

"I would take the deal if I were you, Mr. Canard," Samantha said from the doorway.

George straightened as she entered the room.

"I couldn't help overhearing," she said, tossing the newspaper onto an empty chair. "And that account, at least"–she nodded to the paper—"was short and uninformative. I'm certain that every newspaper in the city would pay a fortune for an interview with me. Are you actually going to pass up the opportunity because you're worried I might cut out a few words?"

George grinned. "I never say yes right away, Miss Kingston. It's good business practice. But I would be mad to pass this up. When will you be ready?"

"I am ready," she said.

"Are you chaperoning?" George asked Wyatt as Samantha sat in the chair beside him.

"I know you too well not to," Wyatt answered. He leaned back and folded his arms.

"Quite the protector you've chosen for yourself," George said, turning back to Samantha.

She smiled thinly, and for the first time, Wyatt thought through the implications of the story she was about to tell. By pretending she had come running to him right away, she was concealing her own bravery and the strength she had drawn on to live on her own for so long. Instead of a story of survival against all odds, hers became one of mere existence, hiding for days on end. Yet, if she told the truth, she would be ostracized by her peers, possibly even arrested for breaking and entering.

George was direct in his questioning, unabashed in his quest for as many details as he could pull from her memory. Samantha answered hesitantly at first but grew more confident as the minutes passed. Madge joined them eventually and added the weight of her name to the story. When he had finished, George gathered up his notes and hurried out the door, promising to send them a copy in a matter of hours.

*****

Samantha was not as sanguine as she had appeared. Her mind was reeling with the morning's revelations. She could not believe it had been Cyril all along. True, even as a child he'd been a sore loser, but to resort to such theatrics and such villainy was beyond even his youthful tantrums. And then to take his own life when he had a wife and child to care for and an estate that depended on him? She didn't want to believe it. She couldn't believe it. She had always considered herself a good judge of character, and she knew it was not in Cyril to have done something so selfish, cruel, and foolhardy.

She sat through the interview with Mr. Canard, answering his questions and feeling the knot in her stomach grow larger and tighter with each passing minute. Now was the time when her lies would be tested and her story revealed to the world. What would be the outcome? Would she have any friends left? Had she had any before?

Charles arrived as Mr. Canard was leaving. "Who was that man?" he asked Samantha when he entered the parlor, having passed the reporter in the street.

"That was Mr. Wyatt's friend, George Canard, a reporter for *The London Inquirer*. He was interviewing me for his newspaper."

"He was what?" Charles asked, his eyes wide with surprise.

She bit her lip, afraid he might not know. She did not want to always be the bearer of bad news to him.

"Did you read the newspapers this morning?" she asked, motioning for him to sit beside her on the settee.

"Of course I read the papers," Charles blustered. "That's why I'm here."

She breathed a silent sigh of relief. "Then you will agree that the time for me to come forward is now. Mr. Canard has been offered an exclusive in return for giving me control over what he writes."

"I suppose it's for the best," Charles conceded, rubbing his temple. "The newspapers are what made this tragedy a spectacle. They may as well finish it out."

"How are you feeling?" Samantha asked with concern. "Now that you know who was responsible for what happened to your father?"

He shrugged. "Not what I should be, I'm sure. Relief that it's over. Dread of dealing with Society's reactions. Exhaustion. What about you? How do you feel?"

"I don't know," she said. "I thought I would feel relieved, but I don't. Cyril and I may never have been friends, but we were family. I never could have imagined the boy I played with as a child would grow up to hurt me in such a way. I'm not sure I believe he did."

He frowned at her. "What do you mean by that?"

"I don't know." She blew out a breath and brushed away the curls that tickled her face. Then she laughed.

"What's so funny?"

"It's been such a morning. I forgot I hadn't even put my hair up yet."

He smiled. "I can't say I mind. I think I prefer it this way."

She looked away, unsure how to take the compliment, especially considering her own shifting emotions towards him.

"Oh, pardon me."

Samantha turned to see to see Madge, standing in the doorway, clearly amused.

"I came to find my magazine," she said. "I've nearly finished it."

"It's by the hearth," Samantha said. "You left it in your sewing basket."

"So I did. Yes, I see it." She bustled across the room and bent to retrieve her magazine, then straightened. "I hadn't realized you were entertaining. Though I should have guessed that Mr. Prescott would rally 'round after the news of the morning."

"I was just leaving, actually," Charles said, standing.

"You were?" Samantha asked in surprise.

He looked down at her and gave her a fleeting smile. "Yes. I'm sorry. I only came to make sure you were alright. There is much I have to attend to today. I will return tomorrow, and we can talk more then."

"Very well. Good luck."

Mr. Canard was true to his word, and that evening, the interview he had sent for her review appeared in a special edition of his paper. The first reporter arrived on their doorstep at eight the next morning and was followed by so many insistently curious people that constables were sent from Scotland Yard to keep them from breaking down the door. Samantha hid inside with Madge, all the curtains drawn.

Wyatt, who had gone to the Yard to request the constables, returned at ten with Inspector Whicher. The shouting from the front of the house increased greatly when they arrived, and Samantha watched through a gap in the draperies as Wyatt and the inspector pushed their way through the crowd of reporters to the front door. The sound from outside was deafening as they opened the door, and she heard the inspector threaten to incarcerate the lot of them if they did not let him through. Then the door shut, and the still of the house was restored.

"I don't have much time," the inspector said when he and Wyatt had joined her in the parlor, "but I wanted to offer my condolences in person. It was a violent and tragic way for these events to end."

"Thank you," Samantha said.

"Your cousin's wife is handling all the particulars, so you needn't concern yourself with any of that. There is some unpleasant business that does concern you, however." He paused to clear his throat. "Your cousin's confession has brought new evidence to light in what was the Avery case. For that reason, a new inquest has been formed. It's mostly a formality, but I think it highly likely that you will be called upon as a witness when the court meets."

"I see," Samantha said, looking at Wyatt. He offered her a reassuring smile.

"I don't know when the inquest will be held, but I wanted to see that you were prepared. Also, I'm not sure if you are aware, but when your aunt's and uncle's bodies were unclaimed, they were taken by rail to Brookwood Cemetery. Now that they have been identified, arrangements for their reinterment need to be made."

"I see," she said again.

"I've spoken with Sir Arthur's son, and I believe he plans to have them moved to the family home in Kent. He'll likely call soon to discuss funeral arrangements." Whicher paused, then went on brusquely. "Again, please accept my condolences. I know this is a difficult time. I'll see myself out."

"Thank you for your concern, Inspector," Samantha said.

He bowed and took his leave. Samantha turned to Wyatt, her panic rising. "What do I do if they ask me where I've been all this time? I can't lie in court. And what if they find Palmer in time for the inquest and he recognizes me? He could reveal that I was a snakesman. And then Skinny Jim would know who I was, too."

"It was always a possibility," Wyatt said, running a hand over his face, "but I hoped a confession would preclude a trial with witnesses called up. It might be time we told Prescott the truth."

"What?" Samantha exclaimed. "Why?"

"He's next of kin. I don't know what kind of influence that will grant him, but certainly more than mine or even yours. He may be able to push for a speedy inquest or claim satisfaction with the facts as they are. Or there may be a legal way we can keep you from testifying. I have friends in the profession I can speak to."

Samantha sighed. "I'll talk to Charles. Let's see what he can do before we try other avenues."

Charles arrived later that afternoon. Many of the reporters had given up and gone to seek other, more cooperative subjects, but there were still a few to question him as he walked up the steps.

"What parasites they are," he commented as he handed Mrs. Hexam his hat and cane.

"Indeed," Mrs. Hexam sniffed.

"It is much improved from earlier," Samantha explained as she led him into the parlor. "There are not half so many as there were this morning."

"I've had just as many following me around the city all day," he said, settling into a chair and taking the teacup she handed him. "Asking the most impertinent questions and making it difficult to get anything done. I'll be glad when the fuss has died down, and we can live in peace."

"The inspector was here earlier," Samantha said. "He told me you are reburying your father and my aunt in Kent."

"I am," Charles said solemnly. "It's what my father would have wanted, to be brought back home. The funeral will be well attended, with all of this attention, and I am sure he would have been happy with that, as well."

"I know he would have been," she said with a wry smile.

"I would like your help," Charles said. "If I may. I have no experience with hosting. I don't know how to begin arranging it."

Samantha hesitated. Returning to Kent as Charles' hostess might be seen by some as a sign of their intention to marry. On the other hand, it was her aunt's and uncle's funeral, and what could be more natural than that she would be hosting it?

"I am sure I have even less experience than you," she said, "but I will offer what services I can. It should take place without delay, and I think people will understand if it's less than it ought to be under the circumstances."

"Yes," he said gravely. "The circumstances. Did the inspector also make you aware of the inquest?"

"He did, and that is something that concerns me, Charles."

"It's just a formality."

"I know, but I will be under oath and there are some things —"

"Say no more," he said, holding up a hand. "I don't want to force your confidence. I understand. I'll do my best to see that you are not needed to testify."

"Thank you," she said with relief, surprised, but glad he had not pressed her for details.

FIFTEEN

The funeral was set for Thursday. Invitations were sent out to all of Sir Arthur's and Aunt Victoria's friends and family, and not one person declined. To Samantha's relief, Madge seemed to take it for granted that she would be continuing as Samantha's companion until a replacement could be found. The two of them traveled to Kent on Monday to prepare for the event.

Hampton House, Sir Arthur's estate, was a neat Georgian mansion, square and symmetrical, surrounded by equally symmetrical gardens. As the carriage rattled towards it, Samantha was surprised to note how ordinary it looked. Those whitewashed walls that had once seemed to mock her in her misery were just flat and dull. The hedgerows that had hemmed her in were simply unimaginative landscaping.

"It certainly makes an impression," Madge said, leaning out the window as they came up the drive. "I can see why you prefer Derbyshire."

"What do you mean?" Samantha asked.

Madge pulled her head back in and grimaced. "It's too tame. It's been beaten back by man and forced into an unnatural shape. I'm all for a lovely English garden, but this"—she swept an arm out to indicate the park— "this is too French."

Samantha laughed, but she thought privately how rightly Madge had described what she hated about the place, and the man who had ruled it.

Andrews opened the door for them as the carriage pulled to a stop, and his normally placid face stretched into a wide smile.

"Miss Kingston," he said. "I can't tell you how relieved we are to see you safe and well. We've been so worried."

"I'm sorry I was unable to get word to you sooner," Samantha said, surprised to feel a tightness in her throat. It meant more than she would have thought to see him again.

"I understand why you could not."

He didn't, of course, but she accepted his words with a grateful smile.

"If you will follow me," he continued. "I'll lead you to your rooms."

Her old room had been made ready for her. She hesitated on the threshold as an odd sensation of going back in time settled over her. The last time she had been in this room, Sir Arthur and Aunt Victoria had been alive and she had been fretting about her upcoming Season.

As she stepped inside, she had barely a second to note that nothing in the room appeared to have changed, when Alice ran forward and threw her arms around her.

"I was so worried for you!" Alice exclaimed as she squeezed the breath from Samantha's lungs.

She froze just then, and Samantha knew what she was thinking. It was a line she had never crossed before. Though they had always been close and though she had been witness to some of Samantha's darkest moments, offering what comfort she could, Alice had maintained the distance proper to a master/servant relationship, never presuming to treat Samantha as an equal.

Samantha hesitated only a moment before putting her arms around her and returning the embrace. They stood holding each other for a long while, not saying a word. When they finally broke apart, Samantha wiped tears from her eyes and saw Alice do the same.

"Now, miss, come sit down," Alice said, walking over to the dressing table. "Your hair looks a fright. And we need to get you out of those clothes. You're covered in soot from the train."

There was not as much to do as Samantha had feared. The estate staff, being well-used to hosting events of all sizes, were equipped to handle the funeral almost without her help. She chose the menu from a list of options brought to her by the cook. Madge helped her with the seating arrangements and the hiring of extra staff to cater the event. Though the funeral would not take more than a few hours, many of the guests were staying the night, so rooms were made up, linen aired and firewood chopped.

Throughout the week, Samantha kept in communication with Charles, who had stayed behind in the city, dealing with the legal matters surrounding his father's estate. She couldn't, in all propriety, write to Wyatt, and she was afraid to ask Madge, lest she misconstrue her intentions, so she did not know how he fared or what he had been doing.

The day of the funeral was bright and clear. She wished it had been cloudy and dark to reflect her mood. It was strange to see so much sun as she slipped into her heavy black crepe mourning gown.

While Alice arranged her hair, she watched her reflection in the mirror, her pale features even paler with the stark contrast of black. It felt as though she had been in mourning for half her life. First, with her parents, then her grandfather, now her aunt and uncle. At least it couldn't go on, she thought darkly. She had no one left to mourn.

The image of tiny gravestones, those of her baby siblings, floated into her mind, and she wondered what it would have been like if they had lived. Would they be sharing these burdens with her now? Would she even be in the position she was? Two of the babies had been boys.

She sighed as Alice twisted a lock of her hair, pinning it back.

"It won't be so bad, miss," Alice said. "At least you won't be expected to attend the interment."

"True," Samantha conceded. "Small comfort, since it means I will be forced to entertain those who remain behind."

"They won't expect you to be cheerful."

Cheerful, no. No one would expect that. And she wasn't cheerful, but she wasn't sad, either. Was she wrong to feel that way? Sir Arthur had been an overwhelming, menacing presence in her life and, though Aunt Victoria had not joined in his cruelties, she hadn't protected Samantha, either. It had taken returning to Hampton House to fully feel their absence, but now, it was as though the pillow that had been pressed into her nose and mouth, suffocating her for six years, had finally been removed and she could breathe again.

It would be an unusual funeral. Sir Arthur and Lady Prescott had been dead too long to lay them out for the guests to view. Instead, there was to be a small reception for close friends and family in the drawing room before the service. After the service would be a dinner for family and overnight guests, then the interment after dark. It would be a long day, made all the worse by the fact that she would be forced to endure the insincere condolences while wearing a black crepe monstrosity in the heat of August.

As Samantha descended the stairs on her way to the drawing room for the reception, Charles stood at the bottom awaiting her. He had arrived the night before, but they hadn't had much time to talk.

"Samantha." He held out a gloved hand. She took it, allowing him to lead her to the drawing room. As they walked, he leaned over and said in a low voice, "You look lovely, as ever."

She scrunched up her nose and frowned. She was not given to humility when it came to her appearance. She knew she was pretty, but she also knew how frightful she looked in black. The compliment, therefore, felt hollow, and she was disappointed in Charles. The insincerity was unworthy of him. She thanked him, however, as propriety demanded, and he smiled.

"Are you ready for the vultures?" he whispered as Andrews showed them where to stand to receive the guests.

Samantha smiled but, at the same time, felt panic rise within her. No, she was not ready. She wished they would all go back home and leave her in peace. But they had to be faced.

Madge entered just then. She came to stand on Samantha's other side and squeezed her hand.

"There are bound to be some people who are actually sad," she said, lowering her voice so Charles could not hear. "Focus on them and ignore the rest. They only want a story to tell later. Make it as boring as possible."

"It is only a funeral," Samantha said, as though saying so would make it true.

"If only I had thought to sell tickets, rather than issue invitations," Charles said, reading her thoughts.

Madge laughed. "That's the spirit."

There was a knock at the front door. Samantha tensed, and Charles squeezed her hand.

"Just breathe," he said.

The reception was a blur and an experience Samantha wanted never to be repeated. The receiving line was endless. Though she recognized some family members, most of them Sir Arthur's, she was introduced to many people she had never met, all claiming friendship with her uncle. Though most faces were somber, few were sad. Following Madge's advice, she focused on the sad mourners, mostly friends of her aunt, but even doing that, she soon tired of the outpourings of sympathy and lamentations.

When the receiving line ended, the guests mingled in the drawing room, talking in low voices and nibbling on hors d'oeuvres. Their eyes never seemed to leave Samantha, though, and no matter where she stood, she was unable to escape the scrutiny. She felt utterly exposed.

Samantha thought that Charles would have understood, if she could have spoken to him, but every time she escaped a conversation, he was deeply entrenched in another. If only Wyatt had been there, Samantha would have confided in him, but he had yet to arrive. Overwhelmed, she excused herself and left the room. She hurried down the hall and entered the library, shutting the door behind her.

The room was unoccupied. She walked to the fireplace and sat in one of the comfortable armchairs beside it. She had often escaped to this room as a child and from it to endless worlds of adventure and wonder. She felt comforted by its dark wood and dusty smell.

The door opened and Samantha jumped up. To her surprise, it was Wyatt who entered, shutting the door softly behind him.

"What are you doing here?" she asked as he made his way across the room to her.

"Good day to you too," he said with a half smile, taking her hand and kissing it. "I only just arrived and I saw you come in here, so I followed you."

"Would you like to sit down?" She gestured to the chair across from hers.

"Thank you."

They sat. She experienced a sudden awkwardness in his

presence. They weren't in his house anymore. This was her world, and it was odd to see him in it. Wyatt, however, seemed to feel none of her discomfort. He leaned his head back and sighed.

"I hate trains," he said conversationally. "So smelly and loud. I have such a headache from the jostling."

Samantha felt a sudden surge of annoyance. She had expected him hours earlier. She had wanted his support in that awful reception. For him to wander in without so much as an apology was insupportable.

"You're late," she said sharply.

He looked up, and she thought she saw a flash of guilt in his expression, but he schooled his features.

"I'm sorry. I had some business that took longer than I anticipated. I didn't mean to be late."

Samantha narrowed her eyes. "What business?"

He huffed in an irritated manner, and she was certain of the guilt this time.

"Not all my business concerns you, you know."

"Then why do I have the suspicion that this does?"

His mouth twitched and he looked away.

"Wyatt…" Samantha said, drawing out the vowels in his name as she stared him down.

"I'll tell you about it later," he said. Then, when she appeared unconvinced, he added, "I promise. Now isn't the time."

She frowned and turned her gaze to the empty fireplace, staring at it with unfocused eyes.

"How are you feeling?"

She had heard that question so many times that day and yet, for once, it sounded sincere. "I don't know," she admitted. "Mostly tired, I think. Exhausted, really. Ready to be done."

She looked up to gauge his reaction and was relieved to see concern rather than judgment. Perhaps that was why she said what she did.

"I hated him."

It was the first time she had spoken the words aloud, and she was unable to stop herself from flinching, as though his spirit would fly out of the empty flue and slap her for her insolence. Wyatt didn't look shocked at her words, but she thought she saw pity, and she didn't want that, either.

"I don't know if anyone really liked him," she said. "Certainly no one out there did." She nodded towards the drawing room.

"I did hear some crying," Wyatt said.

"That will have been Lady Morley, my aunt's friend," Samantha said with a wry smile. "She has always been a bit melodramatic, but I believe she did genuinely care for Aunt Victoria."

"What made you come in here?"

"I needed a break from all the staring," she said. "I've never been more self-conscious. I was sure I was going to spill my drink or catch my dress on a nail and rip it in view of fifty people."

"That would have been a shame," Wyatt said, a glint of humor in his eye. "It's such an…elegant dress."

"It's horrible, isn't it?"

"I wouldn't say horrible, but…" he trailed off, and she grinned.

"It's the latest in mourning fashion, I am told," she said, smoothing her hands over the skirt, which crinkled loudly. "Madge's modiste had it made up especially for the funeral."

"Did she tell her it was for a mourner? Because she might have thought it was for the corpse."

Samantha gasped and tried to look outraged but could not hold her countenance. Wyatt started to laugh, and she joined him. The happy moment was cut short, however, when a sound in the hallway recalled them to their senses.

"We shouldn't be in here," Samantha said, watching the door for signs that it was opening. "If we're caught…"

"Is there another entrance?"

She nodded. "You go out that door." She pointed to the one he had come through. "I'll take this one."

She went to the bookcase and found the catch that opened the hidden door. She pulled it, and the bookcase slid open, revealing the room beyond—a little-used sitting room. Before she had taken a step into it, Wyatt caught her arm.

"I'm sorry," he said, the intensity of his expression drawing her eyes to his. "I'm sorry for all of it, but I want you to know, you're going to be alright."

"I know."

"I'm not being trite," he insisted. "I mean it. No matter what happens. You are remarkable, and you're going to get through this the same way you've managed everything else—with determination and poise—and they're going to see it."

He released her and walked away before she could respond to his unexpected statement. Opening the library door, he peered into the hall, then left the room, shutting the door behind him.

The ceremony was blessedly short. Samantha wore a veil over her face, more usual in a widow than a niece, but she wanted a shield between her and all the glances directed her way. Charles sat beside her and held her hand and she appreciated his strong presence. When it was over, those guests who were not close friends and family left in a parade of carriages, and Samantha and Charles presided over the evening meal. She wished she could have been veiled then, too, but that would have been impractical, so she was forced to sip her soup with the awareness of twenty-odd pairs of eyes on her.

It was with relief that she announced the end of the meal, and everyone gathered outside to see the funeral procession on its way. Charles and a few of his cousins were the pallbearers, and there were several carriages and a couple of mutes bringing up the rear. Sir Arthur would have been proud to see the honor given him in death, though she doubted it would have been quite so much had he died of something more mundane, like gout.

The remaining guests, most of them ladies, retired to the drawing room. It seemed wrong to resort to the usual entertainments of cards or music, so people paired off for somber, hushed conversations. The sounds of so many whispers traveling around the room made Samantha's ears hurt, as though she were being forced to listen to a concert made up entirely of whistlers. She moved herself to a seat near the door, as far away as she could be from anyone else. Madge came to sit beside her.

"I'm here to convey a message," she said, leaning forward, her voice low. "From Wyatt. He says, 'Now's the time'." She rolled her eyes. "Unnecessarily cryptic, if you ask me. I'm sure he means to tell you whatever it is he's been up to since we left. I get the feeling it's important. I suggest you pretend to fall ill, and I'll help you out and take you to him."

Samantha nodded, happy for any excuse to leave the whisper room, but especially glad to know what secrets Wyatt had been keeping. She put her hands to her temple and massaged it, and Madge immediately became solicitous so that it was only a few minutes before they were able to justify a departure. Madge made her excuses while Samantha looked pained. Through slitted eyes, she saw several looks of sympathy directed her way, though a few were laced with suspicion.

Once in the hall, she dropped her hands to her sides and followed Madge to the library. Wyatt stood waiting for them, his brow furrowed.

"I'll be just over there," Madge said, touching Samantha's arm and pointing to a table at the far end of the long room. Samantha nodded and went to Wyatt.

"Well?" she said when he did not immediately speak.

"Let's sit down."

He gestured to the chairs they had occupied earlier, and she took a seat, wincing as the crepe crunched beneath her. It really was a grating sound. Perhaps she was getting a headache after all.

"You thought it odd, too, did you not," Wyatt said, watching her closely, "that Cyril would do what he did?"

She frowned. "I told you as much at the time. But the note was in his handwriting."

He shifted. "The one found beside him was, yes, but there was another note, it seems, which wasn't."

"What are you talking about?"

"Inspector Whicher arrested a man yesterday," Wyatt said, looking down at his hands. "It was Palmer."

She gasped.

"He claims," Wyatt continued, looking up at her, "that he had nothing to do with the murder of your aunt and uncle."

"He's lying. There were definitely two men there that night."

Wyatt nodded. "Oh, he's not disputing that. He's not even disputing the attempted abduction of you. Either of them."

"What?" Samantha asked skeptically. "He's saying he was with his partner all the other times but not during the murder? Naturally, he wouldn't want to admit to a murder."

"He has admitted to a murder," Wyatt said.

"What murder?" she asked, confused. Then, with dawning comprehension, she breathed, "Cyril?"

Wyatt nodded again.

"But why would he admit to murdering Cyril? How did he do it? How did he get Cyril to write the note? Or is he also a forger?"

"He's not a forger. He doesn't know how to write. And he admitted to murdering Cyril because he claims he can give the police a worse offender than himself, in exchange for a reduction in his sentence. Deportation instead of hanging."

"Worse offender?" Samantha closed her eyes and held up a hand to stop him talking. She wanted to make sense of what he was saying. If Cyril was murdered, why? Was it because he'd done all the things he said he had done, and the men he hired wanted to keep him from revealing their identities? But then who was this worse offender?

She opened her eyes. "Does he say why he killed Cyril?"

"He says he was hired to do it. He claims that the gentleman who hired him wrote a note for him to force Cyril to copy, which he was then to burn. He threatened Cyril with the deaths of his wife and son if he didn't copy the note. In exchange for the murder, Palmer was to have been given money to flee the country and start a new life in America."

"Gentleman?"

Wyatt sighed and scrubbed his face with his hand, letting it fall back into his lap. "I think I was wrong. I found out about your inheritance, and I thought that had to be the reason. After all, you were the one nearly abducted and it was only luck that got you out of that house without being shot. Assuming you were the target all along made me discount anyone who didn't have a motive related to you specifically. I thought the blackmail was a diversion."

"And you don't anymore?" she asked, her apprehension growing.

He stood up and walked to the fireplace, leaning one hand against it and staring into the empty grate. "I want you to know that I wouldn't be telling you this if I didn't think there was strong evidence to support it."

"Telling me what?"

He turned to her, his jaw tight. "Palmer says Charles told him to kill Cyril. Charles killed your aunt and uncle."

SIXTEEN

Samantha stared at him. She could hear the seconds ticking by on the clock above the mantle. Four seconds. Five. Six. Then she breathed in—she hadn't realized she'd been holding her breath—and said, in a tone much sharper than her usual, "What?"

"Think about it, Samantha," he said, returning to his seat and leaning forward, elbows on his knees. "You know he gambles. And you know his father cut him off. If he got in deep enough, he would have needed the money. He could have written those blackmail notes, hoping to get something from his father without his knowing. Then, when that didn't work and he got desperate, he staged your abduction to get ransom money. When that didn't work, he went to the house—"

"And what?" Samantha interrupted. "Shot his father?"

"Yes," Wyatt said with maddening patience. "With his father dead, he inherits. He can pay off his debts. It makes sense."

"No, it doesn't," Samantha objected hotly. "The person you're describing, this person who acts selfishly and recklessly, that's not Charles."

"How do you know?" Wyatt asked, his voice even. "You haven't seen him in years. People change."

"No, they don't," she insisted. "Not as much as people like to think. Who they are in here"—she pointed to her chest— "doesn't change. And Charles is a good man. He defends those who can't protect themselves. He would never do anything to put me in that kind of danger. Never."

She stood up, breathing heavily, feeling the suffocating weight of the fabric that clung to her more tightly than she would have liked in that heat.

"Samantha…" Wyatt began, but she held up a hand. She didn't want to hear any more. Especially because, despite her defense of Charles, a small part of her could see the merit in Wyatt's argument.

"I have to go," she said, and she hurried out of the room before he could stop her.

*****

Wyatt watched her leave, wanting to call after her, but knowing it would be pointless.

"Well, that could have gone better," Madge said, walking towards him.

Wyatt grunted.

"Do you really think it was him?" she asked in a more serious tone.

"I admit that I don't have an answer for everything yet." He blew out a breath. "There's a lot that doesn't match up, but then a lot of questions I had make sense if he's the answer."

"What are you planning to do?"

"Palmer—the man in custody—gave us the note he claims Prescott gave him for Lord Etwall to copy. If I can get something in Prescott's hand, we can compare the two. It won't help with charging him for the other murders, but it should go a long way to convicting him for his part in Lord Etwall's."

Madge looked thoughtful. "He's been writing back and forth to Samantha all week. I don't know if she kept his letters, but I could find out."

Wyatt winced. "I don't know if that's a good idea."

"I'm not going to ask her for them," Madge said with an exasperated huff. "Trust me. I can be subtle."

He quirked an eyebrow. "You? Subtle?"

She tapped him playfully with her fan. "Don't be disrespectful. I am your elder. Now, run along. I'll be back down with your evidence before you're ready to leave."

*****

Samantha sat at her dressing table waiting for Alice to come help her out of her awful dress. The face that reflected back to her was a sight to see. Her skin was ghostly white and her eyes, red-rimmed and glassy, were almost nightmarish. There was a knock at the door, and she hastily wiped her eyes with the back of her hand.

"Come in," she said.

"I thought you might like some tea," said Madge. She stepped aside as a housemaid carrying a tray with a pot and two cups entered, laid them on the table, and left.

"Thank you," Samantha said, managing a weak smile.

Madge poured the tea into the cups and handed one to Samantha.

"You've had a long day," she said sympathetically.

"Yes," Samantha agreed. She wasn't in the mood for conversation so she sipped her tea, pretending more thirst than she felt. To her relief, Madge seemed to sense her feelings.

"I won't keep you," she said. "I did hope I might borrow some paper, though. I've run out, and I need to write to my husband."

Samantha nodded and gestured to her writing desk. "Take as

much as you like."

There was a creak and the sound of paper shuffling, then the tap of the lid shutting.

"Thank you, dear." Madge joined her at the mirror and smiled sadly down at her. "It will be alright," she said, and she kissed the top of Samantha's head.

When she had gone, Samantha closed her eyes and massaged her temples. Wyatt's accusations filled her mind. No matter how hard she tried, she could not dismiss them. A seed of doubt had been planted in her heart and she hated herself for it. She hated Wyatt for putting it there.

Charles was not the blackmailer. He could not be the blackmailer. He was her friend. He had cared for her when no one else had. The last two months had been terrible. He would not have done that to her. He wouldn't have lied to her.

She thought back to their meeting at the masquerade. He had been happy to see her, of that she was sure. And he hadn't believed her when she told him his father was dead. He had been shocked. Or had that all been an act?

Samantha banged her fist on the table. No. She would not doubt him. He had always supported her. She would do the same for him.

And yet, he hadn't supported her when she wanted to postpone informing the police. He had pushed her, argued against her. She had thought at the time that he didn't understand her fears, that he thought he was acting in her best interests, despite her wishes. But if what Wyatt had said was true, if he killed his father for the money, he would need him declared dead to access it. He would need the police involved.

Samantha pushed her chair back and stood up. As she paced the room, she searched her memory for absolute proof of Charles' innocence or, though her feelings balked, his guilt. She couldn't find any one way or the other. Every interaction, every conversation, could be explained to satisfy either conclusion.

Charles was a good man, she reminded herself. And even if he hadn't been, it was only right that he be presumed innocent until he was proven to be guilty. She did not consider the word of a criminal, scrambling to save his own skin as Palmer was, to be proof.

She slept fitfully that night and when she woke, early, her eyes were still red-rimmed, though from lack of sleep rather than crying. She did not engage Alice in conversation as she dressed, and she went down to breakfast in a haze of exhaustion.

Madge wasn't there, having gone for her morning ride, but Charles was. The other guests were presumably still in bed.

Samantha watched him as she sat down. She had half expected him to look different, and the fact that he wore the same smile he always did when he saw her made her feel more confused than ever.

"Are you well?" he asked, his voice tinged with concern.

"I'm tired," she said. "I didn't sleep well last night."

"I'm sorry. Would you like some coffee?"

"No, thank you. Tea will do fine."

She rubbed her eyes and leaned forward to reach the toast rack. As she sat back, she discovered that she had trailed her sleeve through the jam. With a grunt of frustration, she scrubbed at the spot with a napkin.

"I have to return to London this afternoon," Charles said, oblivious to her struggle as he read through the mail. He looked up as she set her napkin down. "I hoped I might have the pleasure of your company before I leave. A stroll through the gardens after luncheon, perhaps?"

"I…yes. That would be lovely."

She wondered whether she ought to have refused him and

immediately felt guilty for the thought. Hadn't she just decided to presume his innocence? To rely on what she knew of his character?

And yet, though she hadn't known Wyatt as long as Charles or even very long at all, she knew enough of his character to know he wouldn't have taken the accusations against Charles lightly. Nor would he have brought them to her unless he believed they had merit, knowing how important Charles was to her.

Samantha spent the morning in the music room, avoiding everyone. It had been so long since she had been near a piano that she lost herself in the experience of playing and was unaware of the time until Andrews called her to bid farewell to the guests. There followed nearly an hour of awkward embracing, strained smiles, and numerous invitations to visit once the mourning period was over. She was relieved when the last guest left and luncheon was announced. Conversation was stilted. Madge seemed less vibrant than usual, and Samantha wondered if she was tired of following her around. No doubt the letter to her husband had her missing home more than ever. Samantha determined to start the process of finding a more permanent companion once Charles had left that afternoon. She might even ask him to take a few letters to London for her.

"Shall we?" Charles asked when the meal had ended. He stood up and held out a hand.

"Shall we what?" Madge asked.

"Charles and I are going for a walk around the gardens," Samantha said, joining him. She hadn't spoken with Madge since the night before, but she knew Madge must be surprised to see her go out alone with Charles after what Wyatt had said, so she added, "You can see them from the south window. We won't be gone long."

Madge frowned, but she could not deny the propriety of the venture, so she let them leave.

"I was worried she was going to insist on joining us," Charles whispered as they walked down the long hall to the back of the house.

"I'm sure she's happy not to have to," Samantha assured him. "I fear she's growing bored of me."

"I find that hard to believe."

Samantha offered him a strained smile and put up a hand, squinting her eyes against the sunlight as they stepped outside. Charles led them down the path, past the kitchen garden, and into the ornamental gardens. Though not as beautiful as when they were in full bloom, the gardens of Hampton House were still a pleasure to behold, and Samantha breathed in the fresh air.

"Samantha," Charles said, stopping in front of an ivy-covered fountain. He turned to face her, shifting his weight from one foot to the other and clenching his jaw. "There is something I need to tell you."

She waited, but it was a moment before he spoke again.

"We've known each other a long time," he began finally. "I made you a promise once, one that I broke rather badly when I left home."

She started to respond, but he held up a hand.

"It has always been one of my biggest regrets that I left you to my father. I knew you needed me, but I was more worried about myself than anyone else. I told myself that I would make up for it one day. I don't know how I thought I would do that—how I thought I *could* do that. Recently, however, I have begun to hope that you might allow me to try."

He gave her a sad, almost shy smile. Charles was never shy. Samantha felt a sense of foreboding.

"I love you, Samantha," he said. "I love your kindness, your wit, your vivacity. I've never known anyone like you. I want you to be my wife."

She didn't know what to say. She had known he liked her, had sensed his attraction to her, but she had not expected this.

Charles laughed nervously, watching her face. "Will you? Be my wife, I mean."

"I…"

The silence stretched out between them. He looked down at his feet and kicked out at the pebbles that lined the path.

"I understand," he said.

"No," she said hastily, hating the sadness in his expression. "It's just—this is so sudden."

"I thought I had made my feelings clear," he said, looking up with a frown.

"Not to me," she said. "I had no idea of your intentions. But even if I had…" She paused, trying to sort through her jumbled thoughts. She brushed aside her doubts about his innocence and focused on how she would feel if Wyatt had never planted them in her mind. "Even if I had known what you intended, I would be unsure how to answer. So much has happened in such a short time. With Sir Arthur and Aunt Victoria killed and discovering my inheritance, and then Cyril—"

"You can't think I want to marry you for your money," he interrupted, and he was so earnest that she laughed.

"I don't," she said. "But I need time to recover from all that has happened."

"We can recover together," he insisted, taking her hands in his.

She frowned. He didn't understand. He thought he had all the answers, but he wasn't listening to her.

"There's something you should know," she said, before she could stop herself.

"What?" he asked with a smile.

She hesitated. But Charles would learn sooner or later what he was being accused of. If he was innocent, it was better coming from a friend. And if he wasn't, she deserved to hear it from him.

"Mr. Wyatt brought some news with him yesterday," she said.

His smile disappeared. "What did he want?"

"He said that Inspector Whicher has made an arrest."

"An arrest?" Was she imagining it, or did he look wary? "Yes. A man named Palmer. The partner of that man who was killed earlier."

He stilled.

"Apparently, he denies that he was with his partner when Sir Arthur and Aunt Victoria were murdered. He claims he was innocent."

Charles said nothing, and the wisps of doubt that had settled in Samantha's heart since her conversation with Wyatt began to swirl and grow.

"He's made a lot of claims," she continued, uncomfortably aware of her hands, still held in his. She tried to pull away, but he held tight.

"Like what?" he asked, his voice raspy.

"Well, he says he was there during both of my attempted abductions," she said lightly.

"And?"

He watched her, his eyes boring into hers with an intensity she hadn't seen in him before. Her doubts solidified.

"Tell me he's wrong," she pleaded, her voice barely a whisper.

He blanched, and a series of emotions flitted across his face so rapidly, she barely registered them. What he settled on, finally, was panic, and her heart sank.

"He's wrong," he said hoarsely as he dropped her hands and stepped back. "Whatever he says, it's a lie. He's a criminal, a liar."

"He has a note, Charles. A note you wrote."

He went even paler as he stared at her, wide-eyed. "It was an accident," he said, running a hand over his mouth. "You have to believe me."

"What was an accident?" she asked, the pitch of her voice rising. "What part of it was an accident?"

"My father," he said. "I only meant to scare him, but he recognized me through the disguise, and he mocked me. He called me a wastrel and a good for nothing and said he should have guessed only I would come up with such a ridiculous scheme and I got so angry I…"

"And my aunt?" she asked in horror.

"She screamed," he said, turning hollow eyes to her. "I panicked. I knew I would hang."

Samantha sank onto the edge of the fountain. Charles knelt down in front of her.

"It was an accident," he said earnestly. "I swear."

"How did you even know we were there?" she asked.

"Palmer and his partner Slater have a lot of friends across the city. They found you."

"But why? Why any of it? Why the blackmail?"

He sighed and lowered his head. "I lost a lot of money. Money I didn't have. It's happened before, but this time I lost it to some dangerous people." He looked up at her, his eyes seeking reassurance she was unable to give. "When I told them I couldn't pay, they were going to kill me, to set an example. I begged them not to. I told them I could get the money out of my father. But he wouldn't respond to the notes I sent him."

"They weren't very specific," Samantha said. "He didn't think they were much of a threat."

He groaned and stood up. "I know. I should have approached him differently. Then, when he failed to respond, the man I owed money to—"

"Skinny Jim," Samantha supplied.

"How did you—"

"We met."

He gave her a long, searching look. "Then you know what he's like. He said we had to threaten my father. He said he would send people to abduct you."

"Why did you let him?" she asked in a small voice.

"What choice did I have?" He scrubbed his face with his hands and started pacing in front of her. "They swore they wouldn't hurt you."

"And you believed them?" she asked incredulously.

"I wanted to. Look, I know it was bad, but it was going to be quick, and then I'd hand over the money and it would all be over. Only, it failed, and my father whisked you all away. It took days to track him down. When we did, Skinny Jim insisted I take Slater with me. We would hold my father at gunpoint until he gave me what I needed. Except, well, you know."

Samantha stood up and began to walk away, then rounded on him. "And after all that, you thought it was a good idea to propose to me?"

"Yes." He tried to take her hands again but she pulled away.

"Things are different now," he said. "I can support you. You're free of my father. And it's not as though anyone mourned him."

"You're forgetting about Cyril," she said hotly. "He had a wife and a son. You let them believe he killed himself. I suppose you thought you could put the blame on him and go your merry way? And what about my aunt? And Mrs. Dunbar, the housekeeper? And Slater? Did you shoot him too?"

"He was a criminal, Samantha," Charles said. "He robbed people and beat them. He abducted you. He hit you."

"Yes, he did," she said, her voice rising. "That was after I met you again, when you were pretending not to know what had happened. You were behind that, too, weren't you?"

"I needed to convince you the situation was dire enough to involve the police," he said, throwing up his hands. "I needed my father declared dead so I could claim my inheritance and pay Skinny Jim. He'd been forcing me to help Slater and Palmer rob people I knew to pay him back. I couldn't keep doing that."

"You were responsible for the robberies?" Samantha asked, momentarily distracted.

"I gave Slater information about when people would be away from home and what I knew about their houses and jewels. That's all. I didn't want to, but I was forced to." He looked at her with pleading eyes. "That's why it was so important that I got my inheritance—so I could stop."

"And you were happy to sacrifice me in the process?"

"No," he said vehemently. "Never. Slater wasn't supposed to hurt you, just scare you enough to go to the police. When I saw what he did to you—" He broke off and ran a hand over his face. "I confronted him about it and he attacked me. That's why I shot him. I was defending myself. And you."

"No." Samantha jabbed her finger at him. "Don't you blame any of your actions on me. How could you do that to me, Charles? I was scared to death. He might have killed me."

"I'm sorry, Samantha. I truly am. I was in so deep I didn't know how to get out. I made some horrible decisions. And I hate what that did to you."

"Do you?" Samantha said, her voice thick with emotion, blinking back the hot, angry tears that welled up in her eyes. "Do you even know what that did to me? Do you know what it's doing to me now? To know that my oldest friend put my life in danger to save his own? That he killed five people? Do you know what it's doing to me?" She choked out a sob. "You're breaking my heart, Charles."

She collapsed back down on the fountain, her whole body

shaking.

"I am so sorry," Charles said, sitting beside her. "If I could take it all back, I would. I never meant any of it to happen."

He reached into his pocket and drew out a handkerchief, handing it to her. She took it automatically and dabbed her eyes.

"Come with me," he said in a soft voice. "We can go to America. I have a cousin in New York who will take us in until we're on our feet. Let me fix this."

The hand holding the handkerchief stilled and she turned to stare at him, her mouth agape. It was several seconds before she could form any response.

"Fix this?" she said finally. "Fix this? You've killed five people, Charles. You're a murderer."

"And if I stay here, I'll hang." His eyes searched hers. "You can't want that for me. You have to help me."

"Have to?" She scoffed. "Why? Because of our friendship? The one you valued so highly?"

He frowned. "You won't help me?"

"How could you even ask me that?"

He stood and started pacing again, a wild, panicked look in his eye.

"It won't work, Charles," she said, trying to calm him with her voice. "Wyatt knows. Inspector Whicher knows. They'll come for you."

"Yes, they will." He glanced at her, and then at the house. "But they can't find me if I'm not here. I know running is the coward's way—not very English—but I don't seem to have much of a choice."

"How will you get to America?" Samantha asked. "As soon as the police know you've run, they'll be searching the ports and the train stations."

"I'll buy myself as much time as I can." He looked back at her and she was startled by the blandness of his expression. The panic had gone from his eyes and what remained was an emptiness. "I'll start by making sure you don't send them after me."

"What do you mean?" She stood and backed slowly away from him.

He watched her with the same bland expression, all emotion gone.

"You can't do anything to me here," she said, trying to keep the tremor from her voice. "We're in full view of the house. Madge or any of the servants could be looking out right now."

"It's a good thing I brought this then." He pulled a revolver from his inner coat pocket.

Samantha froze. "You've been carrying that this whole time?"

"I'm always carrying it."

"Charles," Samantha said breathlessly, as she watched him check the cylinder with an air of cool indifference. "What are you doing? This isn't like you."

He looked up and their eyes met. His were cold and hard and she could see no trace of her friend in them.

"Now," he said, holding out a hand to her. "I want you to come over to me and take my arm. We're going for a walk."

*****

The train ride back to Kent was one of the longest of Wyatt's life. No one spoke. Inspector Whicher was reading the newspaper, and the three constables he'd brought with him stared stoically ahead. Wyatt gazed out the window, swaying with the motion of the carriage. The handwriting on the notes had matched. It wasn't conclusive proof, but Whicher was confident that he could use it to scare a confession out of Prescott. The constables were backup, in case he ran. Wyatt wished he could feel relief that it would all soon be over, but all he could think about was how upset Samantha would be. After everything she'd been through, this would be the biggest blow.

When they arrived at the station, Wyatt hired a gig for himself and Whicher. The constables hired horses. They would arrive separately, hiding themselves within sight of the house.

"What if he won't confess?" Wyatt asked, pulling on the reins to guide the horses around a bend in the road.

"He will."

"I wish I shared your confidence."

Whicher grunted. "When he has time to plan something it's theatrical—a bit overdone."

"Like the blackmail."

"Yes, and the murder of Cyril. When he doesn't have a plan, or his plans go awry, he panics. He's reactionary. If he's backed into a corner, he won't act rashly. I'll get a confession."

It made sense, Wyatt thought. However, the fact that Prescott was reactionary was less than comforting considering that he was currently at the house with Samantha. She had been quite upset at Wyatt's accusations the night before. He didn't think she would do anything foolish if she knew she was in danger, but if she believed Prescott innocent, she might feel it was her duty to warn him that Palmer had accused him. And if Prescott panicked… He'd already shown that he was willing to put her in danger to protect himself. Wyatt snapped the reins to hurry the horses along.

When they pulled up in front of the house, he jumped down and hurried to the door. The butler, Andrews, opened it, and Wyatt pushed past him.

"Is Samantha here?" he asked Madge, who had come to greet him.

"Where else would she be?" she asked, raising an eyebrow. "What happened? You're flushed."

"It's hot," Wyatt said. "I was in a hurry. Where is she?"

"In the gardens with Mr. Prescott. But don't worry, I've been watching them."

He hurried down the hall, Madge at his heels. When he got to the library, with its wide windows, he looked out, but he couldn't see any sign of Samantha or Prescott.

"They were just there," Madge said, leaning forward and squinting. "I've been checking every few minutes. You haven't answered my question. What's wrong?"

"It was a match," Wyatt said. "I've come with Inspector Whicher to confront him. But I'm worried Samantha may have said something to him of my suspicions, and he may have panicked."

Madge's eyes grew wide. "Well, they can't have gone far," she said, hurrying past him to the door. "They were on foot, after all. I'll gather the footmen—"

"No," Wyatt said firmly. "I don't know what he'll do if he feels cornered. He might hurt her. I'll go."

"Well then, take this." Madge ran to an ornate table and opened a drawer beneath it, pulling out an old, single-shot pistol.

"I found it the other day when I was looking for a pen," she said, handing it to him. "I couldn't find any ammunition or powder. It looks threatening enough, though."

"Thank you," Wyatt said, checking it over to confirm that it wasn't primed. "Inspector Whicher will be here soon. I left him to deal with the horses. Let him know where I've gone."

*****

"Where are you taking me?" Samantha asked as they trudged through the small woods behind the house, Charles' gun at her back.

"Do you remember that old well we found the year you arrived?"

She stumbled, and he grabbed her arm to steady her. She turned her head to look at him, her eyes wide.

"Please don't," she begged.

He looked down at her, and for a moment, she saw his expression soften. Then he clenched his jaw and his eyes became hardened again. "I don't have a choice."

"You always have a choice."

A vein pulsed in his temple as he regarded her, his expression unmoving. Out of the corner of her eye, she noticed the revolver was pointing uselessly at the ground. Seizing the opportunity, she twisted her body and slammed her left knee between his legs.

He released her immediately and fell to his knees. The gun dropped from his hands. She started to go for it, but she could see that he would beat her to it, so instead she ran. His curses followed her as she crashed through the underbrush.

"Stop!" he yelled. "I'll shoot!"

She ignored him. He had never been a good shot. As long as she could outrun him, she would be safe. A crack split the air, and her breathing hitched as she wondered, for a moment, if she'd been hit, but she didn't stop. Soon, different sounds came from behind her. Footsteps pounding across the damp ground, twigs snapping, leaves crunching. He must have given up on shooting and decided to run after her. She put on a spurt of speed. But then, just as she caught her first glimpse of the house in the distance, her skirt caught on a shrub and yanked her back.

She landed hard, knocking the breath from her lungs. Dazed, she struggled to rise, slipping on the muddy ground. Behind her, crunching leaves announced Charles' arrival. He grabbed at her wrist and yanked her up. She twisted away and he tackled her to the ground, pinning her arms beneath her. She could feel his breath on her neck and smelled sweat. Fear coursed through her and she thrashed wildly, desperate to escape. The weight of his body on hers was suffocating and she gasped for air.

"I've made my choice," he panted as she struggled against him. "I can't go back."

"Let her go."

Samantha twisted her head up to see Wyatt standing in front of them, an old, tarnished pistol trained on Charles. Her heart leapt at the sight. Charles lifted himself off of her and sat back. She pushed up onto her knees, panting. But then, faster than she would have believed possible, Charles grabbed her arm and yanked her back against him, the revolver pressed against her head.

"I don't think so," he said. "It looks like I won't be able to make my escape in secret anymore, so I suppose I'll have to take her with me to keep you from following."

"I'll shoot you first," Wyatt said evenly.

"With that?" Charles laughed. "Have you shot it before? You'd be as likely to shoot her as me. Are you willing to risk that?"

Wyatt's eyes flicked to Samantha. He lowered the gun.

"Now tell me," Charles said, digging his fingers into Samantha's arm. "You didn't come here by yourself, did you?"

Wyatt shook his head. "If you guessed that, then surely you must realize that you won't get away."

"I'll think of something," Charles said. "I always do."

He started walking around Wyatt, yanking Samantha with him, the gun still pointed at her head. She watched Wyatt's face as they went. His eyes flicked between her and Charles and the woods around them as though looking for something. Then he stilled, his gaze resting on a point behind her. His eyes flicked back to her and he jerked his head slightly, looking back at the spot. There must be someone there—a constable or the inspector—and Charles hadn't noticed yet. She knew whoever it was would be afraid to make a move while she was in peril. She considered her options. Sudden movement might set Charles off. She glanced down and saw a thick, broken branch below her. An idea formed.

"Charles," she said softly. "Charles, I think I'm going to be sick."

"Don't," he said gruffly.

"I can't help it. I…"

She made a convulsive movement and he let go of her immediately. She bent double and, as she did, she snatched up the branch and jabbed it behind her, up into his abdomen. He gasped and staggered back, and she hit the ground, rolling away. There were shouts and scuffling, and she heard running footsteps coming from all around. Pushing up onto her knees, she saw Charles being brought to the ground by Inspector Whicher and two constables.

"Are you hurt?" Wyatt asked, hurrying over and falling to his knees beside her. He grabbed her hands and turned them over, checking her for injuries.

"I'm fine," she said breathlessly, watching as Charles' arms were bent behind his back.

"Are you certain?"

He took her face in his hands and turned her to him. His eyes searched hers with an intensity that surprised her.

"Yes," she said. "He didn't hurt me."

He held her gaze for a moment longer. She thought he was about to say something, but then he stood and helped her to her feet. Nearby, the constables were doing the same to Charles, whose hands were now shackled, one to each constable. Inspector Whicher instructed them to take Charles to the house, then he made his way over to Wyatt and Samantha. As Charles was led away, he cast one last glance at Samantha. She could see the panic returned to his eyes.

"I want to thank you for your help," Inspector Whicher said. Samantha was only half paying attention, her eyes still on the retreating form of Charles. She wondered what was going through his mind. "Not just in this moment, but throughout, your cooperation has been invaluable. Both of you."

"Thank you," Wyatt said. "I apologize for my initial animosity. You're a good detective, Inspector. I hope this arrest might do something to restore some of your reputation. I'm beginning to think you must have been right about Miss Kent, as well."

Charles and the constables disappeared in the trees and Samantha returned her gaze to the inspector in time to see an ironic smile play across his lips.

"Are you indeed?" he said. "I appreciate the sentiment, but it will only really make a difference if we can get a conviction. That will be a harder road. I'll be counting on you both to testify."

Samantha nodded resignedly. She couldn't summon up the energy to be worried about the trial anymore. It hardly seemed to matter.

"I'll be in touch," Inspector Whicher said. "Usually, these proceedings take time, but with all the attention this case has gotten, I expect the trial will begin within the week."

He shook Wyatt's hand, tipped his hat to Samantha and set off back to the house, leaving the two of them alone.

They stood in silence for a moment. Samantha stared up at the tall, narrow trees, watching their upper branches sway gently in the breeze. She closed her eyes as a small gust of wind blew her disordered curls across her face, and she sighed.

"I want to apologize for last night," she said. "I shouldn't have doubted you." She glanced at Wyatt, then returned her gaze to the trees. "You were right. And I was so very, very wrong."

"There's no need to apologize," he said evenly. "He was your friend, your family. It's only natural you would defend him."

"Wrongly, as it happens," she said, her voice breaking with barely suppressed emotion. "He did it. You were right; people change." She sighed again and looked back at him. He watched her with a serious expression. She put on a false smile and went on in a lighter voice. "We should get back before Madge wonders what has become of us."

Wyatt held out an arm, and she took it out of politeness, though in that moment she didn't want to be near another person, much less touch one. She wanted to run and scream and rail against the injustice of the universe.

"I think you're wrong," he said, holding aside a branch so she could duck under it. "I don't mean in thinking Prescott was innocent. I think you're wrong in saying that I was right about people changing. I've been giving it some thought, and I think your position has merit. People don't really change at their core."

"Charles did."

"I don't think he did. And before you attack me for saying that, hear me out." She closed her mouth, biting back the retort that he'd been right to assume was coming. Out of the corner of her eye, she saw an amused smile tug his lips, but when he spoke, it was in perfect seriousness. "You've built him up to be this paragon of virtue in your mind. He was your friend when you didn't have any others, so naturally he would have a special place in your affections, but don't give him qualities he never had. If he truly cared about you, he would have made an effort to stay in contact with you when he left home. He would have made sure you were safe and well and found a way to help you if you weren't. He didn't do any of that. When the situation was difficult, he ran. He protected himself. Just like he's done ever since."

Samantha didn't respond right away, mulling over his words in her mind. Perhaps she had elevated Charles a little, but she still would never have believed him capable of what he had done.

"What does that say about me?" Samantha asked. "That I have no judgment? That I'm blind?"

"It says that you were a lonely little girl who wanted a friend and got what she wanted." He stopped and turned to face her, his expression earnest. "Please don't punish yourself for his actions. Don't give him that power. Let it go."

If only it were that simple. Samantha wanted to let it go. She saw the wisdom in Wyatt's words, but she couldn't do it. She kept replaying every encounter with Charles since she'd seen him at the masquerade, looking for clues she had missed. She ran through every conversation they'd had, searching for evidence that he'd been a selfish, lying murderer all along. But she couldn't find any. He'd been so kind to her and so considerate. Yet now, every memory was tainted. All the smiles seemed false, every word calculated. How could they not be, when he had known his own guilt all along and continued to pretend to seek answers with them? She wondered if he had ever cared about her at all—if his proposal had been genuine, or if he had only wanted her fortune, as he had wanted his father's. And yet, even if he had loved her, it hadn't been enough for him to value her life above his own freedom.

*****

That night, Samantha couldn't sleep. She threw on her dressing gown and slipped downstairs and out the back door. In the dim light of the moon, she headed down the path, the crunch of her slippers in the gravel the only sound apart from the hum of the crickets. The warm air felt heavy against her skin. She could still smell the remnants of the brief rain shower that had fallen that evening.

Up ahead, the dark outline of a tree became visible, its shape oddly distorted by the sharp angles of a treehouse. She quickened her pace. When she had reached it, she stretched a hand up and undid the clasp she knew to be there. A short rope ladder unrolled itself, ending with a *thunk* and swaying from side to side. Samantha grabbed hold of the sides of the ladder and climbed.

When she reached the trapdoor, she pushed it open and hauled herself inside, then sat down and closed the door behind her. She dusted the rope fragments from her hands and looked around. The wooden platform that formed the base of the treehouse was small, barely large enough for two people to sit cross-legged. Windows on each side gave views of Hampton House and the park. The ceiling was low. Even on her first visit, when she was fourteen, her head had almost grazed it.

Drawing her knees up to her chest, Samantha gazed out the window that faced the house. She had sat in almost the same position her first afternoon there, watching for signs that she had been followed. She had nearly cracked her head on the ceiling when the door opened and Charles popped his head in. She had met him before, a handful of times since her aunt had married his father. His wide, cheeky smile had instantly endeared him to her. He had been on a break from school, and she was fascinated to hear about his studies, though he preferred to share stories of his friends and their juvenile antics. For two hours, he had sat with her, making her laugh and helping her to forget how much she missed her grandfather. Then, when they saw Aunt Victoria in the garden looking for them, he had shown her how to sneak back to the house so that it seemed she'd been there all along.

The treehouse had been their special place after that. They snuck food from the kitchen and talked and hid from his father. He taught her how to play piquet and whist. When he was at school, she went there on her own and sometimes pretended he was there, too, just so that she had someone to talk to.

Tears formed in Samantha's eyes as she traced her fingers over the letters of her name, carved into the wall many years before. When she reached the end, she stopped. There, right beside hers, was his name. The last time her fingers had traced those letters, she had been missing him, wishing to see him again, confident in his friendship. Those letters were a window to the past, tangible proof that there was once a Charles who loved her, who had spent an afternoon laughing with her and carving their names on the wall of their treehouse. She pulled her hand away, unwilling to taint the letters with what she knew now.

Wrapping her dressing gown around her tighter, Samantha lay on the floor beside the names, turning her face to them, though she couldn't see them in the dark. She reached out a hand and laid it against the wall, holding it there, as though by doing so she could be transported back in time to when life was simpler and Charles was her friend.

She closed her eyes and was soon asleep.

SEVENTEEN

When it became known to the general public that, not only had Lord Etwall not killed himself, but he had been murdered and had written his suicide note under threat of violence to his wife and child, the city was thrown into uproar. Those men of high society still in town who had country homes immediately sent their wives and children packing. There were calls for an emergency session of Parliament to be convened and for the city police force to be doubled in size. Fear of revolution—never far from the minds of the aristocracy—was high. A man's home was his castle. The idea that a member of the criminal classes would dare assault a man of rank and fortune at all, much less in his own home, was unthinkable.

As Wyatt was quick to point out to those who spoke to him of their fears of an English Reign of Terror, Palmer would never have done the deed without Charles Prescott's inciting. And, too, it was Prescott's knowledge that had made the rash of home invasions that summer possible. The deaths of Mr. and Mrs. Avery, which had not long before thrown the city into a panic, had not been the start of a spree of random killings, but a domestic matter, again instigated by Prescott.

The fact that Charles Prescott—Sir Charles—was a member of the landed gentry and a baronet at that, was a double-edged sword. Even as it lessened the fears of uprising, it gave rise to a sense of unease among the upper classes. Sir Charles had betrayed his own kind. He had taken what he knew of friends and acquaintances and fed that information to thieves and murderers. He had led vipers into the nest, and if he could do it, why not others?

By the end of the week, the hysteria had diminished, to be replaced by a growing obsession with the upcoming trial of the now-infamous Sir Charles. Wyatt found himself an object of unusual interest, receiving more invitations to dine than he could accept and being asked to retell his fictionalized version of events so many times that he could not believe his listeners were not as bored hearing it as he was telling it.

To Wyatt's relief, Samantha had heeded Madge's suggestion that the two of them stay in Kent until the trial. Her respite wouldn't last, and she would soon be subjected to an even greater fervor of interest than he had, but at least she'd had some time to grieve and reflect on her situation—which would, he hoped, make the coming onslaught easier to bear.

The day of the trial, Wyatt was to pick up Madge and Samantha from the train station to take them to the courthouse. The trial was in the afternoon, and they weren't set to arrive until just before it, so he spent the morning in the United. It was emptier than Boodle's that week, and he was happy to find the library sparsely populated.

He had finished his paper and was sipping his tea when a familiar, unwelcome voice entered the room. He looked up to see a man striding towards him with eyebrows lowered in displeasure. The man had evidently just arrived—his dark hair, due for a trim, was windswept, and the red glow in his cheeks could not all be from anger. Wyatt folded up his paper with deliberate calm and stood to greet his brother.

"Tom," he said with more warmth than he felt. "In London. Don't you usually stay at White's?"

"I am staying at White's," his brother said, taking Wyatt's hand in a crushing grip. "I thought I would surprise you this morning."

"You certainly succeeded."

"Good. I hope you don't mind, but I took the liberty of hiring a room. We've both been so busy lately, and I miss our conversations."

Wyatt glanced around the library. Its few occupants sat pretending to read, their eyes not moving. "Very well," he agreed reluctantly, allowing himself to be led away.

Tom walked quickly, his long, purposeful strides carrying him down the hall and around the corner, leaving Wyatt in his wake. Wyatt slowed his pace, walking to the beat of a funeral dirge playing in his head. He had to suppress a laugh when Tom's irritated face appeared around the corner and beckoned Wyatt further.

When they had entered the small room Tom had rented unnecessarily, Wyatt leaned back against the windowsill, crossing his arms and affecting a pose of unconcern.

"This surprise would not have been necessary," Tom began, rounding on him as soon as the door had closed, "if you had answered my letters."

"I've been busy." Wyatt shrugged.

"Too busy to answer even one of the dozen letters I've sent you?"

"Answer?" Wyatt said mildly. "Was there a question in them? They read more like tirades to me."

"There were several questions," Tom pressed. "Among them, 'What in blazes did you think you were doing?'"

"I must have missed that one."

"Do you find this amusing?" Tom asked, narrowing his eyes. "The near-ruination of our family name makes you laugh?"

"Near ruina— Don't exaggerate, Tom."

"You think I'm exaggerating? Are you aware of how many fires I've had to put out? How many people I've had to speak to, trying to explain the sheer lunacy of your actions in a way that makes you appear sane? You involved us in one of the biggest scandals in a decade, V.T., and that is not an exaggeration!"

Wyatt was silent, waiting for his brother's anger to blow over.

"When you took Aunt Augusta's house in London, I let you go because I hoped you had plans to make something of yourself. I thought, after rejecting the living I offered you, that you had plans to go in for the law—something respectable. Instead, I find you are some sort of private inquiry agent? You may as well have deflowered the Duke of Marlborough's daughter for all the difficulty this has caused us. In fact, I wish you had, because then the solution would have been simple."

"'Let me go'?" Wyatt repeated. "What do you mean, let me go?"

"As the head of the family—" Tom began pompously.

"Bilge."

"With Father gone—"

"With Father gone, you're the title holder," Wyatt said, "and Mother's errand boy. You're not the head of anything. Certainly not my life. Aunt Augusta left me the house, and what I choose to do in it is my business. Now, if you'll excuse me, there's somewhere I need to be." He pushed off the wall and strode across the room.

"It isn't just your business," Tom said, grabbing his arm and halting him. "That's the whole point. The name you carry, the only one you use, it's important."

"Believe me," Wyatt said, shrugging his brother's hand off

and stepping back from him. "If I had a better one, I'd use it. What would you have had me do? A young woman came to me for help. Would you rather I had turned her away? Left her to an uncertain fate?"

"I would have had you hand her over to the proper authorities."

"She was wrongly suspected!" Wyatt said heatedly. "If I had turned her in, she would have been held for trial."

"And the courts would have found her innocent," Tom insisted. "And she would have walked free, as she does now, but with no connection to us."

"Even were that true, which I am not wholly convinced of, what sort of life would she have had as a once-suspected killer, cleared or not? Society makes its own convictions, irrespective of the courts."

"That is no concern of ours."

Wyatt snorted. "I wish I could be as dispassionate as you."

"I wish you could too."

They glared at each other.

"Heaven help the poor soul who makes the mistake of coming to you for help," Wyatt said.

Tom's eyes narrowed. "Don't turn this around on me, V.T. It won't work. Everything I do is for other people. What do you think would happen to our tenants if I weren't managing the lands properly? And don't forget it is I who takes care of Mother. If you are in need of a poor soul to help, I'd be happy to deliver her to you."

Wyatt laughed and walked past his brother to the door. "Don't be ridiculous," he said over his shoulder. "Mother is no poor soul. And, anyway, she hates the city."

"She has expressed a desire to return for a final season sometime soon."

Wyatt froze with his hand on the doorknob.

"Yes," Tom said, his smirk audible. "And I am certain she would love a visit to your new place."

Wyatt took a step back. His mother would skin him alive if she saw the conditions he lived in now. No carriage, few servants. At least he had finally replaced his valet.

"Take a seat," Tom said, lowering himself into one of the elegant chairs by the empty fireplace and gesturing for Wyatt to do the same. "There is something else I need to ask you."

Wyatt sat, crossing his arms in front of him. Tom leaned forward and lowered his voice.

"Is there anything untoward between you and Miss Kingston?" he asked.

Wyatt had been expecting the question, but that did not make him any less angry to hear it actually cross his brother's lips. "Untoward?" he asked through gritted teeth.

Tom shrugged. "From what I've heard, she's quite pretty. She was young…and vulnerable."

"And so, naturally, I took advantage of her vulnerability, cad that I am, to satisfy my own selfish desires. Honestly, Tom, if that's what you think of me…"

"I'm not saying you set out to do it," Tom said quickly, "but the temptation would have been great. Just the two of you, alone in that house…" He trailed off suggestively.

Wyatt stood up and walked to the other side of the room. "First," he said, barely controlling his temper, "it wasn't just the two of us. There was Cousin Madge, as you well know. And second, I was hardly even in the house. I spent most of my time at the club, as anyone can verify."

Tom remained calm, irritating Wyatt further. "I'm only asking what everyone else will, once things have settled. If anything did happen, it would be better for the family if you would tell me now, so I could handle it."

Wyatt pinched the bridge of his nose. "You're unbelievable."

"I know you're holding something back, V.T.," Tom said, leaning back in his chair and drumming his fingers on the table. "I had hoped you could be honest with me. I can help."

Wyatt laughed, crossing his arms again as he leaned against the wall. "Honest? With you? What made you think that?"

Tom frowned but said nothing. After a moment, he stood. "You're coming home with me. Monday morning."

"Am I?"

"Mother asked for you. You owe her an explanation. And I've organized a few suppers. It's time you took some responsibility in restoring the family honor."

"If my helping a young lady in need destroyed it, it isn't worth saving."

Tom glared at him. "That is exactly the sort of comment you had better avoid making."

"I'll come," Wyatt said, "to appease Mother. But don't expect me to apologize to your useless friends."

Tom looked as though he wanted to argue, but checked himself. "I'll see you Monday, then," he said, striding to the door. He paused, his hand on the knob, and turned to Wyatt. "And don't wear that coat again. You know the one I mean. People will think you can't afford another." With that, he left.

Wyatt stayed a moment to collect himself. He didn't get angry often—he was usually even-tempered to a fault—but Tom was one of those few who brought it out of him.

*****

It wasn't a long ride from Kent to London, but Madge still managed to fall asleep. They were the only ones in their carriage and Samantha didn't want to wake her, so she watched out the window instead. When fields and villages gave way to tightly packed soot-stained buildings, Samantha sat up straighter, her body tensing. She had been blissfully unaware of the mood of the city, tucked away in the country, and she was worried about what she might find.

The whistle blew, startling Madge awake. As the train slowed to a stop, Samantha stood, brushing her hands down her skirt as she peered out the window. The platform was crowded. She clutched the handle of her small traveling case tighter in her hands and searched for Wyatt, but it was impossible to distinguish anyone.

When the doors were opened, Samantha stood at the top of the steps and scanned the platform. She spotted him, weaving his way through the crowd, searching the compartments. She waved and he looked over. A smile lit his face as he recognized her, and she found herself smiling back as she stepped down to greet him. There was something reassuring about his presence. She had missed him.

"How was your journey?" he asked, taking her bag and leaning across her to kiss Madge on the cheek.

"Uneventful," Samantha said.

"I wouldn't know," Madge said with a laugh. She coughed, waving away the steam that surrounded them, mingling with the smoke from nearby chimneys. "This is why I hate London."

"Then let's get out of the station," Wyatt said. "I have a carriage waiting."

He escorted them through the press of people to a line of carriages. As he approached one, a coachman jumped down to open the door. Wyatt handed Samantha up, then Madge, before climbing in himself. He sat across from them, facing backwards.

"Has it been awful?" Samantha asked, twisting her hands in her lap as she tried to calm her mounting nerves.

"Not worse than we anticipated, I think," was his response. He smiled reassuringly at her, but she couldn't reciprocate. Her stomach was churning and she could feel a headache coming on.

"You're not the one on trial today," he said, leaning forward and fixing her with an earnest expression.

"Then why does it feel like it?"

He didn't respond—what could he say? —but he gave her a sympathetic look.

The trip to the Old Bailey should not have taken long, but as they drew closer to the heart of the city, the traffic worsened. Once they were near the courthouse, the carriage had to slow considerably as the large crowd that had gathered outside the building pressed in all around.

"Why are there so many people?" Madge asked, looking aghast out the window. "It will all be in the Proceedings soon, and it is not as though they can see anything from out here."

"They're hoping to get tickets, I expect," Wyatt said dryly. "I heard the warder is charging a premium."

Samantha's eyes widened in horror. She had not thought of spectators.

Soon, they were past the crowd and pulling into the covered colonnade that was the carriage entrance. A coachman opened the door, and Wyatt stepped out, holding out a hand to help Madge down. When Samantha alighted, he took her arm, and together they entered the building.

Once inside, they were directed to the witnesses' room to await the start of the trial. It was a well-appointed room with comfortable chairs but no windows. The other witnesses were there. Apart from Cyril's butler, Samantha did not recognize any of them. Inspector Whicher stood in a corner looking morose. After briefly greeting him, Madge took a seat near the door. Samantha, however, could not contain her nervous energy and paced instead.

"Shall I order us some tea?" Madge asked kindly, watching Samantha walk to the door and back.

"It should be starting soon," Wyatt said, pulling out his fob watch.

"Yes," Inspector Whicher agreed. He pushed off from the wall he had been leaning against. "It should be, but they're often late. I wouldn't bother with the tea, all the same. The moment it arrives, they'll call us. It always happens."

In fact, Samantha and the other witnesses only had to wait ten minutes, according to the clock in the room, before a page was sent to take them to the courtroom. They crossed into the annexed building and were suddenly surrounded by people. Lawyers and trial clerks and court officers milled about, adjusting their wigs, exchanging greetings and balancing piles of paper in their arms. There were a few spectators as well, though most filed into the courtroom. Among these, she spotted Wyatt's reporter friend, Mr. Canard. He winked at Wyatt before proceeding inside.

The page motioned for them all to step aside as the minor officers of the court entered. As they shuffled in nonchalantly, discussing their dinner plans, a door opened at the end of the hall. Two prison guards entered. Behind them, partially obscured by their bulk, came a man, followed by two more guards.

Samantha inhaled sharply when she saw Charles. It had been only a week since their last meeting, and yet how different he appeared. He was thinner; his coat hung loose on his frame. There were dark circles under his eyes and a shining bruise under his chin. His shoulders slumped and his feet dragged the ground. In spite of everything, Samantha couldn't help but pity the diminished man before her. He looked up, and their eyes met.

They were Charles' eyes again, not the emotionless, empty orbs she had seen the week before. She searched his face for some sign of remorse, some acknowledgement of shame that would help her make sense of what he had done.

Suddenly, a shrill whistle filled the air. As heads turned in confusion, another, louder sound echoed through the hall.

A gunshot.

Someone screamed. There was another loud crack of gunfire, and she saw Charles fall to his knees, blood blooming from a spot on his chest. More screams. Someone, probably Wyatt, pulled her to the ground as the deep voice of Inspector Whicher shouted out orders to the guards. Behind her, the other witnesses had all taken cover, hands over their heads. She could not see Madge.

The officers of the court were struggling to enter the courtroom, out of the line of fire. From the other side and pushing hard against them, the mass of spectators was fighting to enter the hall, calling out questions about what was happening. The shouting, screaming, and crying was deafening, but Samantha ignored it, struggling against Wyatt's hold, twisting her head to see Charles.

He was on the ground, lying on his side. One of the guards knelt beside him. The others had gone, presumably after the shooter. He was gasping and coughing up blood. There was so much blood. Bright red. Wyatt was trying to shield her view, but she resisted.

"Charles!" she cried out.

He turned his face to her and she saw eyes wide with fear and panic. She struggled for something to say, something to comfort him, but no words came. Instead, she merely watched him, as he watched her, until the light in his eyes began to dim.

"Charles!" she shouted again, more frantically. But it was too late. With a last shuddering gasp, his eyes slid out of focus and his body stilled.

The next several minutes passed with the haze of a dream.

Samantha was vaguely aware of being shepherded out of the building. Madge appeared by her side, and she and Wyatt propelled Samantha into a waiting carriage. Wyatt stayed beside her on the seat, connected to her by the hand he had offered to help her up, which she had yet to relinquish.

She felt numb. It was as though she were still living in that moment when Charles had taken his last breath, frozen in time. If she moved, time would start again and she would be forced to comprehend the reality of what had just happened.

"Samantha." Wyatt's voice seemed to come from a long way off. "Samantha!"

He squeezed her hand and she became aware that he was kneeling in front of her. She blinked as he came into focus. His face was a mask of concern. "You're pale. How do you feel?"

She didn't know how to respond. Her teeth started chattering and her body began to shake. Wyatt shrugged out of his coat and draped it over her shoulders.

"We're getting you out of the city," he said, returning to the seat and taking her hand once more. "It's going to be a circus. Will you go with Madge? She's offered to take you to her home in Derbyshire."

Samantha felt sluggish. It took her a moment to understand what he was saying. "Derbyshire? Yes. I'll go. But, what about you?"

He looked down at her and brushed a hair out of her eyes. "I'm staying here. I'm going to try to help Inspector Whicher."

She nodded woodenly and wrapped his coat more tightly around her. Madge and Wyatt continued to talk, but she let their words wash over her. When they arrived at the train station, Wyatt gave her the support of his arm and Madge walked on her other side. There was a train leaving for Derbyshire in five minutes. Wyatt bought the tickets and the three of them crossed the platform, jostled by the crowd. Madge climbed onto the train and went to find a compartment.

Samantha turned to Wyatt. "Thank you," she said quietly. "For everything."

He nodded. "I'm sorry it turned out the way it did. I'm sorry about Charles."

She glanced up at the overcast sky. "So am I." Then she sighed and looked back at Wyatt. "I hope you find who…did it."

"I plan to." He took her hand in his. She watched as he raised it to his lips and kissed it. "Take care of yourself," he said.

"You will let me know, won't you," she said a little shakily, "how you are? When you write to Madge."

"Of course."

Wyatt helped her onto the train. She grabbed the rail to steady herself and turned back. Her left hand was still held in his. She looked down and their eyes met. She couldn't read his expression, but she sensed that he was as reluctant to break the connection as she was.

A train whistle sounded, startling Samantha. She and Wyatt let go at almost the same moment. Beneath her, she could feel the rumbling of the engine. The hiss of pistons filled the air and the steam began to thicken.

Wyatt lifted his hand and waved. Samantha waved back, feeling that she ought to say something else, but her mind was in such a haze that no words came to her. The noise of the engine increased and she saw a conductor walking down the platform, closing compartment doors. When she looked back, Wyatt was gone.

It wasn't until she had reached the compartment she would share with Madge that Samantha realized she had forgotten to return his coat. She looked out the window, but she couldn't see him anywhere on the platform.

"You can return it next time you see him," Madge said unconcernedly, guiding her into her seat. "Can I get you anything? Water? A blanket?"

Samantha shook her head.

"I'm fine," she said, forcing a smile. She didn't want Madge to worry about her.

Madge watched her a moment longer before nodding and turning to look out the window. Samantha settled into her seat, wrapping the arms of Wyatt's coat around her. She could hardly believe that, after so many years away, she would be returning to Derbyshire. It was the county she had grown up in, the home of her grandfather—her true home. She wondered if it would have changed as much as she had in the intervening years. She hoped not.

But as she closed her eyes, hoping for rest, it wasn't visions of the green pastures and rolling hills of Derbyshire that filled her mind. Instead, she saw Charles' eyes, wide and fearful, looking at her pleadingly as the life drained from them.

Author's Note

Inspector Jack Whicher was a real historical figure. In 1860, the year before this book takes place, he was one of the most successful detectives in the relatively new detective branch of Scotland Yard, publicly praised by no less than Charles Dickens. The brutal murder of a small child in the relatively isolated estate of a wealthy businessman drew the attention of the country and Whicher was sent from London to aid the investigation. Early bumbling by local officials, pressure from the commissioner to convict quickly, and a lack of cooperation from the family and locals hampered Whicher's efforts, and when a vital piece of evidence needed to convict Whicher's prime suspect—one of the daughters of the house—was found to have been lost, so was the case. The lack of a conviction angered the public and Whicher was an easy scapegoat for their frustration. It wasn't until five years later, when Whicher's suspect turned herself in and confessed, that his reputation was fully restored.

In researching for this book, I found myself intrigued by Whicher's story and liked the idea of exploring how the detective branch might have handled another high profile murder so swift on the heels of such a public failure. If you want to learn more about Inspector Whicher, I suggest *The Suspicions of Mr. Whicher: A Shocking Murder and the Undoing of a Great Victorian Detective* by Kate Summerscale or *Brilliant Deduction: The Story of Real-Life Great Detectives* by Matt Kuhns, which has a chapter on Whicher.

Thank you for reading *Masquerade in London*! If you liked it, please consider posting a review. If you would like to read more of Samantha and Wyatt's story, join my newsletter at www.emilylfinch.com to be notified when the next book releases. You can also follow me on Facebook or on Instagram @writer_elf.

Acknowledgements

As the great Leslie Knope once said, "No one achieves anything alone." That is certainly true when it comes to writing and publishing a book.

First and foremost, I want to thank my husband, Brandon, without whom none of this would have happened. You have been there for me from the beginning, always supportive, always encouraging. You've listened to me read for hours through multiple drafts. You've had long conversations with me about the characters like they're real people. You've made suggestions, offered feedback, been a sounding board, and reassured me when I felt like giving up. You are my best friend and my champion, and I cannot thank you enough. I love you.

Thank you to my book club readers, Jen, Meredith, and Shanta, for reading a somewhat messy draft and giving helpful feedback. A special thanks to Lisa whose early support and enthusiasm was invaluable.

Thank you to my fabulous editor, Meredith Spears. Your suggestions were pure gold and your encouragement was just what I needed.

Thank you also to Bonnie for your positivity and love, and to Bethany for that fabulous poster. You don't know how much that meant to me.

To Aunt Cindy, for talking through several plot points with me. The last few pages are mostly down to you.

Thank you Dad for your support even after reading a very unpolished early draft.

To Mom for reading several drafts, polishing the final one with your copyediting expertise and for listening to me talk about my book during so many phone calls.

Finally, thank you to D'Atra for being in my corner from day one. I cannot express how much your unrelenting support has meant to me.

Acknowledgments

Made in United States
Orlando, FL
11 April 2024

45703860R00200